STRANGER

BOOKS BY JAKE CROSS

*The Choice*
*The Family Lie*

# PERFECT STRANGER

## JAKE CROSS

bookouture

Published by Bookouture in 2019

An imprint of StoryFire Ltd.

Carmelite House
50 Victoria Embankment
London EC4Y 0DZ

www.bookouture.com

ISBN: 978-1-78681-443-2
eBook ISBN: 978-1-78681-442-5

# MONDAY

# CHAPTER ONE

'What on earth is this?'

Chris's wife walked into the kitchen, mail in hand and favouring her right ankle today. She held up a note.

It was a piece of thick white paper the size of a postcard. It was blank. Blank except for those eight words which he could read even from six feet away.

*I KNOW WHAT YOU DID TO EVE LEVINE*

'Who's that addressed to?' Chris asked.

'No envelope.' Rose turned the note over. 'And it's not stamped.'

He took the note, turning it over carefully, hoping she was wrong. She wasn't. No stamp. The sender hadn't dropped the envelope into a post box half a country away. He or she had approached the house, had stood right at the front door and slotted it into their home, to guarantee the recipient would find it, read it, be shocked by it.

'This can't be for us,' he said. 'It must be a mistake.'

Julia sauntered into the kitchen, eye make-up smudged and long oak hair from her mother a wild mess. Her blue dressing gown was similar to Rose's, but Julia's had a frayed collar where she liked to chew it. Rose grabbed the note and slotted it into the mass of mail to hide it, and then put the mass into Chris's hands. She needn't have bothered because their eighteen-year-old was hypnotised by her phone yet again, which made the rest of the world white noise.

Rose put the kettle on then started to fix hair that had escaped from her messy bun.

'Remember I've got the physiotherapist and then I'm off to Meadowhall. And you're buying, remember?'

He did remember. He'd bought her the wrong phone charger. The last thing on his mind at the moment.

With both girls distracted, he went to the front door and peered out, left and right. No strange cars or faces. The same schoolkids drifting past, the same neighbours leaving for work, and not a one amongst them with a guilty look. He walked halfway down his path just to make sure there was no damage to his car or Rose's or to the house. If someone was bold enough to post unsettling notes through their letterbox, who knows what else they might do? But the cars were fine. It was just another Monday morning no one would remember on their deathbed in a Sheffield suburb on nobody's 'places-to-die' list.

Back in the kitchen, Julia was still hooked to her mobile, and Rose was writing on a sheet of paper stuck to the fridge door, using her special big pen and big letters because of her arthritic wrist. Always chirpy in the morning, she was mouthing the words to some song as she scribbled the day's important tasks. A routine morning in the Redfern household. Same scene as yesterday, and the day before, and countless previous. Save for the note that Chris couldn't get out of his head.

'Grab my slippers, please. From the en suite,' Rose said.

He did as asked, trudging up the stairs.

But when he came out of the bathroom, she was standing in front of their closed bedroom door. Clearly, she didn't want this conversation to happen in front of Julia.

Chris noticed that he still had the mail clutched tightly in one hand, Rose's slippers in the other. Rose took the lot and dropped everything but the note.

'I just asked Julia if she knew the name Eve Levine. No. And it's a no from me, too.'

She was awaiting something, leaning against the door with her arms folded. With her long bob now free of its bun, she looked healthy and radiant.

Chris said, 'Same here.'

'What about your work?'

Chris paused to think. As a microbiologist, he was often instrumental in saving lives, but not always. Sometimes patients were just too ill to save. But that didn't mean…

'Do you think this could be about my job? Someone blaming me because my lab failed to save Eve from her cancer?'

She stepped forward and touched his arm reassuringly. 'Don't panic yet. It could just be some kids playing silly buggers.' Rose glanced down at the note in her hand. 'But we have to be sure. So, when you go in today, would you ask about it?'

He nodded. She left and he took a shower and dressed.

But when he came out of the en suite, his wife was back. And was sitting on the bed with his phone.

'What are you doing?'

She showed him. She'd loaded his Facebook app and sent a message:

You know what I did, do you? HA HA. PM me

'I sent this to all your friends, even those old college pals you've not seen in nearly twenty years after you just walked out. It'll sound vague to most of them. But if someone's playing a game, they'll think they've been found out and so they'll private message you. I've done the same on mine and I'll do Julia's if she ever lets it go. So now all you have to do is swoon over your wife's computer brain and then wait. Help me dress.'

While childbirth had put a little stubborn weight on her, and arthritis had stolen her ability to exercise, teenage years of gymnastics had kept her slender and young-looking. He kissed her insteps as he helped her into socks, and the smooth skin of her shoulders as he clumsily worked the clasp of her bra. She cast her hair aside so he could nibble her neck, but giggled and playfully slapped his hands when they tried to wander.

The rest of her clothing she could manage alone, so he went downstairs. She had left his packed lunch in the fridge. Another cold meal, yippee.

There was a note on the fridge.

*Buy whiteboard so don't have to stick paper on fridge and read what's on damn paper stuck on fridge.*

He was always forgetting to check the notes. He wrote 'WHITEBOARD' on his hand. He grabbed his coat. Julia didn't even glance up from her phone, but en route to the car he got a text from her reminding him that it was their wedding anniversary on Saturday. He smiled. Sometimes it was easy to forget how sweet she could be.

Then he set off for another day of work, trying to ignore the ball of dread in the pit of his stomach. This was the only family he had, and he couldn't let anything happen to it.

# CHAPTER TWO

*Saturday, 16 November*

DOUBLE TRAGEDY AS MOTHER OF ONE TAKES OWN LIFE
FOLLOWING BOYFRIEND'S MURDER

*Eve Levine, 40, was found dead at her home in Bradford by her sister, Elaine, 44, early on Friday morning. Eve had been living with a terminal cancer diagnosis when Ron Hugill, 48, her long-term boyfriend and father to her daughter, was murdered in an altercation with a mugger at the gym where he was employed on 9 November. His funeral is on Monday.*

*Eve's sister says, 'I want to remember Eve in life, not death. She was suffering at the end, and Ron's murder hit her hard. I hope there is a heaven and she's finally at peace.'*

*Eve, whose funeral is on 22 November, is survived by her estranged sister and a young daughter.*

'Did you click the link in my text?' Rose said as soon as she answered the phone. Chris had been walking across the car park to the lab when her message had pinged through, stopping him dead in his tracks. The concern in her voice upped his own store of anxiety tenfold.

'Yes. What the hell is it?'

'A newspaper article. Look at the date. I searched for the name Eve Levine online. It took some time because it's a popular name, but I found her. This was the only mention of her that I could find. She was from Bradford, so it's got to be her. Look, cancer. So she would have had tests. This really could be about your work after all.'

He stopped and leaned against someone else's car in the car park to get his head around this.

'Not possible, Rose. Cancer, it says. And even if I'd done something to cause this woman harm, and her family is pissed off, they would blame the GP first. They couldn't get my name except through official channels, probably not even then. It would involve a complaint and I'd know about it. Rose, it's just a big mistake. Forget about it.'

'I can't. Just make sure you ask your boss about it. I also searched for Eve's sister, Elaine. But there's nothing online or on Facebook or anything. I couldn't find anything about her daughter, either. The one mentioned in the article. Poor girl, losing her mother to suicide. And her father, if that's what the man who got killed was to her. The article doesn't really say, does it? I hope she's not a small child. How old do you think she is?'

'How should I know?' he snapped before he could stop himself. 'Sorry, Rose. I just— I just don't know why someone would want to mess with us like this.'

Rose's voice came back softly. 'It's okay, Chris. You're worried, I'm worried, and I guess it's making us a bit snappy. But we'll figure this out, together.'

'You're right, you always are. But right now I'm still sorry. And I'll always love you.'

'I love you too. Also always.' Rose paused. 'But, even if it's just for peace of mind, would you ask at work? You never know.'

Chris sighed. 'I will. I'll ask.'

She thanked him and hung up. But he knew she was still upset at his outburst.

A headache was forming, and he didn't expect it to go away anytime soon.

# CHAPTER THREE

Sheffield Royal Infirmary's microbiology lab. Here were the guys and gals who poked and prodded at blood or tissue or whatever else the nurse or doctor took from you. Their job was to work out what was messing you up. You'd never meet them, but they'd know you had HIV or Ebola long before you did.

Chris worked on Sterile Fluids, which the staff called 'body bench': a name that to the uninitiated painted a picture of corpses laid out for dissection. Body parts were not uncommon, but mostly Chris dealt with blood samples. One of the keen-to-please Medical Lab assistants had already taken all positive blood cultures from the machine and dumped them on his bench. Chris would go through the robotic routine of applying coloured dyes to highlight the invisible little alien intruders, so he could work out what kind they were. Then he'd call the medical staff in charge of the respective patients with news of how to wipe out whatever he'd found.

An intruder. Like the one who'd posted the threatening note.

Chris waited until Alan, his gangly boss, went into his office, then he sat at one of the computers and loaded I-Lab, the laboratory's filing system. On his way upstairs, he'd copied Rose's idea and checked Facebook for Eve Levine, but the result had mirrored what I-Lab now showed him. Nothing. Rose's Facebook message had already fielded a blitz of replies that ended in question marks or puzzled-face emojis.

'So, sixteenth anniversary on Saturday. That's silver hollowware, by the way. Like a teapot. If you'd killed her on your wedding day, you'd be out of prison and a free man by now.'

He turned his chair. Hovering far too close was Louise, twenty-six going on fifteen with two oblivious-to-each-other boyfriends, and a habit of shoplifting cosmetics. Chris stood in order to hide the screen.

'Dobbo, you done that shift swap form yet? You're my last hope, remember?' Louise asked, tapping at her lower lip with a forefinger. It was her bizarre version of fluttering the eyelids.

'I'll sort it.'

'And while you're not busy, order me an urgent BDMAX Enterics kit.'

He gave her a thumbs up and she meandered away.

Still hopeful the computer could shed light, Chris delved into Medway, the national system, and found an abundance of historical information about Eve Levine. Every test performed, treatment given, appointment made, the works. Even her GP's name. All to do with her cancer, because anything much older wouldn't have been transferred from dusty cardboard to digital yet. But what he wanted was her address.

The Blue Swan, Shipley, Bradford.

It stirred something deep down, almost lost within his memory banks, like a mild bout of déjà vu.

A quick scan down the list of websites containing 'The Blue Swan' paid a jackpot. A newspaper article, dated fifteen months ago, about a charity fun day held in the beer garden of The Blue Swan pub. And Eve Levine was pictured surrounded by playing kids, although none clung to her or otherwise appeared to be her daughter. She was standing with a thick-set middle-aged man with a completely bald head and a boxer's twisted nose. The photo's caption was '*Eve and Ron, proprietors of The Blue Swan public house in Bradford*'.

He zoomed in with shaking fingers, cutting Ron Hugill and the children out of the image. Amongst fun day revellers, Eve posed in a dress that hung on her bone-thin frame. So she already had cancer chewing her up from the inside out. Short hair, no style, messy: a cut designed only for comfort, and screaming that there was no one in her life to impress. Forty years old, so only a couple of years his senior, but while he still had youthful brown hair and very few lines on his face, she was grey and wrinkled. Good health and humorous times had kept him fresh, but Eve looked like she had been through the wringer. A clearly fake smile added to the impression that her life had been one of far fewer fun days than miserable ones.

The note flashed through his mind again.

*I know what you did to Eve Levine.*

But he wasn't responsible for what had happened to this woman. He couldn't be. Could he? Even if one look at Eve's wasted face showed him features he knew he'd seen before.


On the way home, Chris stopped to buy a whiteboard. Hopefully, remembering would win him brownie points with Rose. On the corner of his street, the Swift sons, strapping twenty-year-old university rugby players, were finally getting around to fixing their garden fence, which some idiot had cut down with his car late at night two Saturdays ago. Chris waved as he passed.

As soon as he stepped through his front door, a heavy tension burst from his chest in a thick, loud sigh. He hadn't realised how worked up he'd been. Someone who might have bad intentions knew where he lived, and by extension, where his wife and daughter slept, too. But Chris was blind and deaf to his enemy. They could be anyone. They were a stranger, and according to Chris's Facebook profile all but 217 of the 6 billion people in the world were strangers to him. They existed in the aisles of the local supermarket, in the corridors of his hospital, on the pavements criss-crossing the city. They were everywhere, the world across, infesting it, and he couldn't get from A to B without crossing their paths. His enemy could just as easily get to him in the town centre in broad daylight as in his bedroom during the dead hours. And Chris wouldn't know the face of that enemy until it was too late.

'Is that you, darling?' Rose called out.

Chris found Rose and Julia eating in the kitchen. Theirs were hot meals, but Rose had prepared him a salad because she never knew exactly how long it would take him to get home – so she always claimed. He figured it was because he'd hit midlife, that period when fending away illness and weight gain became an uphill struggle.

He showed Rose the whiteboard and gave her a look that said he wanted a quiet word.

'Love, there's a problem with the bedroom curtains. Come up with me and have a look?' Rose asked.

'I'm not a fool, Mum. If you want to talk to Dad about things I'm not supposed to hear, you don't need to make up an excuse to leave the room.'

Fair enough. A particularly bad day for Rose's joints meant it took a while for her to get up the stairs, even with his help. And that she didn't laugh when he pinched her bum on the way up.

'How did your physio appointment go?' Chris asked.

'Yeah, it went fine,' she said, sounding as if it had been anything but. She was happy to talk about her arthritis on good days, but the bad ones made her feel inept and embarrassed. He knew not to push the conversation. But she had more pressing worries, anyway.

Once in the bedroom, she shut the door and came right out with it.

'So, did you ask at work?'

'No, but I searched for her in the system and checked her file. She hasn't had any treatment at my hospital.'

'Maybe she went to the doctor under a false name,' Rose said, taking a seat on the bed, leaning slightly to one side because it was more comfortable on her hips. 'Makes sense if it was a sexual disease. So nobody would know.'

'Perhaps, but I'm not sure that's possible. She'd have to prove her identity before a surgery would put her on its books.'

'Stranger things have happened. It's just… I mean, I can't help but think about what happened with Dana.'

Chris nodded, frowning slightly at the memory. Dana, while working Respiratory, had committed the cardinal sin of contacting a patient whose results she knew before the patient did. She had commented on one of his Facebook posts.

He'd written:

Going to get my suit tomorrow. Vegas in three sleeps, baby!

And she'd replied:

Don't bother, get some pyjamas and a big book instead.

A throwaway comment no one gave a shit about, until two days later when the guy was in pyjamas in hospital, tuberculosis confirmed, and Infection Control was probing into his nearest and dearest. A sleuth-like friend of his put two and two together, kicked up a stink, and now Dana was suspended.

Chris sat beside Rose and took her hands in his. 'You know I'd never do anything as reckless as that.'

'I know,' she said. 'But if anything else comes through the door, we go to the police.'

He gave her a hug, told her not to worry and silently prayed that there would be no more notes.

As Chris made his way downstairs to half-heartedly eat his salad, he caught a snippet of conversation leaking through the gap in Julia's bedroom door. Something she said stopped him in his tracks.

'—kill herself.'

He virtually kicked the door open. Julia yelped, her phone now clutched to her chest in shock.

'Christ, Dad, try knock—'

'Who's killed herself? What do you know about it, Julia?'

'About what?'

He thundered across the room and snatched the mobile from her hand. She looked almost scared, but mostly annoyed.

'Who's this?' he snapped into the phone.

Julia snatched it back. 'What are you doing? I'm on the phone.' She told the person on the phone she'd call back and hung up. 'What's going on?'

'You said something about someone killing herself. What was it?'

'Simone. My friend. She's coming down from uni tomorrow. Why?'

'And? What's this got to do with…' He left it there, because he was already starting to think he'd got the wrong end of this stick.

'It's her ex. He knows she's in town soon. He's been on Facebook saying she better not cross paths with him when she comes down.'

'And?'

'Calm down, Dad. What's this about?'

'Has someone killed herself?'

'No. Marc said—'

'Who's Marc?' he asked, more exasperated than afraid, now.

'Simone's ex. He reckons he'll kill Simone's new boyfriend if he comes down with her. He wants Simone to kill herself.'

'Why?'

'Because he's a togmuppet. Why are you so bothered?'

He relaxed – somewhat. False alarm.

'You think I should tell Simone what he's said? She's not on his Facebook and—'

'You've got a good head on your shoulders,' Chris cut in, turning to leave. 'I know you'll do what's best.'

He paused at the door.

'Sorry,' he said. 'If I scared you, I mean.'

Julia shrugged. 'Whatever, it's fine. Just don't go morphing into the overprotective dad, okay?'

'Okay,' Chris said with a small smile.

But the note was already changing him, and with someone out there watching his family, he knew his promise to Julia was one he couldn't keep.

On the stairs, Rose was giving him a burning look.

'We can't let this note get to us, okay?' she said.

Chris rubbed a hand across his brow, sighed, and nodded. Rose was always right.

'Good,' she continued. 'It'll be good for us to get out of the house, have some fun. You drive because my hands are playing up.'

Rose clocked the quizzical look on Chris's face.

'How could you forget? The cinema.'

'Sorry, yes, of course,' he said. The cinema, every Monday evening. That damned note was eroding his concentration.

She stepped towards her husband and gave him a reassuring kiss. 'Make sure you don't bring Eve Levine out with us. Her and her ilk are not going to ruin our evening.'

He almost laughed. His entire day had already been torpedoed.

# CHAPTER FOUR

The local cinema was only half a mile away, but walls of woodland sent them on a circuitous route that increased journey time. Indefinitely, as it happened, because they had to ride Herries Road South, and that was where it happened.

Trees lined each side, cutting off the rest of the world, leaving them alone for the short drive through the dark woodland. Just them and whoever was in the car parked ahead by the side of the road. Its hazards were on, so Chris veered to the right to bypass it, edging into the opposite lane.

No cars swung around the corner towards him, but that was where he was looking when the C-Max, hazards still flashing, leaped into the road. Right into his line. No time to avoid it.

'Chris, watch out!' Rose yelled. But too late.

He crushed the brake pedal but had no doubt that the cinema was now a no-go. With luck, they'd drive away from this one, but this one was definitely happening.

He was almost cut in half by his seatbelt as his car struck the other's rear. It was all over in the next second. A soft impact, no write-off, maybe no pain in the ass of awaiting a tow truck. With the stoppage of both cars, the whole world seemed to pause.

'Everyone okay?' He put his hand on Rose's arm and looked at Julia in the back seat.

'What happened?' Julia said, unhurt but shocked. She'd been watching her phone when the crash happened.

'Idiots,' Rose snapped, as if that explained everything.

But Chris didn't agree. He'd noted the grimy paintwork of the C-Max, and the dents and the old registration. And the paranoid part of him made a leap. Not the crash-for-cash scam leap, though.

Two guys jumped out of the Ford. Big guys. With baseball bats. Not crash-for-cash, and not an act of road rage. No matter how paranoid somebody was about confrontation, nobody kept a pair of long baseball bats sitting there in the front of the car.

*

Dark road, nobody about, and two guys who'd been sitting there, no seatbelts on, bats in hand, like army guys ready to deploy the second the chopper touches down. Prepared. With an intention. Following a plan.

'Oh, God. Chris, what do we do?' Rose asked. She looked round at their daughter, and a boosted expression of shock told him Julia must be terrified.

'Julia, it's fine, don't worry. Nor you, Rose. I'll handle this,' Chris said.

When the two guys passed the back of their C-Max, they didn't even look at the damage. That was what you did, no matter how angry. You checked out the damage in order to make a quick assessment of how much of your time and money had just burned, and maybe to decide just how much rage you were going to employ.

Instead, the men walked past their own car and alongside Rose's. One down the left side of the bonnet, one down the right. Rose quickly buzzed her window up, and Chris jabbed the central locking button hard enough to hurt his finger.

Julia slid into the centre of the back seat. 'Is this a trick to rob us or something?' she said, throat croaky with fear.

'Everything's going to be okay,' Rose whispered to her. She didn't sound like she believed it herself.

The headlights were kissing the back of the C-Max, so there wasn't much illumination. One of the guys was heavyset, bearded and wore a cap that a fisherman grandfather might have handed down. A versatile look. With a comic book in hand, he might have seemed like the neighbourhood weirdo. But here he definitely fit the profile of a thug.

His bat slammed down on the bonnet. It was a one-handed strike, designed to pass a message rather than cause damage. 'Money or the bat,' he said, very matter-of-factly. He sounded like a guy who'd done this before and had had it go his way far more often than not.

Chris already knew it was going to go this guy's way tonight, too.

The guy on Rose's side was skinnier, taller, with a shaved head and long arms like some cartoon character who'd had them stretched by lifting a too-heavy weight. He tapped the windscreen with his bat, also softly. Another message: locked doors weren't going to save them here.

'Toss your purse out,' Chris said. Rose started to object. 'Just do it.'

Chris lowered both front windows, a couple of inches each, just shy of thug-arm width, and a purse and a wallet thumped to the tarmac in unison.

Both guys bent down. Wallet and purse lifted off the ground in unison.

Two bats tapped the windscreen. The bearded guy Chris's side said, 'Jewellery.'

Rose gasped and threw her hands to her throat, as if to protect her necklace at all costs.

'You'll have to give it them, Rose.'

'It's my mother's, Chris, I can't just—'

Her words were cut off by a loud prompt from the skinny guy's bat. Two-handed this time. It hit the roof with a mighty dong. A much clearer message.

'Jewellery,' the bearded guy repeated, nice and loud. He shifted his stance and swung back his bat. His intention was clear: the windscreen was going in if more goodies didn't quickly appear.

Now Julia burst into tears, too. Rose's hands were shaking so badly she couldn't get the necklace off and resorted to trying to yank it free, although it held. Their panic hit him hard and he grabbed the door handle, knowing he had no choice but to try to reason with these men. Out there, where he could draw their focus away from his wife and only child. He grabbed the satnav from its dashboard cradle as a bargaining chip.

'Rose, you're going to have to drive away if this goes bad for me—'

He stopped as white sliced through black far ahead. A single, powerful ball of light like a moon dropped from the sky into their small patch of forest. A headlight. Both batsmen looked round, and then looked at each other. The skinny guy pointed his bat at the windscreen.

'You're one lucky bastard.'

Amazingly, beautifully, both men turned their backs and ran to their C-Max. Chris didn't dare believe it was over, until it was. The C-Max leaped away and shrank ahead of them in the headlights, passed the oncoming car, turned the corner and was gone. Just like that. Like a magic trick.

In the back, Julia hugged herself and cried, and Rose tried to calm her down. Chris's hands throttled the steering wheel as dwindling fear cleared a path for anger.

Those thugs had tried to rob his family. First the note, then this: two major headaches on the same day. And the thug had the nerve to call him 'lucky'. Lucky! He was anything but.

Worse, he couldn't shake the words he'd so often heard Rose say.

Bad things always come in threes.

# CHAPTER FIVE

It soon became clear that the bright light that had been the family's saving grace was not a car but a motorbike. It pulled up a few metres ahead, same side of the road, headlights of both vehicles creating a dazzling white sun in the space between. Beyond, the rider, a tall silhouette, climbed off.

Rose pulled out her mobile and struggled to get her shaking hands to dial.

The silhouette removed its helmet and, holding it, stepped into the middle of the road, out of the obsidian abyss and into the overflow from the headlights. Better lit, some of his textures appeared. A young man with a beanie cap, young-looking, in jeans and a wax jacket. There was something on the side of his face. He spent a few seconds staring at the minor damage on the front of their Kia, then approached Chris's side. That was when Chris saw big eyes and a petite nose and noted clumped blonde hair that protruded from between the cap and the ears, and he realised his error. Not a man at all. A young woman. Maybe Julia's age. He started to open his door.

'Oh, no, you just stay indoors, please,' she said, a hand raised to say *stop*. Her voice was deeper than he'd expected, a gravelly purr that reminded him of Eighties singer Bonnie Tyler.

Chris closed the door. The woman pulled a small torch from her pocket and did a full revolution of the car, slowly, and at each side window she put the beam inside, taking turns to light up the faces of Julia and Rose.

'What are you doing?' Rose almost yelled as the light stung her eyes. She had her phone to her ear.

The woman flicked off the torch, circled around the bonnet and retook almost the exact same spot on the driver's side of the car. A few careful feet away.

'Hello, police, please,' Rose said, and then 'Hey!' as Chris snatched her phone.

'Don't phone the police yet.'

'Why? Chris, those bastards just took our stuff. They robbed us.'

'I know, I know. But just wait a minute.'

'Why?'

'Just wait while I talk to this girl.'

The girl stepped forward and knocked on Chris's window, then moved away again. That safe distance.

'So, what happened here?' she said, suspicious. 'Why did that other driver speed off?'

Chris buzzed his window down a couple of inches so he could speak quietly. 'Two men mugged us. They had bats. You scared them off. Thank you.'

In the pause, the two seconds of silence before she replied, Chris heard something strange from the woman. A ticking sound.

'Right, right. Muggers. Of course.' She couldn't have sounded like she believed him less. 'Can I see your licence?'

'Why?' Rose said. 'Chris, let's just go.'

The woman squeezed both wrists in a fist, one at a time, and cracked them. As if gearing up for trouble. 'Ms, excuse me, but this road's had its share of late-night wacky trickery. Like muggings when some poor young woman like me stops to help someone who's claiming to have broken down or crashed. So, if you don't mind, all of you stay right there in the car. I want a name to give the authorities if I end up having to walk home.' She pulled out her mobile and waved it to highlight her point.

Rose snorted derision. 'Did you not see that other car race away from here? Do we look like—'

Chris put a hand on her shoulder. 'It's okay, Rose.'

'It's not okay, Chris. I just want to go. After what we went through, I'm supposed to have this girl waste our time? And Julia's upset. And we need to call the police.'

Chris leaned towards Rose. 'You made me drive, and I've had half a bottle of wine. If I get caught out by the police, I could lose my damn job. Let's just go through with this and get home. Keep calm for thirty seconds and we'll be out of here and we'll call the police when we get in.'

She gave him a long, unhappy look that said he'd pay for this later, but she didn't object. He pulled his licence from a pocket in the driver's sun visor and slapped it against the glass. The woman stepped forward to look, using her torch. Backlash off the glass lit her up and Chris saw clearly exactly what was on the side of her face.

'God, that scar…' Julia said.

*That scar* ran diagonally from just below the earlobe to just beside the nose. A rugged line, sunken and pinched, like a dry riverbed, but old and not discoloured. Certainly not a surgical scar but something left to fix itself. Chris saw the woman look to her left, at Julia, and he hoped his daughter hadn't just caused a big problem with her even bigger mouth.

No problem. The girl smiled at Julia. 'Impressive, isn't it?' She returned to the licence. And that grin instantly vanished, her eyes wide in surprise. Or was it fear?

She backed off, turned away and climbed on her bike. Chris watched as the girl put her helmet on and started the bike. It moved forward. Closer.

'What's she doing?' Rose asked.

But Chris's attention was fixed on the girl's movements, her bike now parallel with his window. He dragged his gaze from her eyes and down to her hand. It was extended, and it was holding a small white envelope.

'Don't take that, Chris!'

Too late. Autopilot threw out his hand and wrapped his fingers around the envelope. It was bloated with something bulky inside.

'Chris, don't take that. Let's just go.'

But it was the biker who left. The big black machine leaped away like a runner off the blocks. He watched it cut a U-turn and race away. He couldn't avert his eyes until the bike slid around a corner and seemed to slip into a rent in the black blanket of night. He felt a little dazed.

'What is it?' Rose asked. She tried to take the envelope, but he threw the item into his door pocket and started the engine. There was a knocking noise from the dented front end, but the car seemed to move just fine. He built up speed quickly.

Rose watched her husband in concern. 'Chris, what's going on?'

'I don't know.'

He could feel her eyes on him, worry radiating out from her in waves. He kept his own eyes locked on the black road, and he drove fast, saying nothing further.

*

They got home without another word, except for Rose's call to the police and announcement that officers would come to the house soon for statements. Even the ever-curious Julia, sensing tension between her parents, knew not to ask questions.

Chris sat in the car as the girls got out and went up the path. He watched Julia enter the house, but Rose hung back. Then she shut the door and returned to him. She got in but said nothing. Her eyes were on the envelope, now in his lap.

Subdued, he didn't even react, and didn't lift his eyes from the little oblong slip of paper in his hands. She closed the door and waited for him to speak.

'She could have blurted it all out in two seconds.'

She knew he meant the biker. 'Who is she, Chris?'

His eyes stayed on the slip of paper, no bigger than the kind found in a cracker and bearing a joke. But whatever was on it was nothing funny.

'Maybe she opted for a method with maximum shock. Maybe she wanted to... to distance herself from... from the actual act of telling me. But she's had a long time to think about the best way forward.'

'Who, Chris? Who is she? What are you talking about?' No answer, so she snatched the slip of paper. It was missing one little corner. It bore a scribbled mobile phone number, nothing more.

'Is this hers? Did you phone her?'

He shook his head.

She said, 'The envelope had something heavier in it.'

He reached into the door pocket, paused a few seconds, and took out a silver necklace chain, worn with age. No pendant, but a twisted link where one had once hung. Her stiff fingers could barely take it. It was no answer and he knew it.

'It was a week before I met you. The twenty-fourth of September 2000...'

...in Indianapolis, Indiana, home of the United States Grand Prix. He and some college friends, on a holiday paid for by a pal's rich mother, had bought tickets from a tout after losing theirs when a bag was stolen. But at the Indianapolis Motor Speedway, an ape-like guard had claimed his ticket was fake and refused entry. Lurking outside while his friends went in for the fifteenth race of the 2000 Formula 1 World Championship, he'd met a girl with the same problem. A striking young woman with beautiful big eyes. Two strangers in a foreign place. Of course they would hang out.

The rain had stopped, so they visited White River State Park, only a few miles away. Walking along the riverside, they chatted like old friends. They ate on a patch of grass by the Medal of Honor Memorial, shoulders touching as they scanned the names of nearly 3,500 recipients of the country's most prestigious military award. And at the zoo, while he made her laugh with pretty good animal impressions, they had their first kiss.

Later in the day, runaway emotions had ignited at a hotel. Neither cared that they had missed Michael Schumacher win the Formula 1 World Championship. In the late afternoon they had said their goodbyes in order to locate their friends, but had promised to meet the next day at the location that both felt had been pivotal in their union: Indianapolis City Market. It was where, the day before, Saturday, each had both bought overpriced bogus tickets, thus propelling them towards their fateful encounter...

'But I didn't turn up. I don't even know if she did. But I abandoned her. Neither of us had a hotel or number for the other. I didn't even give her my real name. It was only meant to be a one-day fling, so I just used a fake one. And then the holiday was over and I went home. I never saw her again.'

Rose hesitated. She'd known about his failed attempt to get in to watch the Formula 1 race. But not that he'd spent the day with a girl. And she had a rising suspicion who that girl had been.

'Eve Levine,' she said. It wasn't a question.

He nodded. 'I gave her that chain.'

She looked at it. Plain, no markings, like a thousand others. She had no idea how he could be so sure. 'There's no pendant.'

'There was never a pendant, but I'm sure it's the same one,' Chris answered. 'But I think I already knew who she was, even before I saw the chain. I read about a pub her parents owned, The Blue Swan. When I looked at it online, I realised I'd heard of it before. I suspected back then. That necklace was the final piece of proof. I just didn't remember her name. It was so long ago.'

'The note claimed you did something to her. Eve's daughter's not a young child, is she? That woman on the bike… she's Eve's daughter, isn't she?'

Chris said nothing, but that was answer enough. Rose let the chain slip from her fingers as the horror dawned.

'And she's about eighteen. You met Eve eighteen years ago…'

# CHAPTER SIX

Chris thumped a fist against the car window.

'It was damn stupid. Didn't she realise how this was going to affect me? That sending me that damn note would make me panic that I was someone's target?'

Rose didn't know what to say. Her husband, her darling Chris, might have another daughter. By another woman. But if it had sent her mind into a tailspin, Chris's would be a twisted, fiery wreck on the ground. She knew she had to put him first. A calming hand stroked his arm.

'Imagine that she didn't know about you until after the murder of the man she thought was her father.'

'Murder?'

'Eve's boyfriend. Remember? It said in that newspaper article that Eve's boyfriend had been murdered.'

'Oh. Right. Yes. But I don't understand.'

'She would have been distraught at losing her father. Picture her mother, who would also be hurt and confused, telling her daughter that her real father might not be dead at all. Maybe Eve hoped her daughter would be happy about it. Then picture Eve dying. That's three big bombshells in her daughter's life, one after the other, any one of which is enough to knock the sense out of anyone. She wanted to find you, and somehow she did, but the shock of three big hits means she's not thinking straight. She's had no time to adjust because her mother's suicide was only last week. She was unsure how to proceed and came up with the idea about posting you a note as a way of letting you know her mother had died.'

His eyes were ahead, remote, away somewhere beyond the windscreen. She used his chin to turn his head her way.

'I saw the surprise in her eyes when she saw your licence. I think she had a plan to post that necklace to us, but by freak luck she found herself face-to-face with the man who could be her real father. She panicked. She didn't know how to act, so she handed that envelope over and left. That's the behaviour of someone scared, especially after what she went through today.'

'Today? What do you mean?'

'Ron Hugill's funeral. The man she thought was her father. His funeral was today, Chris. Her mother's is on Friday, his was today, so she's obviously shell-shocked. Don't you agree?'

He didn't answer that. He stared out of the side window, at the black world. 'But why? What does she want?'

'Don't try to assume what she's thinking, Chris. Neither one of you is level-headed at the minute, so it would be impossible. Maybe she just wanted you to know the full story. Do you worry that she might want to start a relationship?'

Chris took a long time before shrugging.

'I know you,' she said. 'You don't like an upset to routines. Like not letting me replace the wallpaper. I swear an assessment would diagnose Asperger's. I can't imagine a bigger shift in the balance than a new family member.'

Chris took a long time before sighing.

Rose continued, 'And she's a grown woman, with a life behind her already. She'll have friends. Her own likes and dislikes. She's not necessarily trying to find a new father to fit into all that.'

Chris took a little time before nodding.

'We can't know what she wants, Chris. She probably doesn't even know what she wants. And bear in mind that nothing is concrete yet.'

He turned to her, puzzled.

'What I mean is this could be a mistake. Your next step is to find out if it's true. Find out if this young woman really is your daughter. A paternity test. After that, you have a big decision to make. But don't make it now. You need to put sleep between getting this news and making a decision about it, as hard as that might be. Now, are you okay to go inside?'

He nodded. 'Julia needs to know. To know she's got a sister about the same age.'

Rose felt a jolt. Julia had been conceived in 2000 at the start of October, their second time sleeping together, just a few days after he and Rose had met… and this meant she would have been pregnant at the same time as Eve Levine. Two mothers, both carrying Chris's child, both unaware of the other. Two girls, oblivious to their sisterhood. Refocussing on the moment was a struggle.

'Julia doesn't need to know yet. She needs to be told only if that girl is really your daughter. She won't hear a word of this otherwise. The same for the rest of our family.'

Not conversations he would enjoy, she knew. She would tell Julia, though, because that had to be done correctly and she wasn't sure he could manage that. The rest of their small family was scattered, so he could deal with them in his own time. It made her think of Chris's father and she had to stop herself from bringing that subject up.

He rubbed his face with both hands.

'I'm sorry I lied to you. I know you doubted me when I said I didn't know the name Eve Levine. I mean, I suspected, but I didn't know for sure. But I wasn't upfront with you. I didn't admit the truth, because…' Here he fell short of words.

'Because you wanted it to not be real. You wanted this problem to just go away.'

He gave no answer. But he didn't need to.

'We won't get any more answers tonight, Chris, so you have to try to put this a little bit further back in your mind. It could take a while, and you can't wander about in a daze like a zombie until then.'

He gave a bizarre cackle and she knew why. Put it to the back of his mind? She knew her husband and tonight's bombshell would stay dead centre, in the limelight, perhaps for ever. For her, too.

# TUESDAY

# CHAPTER SEVEN

Rose woke from a wild dream to find Chris sitting on the edge of the bed with his back to her. It was still midnight-black outside, the room cloaked in shadow. She reached towards her husband, laid a hand softly on his shoulder. He took her hand in his and kissed her fingers.

Rose spotted a rectangle of white brightness in his lap. His phone.

'Call her,' she said.

But he shook his head.

'It's not about the girl.'

She twisted his wrist so the phone washed her in light. On the screen, a newspaper article. She squinted. By the third word – MURDERED – she forgot all about the pain in her shoulder from having slept on one side too long.

*Monday, 11 November*

Local father found murdered at workplace

*Ron Hugill, 48, has been found dead at MuscleBound, where he taught boxing classes. The attack is thought to have happened late Saturday night, after Hugill had locked up. A witness reports hearing screams and then calling the police, who found the cash register empty and Hugill unresponsive on the scene.*

*While no one has yet been taken into custody, police are seeking the whereabouts of a prolific lawbreaker called Dominic Everton, who has prior convictions for robbery and assault. It is believed that Hugill returned to the gym to fetch his laptop, interrupted the burglar and paid the ultimate price. Everton is presently missing from his home, believed to be on the run in Sheffield or Newcastle, where he has contacts. News of the brutal murder has been delivered to Hugill's long-term girlfriend and daughter.*

Rose had remembered the mention of a murdered boyfriend from the suicide article, but hadn't thought to look into it. But Chris had. And now she had. And she wished they hadn't. Reading the word 'murdered' was one thing, but knowing the whole story was so much worse. And this gruesome story would have been relayed to Eve, fresh and right to her face, while she lay dying of cancer. It explained Eve's suicide, although Rose couldn't fathom the selfishness required to heap even more tragedy upon a daughter.

'Too late,' she said.

'I know,' Chris replied.

'No, I mean… too early. It's too early in the morning to worry about this.'

She pulled, and he moved. Back into his space in the bed, cold now. She flipped the quilt over him. Then turned him away so she could mould herself to his warm back, legs against his own. Her weight upon her shoulder hurt like hell, but the warm embrace was preferable.

'Eve's daughter is asleep now. She's not worrying about Ron Hugill right now, so don't worry about her. You have to try to sleep.'

'It explains why Eve killed herself. Does it explain why her daughter came to me? She lost her father; is she trying to replace him?'

'All you can do is contact her tomorrow. When the sun is up. Now you have to do nothing but sleep.'

The correct advice, but she didn't doubt they were wasted words.

*

Once more cast out of a strange dream, Rose woke to find Chris again sitting on the edge of the bed, his back to her. The curtains were drawn, but their thin texture glowed with sunlight. She reached out to him. Pain cruised circuits in her left shoulder and she loosed a moan.

'Oh, God, sorry,' he said. 'I forgot to turn you.'

His phone was in his lap again. She had managed to put this mess aside to sleep. Chris hadn't. Now, with the sun up and sleep gone, she twisted his wrist so she could see the device. On the screen, a recently sent text message to: 'EVE DAUGHTER'. She read the text:

*'We should meet for a chat.'*

She pulled, and he moved, but not back into his sun-warmed space in the bed. He got up and went into the en-suite bathroom. His agitation kindled pity and she threw off the covers.

Standing naked behind him, she watched him shave. 'You've had time to think.'

'Parents have a bond with children. It's ingrained. Biology. You have this weak little human that'll die without your care.'

She considered this. 'You're saying that kind of bond can't exist with a child that's already fully grown? People take on other people's children all the time.'

'Below adult age, maybe it's different. They still need care. There's still a sort of child and adult relationship. What if I'm too late? Christ, she's already almost as tall as me.'

'By sixteen I was taller than my mother. From that point we became more like sisters. When my dad died a few months later and Mum lost her job, I got one. I provided for us. It was almost as if our roles reversed. It didn't affect us. In fact, the changing relationship made us happier. It was new and different. Like a change of scenery. Or like a holiday.'

'But you already had that bond. You had the… I don't know… *roots*. You weren't strangers. And maybe it's different for mothers than it is for fathers.'

She took his wrist in one hand and pulled the razor from his grip with her other. 'The girl is only a stranger to you because we don't have the results yet. We don't know for sure. Wait and see. And the fact that she's fully grown already can be a good thing. You skipped all the hard baby and toddler work.'

He grunted. 'You think I'll be sad that I missed her firsts, like first bike ride, first day at school, losing her first tooth?'

She started to shave him. Her frozen wrist made it awkward for her, but she ignored the pain enough to be careful with the tool. 'It's a thought. I'd hate to have missed any of that with Julia. Normally I can read you, Chris, but you have me stumped here.'

Finished, she lay down the razor while he stripped off his boxer shorts and turned on the shower. 'I have me stumped, too. But that says something, doesn't it? That I'm not jumping for joy after what I just found out.'

'What does it say? That you don't want the girl to be your daughter? I don't see it saying anything other than your mind is still scrambled. Which I understand. You just got hit with a haymaker. It's a form of concussion. Give it time. Besides, none of this means anything. Like I said before, it doesn't mean Eve's daughter wants to enter our lives.'

'Oh, but it does,' he blurted. 'She wants me to be her father. She wants to come right on into our life—'

'No, you don't know that. The girl heard a story and now she's told it to you – in her own way. That could be the end of it.'

He shook his head. 'No, no. That's why she came, Rose. Why else? Her other dad's dead, so she wants a new one. Like you replacing your broken phone charger. I'm her new phone charger.'

He looked ready to shed tears, so she took his hand. 'Well, that's just silly, Chris. But do you remember the charger you bought?

Didn't fit, did it? Wrong one. You assumed and got it wrong. You just remember that until you know for sure. You might be the wrong charger.'

\*

'Does this make you think about your own father?'

When Chris didn't answer her question, she turned to him. They were sharing the shower, their backs to each other. She put a hand on his shoulder, and that was when he spoke.

'That's not the same. Not at all.'

He left the shower, still soapy. She gave him a minute then followed. He was sitting on the bed with a towel around his waist, torso still wet and his phone in his hand.

'Nothing yet,' he said.

'Too early,' she answered.

They dressed. He finished first, but waited so he could towel dry her hair. Like clipping her toenails, it was one of a few activities she didn't mind needing help with.

'Did you never suspect? Never wonder? With Eve. About a pregnancy. If you knew you hadn't used protection.'

Behind her on the bed, he stopped rubbing her hair. 'No. It was a drunken late night. I didn't think about it at the time. And I guess I just assumed afterwards that… we'd been lucky.'

He continued rubbing her hair. When it was dry, he left the bedroom a step ahead of her.

Julia's door opened and she stepped out. She wore jeans and a *Baywatch* T-shirt with doll-like people in swimwear running along a hot beach. Perhaps sensing parent-talk had been interrupted, she quietly rushed past. Chris got a whiff of deodorant from her room. It wasn't a feminine smell.

'Morning, old ones,' she said as she glided down the stairs. She waved her phone over her shoulder. 'My pal Simone is down today, remember? Can she stay here?'

'Of course,' Rose said.

'The one with the togmuppet ex?' Chris asked.

Rose looked puzzled. Julia stopped and turned, quickly explaining a story Chris had already got. She added: 'Simone moved out of their flat, so she's got nowhere to stay. Can you take me to pick her up from the Lost Valley?'

A question for Chris. She laughed at his puzzled face. 'It's a pub in Sheffield, near the train station. We want a quick drink before we come back. But can you wait in the car? About nine o'clock okay?'

'What if people see her in my car and think I'm her boyfriend?'

'What do you mean?'

'The togmuppet's going to kill her boyfriend, isn't he?'

Julia had to quickly explain that for her mother, too. 'But Marc's not going to chase her or anything. He won't come here looking for her. There's nothing to worry about. Can she stay?'

Again, a question for Chris. 'Your mum just said it was okay, so I haven't got a say.'

Like a striking cobra, she darted up the stairs, kissed his cheek, and was on the ground floor two seconds later. Chris made a mental note to remind her not to bounce around like a ninja in front of her frail mother. He went to her open door and sniffed.

'What are you doing?' Rose said. 'Look, I want you to ask Simone not to call this Marc fellow while she's staying here, okay? Not from the house phone.'

'She won't, believe me. Listen, you were out yesterday afternoon, right? So Julia was alone in the house?'

'No, Julia went out, too. What's with sniffing the air like a dog?'

'Maybe she sneaked back while you were out. Why am I smelling male deodorant from her room? Has she had a boy here?'

'Not that I know of. No. Come on.'

They started down the stairs, Chris leading in case Rose fell. In the kitchen, she asked if he'd made up with 'her'.

'Who?'

'Simone. You had that spat at that party.'

He nearly dropped the kettle. 'Christ, that was her? The leprechaun hat?'

'Yes. I'm surprised you said she could stay if you hadn't made up. You ruined that party.'

'Well, she was abusive.'

'I heard that you got offended by some drunken joke she made. You were snippy with her.'

How could he forget? He'd dropped Julia at a flat party, but had peeked inside to make sure it wasn't a bunch of college idiots snorting drugs. Drunk, a girl in a silly leprechaun hat – Simone – had made some crack about him being too old for parties.

'I responded, that's all. Things got out of hand. Some of the boys there tried to act macho by sticking their oars in.'

'You were embarrassing, I heard. Julia refused to bring friends to the house for weeks afterwards. You remember that?'

He did, unfortunately. He grabbed teacups. 'She can't stay here, then. We'll have to tell her no.'

'No, we've promised Julia now. You can pick Simone up and see how she is with you. Maybe she's forgotten. You can apologise.'

He slinked into the living room and checked his phone. Goddamn leprechaun hat, coming here. To stay!

But he got his mind onto things more important. No return text from the girl. He half hoped there never would be. Rose had been right: he was worried about *scorpions in the closet*, as Julia had so beautifully misused the term only a few months ago. And a murdered father was a big scorpion that Eve's daughter would carry around for ever. Chris didn't like to deal with other people's problems, and a grieving brand-new daughter could become one big enough to for ever upset the balance he so craved. And he knew almost nothing about the girl, which meant…

…There could be other scorpions.

# CHAPTER EIGHT

Eight times according to his call log. A number dialled, but a call terminated before the other end could be picked up. He was worried what the girl would think if the text hadn't arrived. How would it look? Like he didn't give a shit? But he didn't complete a single call. Of eight. He wanted to vent his frustration with fists against a wall.

Two had been made by the time he set off for work. He drove in a daze and barely remembered the journey. But he got there in one piece somehow. After call three, made en route, his phone rang and his heart leaped. But it was just Rose.

'The police finally turned up. What was that, thirteen hours to respond? They said it was a busy night and we didn't sound that distressed. Anyway, I gave a basic description of the car and the men. And that our purses were taken. They took my statement but you'll have to go give yours at the station. They won't come back.'

'I will,' he said, but it was a lie. The capture of a couple of lowlifes was the last thing he cared about right now.

Chris had cancelled another call to the girl by the time he got to the hospital. He walked fast to the lab because he didn't want time to let his mind run wild. Once he was inside, though, he regretted not having taken a pause to wind himself in. He doubted he was in a fit state for work. He'd made some gruesome errors so far this week, and today his head was even less focussed. And so:

*Redfern, get your head in gear.*
*Redfern, concentrate.*

*Redfern, you're in trouble if this happens again.*

Three mistakes in an hour, none really costly, but all indicative of a mind in turmoil.

The girl called.

No, she didn't. He thought he'd felt his phone vibrate, but no. Ringxiety, or Phantom Phone Vibration, or whatever it was called. Seemingly every minute his brain read the movement of clothing or a faint muscle contraction as a call. While it was in his hand, he made call eight and this time waited five rings before hanging up.

'Hey, did I mention that fool I got in my room a few days ago, Missus Chiclets? About her second set of teeth? Christ. Full-grown woman, in she comes…'

Chris listened as the radiographer moaned to the gastroenterologist about a woman who'd come in for an X-ray because she thought she had a second full set of teeth growing in her gums. Normally he found these overheard lunchtime conversations fascinating, but not today. Maybe never again. Just as the radiographer got heated about his freaky patient, Chris swallowed his last piece of sausage roll and headed out of the Pitstop, an open-plan café in the hospital foyer. On his way to the lift, he pulled his phone to perform a brand-new aborted call to the girl. But he didn't get the chance, and the option was about to become obsolete.

It rang as he was about to dial. Rose.

'Hello, Ro—'

'Chris?' she cut in. 'Can you come back? Eve's daughter… she's here.'

At the house? She was at his home, with Rose?

She started to say more, but he killed the call. Heads turned to watch as he bolted down the corridor.


The journey was as much a misty haze as three hours earlier, but again he somehow avoided tying his car in a bow around a tree.

The driveway ran alongside the house to a garage in the backyard that was full of junk. Sitting before the garage was a motorbike. And standing by it were Julia and someone nobody could mistake for a man this time. She wore jeans and a long-sleeved black polo neck which was fitted to her feminine form. No beanie cap this time, so the blonde hair was pulled back into a bun. The contrast between this image and his last of her was mammoth, but that scar upon her porcelain cheek was undeniable. It was the same girl. Chris tried to swallow but his throat was a desert.

They were just chatting, though. Everything fine there. Broad daylight, urban environment, and a pair of teenagers talking about a motorbike. Julia had always wanted one, he remembered, so of course she would ask about the bike when it turned up. Nothing suspicious there. She didn't have the demeanour of someone who'd just learned she might have a sister.

Calmer now, he felt silly for rushing back, for his wild and illogical assumption that there was danger to thwart. He slipped towards the front door before he got spotted, unsure why he was trying to avoid the girl. Even so, he crept in like a burglar and found Rose in the kitchen, with her back to him. She was watching the young pair through the window. There was a satchel on the kitchen table. The girl's, surely. For a moment, he remembered how she had ticked. Strange.

When he appeared by Rose's side, she jumped.

'How come she's here? What's she doing with Julia? And why are you hiding?'

'She just knocked on the door, Chris. She's found our stuff. I wasn't hiding. I'm watching how she acts. We never saw how pretty she was last night. But she's stunning.'

He had to admit that was true, especially in daylight, and even with that scar. He wondered why she didn't use her long hair to hide it; in fact, the tight bun seemed to parade it, like a piece of jewellery or a badge. As he watched, she rubbed that centimetre-wide valley between ear and nose. He got the impression Julia had asked about it. He also noted that she stood a good five inches taller than his daughter. His *other* daughter.

'What stuff? What do you mean?'

'Calm down. I'll explain.'

Rose pulled out a chair at the table and he sat. The satchel was right there, and it wasn't ticking. He fought a compulsion to root through it. His jaw started to ache from half an hour of solid tension.

'She found our stuff? Is that why she's here?'

Rose put the kettle on and explained. The girl had spotted Chris's wallet and Rose's purse close to where they'd been snatched. Just lying in the road. She had planned to post them, but then Chris had sent a text about popping round for a cup of tea. So here she was. Rose pointed out the wallet and purse on top of the microwave oven. Chris grabbed both and got no surprises.

'Cash is gone.'

'Not the cards, though. That saves a headache.' Rose hesitated. 'She told me she sent the note. And she told me why she sent it.'

Chris sat again. Rose continued, 'She knows it was a mistake now. Just before she overdosed, Eve told her that her dad… wasn't her real dad. Just as I assumed. Ron Hugill had been in Katherine's life from such an early age, she just assumed he was her father. For all those years. It was a big shock to hear otherwise. Eve gave Katherine your name—'

'Wait, Katherine?' Chris asked, mouth agape in shock.

'Yes,' Rose said with a reassuring smile. 'That's her name. Just like your mother.'

And suddenly it was all beginning to feel more real. Not just that there was a girl, some stranger trying to worm her way into his life. A daughter. Young, beautiful Katherine.

'Wait, but how did she know my name? Eve, I mean?' Chris continued. 'I used a fake. Both times.'

'Both times?'

He lifted the satchel an inch off the table, just to check the weight. 'Yeah, she asked me twice. I had a chance to come clean the second time. I didn't. She never knew my real name.'

'I don't know how she knew, but she found out somehow. So Katherine looked you up. It was easy. Your Facebook told her where you worked.'

'So she could have popped by and said, "Hey, I'm your daughter." That doesn't explain the stupid threatening note.'

Rose pulled out a chair and sat in front of him. His eyes kept jumping to the kitchen window every time he heard a sound outside, so she grabbed his chin and made him look at her.

'Eyes front, soldier. Listen to me. In the same week, the man she thought was her father was murdered, then she found out there was a real dad out there somewhere, and then her mother died. Give the girl a break for not doing a PowerPoint presentation to work out the pros and cons of various ways of contacting you. She wasn't thinking straight, as I always said. So, are we going to give her a chance after what she's been through?'

He nodded. He wasn't sure he meant it, though.

'She wanted you to have time to get used to Eve's death before she hit you with shock number two. A mad idea, sure, but we can understand that, can't we?'

He nodded again. More sincere this time.

'I'm not siding with her, Chris. But we don't know what it's like to go through what she's suffered. She told me she was planning to send a letter of explanation to the house, and that envelope with the necklace chain in it. But then some weird quirk of fate put us all on that road.'

A third nod. Accepted. Somewhat. But as one worry mellowed, another reared up. 'What's she doing out there with Julia? She hasn't told—'

'No, Chris, Julia doesn't know. They're just talking. Our daughter is chatting to a young woman who found our lost property and returned it, that's all. She likes the bike. Your only worry should be that she's probably going to start begging us again to buy her one. And she told Katherine that it's our anniversary on Saturday. Oh, and she asked if she's got kids.'

He felt the bottom drop out of his stomach. That was something he hadn't even considered: that he could have become not just a dad again but also—

'Calm down, you're not a grandfather yet,' she said, the curl of her mouth proving she was having a lark.

He didn't laugh. 'We'll have to tell her who Katherine is at some point, you know?'

'We don't know who she is yet, do we? We still need to do a paternity test. She might just be some girl who returned our stuff, mightn't she?' She grabbed Chris's hand. 'Come on, let's go outside.'

He yanked that hand right back. 'What am I supposed to say to her? I don't know what to say. This is very awkward. We can't mention who she might be in front of Julia. But it'll hang over us like some toxic cloud.'

She shook her head. 'You came back for this. What's the problem?'

'This is easy for you. How would you feel if you suddenly found out you had a long-lost daughter you never knew about?'

It took her baffled laughter to make him fathom the nonsense of his question.

There was a knock at the back door. It opened and Katherine stood there. 'Can I come in?'

Again he noted the husky voice, somewhat... he mentally slapped himself before the word *sexy* could enter his head. Rose got to her feet, but Chris remained seated. Rose waved her in and she crossed the kitchen with enough confidence to wear at his. When he stood to greet her, he was unnerved by something in her features. Was it the lips – so much like Julia's? Those big brown eyes – akin to his own? His hand nervously shook as he clasped the one she offered him. She gripped tight and shook hard, like one of his good buddies.

'My name's Katie. Katherine, but I always go by Katie. I'll just come out and say what I'm sure you already know,' she said. 'I think you might be my father.'

# CHAPTER NINE

The words were still ringing in Chris's ears.

*I think you might be my father.*

He had to look away from Katie's probing eyes, at Rose, who sensed his shock – or figured he was about to say something daft – and put out her own hand in greeting. As the two women shook hands and Rose reintroduced herself, he took a moment, unwatched, to suck in a lungful of air. His head felt light.

When Katie returned those probing eyes to him, he tried to take a step backwards, away, but he was already hard up against the kitchen table. He felt spotlighted, like a kid called upon to speak in class. The first thing that entered his head was: 'You'll have to excuse how I act in the next few minutes. This has come as a very big shock.'

She gave a slow nod, and a warm smile. 'I understand. You need time. That's why I won't stay long. I want to make this easy for you.'

She leaned towards him and for a horrible moment he thought she was going to snatch him into a hug. But her arm snaked past him and then she withdrew, and in her hand was the satchel from the table.

Captivated, he watched her extract a small box from inside. He noticed her nails were long but unpainted, and real, unlike Julia's or Rose's. 'I understand how awkward this is for you, Mr Redfern. My turning up here, like this. But I wanted to get this part out of the way immediately.'

The box had a picture of a smiling man with a grinning kid on his shoulders. Gene Genie – 'fast and accurate home DNA test kit'. As usual when confronted with a surprising blow, Chris's brain sought to joke.

'Maybe a more realistic picture would be a guy strangling his cheating wife.'

Peripherally he saw Rose's jaw drop and realised he must have said the wrong thing.

But Katie didn't react, except to say, 'This is very intrusive of me, I know that. But this will be over in a minute and then I'll get out of your hair.' She lowered her eyes and timidity coated her next words: 'Do I have your permission to contact you when I get the results? They come by email in three to five days.'

'Yes, of course,' Rose answered for him. 'Katie, can I ask your birthday?'

'Of course. The fourth of June 2001,' Katie replied, looking pleased that Rose wanted to know more about her.

Chris looked at Rose, wondering why she'd really asked. He'd already wondered if she'd thought about the fact that she would have been carrying Julia at the same time that Eve bore Katie – Julia was born only a few weeks later. If so, she hadn't mentioned it.

Katie looked at each of them and then lowered her eyes. 'I was wondering what plans you had this evening? I was thinking we could have a sit-down. Have a proper conversation. I know right now you have to get back to work, but it would be nice if you could spare the time later.'

'I can't tonight,' he said, too quickly. He felt Rose stiffen, obviously no fan of his response. But he didn't backtrack. Couldn't. 'One of my daughter's friends is coming up from university for a few days. I have to pick her up. Then it will be a busy evening of settling her in.'

She paused. 'She's staying here?'

'For a few days, yes. So, unfortunately, I can't make tonight. But another time?'

Rose rubbed her chin, one of many giveaways that she was unhappy with his behaviour. But Katie smiled.

'Absolutely fine. Anytime. Anyway, it's three to five days for the result so I will get out of your hair and leave you alone until then.'

'I didn't mean we can't meet up. It's just—'

'No, it's fine,' she cut in. 'You need time to get your head around this. I get it. It really is fine. It's probably best if I stay away until the test results are in.'

'If you're sure. I just don't want you to think I'm trying to avoid you until we know.'

Katie shook her head, but Chris could tell the girl wasn't comfortable. 'No, Katie, we'll grab a drink or something before then. Tonight is just bad timing.'

Some of the warmth radiating off Katie had cooled. It was almost like she'd retreated into a shell of herself. But that sheepishness was absent when she pulled a folded A4 sheet from her pocket and said, 'I need a swab from you, and a signature. Something to do with the Human Tissue Act.'

The sheet was an application form. There was a clear box for including a driving licence, which Katie had already taped hers to, and an invoice at the bottom, to which she'd attached a cheque. And she'd signed the form. There was a line for Chris's signature. He scrawled it with an unsteady hand while Katie extracted oral swabs from the box.

Again, needing to crack a funny, he showed Rose the cheque and said, 'So cheap. We could treat John and Carol. We all know their kid's the spitting image of John's brother Eric.'

This time Rose didn't settle for a sly reprimand, but outright told him to stop acting immature.

Now eager for something serious to say, something unbidden popped out. 'Do you hope it's positive?'

His question seemed to shock Katie.

'Let's wait for the results,' Rose jumped in. 'Katie has business at the garage and Chris, you have to get back to work. Katie, thank you for returning our property and I want—'

'I just want you both to know that I'm sorry for all this,' Katie blurted, wringing her hands. 'I don't mean harm and I'm not trying to create an awkward situation.'

Rose touched Katie's arm. 'No, Katie, it's fine.'

'Yes,' Chris said. Again, all he could think of. Nothing else untoward escaped this time.

'No, I really am sorry.' Katie's expression was remote again, as if she was holding back all emotion. But meekness was once again layered upon her tone of voice. 'I had a father for all my life, and then I got the bombshell that he might not be. I just need to know the truth. If you like, I don't even have to tell you the results. I can just vanish, and you need never know. But I need this for *me*. *I* need to know.'

The tension pulsing off Katie started to harden Chris's spirit, as he realised he might not be the weaker one of the pair. 'No, Katie. No, you go ahead and contact me with the results. Of course I want to know. As soon as you get them. And we'll take it from there.'

Meekly, she stumbled through her next sentence: 'I suppose you'd work it out anyway if I just didn't contact you, and, sorry, I wasn't thinking about how you also need to know the truth.' She held up an oral swab. 'Perhaps we should get this done before my – before your daughter comes in.'

She'd corrected herself sharply, but Chris didn't miss it. It sent a funny tingling through his fingers. *My* changed to *your*. Before she said, *your daughter*, Katie had been about to say *my sister*.

Wishful thinking?

\*

As Rose escorted Katie as she rolled her bike down the driveway, she couldn't help a glance up and down the street: nosy neighbours might be wondering who this young woman was. She also couldn't help noticing a curve to Katie's spine that gave her a slight forward lean, and her own horrible relief that this tall, slim beauty wasn't a perfect human specimen after all.

As Katie swung her leg over the ride, her jeans rode up to expose a sockless ankle. And mottled reddish-white skin, raw and nasty. Rose gave it just a glimpse and looked quickly away, revulsion instantly smothered, but Katie hadn't missed it. Perfectly balanced astride the machine, she raised the same foot onto a handlebar and tugged her trouser leg up another six inches. Now, permission granted, Rose stared. The entire calf was ruined. She knew she was looking at burn scars. This imperfection instilled only pity.

'Engine caught fire at eighty miles an hour,' Katie said.

'My god. What did you do?'

'Trousers caught fire. I slowed to about forty and just leaped off. The road rash on my butt hurt more.' She smiled, a great big grin that eased Rose's awkwardness. 'No big deal, but both ankles look like I wear lava socks.'

There was a moment's silence. Katie cracked her fingers, one at a time. Rose had noticed the young woman cracking her wrists when they first met, and again when Rose had opened the front door to her.

'I have rheumatoid arthritis,' Rose said. 'My immune system attacks my own joints. I've had it since about your age.' She showed her own wrists, which were misshapen, like some of the finger knuckles. 'My hips and shoulders hurt the worst, although I've got three toes that don't bend.'

Katie looked at her own hands. 'Oh, I understand. I'm always cracking my wrists. No, my problem isn't arthritis. My fingers and feet tingle, but it's just a circulation thing. Thin veins or something.'

Rose's hand was still raised and Katie grabbed it. 'I don't want either of you to think that I'm trying to find a new father.'

'We don't... we don't think that.'

'I don't know why he was killed.' Katie let go of Rose's hand and her eyes dropped to her bike, like a sorry child.

It took Rose a second to bridge the gap: Ron Hugill, the man Katie had long called father, in error. 'I read it in the newspaper. His funeral was yesterday. I'm so sorry about that. You've had so much pain recently.'

'Ron was a very good man,' Katie continued. 'Even when my mother was having her bad days because of the cancer, he was a rock, you know? Good to me. I don't know why he was killed. He didn't have any enemies. Everyone liked him. I don't know why he was killed.'

'It was probably just a robbery. Just... wrong place, wrong time. Thugs like that don't care. They don't care who they hurt. Your father was just very unlucky.'

She immediately regretted using the word *father*. Katie only nodded and then started her engine. Rose suddenly hated the thought of Chris and Katie parting with nothing but a plan to wait for the test results.

A neat idea popped up.

# CHAPTER TEN

Chris was late back to work, which pleased his boss, Alan, because he got to vent sarcasm. Chris barely heard the rebuke, though, because everything was blurred background scenery and would probably remain so until he got the paternity results. He now had a new worry because Rose, with her misplaced good intentions, had invited Katie to their wedding anniversary on Saturday.

Her reason was two-fold. Rose had asked if the rest of Katie's family knew about Chris, but the answer had been no. Eve's sister, Elaine, was the only member of a shattered family who'd kept in periodic contact with Eve, but Katie had never liked her. Plus, Katie didn't have many friends. So Rose had wanted to make her feel wanted. But mostly she hoped to make sure Chris and Katie weren't total strangers when gloriously announced as father and daughter. 'What better chance for some bonding than a party?' she'd said.

He didn't like it. 'And what if the result comes back negative?'

'You think I didn't think about that? If we have a negative result by then, Katie might just vanish. But I think the party would be a good way of saying goodbye and good luck. There's no doubting that you knew her mother. That's fact. You and Katie have still had an impact on each other's lives and it wouldn't be right to just shoo her away as if she was nothing more than a waitress who brought food.'

Good point, but he still didn't like it. But the girl had accepted the invite, so it was happening. And his anxiety hadn't been helped by Rose's damn joke that he should be thankful Eve Levine hadn't had triplets.

Even so, he managed to get on with his job. Louise called him over to the Enterics bench. He remembered she wanted that shift swap for this weekend, but he'd forgotten to ask Rose's permission. Which was good, because when he'd told Louise he'd think about it, he had forgotten about the anniversary party. As he walked over, he plucked up the courage to tell her.

'Ask your ball and chain about that swap?' Louise predictably said.

The courage failed him. 'She's checking to see what we've got on. I'll let you know tomorrow.'

She had a stool sample on the bench. He picked up the form. From the Emergency Medicine Unit, a temporary assessment feeder ward from A&E.

'You mean you forgot?' she said.

Raymond Monroe, 34, serious gastroenteritis. Suspected E. coli 0157. An awkward little alien intruder because it was booby trapped. Antibiotics could kill it, but after death it released serious toxins that could turn a host's bad day worse. So right now, Raymond Monroe wouldn't be getting any medicine, not until his carers knew more.

'Oh yes,' Chris answered as he pulled out his phone and booted up Facebook.

'Phone her now, could you? I need to let my boyfriend know.'

'Which one?'

She elbowed his arm and he told her he'd ask tonight. Tomorrow, he'd tell Louise that he'd forgotten about the anniversary party. He was back at his bench only seconds before Louise shouted his name again.

'I'll call her on the way home,' he yelled without looking, and with no intention of doing any such thing.

'Not that. Where's the Enterics kits?'

She was now by the supplies cupboard, looking annoyed. He stared at her and his silence told her what she needed to know.

'Christ, Chris, is there anything you can remember? Is that why you wear a name badge?'

Uncommon anger from her. He told her he'd order the kits right away.

'I need it here right now. It should have been here today. It won't come till tomorrow.'

His own anger started to simmer. He had bigger worries. 'So why didn't Alan order it?'

'He asked me to. And I asked you. I've got this test to do.'

The BDMAX machine was fast and accurate at identifying the presence of certain bacteria, including the nasty E. coli 0157. But the test could still be done manually.

'So do a damn Sorbitol test and stop being lazy,' he snapped. Loud. Others looked around. Louise pulled a face and returned to her bench. Maybe she would have argued further if she wasn't eager for that shift swap. Which she wasn't getting.

Show over, he hopped on the computer to order the kits. As he typed, he wondered what changes to his life a positive paternity result might mean. He'd been terrified about a meteoric shifting of land mass in his world, but that didn't have to be the case, did it? It wasn't as if he and Katie had had a long life together. They barely knew each other, lived in separate worlds; maybe Katie, even following a positive result, had no plans to keep in touch.

He looked over at Alan's office. The boss had a grown son he hardly saw. Plenty of adult children flew the nest and hardly saw their parents thereafter. Maybe Chris and Katie would just shake hands and never see each other again.

That thought eased him a little.

Later, he sat at one of the computers to input a result on a pregnancy test. Louise was already at the other computer. He ignored her, but his peripheral vision caught her staring at him.

'What?' he said.

'I apologise.'

He softened. He turned his chair to face her and she showed her monitor. He saw that she'd written up the result of her test on Raymond Monroe's sample. Negative for E. coli 0157.

'For sure?' he said.

'Yeah, I did the manual. Pink all over the plate. No E. coli.'

'Then he can go ahead and get antibiotics. Well done.'

'Thank you. And I'm sorry for shouting at you earlier. I'm just bitchy today because Joe's not back now until early Friday. But we argued because he wants to pop to Bradford to see his brother before he sees me.'

Joe, one of two boyfriends, worked on an oil rig, two weeks straight then two off. He only got the chance to see Louise for a couple of days a month. Most of the lab joked that he had another family somewhere. Not something Chris would laugh at right now, of course.

But he focussed on something else she'd said. Popping to Bradford. The city was only an hour's drive away.

# CHAPTER ELEVEN

Chris pulled into the car park of The Blue Swan in Bradford and sat staring at the building.

He remembered the first time that Eve had hinted at continuing their relationship. In White River State Park. *If you and your friends are ever on a pub crawl*, she'd said, *I'll get my dad to do happy hour prices for you. We run The Blue Swan.*

*Will do*, he'd replied. Just a throwaway answer at the time, but back home and during a pub crawl with pals, he'd mentioned the happy hour promise. They'd said no, too far away, and besides, he'd started seeing a sexy young gymnast called Rose by then.

He'd given that false name and no address, no place of work or friends' names or anything else Eve could have used to trace him. He wasn't sure why, but once they'd started to enjoy the day, he'd felt that admitting a lie might put her off, so he'd stuck with it. The same weakness that had prevented him from telling Louise why he couldn't do her shift swap. If he had had any plans to see Eve again, of course he would have told her his real name. But he hadn't. So, he hadn't.

He stared at the pub. A two-storey detached red structure with a small white stone outbuilding. It was for sale at just over two hundred thousand, now closed, rundown, and maybe symbolic of Eve's mental state as her efforts to find Katie's father slowed, faltered, stalled and finally died. He pictured her beyond that outer wall, cancer-ridden and popping pills, passing the search for Chris onto Katie with her devastating revelation. Then he imagined the place in its heyday, bloated with customers, Eve working the bar for her parents, while upstairs a baby girl slept. What might have been? Maybe Chris would have ended up running the place with her. He could be chairman of a pool league that Katie played in as a teenager. He could have developed a whole new social circle. His errant sister and Katie, what kind of relationship might they have had? Perhaps in some alternate universe a relationship with Eve Levine might have resulted in his own mother not dying, since she'd been driving to visit Julia with birthday presents when a non-fatal heart attack sent her car into a lethal somersault – ten years next July, that. Maybe she would have had that heart attack at home and got necessary treatment, and survived. Consequently, his sister, Lindsay, might not have gone spinning off the rails, and she'd have a rich husband and a house on the same street. Who knew?

Chris forgot about parallel universes as he spotted a little human figure attached to the keystone above the arched wooden double doors of the pub. He got out of the car and approached for a closer look. It was a doll in a dress, secured there by string around the neck. The plastic skin and the clothing and the hair were grimy, as if from the pollution of a billion passing vehicles. A strange decoration for a pub, but Eve had had a little doll hanging from her keys, way back. He remembered it now, for the first time in all that time. Had she called it a lucky charm? Something passed down the family? He couldn't recall. But the one above the door struck him as a sign of her presence. Like her seal. Or, now, like her ghost's calling card.

He strolled to the large front window, which was whitewashed, and found a gap to peer through. The lounge beyond was dim and empty. No tables or chairs, no jukebox or pool table, and although the bar had pumps, the shelves behind it were bare and there were spaces that he guessed had once contained tall fridges for bottles. The place looked like it had been out of action for a long time. Long before Eve Levine had died.

He tried to picture himself behind that bar, Eve by his side, but quickly shut it down. Looking at the past was such a daft thing to do because you couldn't change it, and there was no guarantee of what might have been even if you could go back. He could have dated Eve and raised Katie and bonded with her entire family, and every single one of them could have died in a gruesome pub fire ten years ago.

But there was one absolute fact: cancer. Chris's presence in her life might have prevented a suicide, but death ultimately wouldn't be denied. As her husband, he would have had to deal with that. He would have had to accept the news of the cancer, and comfort her as she spiralled into depression, and explain to a little girl that her mummy was soon going to vanish.

And there would be no Julia. That was all the reason he needed to be assured that he had done the right thing. Julia was alive and maybe Katie and Eve and that entire extended family had lived much longer than they would have if he'd announced his real name back in Indiana.

He smiled at his own silliness. Parallel universes? Things were as they were and that was the end of it. He may have lost his mother, but he still had Julia and Rose. The grass was definitely greener on this side.

He jerked as he thought he caught a glimpse of movement from within, over by a door near a staircase. He watched for a few seconds, but the scene remained unchanged. Then he backed away and headed for his car, figuring that an empty pub would be Shangri-La to squatters.

As he started his engine, his phone rang. Rose.

'Traffic,' he said, and then instantly regretted the lie. 'Got caught up in it on my way to Bradford.'

'Bradford? What are you doing in Bradford?' Rose asked.

He hesitated, then decided to come clean. 'I popped out to Eve's old pub, just to have a look. I know what you're going to say.'

'Wish you married the pub heiress, eh?' she said, laughter not quite masking her concern. 'Thinking of the life you could have had with her?'

'Don't be silly, Rose. I don't waste my time thinking about what-ifs.'

*

Ringxiety. Chris checked his phone so many times during the first hour at home that Julia snatched it off him and had a look.

'You better not be having an affair,' she said, glaring right into his eyes. It made him laugh. And then hug her. His elegant, beautiful daughter, at times immature and naïve, sometimes logical and serious, but always protective of her mother.

The hug, right out of the blue, freaked Julia out even more and she called for her mother, saying, 'Dad was being weird.'

He laughed until a sudden thought reminded him that he might soon have to refer to her as his *youngest* daughter.

Later, Rose went into the kitchen to work on her non-fiction book for half an hour and Julia shifted upstairs. Chris lounged on the sofa and tried to concentrate on a Netflix programme but couldn't follow the plot with half a mind. He tried a book, but that was worse. So he closed his eyes and put his head back.

A noise woke him forty minutes later, close to eight. Or rather, a series of noises. Rose was in the living room with him, whistling while ironing like a happy old farmer.

'I found what I needed about the Broad Plain Gymnasium,' she said, and then the iron belched a cloud of steam like an old locomotive pulling out of a station.

'Spectacular,' he said, although he had no clue what she meant. She was writing a book about the history of British gymnastics and some of its major players, but, as much as he loved his wife, that was as much as he cared about. She hadn't practised the sport in years, but the interest had never waned. The book was her way of staying involved.

He got up for a drink of water. From the dining room, a blizzard of screeches and roars and crashes. He stopped at the doorway and saw Julia playing her damn Xbox game on her portable TV. Something demonic was hacking away at a bigger monster surrounded by flying creatures. He saw flashing neon blades and fireballs and all manner of kaleidoscopic weirdness, every bit of it accompanied by tremendous noise.

'Julia, it's time to go and get that friend of yours. Turn that off.'

'Can't yet,' she called back without looking away from the screen. 'Need to kill this Cyclops Boss to get the next Save Point Power Medallion.'

'Silly me.'

He got the water and settled on the sofa as Rose tossed aside the last piece of ironing and collapsed the board. Hopefully, Julia's game would consume her for the evening and she'd forget about having to collect Simone, and they could enjoy a quiet evening in as a family.

'Turn that noisy crap off!' Rose yelled towards the dining room.

'Dvark's on half-life-bar!' Julia shouted back.

'Can't save the game until she gets a power jewel or whatever,' he said.

Rose shook her head at him.

For the first time in a couple of days, he found himself content. He was submerged in the normal chaos of his home life, on his own sofa, warm, surrounded by people he loved, all of them happy and there wasn't much more he could ask for.

He didn't want the terrain to change, but he knew the map might soon alter for ever.

# CHAPTER TWELVE

The place they were picking up Simone was called the Lost Valley because it was in a corner of Sheffield's Meadow Park and surrounded by trees. A high wall separated the pub's beer garden from the park, but Julia's friend was coming from the train station on the other side of the park and the walk around was three times as long as a straight trek through. So Simone was going to climb the wall and meet Julia in the beer garden. Chris pulled up in the car park fifteen minutes before Simone's train was due and turned off the satnav. Here he finally got the will to vocalise his thoughts.

'Julia. I think you should ask Simone to stay at her parents' house.'

She gave him a sly smile. 'This is about that crap at her party, isn't it? What do you think she's going to do? She was drunk back then, and you were in a bad mood.'

'It's not about what she'll do. I'm worried it'll make for an uncomfortable atmosphere.'

'Only uncomfortable for you. Simone wouldn't have asked if she felt it would be a problem being around you. Although she did say she would keep out of your way.'

He sighed. 'Well, she shouldn't feel she has to, but okay.'

'Sorry, Dad, but Mum said it was okay, and I didn't think it would be a big deal. Walk me into the garden to wait. Get the awkward first meeting out of the way quickly.'

'No. I'll wait in the car, in the warm.'

'Fair enough, Mr Grumpy.'

Julia headed in.

But Chris didn't wait, instead choosing to take a drive.

*

He was back half an hour later. He parked and washed his hands with a bottle of water before strolling into the garden. Each table was on a circle of concrete and had an inviting-looking outdoor heater. Peaceful, apart from the thump of rock music from inside the pub. Julia had chosen the closest table to the garden wall. She sat alone.

'She's not here,' Julia said as Chris rubbed his cold hands before the pot-bellied heater. 'But the train was on time.'

'Maybe she bumped into the togmuppet.'

'Funny.' Julia tugged her eyes away to glance at the wall. Nobody toppled off it and came running. 'I'll call her again.' She got up to make a call out of his earshot. It took only seconds. 'No answer. Again! Dead tone. If that bitch didn't even get the train, I'll kill her.'

'Bitch? Sorry, I thought we were meeting your good friend.'

'She's a grand master at cancelling without telling people. She's got our postcode. If she's not here by ten, she can get a taxi.'

They chatted about nothing for a while. Two chicken wrap meals were brought out by a young woman who looked real pissed off that she had to travel to the furthest table in the garden. Her long face made Chris put away the small tip he had ready for her.

'You can have Simone's, Dad. I ordered for us both, but she's so late she can get stuffed.'

They ate, and Chris tried not to feel ignored as Julia played with her phone.

'Is that Facebook? I was just thinking how long it's been since I checked it to see whose dog has been photographed sleeping,' he said.

She just nodded, barely hearing.

'I could be missing out on seeing what someone's cooked for dinner,' he continued.

'Huhum,' she said, still hypnotised.

'I should upload the photos of that time aliens abducted me for mating with their women.'

'Sure,' she murmured.

He was white noise to her, so he played a game on his own phone until ten o'clock rolled around. Julia went to the wall and found a hole for her toes so she could peek her head over, into the black woody gloom beyond.

'Is she frozen into a block of ice out there?' Chris called out.

'It's a fifteen-minute walk from the station.'

She retook her seat. The heater was coin-operated and Chris didn't have another coin. They both started to feel the cold, and Chris was relieved when Julia reached a critical level of boredom and frustration. She sent her friend a text and left a voicemail, and they headed home.

*

Chris woke in the dead hours and immediately worried why. Normally, he'd go downstairs and check the windows, in case a noise had stirred him. But he didn't doubt that some unremembered dream about Katie had done the job tonight. Rose was on her left side, left forearm poking straight out. Once, he'd found her in that position and been unable to resist a joke. A Dear Jane letter slotted into her fingers, which she'd found upon waking. She'd been quite upset. She tried to hide her fears that he'd leave her for someone with pretty fingers and spreadable legs, but she wasn't the only one who could read a spouse's mind.

And that had been back before sleeping on the same side all night could wreck her for two days. So he rolled her onto her back and got up.

Out on the landing, he opened the attic trapdoor and jumped to latch his fingers over the edge. It was far more of a struggle than last time to haul himself through the hatch and into the attic, and he wondered if the last few weeks of Rose's healthy food had actually put weight on him. But he was in. He flicked on the light and crossed the grid of beams to a space cleared amid old junk where he had a plastic outdoor chair next to a tiny coffee table. Both were dusty, as too was the half-empty bottle of Proper Twelve whiskey that sat alone on the table. The last time he had sat here, in his private hideaway, to sip and blot out the world, had been five weeks earlier, when Rose's mother had a mini stroke and Rose had withdrawn internally while she recovered. The time before that had been because of a friend's death, some five months ago.

Only now, remembering those tragedies, did he realise that he was putting this latest life development in the same category. Perhaps not quite a tragedy, but certainly a hammer blow that was going to send his life down a new track. Unless the paternity test came back negative. Maybe even then.

This was his private room, the Manor, for emptying the mind, so he sat and he sipped and he worked on doing that. It was the only place he could manage it. It was why he'd removed the trap ladder, so nobody could see his private little domain, let alone enter it. No one knew he came up here and he even got a mild sort of kick from the secret. Here, he easily managed to shut down the voice that was telling him his life would run smoother if Katie's real father turned out to be the one who'd got beaten to death.

# WEDNESDAY

# CHAPTER THIRTEEN

When Chris arrived at work the next day, he noticed there were four police cars parked outside the hospital's main entrance but gave them no further thought.

He soon would.

He trekked to the lab, dumped his coat and went to his bench. But before he could begin lifesaving, Alan collared him.

'Carla phoned in. Hurt her foot on that damn car of hers. Won't be in, surprise, surprise. Guess she can't read.' He jerked his head at a plaque above his office door which contained a long-winded warning about the menace of missed workdays. 'You do HVS as well as your own department today, Redfern.'

HVS was the department that dealt with samples taken from more *intimate* areas of the body.

Chris shifted reluctantly over to the HVS bench. An hour later, someone brought up the microbiology box from Specimen Collection, which was where all samples from the wards were assembled. Chris decided to wait until the throng around the box had dispersed before he looked for the HVS samples, but a gangly guy called Lionel Parrott, a twenty-two-year-old Medical Lab assistant rumoured to enjoy kicking the daylights out of homeless men with his mates at the weekend, appeared by his side with a bag and a grin.

'You want to swap benches for a while? I want to do Meadow Moll's sample.'

'Who?'

'Have you been in a cave?' Parrott asked. 'The girl that got attacked last night.'

No gossip pleased Parrot more than crime and violence. He gleefully explained that an early morning jogger had found an unconscious young blonde woman half battered to death, babbling incoherently: possibly drugged. And possibly sexually assaulted, because the bag in Parrott's hand apparently contained an intimate sample.

That explained all the cops downstairs. They were waiting for this Meadow Moll to blurt a name so they could go crack the corresponding head. Chris reached for the bag, but Parrott kept it out of reach, like a treasure.

'We could crack this case,' Parrott said.

'She came in this morning, Lionel. She's not going to show sexual disease symptoms in a couple of hours. If she's got something, she already had it.'

'Doesn't mean she wasn't raped,' was Parrott's answer.

Chris tried his best not to frown. 'All her sample will tell us is what infection she has. We're not going to get her attacker's name. You won't get your picture in the *Journal of Forensic Science.*'

'If she's got something and she was raped, he'll get it, won't he? It could be something tying him to all his victims.'

'All? What are you talking about?'

Lionel nodded rapidly. 'This guy will get bolder, and start killing. This is the low-key start of some serial killing spree that'll shock the world, Chris. Just watch—'

'Piss off, Lionel. You'd love that, I know. Not every attack is some serial killer.'

'No, no, trust me. They start like this. I read about it. The Yorkshire Ripper, the Suffolk Strangler. You watch. Meadow Moll is just a warm-up.'

'What's with that name? Meadow Moll?'

'Moll. Prostitute. Like Moll Flanders. That's the nickname going round the hospital. You really haven't heard this story? Everyone's been talking about it.'

He hadn't. And the normal humdrum atmosphere in the lab said nobody but Lionel thought this was the biggest story ever.

'Who says she was a prostitute?' Chris asked.

'Oh, I'm sure the police won't say that. But that'll just be bullshit for her family. Meadow Park's known for the ladies of the night. She was a whore and this guy was a punter—'

Chris snatched the bag from Parrott and checked the label.

His breath caught.

*

Chris's phone rang, cutting his interest in the next table, where a McDonald's employee chatted with a patient in a dressing gown. Lunchtime at the Pitstop café, and he was still waiting for his daughter to call him back – *youngest* daughter, perhaps. Immediately after reading the name on Parrott's bag, he'd darted out of the lab for privacy to send her a text.

*'Call me as soon as you get this. Dad x'*

'Did you hear anything from Simone?' Julia said, stress evident in her voice. 'I still can't reach her. I just called the flat she shares at university and I called her parents. No one's heard from her; they thought she was with me. What if she went off with some lad and something's happened?'

'Something's happened,' Chris said, and then he told her that Simone had been attacked. She was now a patient in his hospital.

Cut to pieces, Julia excused herself from the call in order to find her mother.

Chris sat quietly for a few minutes, chewing chocolate cake and trying to process what had happened. He was almost ready to make his way back to the lab when Julia's name flashed up on his phone screen again.

'Hello? How are you, love?' he asked.

'The police just called me,' Julia blurted. 'Simone's parents told them she was meeting me. They said they want me to go to the station. They're sending a car. What do I do? Mum says I just have to tell the truth.'

Fearful that a nosy sod like himself might overhear, Chris kept his voice low and rubbed his nose to hide his mouth. 'She's right. Just tell them what happened. Just say we both waited at the pub for her.'

'What if they know about the argument? I argued with Simone earlier that day. And then I sent her a voicemail after we got home and said I'd beat her silly if she stood me up for a boy. What if the police know that? They can get phone call information from phone companies.'

'Don't be silly. They're not going to think you had anything to do with this, Julia. You're a hundred pounds soaking wet. We were waiting for her. We were at the pub and then at home. Your voicemail proves we were still waiting for her.'

'I know, I know. I just… I know it looks bad. And I feel so guilty. What if it happened after we left? Have you been to see her?'

Simone wasn't allowed visitors and Julia likely thought that by working in the hospital, Chris could get around this. But nobody was allowed near her except the police, close family, and the staff looking after her. He explained this.

'But I'll try to find out how she's doing.'

He wasn't going to tell her that Simone's sample was in his lab, or why.

'She was coming to us, Dad. She had to cross Meadow Park from the train station. It was my fault for picking that pub.'

Her voice was weak, and Chris couldn't help but picture his little girl, half the age she was now, still in pigtails. It broke his heart.

'You didn't tell her to go through the park, Julia, and even if that had been the case, people walk through parks. It's a public place. The guy who attacked her is at fault here and him alone.'

'I know, I know. I just… Dad, this is so awful.'

She was confused and scared. He wasn't sure what he should say to her next.

His phone beeped to alert him to another call. Rose. He knew what it was about.

'Julia, love, your mother's calling. Are you going to be okay if I take this?' he asked.

Julia sniffled. 'Sure, I'll wait. She'll want to talk to you about the police.'

Rose sounded as distressed as their daughter. Sure enough, she'd been with Julia when the police phoned, and had got the story. Her first question after explaining this: why hadn't Chris called her with the news? Answer: he was waiting until he got home, until he knew more.

'God, poor Simone. This is so horrible. How did you find out? Julia said you heard about her being admitted to A&E?'

'That was a lie. I didn't want her to worry even more. Simone had a sample come into the lab. She might have an STI.'

'My God. We won't tell Julia about that. Have the police arrested someone?'

'I don't know anything except she's here. How does Julia seem to you?'

'She's being quiet. She's not telling me much. She went to her room, but I think she's on the phone to someone. It could be Simone's parents, because they'll probably want to get Julia's side of the story.'

'No, it was me. She's worried that the police will blame her somehow.'

'That's so silly. Of course they can't. Nobody knew this was going to happen. Didn't she think she could talk to me about this?'

'It was me and her last night, so maybe that's why I was the one to turn to.'

'I'll talk to her. If Simone's parents call her, I'm not sure we should let them speak to her. Not alone. I feel really bad for them and I understand they'll want answers, but if they're angry they might try to... blame Julia somehow. For picking the meeting place, maybe. I don't know. But I don't like it. What do you think?'

'I think you'd have a better grasp of that than me. It's up to you, Rose. I don't know. But I do know I'm already concerned that they'll want to talk to me about it.'

Rose gave a long pause. 'I could call them first and... no, let's see if they call. I'll see you at home later. I'm going to talk to Julia again.' She hung up, and he returned to Julia with an apology for putting her on hold.

She said, 'So what do I tell the police? And will you come with me?'

'I can't, I'm at work. Have a chat to your mother, Julia. She's about to knock on your door. I'll see you back home. It'll be okay.'

'What? How do you know—'

He heard the knock that stopped her dead, then Rose calling Julia's name. Then he hung up.

He understood her worry and guilt. While Julia had sat and waited for Simone, someone had been viciously attacking the girl. While Julia drank lager, Simone suffered. While Julia tried to build the courage to try karaoke, Simone bled alone in the dark.

'Hey.'

Suddenly, Simone and Julia and the police were wiped from his head. Katie was standing before him with a nervous smile on her face.

# CHAPTER FOURTEEN

'I got your place of work from your Facebook profile,' she said. 'Hope that's okay?'

She stuck out a hand and he leaned across the table to shake it. The touch felt weird. Normally a pretty young woman's skin against his had something electric about it. This didn't, for obvious reasons. She wore the same type of outfit as she had the day before, but a different pullover this time. Her hair was again tucked into the beanie cap she'd worn the other night, which downplayed her attractiveness. For this, he was relieved. He didn't want colleagues to see him conversing with a pretty girl, in case they started firing questions.

'Have you come to see me?' he asked, eyes darting about in search of curious onlookers. But nobody seemed to care.

'Yeah. I just wondered if perhaps there might be a chance to meet up before the anniversary party on Saturday.' She had a plastic supermarket bag in her hands, something wrapped up in it. 'Maybe just a chat over a drink?'

In a crowded local pub? Him and a pretty girl half his age? No way.

'I… I sent you a text,' Chris said.

'To me? I didn't get it.'

Chris covered the uncomfortable silence that followed by checking his phone. He saw that the text was in his outbox, undelivered for some reason. 'Sorry. It didn't send.'

Katie was rubbing the back of her neck. He remembered her circulation problem. Did she get that from his side of the family? His uncle had died of circulation problems, now he thought about it.

'Sorry about turning up like this. I remembered that I didn't say thank you to you for inviting me to the party on Saturday night. I'm so looking forward to it. There's so much I want to say to the family.'

He had to watch how much he opened his life to this girl, how close he allowed Katie to get to his family. It wouldn't be a good idea to let her get too friendly with Rose or Julia, because in a few days they might be parting ways for ever.

'Sorry for interrupting your lunch. I was just passing and thought I'd pop by. I'll get going. Like I said, I'll contact you about the result.'

He realised he hadn't responded to her offer. 'Wait. On Friday I'm on lates, which means working from midday till eight. But other than that, I'm free. Rose has a friend's party to go to, so if you want, if you like, we can—'

'That's perfect.' Katie sat at the table.

'Good. So after work—'

'My mother's funeral is on Friday at ten in the morning.'

Words clogged in Chris's throat like a motorway pile-up.

'It's perfect,' Katie said. 'If you don't start work until midday, you can be back in time. It's in Bradford. You won't be late back. And we can still have that drink after work. Although it'll be non-alcoholic for me. I'm not much of a drinker.'

'I didn't know your mum, Katie. I mean, not that well. I don't know the family. I'm... not sure that's a good idea.'

Katie seemed unfazed. 'You know me, so it will be fine. You can meet all the others and get to know them.'

'I don't know, Katie. They might hate me being there.'

'Why?'

'Because I—' *got their Eve pregnant and then ran away* – 'don't know them. I'm not part of the family, Katie, and we have to remember that I might never be. At the minute, all we have is what your mother told you.'

Katie looked crestfallen. 'She wouldn't lie.'

'I'm not saying she's lying, Katie. She could be wrong. Until then we should…'

He went blank, unsure of how to continue, but Katie nodded, avoiding eye contact.

'Be careful. We should be careful,' Katie said. 'Have I ruined this before it's even started?'

'No, you haven't. I just feel…' Chris stopped, aware that he was focussed only on self, self, self. This was difficult for them both, and he hadn't also recently lost a mother.

'I'll come. It's the respectful thing to do. I'll come to the funeral.'

Katie grinned. 'Thank you. Look, I should leave you to your lunch break. See you Friday about eight in the morning?'

But she didn't make a move to leave.

'Say what's on your mind, Katie.'

'It's just… with my being older. Fathers want to bring their children up. Do all those first-time things with them. But you never even got to pick my name.'

'Katie, conversations like this… Please, let's just wait for the result first.'

'I know, I know. It's just… Well, maybe you don't like the name Katie. I could change it.'

Change her name? This was becoming surreal. 'We shouldn't be talking like this yet, Katie.'

'I know, I know. But I just wanted to say it's easy to change a name. I could, if you like. If there's other names you prefer. But you're right, let's wait for the result. I'll get going. Oh, but I wanted to show you this, first.'

From the bag she extracted a small trophy. And slid it across the table. He lifted it. On a wooden base was a go-kart with wings, made of plastic gold. It said 'UNDER-7S RIDER OF THE YEAR'. There was no plaque, just an oblong of stickiness where one had once been. Inked into the furry felt baize base was 'COOPER & SONS LTD'.

'I won that. I just wanted to show you. I know you like racing – Mum told me how you two met. I guess maybe it runs in the family.'

Her big grin only heaved awkwardness over him. What was he supposed to do, reward her? 'It's nice. Well done. But, again, conversations like this—'

Two men carrying gear came through the entrance at a rush, which got everyone staring. An interruption Chris was thankful for. One, suited, carried a microphone and a briefcase. The other guy was in jeans and a T-shirt because he wasn't going to parade in front of the big video camera he lugged. Everybody stopped to watch, perhaps wondering if an episode of *Casualty* was going to be filmed here.

When the two guys had gone, the woman at the nearby table said, 'I bet they're here for a TV interview. That girl that was brought in last night.'

'You mean Meadow Moll?' her boyfriend replied.

'Would you not use that name, please,' Chris said, glaring at them. It was the first time he'd ever jumped into a private conversation here at the Pitstop. The pair looked at him like something brought in on their shoes, then spoke quickly in a whisper, got up and left.

Embarrassed, Chris turned back to Katie, but the young woman was walking away, trophy in hand. He wasn't sure if she was upset with him. But he didn't call her back.


Rose opened the front door before he got there, a solid and concerned frown on her face. He knew why. She stepped backwards as he came in. He back-kicked the door shut and told her there was no further news about Simone.

'I went to the police station with her,' Rose said. 'Nobody treated her with suspicion, but they wanted to seize her phone. I kicked up a stink and they settled for a quick read through her messages. They asked about Simone's past and her boyfriends.'

'You tell them about the togmuppet?'

'Yes, but for some weird reason I used the name Marc Woodley.' She handed him a business card. For a Detective Johnson. Sans glamour and cheap.

'I have to go and give a statement, too?'

'Call him to arrange a time.'

'But I thought Julia told them we both waited at the pub.'

'She did. But they have to hear it from you, don't they? You just have to tell them you both waited at the pub for Simone. What's the problem?'

He paused. 'I was in the car at first. I waited in the car.'

'Just call the man. Look, Chris, don't talk about Simone in the house, okay? It's sore for Julia, so wait until she brings it up.'

He looked over her shoulder, wondering where his daughter was.

'She went for a walk,' Rose said, ever the mind-reader. 'Just promise me you'll keep a rein on that big mouth of yours.'

'Okay. Katie came to the hospital, by the way. I was in the Pitstop. And I nearly choked on my cake. She asked me to come to her mother's funeral on Friday morning.'

He'd wanted a companion in shock and outrage, but her response left him yearning.

'Good idea? Are you kidding?'

'It's a *great* idea, Chris. Bonding time with tears. It will bring you closer together.'

'And if one of the tearful family asks who I am?'

She flicked a hand. 'Meh! Just say you're the guy who knocked her up on holiday eighteen years ago.'

Chris glowered at her, but it only made her laugh. 'Calm down. Katie will have told them who you are—'

'*Might* be, Rose. Who I *might* be.'

'Okay, who you *might* be. Or maybe Eve told some of them years ago. Because they might have wondered when she suddenly had a baby. But you did know her.'

'Not really.'

'She's one of only a few women you've seen naked. It's still a connection, if loose. You won't feel out of place. We went to Josephine's funeral earlier this year, didn't we? She was only one of your colleague's friends. Tell me that's not a loose connection.'

'Er, little bit different, that. But if I'm not her dad, I… Look, I don't want to go.'

'Okay, phone her. Tell her you're not going. That you changed your mind.'

He couldn't fathom doing that.

She rubbed a hip, obviously in pain. They headed into the living room and she dropped into her favourite armchair and rubbed some more. He was too wired to sit. 'Chris, if the results come back early on Friday, think about how much easier the funeral will be.'

'And if they don't?'

'You'll know the kid a lot more, and that'll make it easier to be around her. I watched you with her. You don't look right. You don't act right.'

'She's a little bit weird, Rose.'

'No, she's a little bit confused and knocked for six and desperate not to say the wrong thing in front of us. In front of you.'

'She showed me an old go-karting trophy, Rose. Something she won as a kid. And she asked me if I liked her name. Actually, she said I could change it. If I'm acting funny, it's because I find it all – and her – a bit weird.'

'I know the reason, Chris. You feel she's being too pushy. You feel uncomfortable. Look, if the results come back negative before the funeral, even if we're halfway driving there, just cancel it. At that point, she won't mind. We'll offer her help to find her real dad, and then we'll part ways.'

He considered this. He didn't like it, but it beat calling Katie right now to cancel. Or would such a last-minute cancellation hit Katie harder?

Rose sighed at his indecision. 'Do what you want. I'm going for a bath, and then I'm starting dinner and going to work on my book.'

As promised, she got up and left the room. The house was silent, which he wasn't used to, and it allowed uncomfortable thoughts to kick up a storm. He wanted to visit the Manor, but Rose would be walking about upstairs while she got ready for her bath. And supping whiskey this early was a bad sign. He put the TV on, but nothing sank in, so the storm continued. He went into the kitchen, meaning to put the whiteboard up, but that was a brainless exercise and wouldn't calm the bad weather in his head.

He decided to see what his colleagues and friends were up to on Facebook.

Brand new in, a post from Lionel Parrott.

Guess we gotta wait for the next infamous Brit slasher

There was a link to a blog he followed. Chris ignored the narrative because the post began with reader replies that gave him all he needed.

*Weds 20 November*

TEENAGE GIRL LEFT FOR DEAD – ARREST MADE
  [FBIguy32]cops got someone for #meadowmoll I hear. Per law, only giving out 21 male from Manor Castle. Attempted murder, man.

[TheChoiceNovel] yeah its marc Woodley I know. Ex-boyfriend and #nobhead. Retweet this.

[gamergirl567] she dumped him like a week ago, threatened her with a #baseball bat for shagging his friend.

[TheChoiceNovel] yeah, marc Woodley, I already posted name all over.

[BabeInTheWud] I was there didn't shag his friend she bought a short skirt and he flipped in Meadowhall thought she was cheating.

[gamergirl567] some of his texts said he didn't exactly take being single with pride & honour.

[TheFamilyLie] my pal works at train station and says cops been after CCTV n asking about a car.

[AndiJ1994] marc woodleys the name I got too. Sharing now 2000 friends.

[FBIguy32] she dead yet?

[BabeInTheWud] cops move fast already searched his flat I saw it.

[CryBaby645533] yeah CCTV car matches his I heard.

[AndiJ1994] yeah they found a hooded top like the one in that leaked CCTV footage from station.

[TheFamilyLie] that's my mate that, he leaked it, works there.

[BabeInTheWud] I saw the bastard get arrested. Grabbed him on his way to college. Impounded his car. Slam dunk.

[IamBetterThanYou] I had Simone, ha ha

No wonder Lionel seemed annoyed. His dream of another British kill spree to go in the crime annals had been thwarted, or at least postponed. Here, just a run-of-the-mill *jilted/jealous-boyfriend-half-kills-ex-girlfriend* story. Booooriiiiiiing.

Under 'MORE ON THIS' was a link to

TEENAGE GIRL LEFT FOR DEAD SPEAKS ABOUT HER ORDEAL

Chris clicked it and was whisked away from the blog. Here, a video shot in darkness. Small room, window blinds shut and two figures facing each other in chairs. Both were just black forms, but one had long hair. Simone Baker and a reporter. Chris's brain decoded dark lumps in the room as hospital equipment even before a news ticker slid into view and told him so.

Simone Baker Speaks Exclusively to our Reporter from her Hospital Room

That explained the guy with the mic and the guy with the camera earlier that day, rushing into the hospital to record Simone's words before she changed her mind about giving them up. They hadn't brought any special lighting, so maybe they had had to improvise when she said she didn't want her face shown to the country. Hence why the interviewer was faceless, too. At least the dark hid his annoyed expression.

She had some memories back, she said. The interviewer might have had a series of linear questions planned, but either he didn't stick to it or the video had been edited, because Simone Baker had refused to answer this or that. Either way, it was a bit of a disjointed shambles, like a dodgy highlight reel.

'Did you see your attacker's face?' the interviewer asked.

'I didn't. He was masked, and it was dark. The park was dark. I didn't hear him coming. He grabbed me from behind.'

'And how are you feeling?'

'I'm okay. The bruising is healing. He broke two of my fingers, but I think that was when I tried to defend myself. He hit me with a pipe: I remember seeing copper. Like a copper pipe. But it had foam padding on. I remember that, too. Foam padding. He hit me with a pipe but it had foam padding. It must by why I survived.' She paused. 'I am waiting for test results. I'm not ready to go back out yet. Nightmares and things. Not yet. But I'm taking up a bed. I don't want to take a bed someone ill needs.'

'What about the voice? Did you recognise the man's voice?'

'I didn't. But he knew me. I know he knew me.'

'And how's your family coping?'

'As well as they can, I guess.'

'The police just released details of an arrest made this morning. A 21 year-old man from Manor Castle. Do you know who this man is? Is he your attacker?'

Simone's silhouette shifted uncomfortably. 'I'm not supposed to say anything about that.'

'But you said your attacker knew you. What makes you think this?'

And here she gave a lengthy statement which perhaps explained the rough cut. Maybe the segment had been allocated only a couple of minutes, but the editor had dumped other portions of the interview to focus on this gold mine.

'"You expected to be happy, didn't you?" That was what he said. I remember it now. "You cut me out of your life and ruined mine. You expected a long life, but you cut me out and now look! Are you happy now without me?" That was what he said each time he struck me. "Are you happy right now without me? Are you happy right now without me?"'

Here the interviewer turned his head from her and there was a commotion offscreen.

The video cut to the interviewer, standing in a hospital corridor with his face returned and his smart suit on show, telling the camera, the captivated world, that the hospital staff and the police had intervened to terminate the interview.

It was obvious why, Chris thought. Her words – *Are you happy now without me? You cut me out of your life* – had given the game away, ruined the police's big reveal. Sounded exactly like the sort of thing a jilted ex-boyfriend would say. Slam dunk.

# CHAPTER FIFTEEN

At dinner, Chris was still thinking about Simone and having to talk to the police, but a nasty event in a nearby city was about to change all that. It started with a ringing doorbell.

Julia jumped out of her seat to answer it. Rose didn't seem to care, but Chris perked up an ear, listening. He remembered smelling male deodorant in her room. If he heard a young man's voice, he was going to go storming out there and interrogate both of them about their relationship.

'Katie? What happened?' Julia said.

Chris and Rose looked at each other. Katie.

Julia returned with Katie behind her. Rose gasped at her appearance. She wore blue jeans and a white Eiffel Tower T-shirt and both were as blackened as her face. She looked like a coal miner. Her smoke-stained hair was still in a bun, but myriad strands had come free and one clump was stuck to her face, right through that scar.

'My god,' Rose said. 'What the heck's happened?'

'I'm sorry,' Katie said, 'but I didn't know where else to go. I lost all my clothing. My flat just burned down.'

Chris didn't move, but Rose got up and rushed to the sink to wet a teatowel. Both girls fired questions as Katie wiped her face. They crowded and fussed over her like A&E staff around a car crash victim, while Chris sat and didn't know what to say or think. Katie seemed emotionless, still numbed by her ordeal.

Rose turned Katie away from Chris, grabbed the blackened T-shirt and tried to lift it, meaning to remove the garment. But

Katie pushed her hands away and tugged the waistband further down, then both cuffs. They were elastic and bit into her skin.

'Don't fuss, please,' she said. 'It's fine. Just smoke. Please. I don't want to be a pain. You're in the middle of dinner. Sorry.'

'I won't hear of it,' Rose snapped. She forced Katie into a chair at the table. Now that it was clear she was unhurt, curiosity set in. Rose and Julia demanded to know what had happened. Chris only wondered why Katie had decided to venture here.

'I was working on my bike,' Katie said, staring down at the table. 'Out in the garden. Then I saw flames in the kitchen. I couldn't believe it. I tried to get inside, but by then it was too late to kill the blaze. I got my bike out of harm's way, the only thing I could save. I called the fire brigade, but there was nothing else I could do. I just stood on my street and just watched everything I owned go up in smoke. It was awful…' She looked like she was on the verge of tears. 'I know I should have waited to talk to the police and fire people, but I just had to get away, get somewhere, see someone. I know it was silly to just ride away like that, but I wasn't thinking straight. I'm sorry.'

'No, don't be,' Rose said. 'You did the right thing coming to somewhere comfortable instead of standing around in the cold like that.'

*Somewhere comfortable?* Chris thought.

'And you can always talk to the authorities later. So don't be sorry.'

'But I am. And I'm sorry about this.' Katie held up the tea towel, which was blackened from her face.

Julia snatched it. 'Don't worry about that. Mum, can she have some of your clothes? She's ruined that Eiffel Tower T-shirt.'

'Yes, of course. Chris, take Katie upstairs and let her use the shower while we find her something to wear.'

'Yes, and then we should take Katie back to her flat,' Chris said. 'Like she said, she should talk to the police about the fire and maybe see the full damage.'

'That can wait,' Rose said, giving him a sharp glance. 'Let her get her wits back about her first.'

'I really don't want to be a pain,' Katie said. 'I'm sorry to interrupt your dinner. I must be smelling out your house. I'm sorry.'

*Yet you came round here*, Chris almost said. This time he decided he was being too harsh. Maybe Ron Hugill's murder, her mother's suicide and now a house fire had weakened an already fragile mind, and like a lost soul she'd sought out the one person everybody at some point looked to for help.

A father.

Chris got up, reached across the table and put a hand on Katie's shoulder, and although the gesture was more act than instinct, it wasn't without sincerity.

'It'll be okay,' he said. 'Let's go get you cleaned and changed.'

\*

Chris quickly made the bed before Katie entered the bedroom. For some reason, he didn't want her to see the sheet that he and Rose slept on. Strange, but there it was. He pointed to the en suite.

'Towels are in the airing cupboard. You okay?'

Katie's eyes soaked up the room. 'Of course. I didn't get hurt. I just don't want to put anyone out by staying here too long.'

And just how long did she think was too long? Three hours? A day? He tried to think of some hints to drop that an overnight stay was out of the question. 'So, you have your own flat? You don't stay at the Blue Swan?'

'No, no, the pub is up for sale. Has been for months. My mum and Ron put it on the market when she got ill. I moved out two years ago.'

'At sixteen? You got your own flat at sixteen?'

She was still looking around the room, which wasn't big or littered enough to warrant such scrutiny. He knew she didn't like his question. Her answer was vague. 'I only recently got the flat. I stayed elsewhere.'

He didn't push it. 'The shower is there. I'll get you some clothing.'

While Katie showered, Chris went downstairs. He found his wife and daughter sorting through clothing in the tumble dryer. Like scavengers, he thought. Going all out to aid Katie. He didn't know why it annoyed him. Rose held up a pleated skirt, but Julia grabbed it and threw it aside.

'No, Mum, I don't get the impression she's into pleated silk. Find jeans. A T-shirt.'

Chris let them ignore him for a few more seconds, then said, 'A bit off that she just rode away to come here without waiting to see the fire brigade and the police.'

Rose tutted. 'Would you want to hang around in the dark and watch your home burn? She can go tomorrow morning.'

Clearly he was the only one who thought Katie's fleeing the scene strange. 'Does that mean you're wanting her to stay the night?'

'She should, she's got no flat,' Julia replied. Rose agreed.

'Just one day, though?' he said. 'We can help her find a place tomorrow. She's probably got friends she can stay with anyway.'

Rose gave him a disapproving look. He added that they had a full house, but that seemed to make things worse. Rose found a pair of jeans and tossed them beside a plain T-shirt Julia had located.

'Dad, Mum told me about Katie's mother's funeral,' Julia said. 'She said it's okay for us all to go. I'd like to come, be supportive.'

'Of course,' he said.

Julie pecked him on the cheek. 'Thanks, Dad.'

Rose jammed the trousers and T-shirt into Julia's hands. 'Take those upstairs.'

As soon as Julia was gone, Rose torched Chris with her eyes. 'What kind of bizarre attitude is that? Are you scared to have her here? She's not a stranger off the street.'

Having his inner feelings exposed irritated him. 'She came right in off the street, Rose, and yes, she is a stranger.'

'But your daughter, maybe.'

'We don't know—'

She thrust a balled pair of socks into his hand. 'I said maybe, didn't I? From what we do know, she's a nice girl. You saw her; she obviously feels put out coming round here.'

'I know. But this isn't easy for me, Rose.'

'It's not a walk in the park for any of us. I agree it's a little bit weird that her first instinct was to drive right here, to another city, but I'm trying to project the right image. What if she reads the bad attitude pulsing off you like a bad smell? I don't want you to mention it in front of her again.'

He fiddled with the socks just to buy time to think.

'You're going to be nice to her, Chris. Long-lost daughter or stranger off the street, I don't care. Her flat just burned down and she narrowly escaped. Stop this weakness—'

'Weakness?'

'Exactly that, Chris. That's all this is. You're scared. Head-in-the-sand. It's understandable. But it has to stop. I want you – *you* – to offer Katie a roof here for a few days.'

'A few days? She might not want—'

'Then she'll leave, won't she? All on her own. A few days. Use those exact words. And ask her if she minds Julia coming to the funeral on Friday.'

Julia thumped back downstairs. Rose pointed at the socks in Chris's hand. 'She'll need those, won't she?'

Another trick, he realised. First, she'd got him alone for a telling-off, and now she was sending him to Katie. Alone.

\*

When Chris carefully leaned into the en suite doorway, he saw Katie at the bathroom mirror, still wearing her ruined Eiffel Tower T-shirt but no bottoms. A towel was wrapped around her waist and legs. She was up close to the glass, analysing her teeth.

Chris froze, staring at Katie's skinny legs. They were raspy and mottled in myriad places – burns, he realised. Not bright and red raw, like the surface of Mars, but insipid and hardened, like the surface of the Moon. From the ankles right up to the knees, where the towel started. And maybe beyond. Chris knew he was looking at ancient fire damage. Katie sensed him and turned.

She didn't seem the least worried about having her terrible skin on show, but Chris felt ashamed that he'd been caught staring. He quickly turned away. 'Rose wants me to ask if Julia is allowed to go to the funeral on Friday.'

There on the floor, next to Katie's smoke-soiled jeans, were two items. One was a small black travel clock. That explained the constant ticking from her. The second, far more intriguing item was a notebook. Pretty old-looking, battered, well-used and clearly a personal treasure. Like a diary. There was a half-moon of something shiny poking out of its pages. A compact disc.

'Of course. I don't mind at all. If you're okay with it.'

The disc said 'MUM' in thick black marker.

'Mr Redfern? Did you hear? I said it's okay.'

Chris turned to face her again, this time embarrassed that he'd probably been spotted staring at the notebook. All he could think of to say was, 'Please, call me Chris. Normally when someone calls me Mr Redfern, it's because I've done something wrong.'

Katie smiled. She held up the T-shirt Julia had given her. 'Okay. Chris it is. I feel cold. Have you got a jumper instead?'

He found an old pullover in the wardrobe. One of his, but he doubted she'd have a problem with that. He handed it and the socks to her and closed the door. When he sat on the bed to wait, the notebook drew his attention once more. He convinced himself he'd get caught red-handed if he touched it, even for a second.

Katie came out the en suite a minute later. Rose was fairly slim, despite inaction because of her arthritis, but even so her jeans and T-shirt highlighted how thin Katie was. She bent to pick up her clock but ignored the notebook. 'I carry this everywhere. I'm funny about time.'

Chris didn't want to mention the annoyingly loud ticking. 'I guess I should get these clothes into the wash.' He turned to go, eager to not be alone with her any longer, but the sound of her voice stopped him at the door.

'Just ask me.'

'Ask what?'

'Drunk people and children. They're the only ones who ask. They ask in the street. They shout it across roads. They don't have that chip in their head that reminds them to be polite. Everyone else pretends they haven't noticed. They make a hard effort not to look. As if everything is normal. But you might be my dad, Chris. You should ask.'

'I don't understand.'

Of course he did, and Katie knew it. 'I was a stupid five-year-old who thought it would be fun to play with fire. Turns out lit polystyrene is its own version of napalm. Sticks to the skin, continues to burn. It was awful.'

Before he could react, Katie abruptly darted into the bathroom again, and closed the door. But in the last moment before she turned away, he sensed bitterness. Possibly because he hadn't displayed more sorrow and horror.

Or because he hadn't been around to stop her getting hurt all those years ago?

\*

Katie stood in the living room doorway, smart and clean, and once more beautiful. Her hair was now in a ponytail, radiant as a summer cornfield. She did a twirl as Julia clapped.

'Makes a change to see someone not grumpy in that pullover,' Julia said.

'Julia used to run off to another room to scratch her bum when she was a toddler,' Chris said. His daughter blew a raspberry at him.

Rose said, 'Chris won't mind. Will you? If Katie keeps that clothing?'

As if he had a choice after that. 'Sure. Christmas is coming and I'll get another tacky jumper.'

Rose flicked him a glance, meaning she'd read the sarcasm behind his joke. 'Thank you, Katie, for inviting us to your mother's funeral. I know this will be a tough day for you. But for now – tea, everyone?'

'I shouldn't,' Katie said. 'You've already got one guest. I don't want to intrude.'

Chris felt his heart lurch. Julia hung her head and scuttled for the door, barely holding back the tears. Rose glared at Chris as she made the connection. 'Ah. I understand. We don't have a guest, Katie. Chris will explain in the kitchen. Do you mind, Chris?'

She went in pursuit of Julia.

Once alone with Katie, he boiled it down. 'Julia's friend got attacked. She's not here.'

'I'm sorry to hear that. Is she okay?'

'She will be. My wife didn't know I'd told you Simone was staying here.'

'I'm sorry.'

'Don't be. You didn't know. You expected Simone to be here. It's fine. But we're sort of not talking about her around Julia unless Julia brings it up first. It's painful for her.'

'I understand. Julia's friend. I won't mention it again.'

'Thank you.'

Julia returned, Rose following. Julia seemed to realise there had been a conversation about her and gave a thumbs up to show she was okay. Katie mirrored the thumbs up and announced she would make the tea. Julia offered to help. Rose waited for his eyes to meet hers, then walked into the hallway. He knew he was meant to follow.

As soon as she whirled on him near the stairs, he blurted an explanation.

'I mentioned Simone staying because Katie wanted to go for a drink yesterday but I couldn't because I was picking Simone up. Katie won't mention her in front of Julia again.'

'Not that. Did you offer her a roof yet?'

Chris shook his head. 'Maybe she won't want to stay. Maybe she shouldn't. She should go see the police to explain what's happened.'

A lame excuse. 'Go in there and find out.'

They returned to the living room. All the recent footwork put a pained expression on Rose's face as she sat. Katie brought the tea and poured for each person. Her own cup was already full. As she took her seat, she caught her cup on the table and splashed tea across the back of her hand. Rose gave a yelp and ordered Julia to grab some ice, but Julia laughed.

'It's cold tea, Mum. Hot tea hurts her chiclets, she told me.'

'Her *what*?' Rose asked.

'It's slang for teeth,' Katie explained. 'Sorry, I use it a lot.'

Julia sipped. 'My friend's mum, Gwyneth, she drinks that iced tea stuff. She's coming to your anniversary party. Are you coming, Katie?'

'Yes, we already asked her,' Rose said. 'And Gwyneth only drinks iced tea, by the way, because she puts vodka in it.'

'So doesn't. I'll ask her!'

''S'what I heard.'

The two women started to argue. The debate was good-natured and Chris injected a joke or two. A minute later, Rose nudged him with her knee. He noticed Katie's chair was empty. She was standing by the door.

'What's wrong, Katie?' Rose asked. But she knew, because Chris knew. Katie had been excluded from a family chat.

'I really don't want to intrude. I should go. Is there a good B&B around?'

A second knee prompted Chris, but Julia got there first.

'Katie can stay here, can't she? I've got a sleeping bag. We can do make-up. You won't even notice her. She'll be like white noise, as Dad says.'

'I was just going to say that,' Chris said. Rose agreed it was a good idea. Katie tried to protest, but the girls rapidly talked her into submission.

'I suppose if you've got a spare room, I could do just one night.'

'There's no spare room,' Julia said. 'They decided they didn't want a second child and so they snaffled it for their en suite.'

Rose and Chris could have fainted. The undertone seemed to have skipped by Katie or was ignored.

'If you're sure. But I really don't like to intrude. I can easily sort out a hotel tomorrow.'

'At least until we get the results,' Rose said. Now Chris swept his knee into Rose's leg, but already she was wide-eyed at her error.

'Results?' Julia said. 'Whose? Katie's results? What results?'

'On whether or not my flat is still habitable,' Katie said.

'That's right,' Rose said. 'Anyway, Katie, you haven't had dinner. We've got some more chicken, if you're hungry.'

'I could eat. Thank you. But I'm vegetarian.'

'I wish Chris was.' Rose patted his gut. It sparked a round of laughter.

As the banter continued, Chris realised his family was comfortable around Katie, which was good, but as always, his thoughts turned bleak. What if Katie was asked to stay another day? Then another? If she was still a guest when the paternity results returned, what would happen?

He saw two ways forward and neither appealed.

a) Congratulations, Katie, you're my daughter – now get out.

b) Sorry, Katie, you're not my daughter – now get out.

There was a third path but it didn't bear thinking about:

c) Letting Katie move in.

# CHAPTER SIXTEEN

'I'm sorry for mentioning your friend. And sorry about what happened to her.'

Julia just shrugged. She placed the footstool down and climbed aboard to reach the airing cupboard. 'It's fine. I just hope she's okay.'

Katie leaned against Julia's computer table. 'Do they know who did it?'

'Not yet. It's probably that vicious ex of hers. But I don't want to talk about that, if you don't mind.'

'Sorry. I lost someone, so I know what it's like.'

Feeling around on the top shelf, Julia said, 'Yes. I'm sorry about your mother.'

'No, I mean like your friend Simone. I lost someone to violence.'

Julia whirled around and almost toppled from the stool. 'Really? What happened? Who?'

Katie shrugged. Her fingers fiddled with a book of jokes on Julia's computer desk. 'Now I really understand your position. I don't like talking about that, either.' She lifted the joke book. 'I didn't think comedians actually told normal jokes. Isn't that plagiarism or something?'

'I do kids' parties. They like normal jokes. Hey, can I ask about your voice? Are you putting that on?'

Katie's big eyes grew wide. 'My scratchy voice? No, why?'

Julia leaped off the stool and approached Katie. 'Vocal fry, that's what it's called. Or creaky voice. Something to do with restricted vocal chords, I think. Bubbling air, something like that. It's the lowest register of the human voice.'

'Wow, this is getting deep. Like my voice.'

'I read up on it; I know this girl who does fake a creaky voice. It's a trend now. I think I even do it on the phone sometimes, although I don't sound as cool as you. I tried to pretend to be my dad once when a loser from college called me up. He saw right through it.'

Katie looked at the hand Julia had put on her arm and it was withdrawn quickly. Embarrassed, she stepped back to create space and sat on a corner of the bed.

'So, how about when we're both ready, we talk about what happened to our friends? Like collective catharsis.' Julia yanked a sleeping bag from the cupboard and tossed it down.

Katie's fingers moved from the book to an open notepad. 'Like, talking about something to get over it?'

'With the right mindset, you can cleanse yourself of any tragedy.'

'Any? Some tragedies can hit the mind hard enough to fracture it.'

'Fractures heal. The mind is powerful. Anything can be overcome. One of my friends told me about something called Benign Violation Theory.'

Katie repeated those three words, as if tasting them. 'Is that something you learned at your college?'

'I'm doing technical theatre. I'm not sure they do such a thing as BVT. I thought you'd know that, being there.'

Katie gave her a puzzled look.

'Your T-shirt. Eiffel Tower. I saw a girl who looked like you in the same T-shirt about a week ago in the refectory,' Julia explained. 'But you had your hair down. It's been up ever since. But I reckon it was you.'

The penny dropped. 'Oh, I don't go there. I was having a sly look around because I'm considering a computer course. I'm self-taught and very good with them, but my word isn't enough to get a job. At the minute, I advertise to fix computers from home. It doesn't make much.'

'You're in Bradford, though. Long trip.'

'I love riding my bike. The longer the better. Anyway, this BVT thing. Benign Violation Theory. It helps people overcome tragedy?'

'I'm sure I don't need psychology to get over this.' Julia stepped up and closed the notebook. 'Talking like this, to people my age, that will help me a lot. I don't want to talk about it to Mum and Dad.'

Katie's fingers picked up a pencil to twiddle with. 'You mentioned that your parents didn't want a second child? Would you have liked a sister to talk to?'

'God no. That would be a living hell on earth. My friend Simone has one, and she's a horror. No, I'd rather have a brother. But it is what it is. And they're too old now.'

Katie took the other end of the bed. 'They look very happy. So many children have broken families, but your parents have remained together.'

'Nineteen years. She proposed as soon as she knew I was in her belly, although they didn't marry for a couple of years. Mum always wanted marriage early because her parents were a bit stiff, you know? Posh types, big on status. I think part of the reason Mum and Dad have lasted is that they've always had this kind of cheeky banter. People who dig at each other a lot in jest tend to brush off actual arguments easier.'

'I can see your dad likes joking around. But he can also be a bit quiet.'

Julia laughed. 'No way. Get him on the right day, he's like a bully with that tongue. But yes, the last few days for some reason he's been a bit subdued. It must be because Mum's arthritis is playing up. She won't say, but I know she worries that her joints will get so bad she'll end up in a wheelchair, and Dad won't have the patience to care for her and he'll skip. So she's been glum-faced a bit, and that's probably making him a bit glum.'

Katie gave a slow nod. 'People have run out for less. And you, you're part of the reason. A baby can sometimes be the glue that holds couples together.'

'I guess. You'd have to think how many couples would have split if they didn't have kids. But some are just meant to be together. Like a couple of chemicals that need each other to work. Anyway, I know you don't have kids. Too young I guess, anyway. What about a boyfriend?'

'No.'

Julia gave her a careful look. 'Girlfriend?'

'Neither. I'm not interested.'

'Bad break-up?'

'No, I mean I'm not interested in sex. I'm not attracted to people in that way.'

'That's why no make-up? To avoid flies? It won't work. You're gorgeous. You'd attract a lot of boys if you tried to.'

'They're scared to approach me. Must be my voice. They must think I'm no pushover because of how I sound. Girls, though, they approach me a lot. Maybe I give off the vibe that they're more my type. But you're proof that appearances can be deceptive. That's probably just me being naïve or old-fashioned.'

Julia gave a crooked smile, as if she was unsure yet if that had been insult or compliment. 'You'll have to explain that one.'

'You like girls, right?'

She laughed. Nothing judgemental in Katie's tone, which was good. 'And what makes you say that?'

Katie pointed at a poster of Joan Crawford on stage, and Julia said, 'Wouldn't I have naked girls on the walls?'

'Not on the walls. In a secret book or something. Joan there, I reckon that's a solidarity thing. Like you like respect her success or something. She's a symbol of what women can do. I don't know what I'm talking about, do I? But it's the feeling I get.'

'That's a leap, isn't it?'

Katie shrugged. 'I don't know. Maybe that's me overthinking things. It's not my business.'

Julia grabbed her phone and tapped away. She gave Katie another careful look before showing her the screen. An app. A dating app.

'*For girls seeking girls,*' Katie said. 'So I was right. But your parents don't know, do they?'

Julia had only shown her because she hated having to hide it, but quickly there was regret. Someone with access to her parents knew something they didn't. Mum and Dad never got to meet certain talkative friends of hers, just in case they let something slip.

Julia virtually begged. 'No, and you can't tell them. You have to promise that.'

Katie tapped her nose and winked. 'From your notebook over there, I see it's not the only secret you have from them.'

Julia's jaw dropped in shock, but quickly she grinned at her new friend. 'Very observant. What if that had been my private diary?'

'Kind of is, in a way. Your parents really don't know?'

Julia shook her head so fast her hair whipped the air. 'No. And you won't be telling them that either, will you?'

Good news that shouldn't have been so was that Katie went out to buy new clothing and visit the 'fire and police people' while Chris was in the bath – that set aside one of his worries. He went there for peace and quiet but not to think. Thinking would have given him a headache, so he read a book instead. But he had to reread paragraphs because nothing stuck and soon gave up. When he came out the bathroom with a towel wrapped around his waist,

Rose was sorting through dirty washing, looking for something she had left in a pocket.

'How's Julia?'

'Brave-face mode,' was Rose's answer. Her grim look said she didn't think Julia was coping well at all. 'They're calling Simone Meadow Moll on the news. Like she was a prostitute.'

So that damn nickname had spread. Perhaps for a good reason? 'Maybe they know something that we don't.'

She threw down a pair of jeans. 'You as well? Christ, Chris. Missing white woman syndrome.'

'You what?'

'There's not much news about Simone. No massive public outcry about this crime. Because she wasn't an upper class and respectable girl. Women from broken homes, or ethnic minorities, or anyone with a shady past, they don't get treated the same.'

'You what?'

'Everyone thinks Simone was on the game because of where she was found, so that makes this a lesser crime, does it?'

'Julia effectively told me that Simone was sleeping about.'

She looked ready to slap him. 'And she was so gagging for it that she stopped for a quickie with a man on her way to meet you and Julia at the pub? Even if that happened, it's far from being a prostitute, isn't it? And why does that mean Simone's attack shouldn't get the same kind of media coverage and nationwide sadness and anger? And don't be saying these things in front of Julia, okay?'

'I know, I know, I won't be saying it. Look, Simone's not dead, is she, so it's not the same. And they arrested her ex-boyfriend for it. He did it, so this is different.'

'I suppose,' she said, not really convinced.

To change the subject, he mentioned Julia's slip earlier, when she told Katie they didn't want more children. They would have to tell Katie the truth about that.

'Yes, you will. When she comes back.'

*

An hour later Julia and Rose were in bed, which left Chris alone with Netflix. But he couldn't relax. Normally late nights were when he unwound with a boxset, but that was because the house was his alone and the only interruption would be if his wife or daughter came down for water. But tonight a woman he barely knew was going to come through the door. Was going to walk in and settle down as if she lived here. The sleeping bag rolled up on the sofa was a solid reminder of it.

He wasn't looking forward to being alone with Katie, especially not late at night. He didn't want to be dragged into a conversation about dead mothers or things Chris had missed seeing Katie achieve. And he didn't want to explain about the lack of a spare room, because he had a fear Katie would find this news... fateful. This tension put him on the edge of the sofa, on standby like some kind of soldier awaiting the order to go. And when he heard the purr of a motorbike approaching, he killed the TV and quickly headed for the stairs. He felt like an intruder in his own house.

He sat on the toilet, door closed over but not shut, so he could hear what Katie did. He heard the front door open and shut, and keys get dumped on the phone table.

And footsteps on the stairs. He froze, listening. He heard the landing creak, and then he heard the ticking of that damn clock Katie always kept with her. It would have been funny if not for the late hour. He wondered what Katie was doing. Just standing there?

Julia's door was closed. Chris and Rose's bedroom door was closed. He pictured Katie close to the bathroom, listening at the crack in the door. He was about to say something, like *hello*, when the ticking noise faded. No creak on the landing this time, and no footsteps on the stairs. The ticking was gone, but he sat, frozen, for another thirty seconds. He heard the TV go on. The rustle of Katie shaking out her sleeping bag.

He didn't flush and crept out quietly. It felt so wrong being secretive in his own house. Tomorrow he would have to have a long chat with Katie, just to make his time here with the girl less awkward. Tomorrow, though, in daylight, when it would be easier.

Rose was awake and playing on her phone. She saluted him. He killed the light and got undressed, lay down and flipped the covers over him. His phoned dinged and he saw she'd invited him to play chess. Without a word, he accepted the online game with a person lying inches from him.

He moved a pawn.

She moved one of her own and spoke for the first time. 'An agent asked me today for a chapter breakdown, did I tell you?'

'No. Is that good?'

'It so is. All I've been sending out is the pitch. This is the next step.'

'Well done.'

'Did you decide yet about telling your grandparents? I'll need to tell my mum at some point.'

Not something he wanted to think about so late. 'Only if the test comes back positive.'

'Of course. At least we don't have a giant family, right? No vast horde to tell the shocking news to.'

Said with a smile, but he could see pain in her eyes. Her father was dead (lung cancer), his mother was dead (heart attack), and their remaining grandparents were living overseas. Rose had no siblings and Chris hadn't seen his sister in years, although he'd heard rumours of gangs, crime, prostitution. And then there was his father… Christmases were simple times.

As if reading his thoughts, Rose said, 'There's that old army friend of your father's…'

'I don't want to talk about this, Rose.'

The room was silent for a minute.

He lost one of his rooks to her knight. 'Do you ever think a life with Eve might have turned out nicely?'

He'd expected this question, eventually. He'd also laboured over his answer. He kicked out his leg from under the covers and showed her his bent big toe, result of a school prank. Someone had sliced open a football and filled it with sand. Ha bleeding ha.

'I wouldn't even change this.'

'What? Why? Is that relevant?'

He shifted his other knight, but she dumped him in check. 'Alternate universes, my dear.'

He expected to have to explain but was quickly reminded that his wife knew him as well as anyone could know another.

'You're saying if you hadn't broken your toe, everything after that point would have been different. No holiday to America, and no Eve Levine. So no Katie. We'd be on a totally different path.'

He moved his king out of check. 'And no you or Julia.'

'So a broken toe made our daughter?'

Rose's phone pinged and she picked it up to make her next move.

He said, 'I just mean there's no point in planning until you know. It's like buying girls' and boys' clothing for a baby when you don't know the sex. We found out and then we bought the clothing.'

'The one time I didn't get my way. I wanted to wait for the birth. But before we knew, we still talked about what it would be like if the baby was a boy, and if it was a girl. We didn't plan but we considered these things. You haven't done that? You really haven't even *considered* what a future with Katie in our lives will be like?'

'No point. It makes sense to wait for the result.'

'That's not your reasoning at all.' His phone dinged, meaning it was his move, but he just stared at Rose. 'This isn't about mistakenly buying male clothing for a baby that turns out to be a girl. This is more like not going to the doctor about a lump on your balls.'

'You think I'm scared about the result? Yes, I am. A positive is going to be a shock to the system. Who wouldn't be worried about that?'

'Everyone would, and so I understand. I just don't know if you're admitting this problem to yourself. You don't want a new path to open up. You don't want to change from the path you're on.'

'You've said that before. Is it really such a big deal? Everyone has a comfort zone.'

'But when the comfort zone is under threat, you prepare. That's all I'm saying. You need to get your head out of the sand.'

He tossed down his phone and lay back. 'Goodnight.'

'You don't want her to be your daughter.'

'Rose, just stop. I didn't say that, because I don't know.' He turned off his bedside lamp. She extinguished hers.

'You don't want Katie to be your daughter so you can avoid self-pity and guilt. You want Katie to be wrong and to not know who her father is.'

'Rose, stop it.'

'You want that test to say it's not you and to leave Katie empty and longing. That way, you've done nothing wrong. You've brought up every child you've ever had, you've been there for all your babies. Look at you, father of the year.'

He said nothing. He dug his fingers into his thighs, to lock his arms in place in case anger chose to lash out.

'I won't judge you badly because of that, Chris. Because I also hope she's not your daughter.'

He hadn't expected that. Her attitude around Katie always suggested she welcomed the idea of a new addition to the family, even a fully grown one. In the dark, he turned to her and hugged her from behind. All anger was gone. 'Why?'

'Because she's not mine.'

\*

Chris awoke with a start and Rose's hand on his face. He swiped it off. Pain in his cheek told him she must have whipped her arm into him like a sling. The room was dark. His phone said it was twenty past three in the morning. The witching hour. He immediately thought of Katie. Still downstairs? Or gone with the family silver?

He got up, unable to beat the desire to see if she was still asleep. He hoped she had left already for a friend's house. Until an official document said they were father and daughter, Katie was a free-roaming stranger in the house. Making scary little noises downstairs in the dead of night.

He grabbed his phone and went slowly downstairs. The living room light was on. He peeked around the doorframe. There was Katie, lying back in her sleeping bag, playing on her phone. Awake. He tried to slink away.

But too late. 'Sir. Have a look at this.'

He went in. Katie sat up. She was still in Rose's T-shirt. She pulled the neck up and the arms down, and then tossed her phone onto the sleeping bag, down by her feet. 'Watch that, please. And take a seat.'

He didn't really want to do either, but he'd promised himself more time alone with Katie in order to make scenes like this less uncomfortable. So he took the phone and a seat.

The screen showed a paused YouTube news video.

'What am I about to see, Katie?'

'Press play. Please.'

Mobile phone footage: a mess of images as the person holding the device moves, then everything settles as the camera points at a window, somewhere inside a house. The camera jerks closer, everything blurs as the lens tries to forget the glass in the window and focus on what's outside. On what made the unseen person grab his or her phone and rush to the window.

Elevated view of a basic urban street. It's dark and the street-lights don't do much. A car is crashed against the back of another, and a police car pulls up behind it, roof lights pulsing. A clean-shaven man in a baseball cap gets out of the crashed car and two uniformed cops exit to meet him. But he's got a machete. The cops rethink their idea to rush him, but he swipes and catches one in the arm. Then he turns and flees as the second cop bends to help his bleeding partner. There's a lot of shouting. Adrenaline is making the cameraman's arm shiver.

It's mobile phone footage that's made its way onto YouTube, but via TV news. There's a news channel logo in the corner and for those who might have misunderstood what they just saw, a caption at the bottom says:

WANTED FUGITIVE HACKS POLICE WITH MACHETE

A disembodied reporter tells the story. 'A man wanted for murder was earlier this evening spotted driving a stolen car in Netherthorpe, Sheffield, and when the police tried to stop him, he slashed one with a machete before making his escape.'

For those who didn't understand what they were seeing and couldn't read.

'What's this got to do with you or me?' Chris said, but in response Katie only tapped her eye. *Keep watching.* They were staring at each other when the reporter finished with:

'The fugitive is believed to be Dominic Everton, prime suspect in the murder of Bradford local man Ron Hugill, who was murdered in cold blood a week ago.'

# CHAPTER SEVENTEEN

'I think Dominic Everton is in Sheffield because of me. I think he's after me.'

Sheffield. That part hadn't registered. Netherthorpe was only three miles from Chris's damn front door. Where had Everton been going? Here? Chris jumped to his feet. The phone thumped to the floor. Katie put both hands up, almost defensively.

'Does this Everton guy know where you are? Does he know you're here?'

'I don't know… I don't see how.'

'Does Everton know the story? Does he know you think I might be your dad?'

Katie seemed to shrink back, and Chris realised he had raised his voice.

'I don't know. I don't know what Eve told Ron. So I don't know what Ron might have told Everton on the night he was… was killed.'

Chris sat again. If Everton had seen Katie arrive here, then a fugitive murderer had this house, had Chris and his family in his crosshairs. He peeled back growing anger, because it didn't seem right to blame Katie. But he needed a target. And he had to say something. 'This is bad, Katie.'

'I'm sorry to show you that, really I am. I just wanted all cards on the table. I don't want anyone to worry.'

Worry would come later, but for now Chris felt only that anger. 'You think the guy might come here? To get you? That he might come to my house?'

'I think Ron might have done something to upset people. The wrong people. I had a feeling Ron had got on the wrong side of the wrong guy. And now he's dead and the man the police think killed him is in Sheffield.'

Chris leaped upon that, desperate. 'Just because he's in the same city as you, that doesn't mean anything. Is there more you're not telling me?'

Katie rubbed her face. 'I know, I know, it's weak. It's paranoid. I just can't help wondering; Everton's on the run, so why not travel far away? He's supposed to have contacts in London. Why hang around Yorkshire? Why not go lose yourself down south?'

He felt a need to calm her – something paternal waking from slumber? 'Sheffield is big also and it's close to Bradford. Maybe it's not easy to travel when the police want you. Everton's probably holing up somewhere where he feels comfortable. He might not know any other cities that well. Now that the police know he's in Sheffield, they're on the lookout for him, so he'll know it's dangerous to stay here. My bet is he'll now run somewhere else.'

Katie nodded again. 'You're probably right. I'm sorry. This is a headache for you all. My worries and fears, me on your sofa. I apologise. I shouldn't have even contacted you. I should have left you and your family in peace. I don't want to bring you any trouble.'

'It's fine.'

Katie's meekness gave him the confidence to broach a subject he'd increasingly wanted to tackle.

'Katie, I want to talk to you about your mother's suicide.'

Katie got up. She was wearing tracksuit bottoms. At first Chris thought she was going to storm off, angry, but Katie took two steps and flopped on the other sofa. Their legs touched. But she didn't look at him. It made their closeness easier for Chris to handle.

'On the day she told me about you,' she began, 'I went out on my bike. For a ride. I just rode. I tried to picture what you looked like, even though all I had was a name. But when I went home again, to ask my mother for more information, that was when she dropped the second bombshell. She wanted to kill herself. She was in her final days and wanted to end it. And she did it, she did it, and I was in the house when she did it. I let it happen.'

Chris felt the words like a smack. He got up and stumbled to the window. The curtains were pulled, but he could see the dots of streetlights through the thin material. He stared at one.

'She begged me. "Make me comfortable," she said. I was in shock, but her face… she looked… certain. Resigned, maybe. I got the feeling it wasn't a rash decision. That she had thought about this for a long time. She said that she had taken care of her affairs, as they say. Made sure bills were paid, letters were written, you know? I knew she was serious, and I knew I couldn't talk her out of it. I could only hope that the next few days would change her mind. But then she showed me the Amitriptyline. Right there in her hands.'

To give his own hands something to do, Chris was running his fingers over his phone. Now, after making sure Katie was still staring at the ceiling, or deep space beyond, he turned his eyes upon that device.

'I wonder constantly: what if? What if she hadn't taken those tablets and somehow her cancer wouldn't have killed her? How might we have spent the next few months? She might have got happier. She might have won the lottery. She might have been able to go out at peace, as God intended. And I would have had time to think about what I said.'

He found a website, and now he knew: 'Amitriptyline: a tricyclic antidepressant for chemical rebalance in the nervous system'. Maybe Eve Levine had been feeling depressed for a long time. Maybe doctors prescribed antidepressants to everyone diagnosed as terminal. He wasn't sure, but for certain her doctor hadn't counted on Eve attempting to un-blacken her mood by removing all moods. For ever.

'You understand what I mean? You can say all you can think of to someone before they go, but there's always going to be something else when it's too late. Something you missed, or something you could have said better, or something you once said that you should have apologised for. Hindsight. Hindsight is twenty-twenty vision. If governments could rewind time by a day whenever they wanted, and do it over, there would be no catastrophes, no wars, no genocide, no starvation in the world.'

Amitriptyline: also used for painkilling, which had been her final use for it. The end of all pain, for ever. He wondered if doctors had to face an inquiry board each time a patient died by overdose of prescribed drugs. In the post-Harold Shipman world, probably.

'She showed me the tablets, as if to say she had it all worked out. I knew there was nothing I could do to stop her. I mean, I'd seen the pain and depression first-hand, hadn't I? So I wasn't shocked about that. Not really. But it was kind of out of the blue, you know? She hadn't mentioned it before, and then, when she did, it was like, bang, we had to do it immediately. Like an alarm had gone off. Everything suddenly had to be dropped, and she wanted to do this. And she had this idea about filming it...'

Average manufacturing cost of a penny and a half for 25 mg tablets, and the minimum lethal dose was set at 120 tablets. It was £400 a night for a hospital bed, but Eve Levine's death had cost the government only £1.80. Actually, they'd profited by £6.80 because of the £8.60 NHS prescription charge. Given her illness, though, she probably had an exception card that allowed her to die for free—

'Film it?' Chris turned.

Katie was lying back, face towards the ceiling, eyes wide open.

'So I waited,' Katie said, as if she hadn't heard Chris's shocked response. 'She was upstairs, I was down. I washed pots and I dithered about and I watered the plants, just doing a bit of housework as normal, and while I did this my mother was killing herself ten feet above me.'

'Did you say she filmed her suicide? Katie?'

She closed her eyes. 'No more for tonight. Please. Overloading you is not what I ever wanted. Please, don't say anything. Just go. We'll talk tomorrow.'

Her eyes closed. He thought about trying to comfort her, but reminded himself that he had no idea of the methods she employed to do that herself. Maybe she needed solitude and prompting her to talk could do more damage than good. That, he told himself, was the reason he walked out. But he knew the truth was rooted in selfishness. He just didn't want any more of this witching hour confessional. He wanted oblivion until the daylight hours, and a return to the placid routine of life.

*

But he didn't go to bed. When he made a floorboard creak in the bedroom, Rose stirred and said, 'Hide bank statements from Katie.' He stared at her, wondering if she was worried that Katie would want money. But her eyes were closed. Just a sleep-mumble, then. He made sure Julia was also asleep, and then he dragged himself through the attic trap, into the Manor.

He swallowed a mouthful of whiskey even before he'd sat down and tried to make sense of the last twenty minutes. But his phone beeped. A text from Katie. It was a shaking hand that opened the message, because he knew that whatever Katie wanted to say, it was something she hadn't been able to voice face-to-face. Even after the other terrible revelations. He didn't look at the screen until after another large swallow of whiskey.

*'I lied about the letter I sent you. I didn't send it to avoid overloading you with her death and who I was all at the same time. I sent it for selfish reasons.'*

He was tempted to ignore the message, and deal with this on a fresh day. But his fingers typed. Faceless, it was easier to talk.

*'Tell me. It's okay.'*

*'I didn't want you to split your feelings between both of us. I wanted you to be over shock of her death when I told you who I was. I wanted all your attention.'*

The response came quickly. Again, he splashed whiskey across his teeth before he replied. He stared at the lightbulb as he waited.

*'I understand. I would have done the same thing.'*

*'It was wrong. Tell me if you want me to be gone when you wake in the morning. I understand if you hope you're not my father.'*

*'I do not know yet, if I am honest. It's early into this whole thing. But I know you believe I am.'*

*'I'm not sure yet, either. Like you say, it's early. We deal with this after the test result.'*

*'Okay. And don't go. Stay.'*

# THURSDAY

# CHAPTER EIGHTEEN

At the breakfast table, Julia was writing comedy material in a jotter and Rose was reading a book about gymnastics. Chris took a seat behind his bowl of cereal, sugarless, of course. A lunch of something fresh and healthy, which meant cold and tasteless, was sitting there wrapped in foil. As always, he'd secretly sell it to a colleague for enough to buy Pitstop cake.

'Where's Katie?'

If there was any hope that she'd left in the night, Rose ended it when she pointed out the kitchen window. He got up to look. Katie was in the garden, trying to unearth an old tree root beside the shed with a spade. She was wearing Chris's old North Face gardening jacket, her own beanie cap and a pair of Rose's jeans ruined by bleach spots.

'I said I'd get around to that tree root. What did you say to her?'

Julia made a crack about past broken housework promises. Katie looked over, saw him, and gave a thumbs up. He returned it then sat again behind his breakfast. Now he could hear heavy thuds from outside.

Rose tapped his cereal bowl as a prompt to eat. 'Leave her to it. Besides, you've got a speech to write.'

'I've never been to a funeral,' Julia said. 'Are you sorry about her being dead, Dad?'

Rose saw his shocked face and scuttled from the kitchen.

He met her in the living room. 'What did you tell Julia about Eve?'

'Not what you look so terrified about. She thinks you knew her as a friend from college.'

'What?'

'Isn't that better than the truth? I had to make something up for now. And how daft would it look if a stranger finds our belongings after the robbery and then invites us to her mother's funeral? So now Julia believes it was a strange coincidence that you just happen to know Katie's mother from way back.'

He didn't like it, but it was done and there was no way to rewind time. As long as Julia didn't ask any more questions about Eve Levine, there wouldn't be a problem. That aside, he focussed on something else.

'What speech?'

'Ah, yes. Katie mentioned something about wanting you to say a few words at the funeral. I said you'd be happy to.'

'Please tell me that's a joke.'

She calmed him and explained. He wouldn't have to stand before a sorrowful crowd, all looking at him and wondering who the hell he was. Katie would be reading notes from those who knew and loved her mother, and Chris's would be one of those. He would cover Eve as a young woman. Relax, man.

Relaxation was impossible. 'But I didn't really know her. Surely there's some old friend who could do a better job?'

'I don't doubt it. But Katie wants you. You might be her dad, remember. It means a lot.'

'I haven't got a clue what to say, Rose. I knew her for one day.'

'If people always knew what to say, there would be no such thing as speechwriting. You've got a day.'

He didn't really know what he was worried about the family thinking of him. Rose had an idea, though, and it was worse than anything he could have dreamed up: 'That you're back after all these years and trying to worm your way into her will?'

A will. He hadn't thought of that. Suicides often planned their deaths and considered their family. Jesus Christ. 'That's exactly what they'll think, Rose. That I'm after bleeding her dry. This is just great.'

'Relax. Look on the bright side. She might be rich. Katie might have been left millions. She can be my long-lost daughter for that much money.'

She was winding him up, he realised. Somewhat childishly, he told her that he'd seen The Blue Swan pub and it was a decrepit wreck, so sod you.

'Oh, I didn't think about that place,' Rose said. 'I wonder why Katie couldn't stay there? What do you mean by a wreck?'

'Katie told me she moved out at sixteen. Eve put it up for sale when she got ill. But it's run down and I think there's a squatter. She seemed like she didn't really want to talk about it.'

Rose rubbed her chin, thinking. 'Where did she go at sixteen?'

'I don't know.' And right now he didn't care because of something far more pressing. 'I can't do it. I didn't know her. I can't write a bloody speech, Rose.'

'Well, consider this…' She insisted that he would appear uncaring if, after discovering she gave birth to his child – *possibly, calm down, just possibly!* – he didn't say something respectful about Eve now that she was gone. So man up. 'Now why don't you go outside and congratulate Katie on the fine job she's doing out in the cold with a tree root that you've spent the last six months giving idle threats to?'

There was no fight left in him. He shuffled back into the kitchen. The thudding from outside drew him to the window. Now Katie had a sledgehammer and was dropping it hard onto the tree stump, and doing it right by raising the hammer with a hand at each end for stability before bending her torso to aid dragging the heavy end downwards. Girl had some power, despite her frail frame.

'Eat,' Julia told him. As he sat, she ripped a page from her notebook and slapped it and her pen in front of him. 'Write.'

He took it like a condemned man being handed his own rope.

*

Rose wanted the satnav because she was getting her eyebrows done ready for their party on Saturday, so he swapped the device into her car while she watched from the doorstep. When he returned, she handed him his healthy and tasteless lunch. 'Maybe we could invite Katie to our bowling tonight.'

He dismissed that idea instantly. People would ask—

Julia appeared at the kitchen doorway, nose deep in her notebook and giggling to herself. She pushed between her parents, felt in a pocket of her coat, and then walked away with a folded sheet of paper, back towards the kitchen.

Rose must have shared his thought because she did some editing. 'Perhaps not bowling. People will ask who she is. We can't tell them before the test result and I don't want to lie to our friends. Friday. Go out to the pub with her on Friday night. She'll need cheering up after her mother's funeral. Ask her about it.'

A better idea, but a concern occurred: surely, if Katie wanted a bonding night, she would have offered—

'And don't be thinking Katie would have invited you for a drink if it was what she wanted. It took me to push you. There's no one to push her. She's probably too nervous to ask in case you say no. Easier to stay in the dark about whether or not you like her. I'm not sure myself on that one.'

He'd sworn to make more of an effort, so, yes, he'd ask Katie today. He promised it aloud to Rose, which made backing out no option. 'And I think she's okay. Early days still.'

'Spectacular.' She opened the front door and handed him his car keys. 'Have a good day at work. And if you decide to give your lunch away to someone else again, tell them not to post a picture of it on Facebook.'

He grinned and turned to go, but she grabbed his arm.

'Do you remember my toothbrush? How that was when you said you knew we were going to be together for a long time? My toothbrush appearing in your bathroom?'

He did. He recalled seeing the toothbrush there in his bathroom and punching the air in triumph, because she was his now. 'Why?'

'Katie told me her go-karting trophy was in her bike pannier from when she'd shown you. So it was the only thing she managed to save from her flat. She brought it in and now it's on the fireplace for all to see.'

She was waiting for his reaction. There was no air-punch. He gave her a nod, and a kiss, and the back of his head as he walked down the path.

As he was about to drive away, the front door opened and Katie jogged down the path. Now out of his jacket and Rose's jeans, she wore jeggings and another tight pullover. If she'd bought them yesterday evening when she went out, she'd used a late-night charity shop because they didn't look brand new. Chris buzzed the window down, expecting to be told or handed something he'd forgotten. But no.

'Can I come with you?'

'Where? I'm going to work.'

'That's what I mean. To your work. I know I can't come inside the lab. I thought we could just have a chat on the way.'

'How will you get back? It's three buses.'

'I don't mind.'

Awkward travel had been his only defence, so a minute later he was driving away with a passenger. Fast, to get there as quickly as possible. But the journey dragged. Every red light seemed twice as long and everyone at zebra crossings sauntered nice and slow. At the hospital car park, Chris chose the nearest free space and shut the engine off. At first, he'd been happy that Katie hadn't spoken, instead had watched the world slip by with her forehead on the window. Now, he worried that there was something wrong.

'Have you got change for the buses?'

She kept her head on the glass, as if transfixed by a sight beyond. But the flank of an old Vauxhall Corsa wasn't that intriguing. 'I thought I'd wait. I don't get bored. I could wait and drive home with you.'

Wait? All day? 'Walk around the hospital too much and security will want a word.'

'I'll think of something to do. I can play on my phone, maybe take a stroll.'

Figuring Katie would regret her plan within a couple of hours, Chris said, 'Okay. I'll be back about ten past five. Gotta rush now.'

'Wait. You always have lunch at the Pitstop, don't you? How about I meet you there?'

'Yes, okay.' He opened his door. She didn't move. It was becoming unnerving. At the Pitstop, he would have to bring up last night, just in case today's attitude was because of things she might wish she'd left unsaid.

He got out. 'See you later.'

She raised a thumb. Said nothing.

Julia called as he was dodging ambulances and taxis while crossing the drop-off zone outside the main entrance.

'I've told Mum already,' she said, her voice husky. 'I've been offered a gig tonight. A birthday party in Dinnington. Can I go? It's two hundred pounds.'

'Video,' he said. Julia had been doing stand-up at kids' parties for a year now, eight or nine gigs, and not once had she provided her parents with a recording. Chris had never even heard her practise a routine because it was shrouded in secrecy. 'But only if your grandmother doesn't cancel again.'

'Thanks, Dad. Sure you're okay with me earning twice what you get and being half your age?'

She still had that breathy voice. 'What's wrong with your croaky throat? And is this why you never show us a video? Because you get the Vaudeville Hook?'

Her voice was back to normal suddenly. 'Funny. Hey, Simone is allowed visitors now. Want to meet for lunch before I go?'

'I'm supposed to meet Katie for lunch.'

'That's fine. Maybe we can all visit her. She'll like Katie. I'll see you later, old one.'

She hung up before he could object.

There was no way he was going to visit Simone.

*

As he walked into the lab, Lionel Parrot held up his phone in one hand, waving it like a treasure.

'Oh yes. Cops just released Meadow Moll's boyfriend. Lack of evidence. Wasn't him. Told you all. This is the start of something big.'

Someone said, 'No, they have to charge or release after twenty-four hours. That proves nothing.'

'Actually, it does,' Lionel said. 'It's morning. I heard he was arrested about 7 a.m. yesterday morning, so it's been over twenty-four hours. They'd go for an extension if they thought he was guilty. Wasn't him. Told you, it was the Meadow Murderer.'

Another voice chimed in. 'What about what Moll said he said? That stuff about her cutting him out of her life. She'd just dumped the boyfriend. Explain that.'

'Could have been a chap she turned down at college, or in a club. Sometimes serial killers stalk people and they don't know they're being stalked. He could have held a grudge for ages. Think she'll remember every date she turned down over the years?'

'No one gives a toss, Lionel,' someone else barked. That did it. All eyes went back onto benches. But Lionel was rolling his shoulders like a man who'd just won the lottery.

Five minutes later, Alan stuck his head out of the office and called for Louise. When their meeting was done, she stomped back to her bench and gave Chris a withering look. Alan's head was again floating in the doorway.

'Redfern.'

When Chris dragged himself in, Alan was on the PC. He didn't look up. 'I've got this action on an E. coli 0157 for a chap called Raymond Monroe. I just called downstairs. The patient is still ill, not responding to treatment. He's getting worse. I wasn't happy sending out this manual negative result Louise did until I could get it in the machine.'

He paused here and Chris knew exactly why. But he said nothing. He looked at Alan's telescope on the windowsill.

'So I just told Louise to run it,' Alan continued. 'But Louise said the Enterics kits are out. She asked you to order some and you forgot. There's an ill patient downstairs who's had to wait longer because we did the test manually.'

And there it was. Alan was trying to pass the buck. Chris wasn't having it. 'But you're the manager and you're supposed to order the kits. Maybe you should have done it instead of dumping it on Louise.'

As far back as the word 'but' Chris knew he was going to say something he'd regret. The brakes were on by the word 'manager' but his anger had greased the road and this juggernaut couldn't stop. By the time 'Louise' had exited his mouth, he was fully aware that irrecoverable injuries might result from this crash.

But Alan didn't explode. 'Louise shouldn't have passed the buck, I agree. But now your manager is telling a member of his team to call and get an ETA on the Enterics kits. That member would be you. There, now we'll have no confusion, will we?'

Chris moved towards the telescope at the window. Some said Alan used it to spy on the girls working the burger van operating in the hospital grounds. When he peeked through the eyepiece, he couldn't help but grin.

'Help yourself to my private property, why don't you?'

Chris turned the telescope, skimming it away from the burger van and over the car park. He found his own vehicle. He refocussed and there was Katie, nice and crisp. Just sitting there in the Mondeo. Her eyes weren't downcast, though, which Chris would have expected if the kid was playing on her phone. In fact, she cracked her wrists, proving both hands were empty. Her eyes were ahead, somewhat glazed, as if transfixed by something beyond the windscreen. But there was nothing out there except more cars.

'Redfern…'

'I'll do it now,' Chris said, and turned to go. As he left the office, he wondered why Katie was willing to just sit in his car all day.

A porter brought supplies, including the Enterics kits, as Chris was about to phone for an ETA. As Louise grabbed the box and set the BDMAX machine running on Raymond Monroe's sample, he got his coat. She ignored him as he left the lab, but less care on his part was impossible.

*

Katie was already in the Pitstop, which annoyed him. Not even five minutes to himself. The kid had a slice of cake awaiting Chris, though. Small graces. He took a seat and a bite. That was when Julia walked in.

Chris noticed she looked a little dazed and perturbed, dancing from foot to foot like someone needing the toilet. Everyone said hi.

'Simone's ready for me. I won't tell Mum you've got cake, by the way.'

'I can't come in with you,' he said, then added his new plan to appease her. 'But Katie might.'

'I don't want to intrude,' Katie said. 'I mean, Simone won't want strangers around.'

'No, no, it's fine,' Julia said. 'Simone already texted to say just me. But I'm nervous for some reason.'

'BVT heal that fractured mind,' Katie told her with a thumbs up.

'What?' Chris said.

Julia gave a snort-like laugh and sat. She slid Chris's cake her way. 'Sugar rush will help me.'

Chris looked up as he saw his colleagues flocking towards the Pitstop. He got up.

'I'm sorry to cut this short, guys, but I need to get back for an important result. I'll see you both later.'

Julia waved and didn't even look up from her cake. Katie looked a little hurt, but he left her that way in order to be far from the table before his work pals saw him with a woman they didn't know. Especially a young, pretty one.

*

Back in the lab, alone, Rose called and didn't even let him say hello. 'Did you tell anyone about Katie yet?'

'At work? No, what's the point of—'

'I mean your grandparents, Chris. And your sister.'

'I don't know where Lindsay is, do I? My grandparents are too senile to register what I say. And I don't want to tell anyone until we know. I already said that.'

There was a pause. He knew he wouldn't like what Rose said next. He expected her to again bring up his father, but her words were far more shocking.

'I looked Lindsay up for you. She's on Facebook.' She paused there. He waited. 'It took some time because there's so many. But I think I found her. But it... she was called Lindsay Masseuse Redfern.'

'Masseuse?'

'I'm sorry.'

He paused. 'Leave it with me, Rose. I'll call her or I won't. Don't bring it up again, please.'

'Okay. I'm sorry. Leave your head in the sand.'

Rose all over: an insult and an apology hand-in-hand. As he nervously paced past the BDMAX machine, he spotted something on the digital readout that made him wobble. He hung up the phone even though Rose was still talking. Unwilling to wait for Alan to return, he rushed for the wall phone and dialled the Emergency Medical Unit extension.

*Shiga toxin Pos.*, the BDMAX's readout had said.

A man answered, professional tone atop a bored base. Chris cut into his well-practised opening. 'This is microbiology. Stop treatment on Raymond Monroe immediately.' He gave the patient's number. The man told him that Raymond Monroe's condition had slipped and he'd been moved to the Intensive Care Unit. Chris hung up, called that ward and repeated his warning. The nurse asked his reason, and he told her:

Shiga Toxin Positive – something nasty confirmed in Raymond Monroe's stool, likely E. coli 0157, which would respond to an ass-kicking from antibiotics by detonating a toxin landmine.

'Stop treatment now. We'll run the stool again to be certain. But stop any antibiotics.'

'Toxins in the head,' he thought the woman said in reply. But that was because the line was crackly. Another phone that Alan had smacked. He got her to repeat it. Toxins in the head sounded bad, if a little strange. The truth was worse.

Toxic shock, she'd said. And: The patient is dead.

# CHAPTER NINETEEN

Chris was ten feet from his car, key in hand, when he saw Katie's smile vanish. A moment later, someone grabbed his shoulder. He jumped and there was sharp pain as fingers dug sharply into him, a nail grazing his neck. He spun, angry.

'What the hell?'

He'd expected Alan. The brass knew about Raymond Monroe's avoidable death and heads would have to roll. The lab had cleared in a flash at home time because nobody wanted to be in the blast radius when the shitstorm exploded.

But it was Louise. And she was enraged.

'It's your own fault for not hearing me shout,' she said.

'So you stick your nails in my flesh? What the hell's going on?'

'You've got to get back in there and tell Alan that you messed up.'

He rubbed his shoulder, skin still burning from the aggressive grab. Any sympathy he might have had for Louise because of the Raymond Monroe fiasco dropped through a trapdoor.

'Tell Alan that *I* messed up? You better not mean that Enterics kit. You missed the E. coli. How's that my fault again?'

'I told you to order the kits.'

And no doubt she'd told Alan exactly that when he'd pulled her into the office.

'You did a manual and messed it up. I'm not to blame.' He mellowed a little now the initial flash of pain had subsided. 'Look, we miss things now and then. It happens.'

'It *happens*? That guy's dead because of you and that's all you can say?'

'Because of me? Piss off,' he shouted.

Other people in the car park were watching them, although pretending not to. He was too angry to care.

'I only said that to try to make you feel better,' Chris said. 'But you can bollocks, Louise. You missed it, not me. Now go away.'

She didn't move. 'You'll tell Alan *you* messed up that poor man's life, or else.'

He was certain that Alan didn't blame him, else he would have had his own office visit.

'That poor man? What's his name, Louise? Do you know it?'

'His name's Raymond Monroe, you obtuse dickhead. Now get walking back there. Don't you dare make me ask you again.'

He looked around. A scattering of people coming and going, and Katie just sitting in the car, watching. Nobody wanted to intrude into what might be a lovers' quarrel. But it would be a different story if things escalated. Louise looked like she really might swing for him, and if he defended himself, who knows how onlookers would interpret the situation?

'That's right,' she said, as if reading his mind. 'You don't want me to make a scene, do you?'

He could see a pair of guys who looked ready to rush at him if he made a move, if only to play hero and impress a lady. They would subdue him and the police would come, and it would be his word against three. He started to back off.

'You're losing your mind, Louise.'

She took a step forward. 'I will in a minute, so help me God. I know about your record, too.'

Chris flinched.

'With your history, I could smack you right now and the police will believe me when I say it was self-defence.'

He didn't doubt an ounce of that. She stepped forward, as if actually about to hit him. He had no choice but to step back, but he also put up a hand to push her away. It got her in the chin and jerked her head.

She stumbled backwards, but only out of surprise. It was a simple touch, no power, nowhere near enough to put her down. But when she heard a close yell from one of the have-a-go-heroes, down she went like a tackled footballer. It was such a supreme piece of bad acting that he actually let out a laugh, couldn't help it.

In the next moment the two guys were in his space, crowding him. One turned to help Louise up. The other guy yelled right into his face: *who the hell did he think he was, hitting a girl?*

'I didn't touch her,' he yelled back. The man grabbed his arm, so Chris pushed him away, hard. The guy stumbled, regained his footing, and bellowed, '*Keep your hands off me.*' Chris became aware of a growing audience and how bad this all looked for him: two guys had come to the aid of a woman knocked to the ground, and now Chris, a man with a record he liked to keep secret, had manhandled one of the saviours. He knew he'd have a problem convincing the police that he hadn't started a whole heap of trouble.

Chris launched himself at his car. The wheels were spinning seconds later. When the car blew past the two saviours, one gave the finger. The other waited until the vehicle was beyond a stone's throw – then threw a stone.

Chris was still shaking. He looked at Katie, who remained silent. 'Are you okay?'

She nodded, but her eyes remained locked on the route ahead. 'That woman said you had a record.'

He took a turn out of the hospital grounds without slowing, which forced an ambulance that was turning in to do the braking instead. It made him swear, which he immediately regretted. He put a hand on her shoulder. 'It was two years ago, and—'

'Don't explain. It doesn't matter. I just didn't like seeing you so angry. But it's okay. Let's forget all that just happened.'

He wanted to, but he also wanted to explain. Torn between the two, he simply apologised. 'I get angry sometimes. You shouldn't have had to see that.'

She nodded, eyes ahead. 'There was a CCTV camera. It will back you up, prove you didn't do anything. So will I.'

He was more worried about the long-term effects of now having an enemy in the same room for the rest of his working life. An upset to the balance he craved. That annoying bitch Louise.

\*

Partway home, Chris jerked the wheel and pulled to the kerb. He hauled out his phone.

'What's wrong?' Katie said.

'Just wait a mo. I have to text work.'

He bent his wrist so Katie couldn't see, because he wasn't texting work at all. He loaded Facebook and typed 'LINDSAY MASSEUSE REDFERN'. It got one hit. The profile picture was of a candle burning next to a bottle of scented massage oil, which seemed innocent enough. Except it wasn't a business page and the account owner listed no details except a brief bio under the picture, and that only said 'RELAXING FUN CHIGWELL' and a mobile number. He captured a screenshot then put the phone away.

It didn't have to be his sister, of course. Last he'd known, about five years ago now, she had relocated to Chigwell in Essex, but that place might have a number of women with that name. But his hands shook at the memory of that profile page. The lack of professionalism reeked of sordidness. And there were rumours of prostitution…

'What's wrong?'

He didn't answer. With Facebook loaded, something occurred to him. Previously, he'd found no Facebook profile for Katherine –

but she didn't use that name. Shielding the mobile, he did another search of the social media service, this time for 'KATIE LEVINE'. There were a number of Katie Levines and he scrolled past those with photos that clearly weren't her. On the third profile with no picture, he got lucky. Katie just waited.

It was a skeleton with no details except one. No friends, no photos, no posts. Nothing listed for birthdate, job, likes. Nothing but a little bio snippet under that blank profile picture:

Conceived during Michael Schumacher's 2000 Formula 1 World Championship win!!

The exclamation marks suggested Katie liked this fact, so maybe that was why it had been the first piece of information listed when she set up the profile, especially if Facebook was something new and intriguing and daunting at the same time. Julia's profile bio said: 'Arrived in the world late and kept up the habit ever since.' So talking about when or where you were born, no problem. But where you were conceived? Strange.

He froze as something hit him. Something from that bio snippet. A snake of fear writhed down his spine.

'Chris, what's wrong?' Katie asked.

'Nothing,' Chris snapped, loud enough to make Katie wide-eyed in surprise. He said nothing further and pulled into traffic, sparking a horn blast from someone unimpressed by his impatience. But just a few seconds later, he once more pulled into the side of the road.

'You've never asked about the rest of my family. So I want to tell you about my own father. He walked out when I was ten. The marriage had been failing, but I was unaware of that. Until my mum and dad sat me down one day and explained. My dad was leaving. From that point on, he would see me only at Christmases and birthdays. But I never saw him again. I got a letter from him congratulating me when Julia was born, and a condolence card years later when my mother died. Nothing since. I don't know where he is or even if he's alive.'

Katie was looking at her lap. 'I had no idea. I'm sorry for your loss.'

'Your finding me has made me think about him. Rose thinks that my father keeps tabs on me through an old army buddy of his who lives just a couple of miles away. I think Rose wants me to reach out to this guy, so I can reconnect with my father. You did the very same thing. I want to know what you think I should do.'

Katie looked at him, but her scrutiny forced his own eyes away. 'Is this why you were so ready to accept me? Because of what happened to you? Is it because you feel sorry for me?'

'I don't know,' he said, but was that true? In the two letters he'd had over the last twenty-eight years, his father had spoken of guilt and self-loathing. By attempting to do the right thing by Katie, was Chris simply erecting defences against those same emotions?

'I think you need more time to think,' Katie said. He nodded, but not because he agreed; he just wanted to end this awkward conversation. Katie didn't press the matter, so he put his father out of his mind and started driving.

# CHAPTER TWENTY

On the corner of Chris's street, the Swift sons were at their garden fence, which was up and good and painted. But they weren't admiring their handiwork, they were talking to a police officer. A patrol car was parked at the kerb and a second cop was between it and his open door, talking on his radio. Chris stopped his car, passenger side against the kerb.

'Don't stop, I want to get home,' Katie said.

'I'm just being nosy.'

He put Katie's window down.

The taller Swift, a tattooed monster, peeled away from his brother and the cop and stepped up. He gave Katie a long, hot-blooded male glare that Chris didn't like, then found the will to drag his eyes to Chris. Katie barely acknowledged the guy existed.

'All right, Mr Redfern?'

'What's with the police? This is my friend, Katie.' He prayed that Katie wouldn't blurt the truth, but Katie didn't blurt anything. She just stared out the windscreen.

Swift said, 'We found something.'

While sowing grass seeds this morning to repair damage from the car that had smashed the fence, he and his brother had found a knife in a corner of their lawn. Already believing the car to be stolen, the police now suspected the driver had tossed the knife while abandoning the scene. They'd collected it with thanks and smiles, but now they were back and suspicious. Prints on the weapon belonged to a man dearly wanted and they suspected he might have friends living nearby.

'What's his name?'

'Can we just get home?' Katie said. 'Who cares about some car thief? I feel ill.'

Katie buzzed her window up, which nearly took off the Swift boy's nose. Chris and his neighbour exchanged a farewell thumbs up.

Soon, they were outside Casa Redfern. Katie kicked open her door before the engine was off. Chris sat and watched a second patrol car cruise down the street. His rear-view mirror showed it pull up in front of the other. Two more cops got out, a man and a woman.

Inside, Rose called him from upstairs.

Katie said she'd put the kettle on. Very make-your-self-at-home.

He found Rose at their bedroom window, peeking out.

'Where's Julia?' he asked.

'Out with a friend somewhere. You see these police on the street?'

She seemed enthralled enough that he might get away with a sarcastic joke. 'No, we teleported into the house from the Starship *Enterprise*.' The joke didn't register, so he got little satisfaction.

She told him to come look. They stood side by side, faces against the glass so they could see down the street to the corner.

'What did the police say to you?' she asked.

She must have been at the window long enough to see his car stop at the Swift house. Minus the swearing, he repeated the Swift boy's story: cops took away a knife the brothers found in the garden; cops found a wanted man's prints on the weapon; cops came back because wanted men needed places to hide, people to help them, and either or both could be why the car thief had been in the area late at night.

'So they think the Swift boys, they were hiding this fellow? Wow.'

'I don't know. They don't seem the sort. Besides, why would they call in about the knife if their pal owned it?'

They watched one of the police cars turn in the road and head this way. And past. It stopped at the other end, near the shops. Their heads turned left and right, like tennis fans watching a ball thunked back and forth. Two cop cars, two cops to each. Four police officers to cover both sides and both ends of the street. Chris realised what was going on at the same time Rose got it.

'Wow. They're knocking on doors. So it might not be the Swift boys. They're going to work their way towards the middle, to us. Look, look.'

'I am, I am.'

'I bet the police think this car thief knows someone else here. He must have crashed on his way to another house here. Wow.' She slapped his arm. 'What about that Lassiter girl, always has those strange men around?'

Her mobile rang.

'Mrs Smith,' she said, reading the screen. She answered the call and immediately waved out the window. Chris saw a woman at a bedroom window across the road, also watching the action. The two women started to natter about possible criminals on the street, and Chris left them to it.

Katie was in the living room, watching cartoons.

He asked if she was okay. 'You staying for dinner?'

Katie nodded. 'Sorry about wanting to run off like that. My belly is aching. Can I use your bathroom?'

*Me casa su casa.*

Katie went upstairs and Rose came down.

'I called Yvonne down at forty-two,' she said. 'Silly mare. Know what she said to me?'

'How could I?'

'They'd just been to her house. I asked her who the fugitive was. Know what she said? "Like you don't know. You know everyone that Julia of yours hangs about with, do you?" How cheeky is that?'

Cheeky, yes, but it made Chris wonder.

# CHAPTER TWENTY-ONE

The police's door-to-door was ongoing, but slowly, and Julia had returned so Rose had started dinner. Even so, she kept coming through from the kitchen to peek out of the living room window, always announcing: 'Not here yet.'

Even Julia, the constantly curious one, got bored of the wait and turned her attention elsewhere. She was texting friends about Simone, who had been buoyant and talkative during their meeting but a little scared of re-entering the big wide world. Katie was still upstairs, lying down on Julia's floor in the sleeping bag because her stomach was playing up.

And then it was their turn.

It was the female cop at the door. Julia and Rose saw her through the window, and then both went to answer the knock. Then they returned. Three of them. Seeing the officer made Chris sit up straight, like a schoolkid caught slouching.

Julia offered the officer a drink, which she refused. Then Julia said, 'We know why you're here,' as if proud of her detective skills.

The officer started with a standard line: in the area making enquiries, wonder if you'd mind answering a few questions.

They didn't.

She asked if they were aware of the events of two Saturdays ago, when a stolen car smashed a fence down on the corner and was abandoned by the thief.

They were.

She said the police now believed that the man driving the stolen car might have had business here on this street – would any of you know why?

They didn't.

She asked if any of them knew, or knew anyone who knew, a twenty-eight-year-old man called Dominic Everton.

They didn't—

'Yes,' Chris said. Everyone looked at him, but he saw only the female cop, intent on her as she got on her radio to basically call in a jackpot hit. His gut was turning. Everton, the man who had killed Ron Hugill, had been watching the family, and almost two weeks ago he had driven here late at night, and crashed, and whatever he'd had planned had been thwarted. A plan possibly involving a knife.

A plan to hurt Chris's family. His eyes darted from Julia to Rose. And then to the ceiling. To Katie.

His phone beeped and he pulled it out for a quick glance, because he didn't want to return the officer's stare.

'Mr Redfern, how do you know Dominic Everton? And did he come here to see you on that Saturday?'

His brain raced. Slotting away the phone, he said, 'He works at my hospital.'

He could feel the shock pulsing off Rose, who had read all about Everton.

'Works with you?' the officer said.

He pulled a bogus puzzled face. 'But surely you don't think an eighty-year-old man drove a stolen car.'

Now Rose looked puzzled. The officer said, 'He's twenty-eight, and—'

A fake laugh. 'Darren Enderton isn't twenty-eight.'

'Enderton? Who is that? I'm here about Dominic Everton.'

Now forged embarrassment. 'I thought you said Darren Enderton. I work with a guy called that. He should have retired, but he does it voluntary now. That's not who you meant?'

'No. No, sir, Dominic Everton.' Still suspicious, she asked twice more if anyone knew the wanted man. Twice more Chris had to summon up every ounce of composure and give the lie. The officer didn't fully look convinced and told him to call the station if he remembered anything, saw anyone, or *changed his mind*. But finally, she left. The pressure wasn't off him yet, he knew. Julia was giving him a curious glare. And then Rose pulled him aside for one of her terrifying private chats.

'What's going on, Chris? Why would this Everton guy be coming here? Is this about Katie?'

'I doubt it. Coincidence. The guy's on the run and he was probably driving all over and just happened to crash here. Let me go tell Katie.'

'Is this man after Katie? Does she know him because of Ron Hugill? Chris, is Katie in danger? Are we in danger?'

'No, no. It's just a coincidence. Everton is in the news and people will be thinking they've spotted him all over the place. I bet the police get calls all the time. It looks bad because he's been to this street and Katie has a connection to him, but it's only a freak bit of luck.'

'Freak bit of luck? What about this man Enderton you mentioned? What was that? Is there even such a person? Do eighty-year-olds work in hospitals? I think you just lied to that police officer. Somehow to protect this Everton criminal.'

'Why would I do that?'

'You tell me. But I'm more amazed about why I just went along with it. Why I didn't just tell that officer that the daughter of the man Everton killed is sitting upstairs.'

That made him think of something. 'Look, Rose, if I'd mentioned Katie, how she's connected to Everton because of Ron Hugill, then that officer would have called her downstairs. And she might have been forced to say who she was. To us. To me.'

She seemed to consider this. 'You were worried that Katie might have had to say she might be your daughter? In front of Julia?'

'Yes.'

She considered some more. The slump of her shoulders, a release of tension, told him she'd accepted his explanation. Barely. 'The police will need to know, though. If there's a violent criminal lurking around, and he's targeting Katie because of something Ron Hugill did, then they need to know. Before something bad happens on my doorstep—'

'I know, I know, and I'll—'

'What you'll do is not interrupt me again, Chris. Go upstairs, tell Katie what happened, and then drive her down to the police station. Because she's going to tell them everything. Both of you are, and then you're going to offer to do whatever it takes to help catch this man. Go now. Upstairs. I'll keep Julia down here.'

He went, but not because of Rose's order. It had been his intention all along, so he could demand an explanation for the text message Katie had sent him while the police officer asked her questions. The text that had forced him to lie to the police, and then to Rose.

*Don't tell them about me or Everton.*

\*

'I committed a crime once,' Katie said. She was in Chris's bedroom now, not Julia's, at the window and staring out at the street. Leaning against the shut door, Chris watched. Waited. 'I was fourteen. I knew Everton back then.'

'You *know* the guy who killed your father?'

'He's not my father, remember.'

Chris didn't respond so there was a moment of silence. Apart from the twin ticks of a wall clock and the louder one Katie always kept with her.

'I don't know Everton,' Katie continued. 'I once did, but I don't see it that way anymore. Years ago, I knew some unpleasant people. A bunch of us hung out because we lived on the same estate. My mum's pub was the main local, so our parents knew each other. Everton and his criminal dad, they were known around the block.'

She paused here again. She glanced at Chris, perhaps just to make sure he was still there, then continued.

'We were brash teenagers, but all any of us ever did was a bit of vandalism, that's all. Until we burgled that house. After that, I saw the error of my ways and promised to change. I grew apart from those guys. I didn't see Everton again, or any of them. I have no idea why Everton might be after me, because we didn't part on bad terms. It's only because he killed Ron that I even wonder if he's targeting me. Could be just coincidence. Ron ran a boxing club and criminals might assume he's got money. Wrong place, wrong time, because he went to that club while it was being robbed. We don't know for sure, me or you, if this is about me now.'

True, but Chris was under orders. 'But we have to consider it, just to be safe. He was here, right here on my street. It's about time we took this threat seriously. We have to tell the police.'

'New people in our lives always have baggage. If Everton is around because of me, then I wholeheartedly apologise for bring-ing danger to your door.'

'I'm not upset with you, and I don't blame you. You didn't know Everton would come here. And maybe this was all a coincidence. But we can't take the risk. If he's going to come after you, and possibly put my family in danger, then the police need to know. They need to know he wasn't just out on a joyride when he crashed into the fence. I still don't know why I didn't decide this when you told me about him last night.'

Still no emotion. Chris yelled her name, which finally drew Katie's eyes. He stepped across half the room. 'Katie, the police need to know Everton might have been coming here to my house that night. With a knife, Katie. With a damn knife.'

Katie closed the distance between them and grabbed Chris's hands in both her own, pleading.

'That burglary I committed was never solved. If the police are told about me, that Everton might be after me, that I knew him, they'll want to talk to me. They'll take my fingerprints and DNA. They'll get a match to that robbery and I'll go to prison.'

Chris had barely seen emotion in this kid, little more than averted eyes. But she stared right into Chris's eyes with clear desperation. He had to look away. 'At some point we'll have to tell them, Katie. Maybe they won't take fingerprints, or maybe they don't have any evidence from that robbery. Or perhaps we can work out a way to keep you out of it. I don't know. But the police have to be told. If Everton ever makes a move—'

'You'll kill me if your family is in danger, I know,' Katie said.

Chris pulled his hands free and grabbed Katie's shoulders. He was aware he was acting the role of a father here, but it didn't feel so alien this time. 'That wasn't what I was going to say. I meant if there's ever another indication that Everton is targeting this house, I go to the police with everything. Okay?'

Katie nodded. 'Perhaps I can fix this. I can arrange to meet Everton, if it really is me he's after. Work it out with him.'

'No, you don't go near this guy. You go to the police. Tonight. Now.'

Katie pulled free and went for the door. Chris called out after her.

'Wait, we need to talk about—'

'You only need to watch,' Katie called back, jabbing a finger at the window.

And then she was gone. Seconds later, the front door opened and closed. At the window, Chris watched Katie run down the path, out onto the street.

Below him, Rose yelled: 'Who's gone out? What's going on?'

Katie crossed the road, waving and calling to the male police officer canvassing the houses across the way.

'Katie went to the police,' Chris called down. 'Just like you wanted.'

Katie met the officer halfway down the neighbour's path, right around the time Rose came into the bedroom, looking flustered. 'Did you tell her what I said?'

'Look.'

When she joined him at the window, to watch Katie talking with the police, he pulled his phone and showed her the text message. And then he explained, while Katie explained. All of it.

'Poor girl,' she said afterwards. Katie, finished with her doorstep confession, walked slowly back to the house. They'd watched the officer take notes and call something in on his radio. But no handcuffs appeared. 'But it needed to be done. I hope you don't feel that she's been a challenge so far.'

A challenge, yes, but completed challenges often rewarded victors with that buzz-like warm feeling of achievement. Something very much like that flowed through Chris now. Because he'd put in effort he wasn't really accustomed to and wasn't scornful of his performance.

Sensing this, in that connected way of hers, Rose took his arm in hers. She looked pleased.

He didn't.

Because the problem wasn't fixed. There still roamed free a man who might have Katie in his crosshairs. And the girl herself might not yet be done unloading scorpions from her closet.

# CHAPTER TWENTY-TWO

Later, the landline rang.

'That'll be your mum cancelling,' Chris said. He was at the mirror above the living room fireplace, trying to decide if he needed a shave. Rose was on the sofa, trying to put a chain around her wrist with one hand. Her arthritis creased her face, but getting ready for special nights out were about pride, not ease.

'Don't tempt fate,' Rose said as she got up to answer the call.

'How can I if she's already ringing?'

Sure enough, when Rose answered the phone: 'Hi. I'm sorry, darling. The committee has called an emergency meeting about the new vandalism. I can't avoid it.'

Rose said, 'We only do this once a week, Mum.'

Hearing Rose's response and making the connection, Chris gave an exasperated laugh.

'It's only bowling, after all,' Rose's mother said. 'This is important. This is about our community, not a game.'

Rose was angry. She bid her mother goodbye and hung up before she heard another sermon about the importance of tackling vandalism.

She went into the kitchen and Chris followed. In there, Katie and Julia were sitting around the table, glued to phones.

Julia saw her mother's face and said, 'Don't tell me your bowling's off?'

'No,' Rose said. She held out her wrist and the bracelet and Chris grabbed both.

'Nothing stops the bowling, Julia,' Chris said. Even two-handed, he had a problem with the bracelet. 'Looks like you'll be waiting for Mum's delivery.'

'I can't. I've got that birthday party gig. It's a lot of money.'

'Someone's got to be here to sign for the delivery,' Rose told her. 'I don't want it being sent back.'

'Mum, this is important.'

'And my health isn't?' Rose snatched the bracelet from Chris and left the room.

'That's not fair.'

It was aimed at Chris. 'The package needs collecting from the depot if delivery fails. It's a four-hundred-quid machine and they won't leave it outside.'

'Katie can wait for it. My gig is—'

'No, Julia, we can't ask Katie to do that.'

Julia made a childlike screech.

Perhaps embarrassed, Katie got up to get a glass of water, into which she sprinkled a small measure of salt from a pot on the worktop. Chris jerked his head at Julia, hoping she understood he wanted a chat in another room. But she shook her head.

Katie slammed her glass down suddenly. She marched across the kitchen and yanked open the junk drawer under the microwave oven. Chris was puzzled until he realised why. He leaped to his feet and cursed under his breath.

A thin wisp of smoke oozed out of the drawer, curling into the air. Katie pulled out a packet of small envelopes. The corners were blackened, the plastic wrapping scorched away.

'Is that a fire?' Julia screeched.

And fire it was half a second later as the black corner ignited. Katie held up the envelopes, watching as a flame danced and grew.

Rose walked into the kitchen, probably alerted by Julia's yell. She just stared, puzzled.

Chris took three big strides towards Katie and took the packet from her. Katie still had that blank look, as if numbed. Chris tossed the pack into the sink and turned the tap on it.

'What's going on?' Rose said to Katie. She was halfway between angry and confused. 'Why did you set those envelopes on fire?'

Katie didn't answer, or even seem to have heard. She was staring at the sink, eyes glazed. Chris immediately thought of the burn damage on her legs. Given a childhood prank gone wrong, and the recent loss of a flat to fire, perhaps the mere sight of a flame, a horrible feeling of repeat, had locked her down.

'She didn't do it,' he said. 'I don't know what happened.'

Rose was all the way angry now. She marched to the sink, barging Chris aside, to make sure the flame was out. She tossed her bracelet onto the worktop. 'Someone answer me. Why were those envelopes on fire? In the house!'

'I think I know,' Katie said. All turned her way. She started rummaging in the drawer and returned with a square battery in one hand, a bunch of paperclips in the other. 'Aha,' she announced, holding them up as if the mystery was solved. But all she got was puzzled glances.

'When I was working on my bike in the garden, I went into my drawer for a spanner. Rooted around in there, found it, came outside. Next thing I know, my kitchen's on fire.' She showed the battery and tapped the two silver connectors. 'These square nine-volt batteries, they have these live ends. I had some of these batteries in my drawer. They'd been sitting harmlessly in there for months, as batteries do in people's houses. When I went rooting in the drawer, I must have dislodged something metal, which ended up touching these live ends.'

'We've had those for ages,' Rose said as she moved across to look into the drawer. 'So they started a fire?'

'People have batteries in drawers, no big deal, for years. Then one day you rummage for something and the live connectors end up being nudged against something metal, like these paperclips here, and it creates a lot of heat. If there's something easily combustible nearby also touching, like those envelopes, a fire can start. Unbelievable. You open and close a drawer, and then the house burns down.'

'Wow,' Julia said. 'Imagine if you had to run from two burning houses for the same reason.'

'I'm sure you've got foot-in-mouth disease,' Rose told her daughter.

Katie didn't mind. 'I'll get some tape. It's wise to tape these live ends up.'

Chris noted that Katie still seemed locked in fear, or whatever the emotion was, and to confirm it she threw another long glance at the sink.

End of the first round of bowling and the women were ahead on points, drinks and insults, so the XY chromosomes went to the bar and their wives hit the outdoor patio to smoke. Rose had an electronic cigarette, but only used it socially.

Rose had known Carol Hutch for thirty years, since they joined the same under-15s football club. Carol knew Rose was going to ask Chris for his hand in marriage before he did. She knew about the existence of Julia before he did. She knew Rose had a doctor's appointment to check a breast lump, and he didn't. So, of course, as soon as the two women had some clear space, and after she'd reminded Rose about her party on Friday, Carol became the fifth person to learn about Katie's parentage.

'Good lord,' she shrieked. Heads turned. Then, lower: 'Leave nothing out, lass.'

So Rose talked. She told it all, starting with the dodgy tout who'd sold Chris a dud ticket to the United States Grand Prix, and ending with the moment Chris got that weird note through the door. She even mentioned Chris's claim that they'd had so much fun they hadn't cared that the Formula 1 World Championship had been won at that race. Carol listened intently and made only one remark.

'My ex, John, that would never have happened to him. He would have climbed the wall to get into that car race and never met this Eve lass.'

But Rose did leave out one portion. She chose not to mention the fugitive Dominic Everton. Upon her return after speaking with the police, Katie had seemed happier. She'd told the police that she knew Everton but had kept this information from the Redferns. She'd asked if Everton might have been in the location to seek out aid from old friends, but the policeman had said no. They now suspected Everton had had business with some lowlifes on the Easterbrook estate, a couple of miles away. Nothing to do with Katie, nothing to do with anyone on this street. That announcement had calmed Chris and Rose, so Rose saw no reason to worry Carol by mentioning runaway killers.

'Does she look like him?'

'No, and she's nothing like Julia, either. I hate to say it, but she's prettier than Julia. She's gorgeous, in fact. Tall and naturally blonde, and her nails are long and real. A real stunner. Wish I looked like her when I was that age. And she has this husky voice that's real hypnotic. Like I could imagine her reading my audiobooks.'

'Wow. So apart from massive envy, how do you feel about her? She's not your daughter, and she's way past any sort of cute-to-be-around age, and piggy-backing her would crack your spine. I'd probably feel like she's an intruder in my house. In my whole life, I'd say.'

Rose thought long about this. Chris probably believed she was taking this thing in her stride, but she had thought long on the subject for two days, every chance she got, every time something immediate didn't hold her. Finally, she had some kind of idea of what her emotions were signalling. Or the alcohol was talking.

'She's a grown woman and there's a difference. She's not a baby, sure, so there won't ever be that chance I could have a proper bond, like a mother does for a daughter, because she doesn't need my care. That's a big part of it, isn't it? You bond because for a long time a baby is helpless. It needs your care. But Katie is fully grown. She can take care of herself. We won't ever have that.'

'Have you seen photos of Eve Levine's daughter?'

Rose sucked on her e-cig and blew a blackcurrant cloud over her head.

'I asked Katie about photos earlier. Photos of her. I figured it would be nice if there was a record of her life, you know, for Chris. But there aren't any. All the photos of her as a child, they all burned up in her flat. So there's nothing. That's something else that will make it harder for me to bond. I hope it doesn't make it harder for Chris, if he is indeed Daddy Dearest. No images of Katie as a child, so in a sense no real proof, as if she beamed down from outer space as a grown woman.'

But something occurred to her. Carol had referred to *Eve Levine's daughter* – not *Katie*.

'That's not what you meant, is it? Photos of Eve's daughter – do you mean, like, proof? Proof that Katie is her daughter? Why wouldn't she be?'

Carol fanned herself with a hand, as if embarrassed. 'Oh, no, no, I just meant, well, are you sure about why she's turned up? Wait, no, I didn't mean it like that. I...'

But Rose understood. 'Are you saying it could be a trick? That she might not be Eve's daughter at all? But why would she say she is?'

'Just some silly idea I had, lass, that's all. That she could be after something. But it was just me being silly.'

'Like money? We don't have money. What reason could she have to get around him if it was all a lie?'

'If she already knew him, perhaps. Had a thing for him. Or maybe Julia is her focus. I mean, you said Julia saw Katie hanging around at her college last week. No, not focus, I didn't mean…'

'You think she might be trying to hook up with him? This whole thing is just a lie to get close to him? But he's not a film star or anything. He's not a sexy hunk. And she could have anyone with her looks. And Julia? That's just daft. Katie was at the college to look for a computer course.'

'There you go, then, like I said, just me being silly. Do you wish she'd turned up earlier, as a child, so you could have taken care of her and bonded that way?'

Aware that Carol was desperate to change angles and eager to do so herself, Rose digested this theory. And quickly jettisoned it.

'No. I simply meant that she's grown-up. Got her own life. She won't need to live with us. Won't need taking care of. Won't impact my life in a major way. May even barely change it. If I get to like her, she'll visit a lot. If I don't, then if Chris needs to see her, he can just leave the house to do it. I don't even need to see her again. I suppose in a way it'll be like you and John and Carter.'

The father of Carol's five-year-old saw his son, Carter, a few times a week. He collected and deposited the boy and the former couple barely exchanged a word during the handover. No two people blew further apart than those once locked together as tightly as possible.

'That mate of your Julia's, who got her hands cut off, your Chris treated her for AIDS, didn't he?'

That shout from Wendy, the gossip hound. Sometimes the big news corporations talked to experts, to those in the thick of the action, and peeled away bullshit to expose the truth. Wendy, though, liked gloss and attitude and fireworks, so got her stories from remote corners of the Internet where the unrestrained roamed.

'She didn't have her hands cut off,' Rose said. She realised she hadn't told anyone but Carol about Simone. Carol had been sworn to secrecy. 'And no to the AIDS.'

All separate conversations merged into a group discussion about the woman being called Meadow Moll, until the last cigarette was crushed underfoot and the girls trekked back to the bowling.

But Rose couldn't get Carol's words out of her head: what if Katie knew she wasn't Chris's daughter, yet had a dark and secretive reason for claiming to be? Rose had wondered about the possibility of Katie seeking money – or Chris – but like Carol had said, it was silly. And that idea about Julia being her focus – preposterous. All of it! Of course it was. Of course.

# CHAPTER TWENTY-THREE

While Julia undressed in her parents' room to use the shower, Katie ran her hand around inside Julia's underwear drawer, stirring the items. When a bright blue bra surfaced, she pulled it out and held it up. She dipped in again, this time removing a pair of white knickers. She tossed them onto her bed.

While Julia soaped her hair, Katie ran her hands along tops that hung in the wardrobe, slowly. She stopped at a red tank top and pulled it out. It had a blue bow on each collar and low sides, which would show off the bra. On the front it said 'NOW'S YOUR CHANCE' and on the back 'TOO LATE', which she figured she understood.

While Julia wrapped herself in towels, Katie rifled through a drawer containing her legwear: three rows of four, folded and stacked three high. She was intrigued by a pair of blue denim jeans with pink seams which turned out not to be denim at all but some kind of stretchy material. The waistband was frilly pink.

When Julia entered her bedroom still wrapped in towels, she stopped in shock. Katie had laid out some of her clothing on the bed. A top above her jeggings, knickers and bra lying alongside. Katie's back was to her as she reached high up onto a top shelf.

Julia couldn't contain a gasp and a step back, and her swinging arm caught the computer table, which jolted the mouse and killed the screensaver. Katie spun around.

'What are you doing?' Julia asked.

Katie stepped forward. She glanced at the computer monitor and saw a Google results page for: 'KATIE LEVINE FACE SCAR'. Eight or so results visible within the screen, all dealing with a musician called 'Karly Katie Levine' who had heavy facial make-up to cover the violent result of a failed guitar swing. So, Julia had tried and failed to find out about her injury. If the story was told online, it was buried deep after so many years.

'What are you doing?' Julia clutched her towel tightly around her.

Katie pulled a lipstick from her pocket and showed her. 'I have a deal for you. And then we're going to talk about first times.'

Inhibitions eroded by alcohol, Chris couldn't fight the urge any longer and scuttled away from the bowling lane with a claim of needing the toilet. But he slipped past the restrooms and outside, where he circled around the smoking area to a small yard for storing used beer barrels and roll cages of empty boxes and cartons. There was a young female employee outside an open fire exit, smoking. She gave him a funny look so he lurked just outside the yard entrance until she left, then he stepped inside and made the call.

'Sunshine Massages,' a female voice said. Either fresh from sleep or deep into an alcohol binge. But he thought he recognised it: at least, he knew the accent wasn't southern. Behind it was dance music and the hubbub of other voices. A party?

'I must have the wrong number. I was looking for my sister, Lindsay.'

He didn't suspect the wrong number at all, but wanted to give the caller an easy out. Or himself an easy out, if he was honest.

'Chris? Is that you? I'm Lindsay. Wow, where are you? Are you still in Sheffield?'

'No, Bradford now. I lost hours at work and had to relocate.' The lie might come back to bite. But he didn't edit it.

'You heard from Grandma and Granddad recently? I ain't got a number for them.'

No lie here as he said he hadn't spoken to them for at least four months.

'So what else is new with you? Jane become a supermodel yet?'

It took him a moment to work that out. Last he'd spoken to Lindsay – what, five years ago? – Julia had wanted a career strutting on catwalks. 'It's Julia, not Jane. She wants to be a stand-up comic now.'

'Oh wow. How's that going? Doing well?'

'So-so.'

She asked a few more small-talk questions, and Chris tried his best to surreptitiously make out that he had no spare money, even though the subject didn't arise. He felt bad assuming she was angling that way, but he was only working off their last conversation. Something warned him against projecting success and happiness when he didn't yet know her situation.

'So what are you up to down there?' he asked.

'Where did you get my number, anyway? Was it from Facebook? I was going to call you with it.'

*Sure you were.* He told her he had his ways, but no, not Facebook. After that, she told him she was working caring for the elderly, something she'd always wanted to do. He didn't remember any such calling and wondered if she'd delayed her answer until certain he hadn't seen the 'masseuse' part of her Facebook profile name.

'So what's up? Why the call, big bro?'

In the background, someone yelled, demanding to know who she was talking to. He heard the word *rozzer*, which meant *police*. She covered the phone when she answered the yeller. Chris couldn't shake the image of a crack den full of pimps and girls and seedy men who'd booked a massage they knew was going to be no such thing. Again he felt low entertaining such thoughts.

When she came back on and apologised and said she had to go because a 'housemate' was awaiting an important call, he blurted: 'I just found out I've got a daughter.'

'What? Oh, well done. Congratulations. To your wife, too.'

He understood she didn't understand. 'No, from years ago. She's a grown-up. She found me. I never knew about her.'

A commotion behind her. The yeller became the bellower.

'Lindsay, I was thinking about trying to contact our dad. Have you heard anything from him?'

The racket behind Lindsay increased. In a clearly panicked voice, she said, 'Chris, I've got to go. I'll call you later to—'

The connection ended.

Chris stood in the dark and tried to make sense of his feelings. Disappointment was there, because he'd made that call to Lindsay only to gauge how his big secret would be received, but she hadn't had time to provide that answer. Shame had a spot because deep down he knew he'd picked her because she was a black sheep, her opinion probably easy to dismiss if not to his liking. And both were wrapped in a big blanket of self-loathing. A real man would already be driving to Chigwell with a baseball bat to help a sister who had once yanked him, like a real superhero, out of the path of a bus. But not stress- and responsibility-shirking Chris, because that might just upset the sweet balance of his neat little life. Far easier to just let his head stay buried in the sand, as Rose had so often said.

Angry, he kicked the fire exit with a gong-like boom, and got out of there before someone opened it.


The entrance to the strip club was just a blank door in a brick wall down a nondescript street of closed commercial joints. A secretive place, although a queue of ten, all men, and a girl made of neon lights above the door gave the game away. The woman with bright red lipstick and bright red bob joined the queue, but was immediately waved forward. The bouncer gave her a quick look up and down, decided her sparkly white jeans and mock-neck purple sweater contained no weapons or drugs, and opened the door. She had to walk a dark corridor to get into the club proper.

Inside, there was no throbbing music, no heaving crowd. Maybe thirty people, low on women. Most were either draped over the bar on the left or were seated before the stage on the right, where three dancers dressed as cavegirls capered. A guy in his fifties, clearly drunk, made a crack about her appearance as he wobbled past. The redhead didn't react. She found a spare table and watched the cavegirls.

Being one of only a handful of females in the room, she wasn't left alone long. A young guy approached. The moment he entered her orbit, and before he could speak, she held up a hand. He wasn't drunk enough to ignore it. Soon after that, the cavegirls wound up their act and left the stage. A voice through the speakers introduced tonight's second special act.

*She's funny, she's crude, she is, of course, Rude Jude.*

No one really gave a damn. No applause, no extra heads turned to the stage and nobody moved closer. Rude Jude strolled on and immediately gave the crowd the middle finger. Those men who'd been at the front to watch the cavegirls booed. She grabbed the microphone.

'Now the true test is to see if I can make you laugh now that you all hate me,' she said. 'We'll start with a knock-knock joke, which is about all you pussy perverts can understand.'

The redhead stood up.

Rude Jude looked her way and her jaw dropped.

*

When Rude Jude's piece was over, she scuttled offstage and the disembodied compere announced the return of the strippers. Jude watched the dancers, now in combat fatigues with foam machine guns, pass her and head out through the curtain. One of them slapped her shoulder.

'Took some balls to go out there and do that,' the dancer said.

'Speak for yourself,' Jude replied, and checked out the girl's butt as she walked past.

She found a door into the club and made her way to the redhead. As she sat, a guy approached and tried to talk to her about one of her jokes. Both women told him to scarper.

'How the hell did you know I was here?' Julia asked.

Katie replied, 'I saw it scribbled in your jotter. I didn't think a children's birthday party would be held at The White Dungeon, and certainly not this late. Couldn't let you miss it because of a silly package delivery. The package came, by the way, and it's safely indoors. So I thought I'd pop along and see the show.'

'I should have figured you knew when you picked out such provocative clothing for me. Hardly right for a kiddie birthday party. I bought that wig for a joke. It suits you, but why have you put it on? Your hair is so pretty, and that natural blonde. I'd kill for that.'

Katie grabbed a handful of the fake hair and looked at it. 'I fancied trying it. I hope you don't mind that I borrowed your jeans and sweater.'

'Not only do I not mind but you can keep them. But I'm surprised you put make-up on. I mean going for the sexy look, as someone with no interest in sex. Have you had to beat men away with a stick coming here?'

'This puts them off, I think,' Katie said, touching her scar.

Julia checked her watch. 'Anyway, we'd better get home before Mum, or she will crush our heads with one of her bowling balls.'

'Of course. I allowed you to go to your gig. Now you owe me.'

'Oh yes. First times. Ask away.'

A woman in blue approached and put her hand on Julia's shoulder. She leaned close to give a compliment. Or the like. Julia couldn't help but glance at big breasts hanging inches from her face. Then at Katie, who was grinning. The woman took Julia's hand and scribbled a phone number, then departed with a wave. And a sly wink at Katie. Julia spat on her hand and erased the number.

'Not your type?' Katie said.

'I'm taken as of today.' She showed Katie her phone. Her dating app and messages from a girl called Donna, who was slim, mixed-race, model-like. Katie leaned close to read the messages. Donna, Julia explained, had texted after seeing her profile on a 'You Might Like' list. 'We've only been talking for the last three hours, but I already feel like I've known her for ever.'

Katie nodded her approval. 'That's a good sign. Might be fake, though. Be careful. Could be a guy in his sixties. What's a pretty girl like that doing with online dating?'

Julia shook a fist. 'Am I not a pretty girl using online dating? Mixed-race people are all beautiful to me. It's a biology-evolution thing. Helps prevent inbreeding.'

'You've lost me.'

'You'll study philosophy in the college refectory if you get that computer course. Come on, let's bounce.'

Katie apologised for her online dating remark, which made Julia laugh. 'Anyway, a sixty-year-old man would be asking sexy questions. Donna seems more interested in my family.'

'Well, they'll be her family if she moves in.'

'No chance.'

On the way out, the same guy who'd made a remark about Katie's scar repeated himself and then claimed Julia was about as funny as syphilis. Julia told the bouncers he was dealing drugs and laughed as they thundered towards him.

Katie had brought her bike, parked around back. She took a second helmet from the pannier, ripped off the wig and put it inside. Two girls in heels stumbling past made a crack about her scar, but Katie didn't bat an eyelid.

'You haven't had a drink, have you?' Julia asked.

'I don't drink.'

'No alcohol, no meat and no sex? What do you do for fun?'

'This,' Katie said as she climbed on the bike.

Julia took the helmet and got on the back, wrapped her arms tightly around the slimmer girl. The closeness, combined with the buffer of the helmet, allowed her to voice something she'd been eager to broach. As Katie turned the bike into the main road and roared off, Julia held her tightly and touched helmets.

'I saw your skin when you were reaching up in my wardrobe. I figure it's why you wore my sweater. You got burned. Your body.'

No answer for a few seconds, which made Julia think the noise of the bike had smothered her words. She didn't ask again. But a few seconds later the bike halted at a red light.

'It was a bonfire. I fell in a bonfire as a kid.'

'Is it your whole…' Julia searched for the word.

'Midsection?' Katie prompted. 'My belly and back, yes. There's your answer for why I don't want to have sex with people. Does it put you off?'

'No, but I feel bad for you. It must be hard to maybe be attracted to someone and be, like, too scared to approach out of fear of what they'll say.'

'It doesn't bother me. I show my facial scar off, don't I? But look, I don't want your mum and dad to know, okay? Don't tell them, please. I don't want them to worry and I don't want to have to answer questions.'

'No problem. But that scar on your face – that's not from a piece of wood on a bonfire.'

'No deal. That will remain a secret.' The light turned green. Katie gunned the engine, and Julia clutched her hard once more. The cold wind made her regret her outfit. She had to shout her next words.

'We'll see.'

# CHAPTER TWENTY-FOUR

'It's not something I ever thought about,' Julia said. 'Why these questions?'

'These questions' had been about what it felt like to have a father with her for every 'first' in her life – riding a bike, learning to speak, going to school. Katie had brought it up once they pulled up outside the house.

'I ask only because I never knew my father. He left before I was born. So I never had those firsts. I wonder if, when I finally meet my father again, what if he's got another adult child? Someone he's already experienced all those firsts with. I won't be first to bring a lover home, or get a first wage packet. Or make him a grandfather. Or a father of the bride. I won't see the joy on his face as we experience these things for the first time, together.'

Julia waited until they were in the house before she answered. 'I never thought about it. Dad was always there, so it was normal and I never considered people who didn't have that. I need to get changed.'

Katie followed her upstairs, but remained outside her room as she stripped off. 'So, is he the best dad in the world?'

'I guess. I bought him a "Best Dad in the World" T-shirt last year, but how silly is that? I mean, those are made in bunches. Hundreds of dads have them. Can they all be the best?'

'To their kids, yes. The best dad ever. Not that they've had more than one to choose between. Some do, though.'

Julia poked her head around the doorway. Katie was rubbing her wrists, that habit of hers. 'I need that clothing back.'

Julia found her pyjamas and slipped into them. 'I remember once wanting my friend Alison's dad. He's a fireman and he can do magic tricks. But then Alison says my dad is like a superhero. And he is, I suppose. Viruses and bacteria could kill us all. Like my dad says, they're invaders that need no ships or planes or bombs, move silently, invisibly, can attack us anywhere. The ultimate soldiers in an army with no manpower limit. And he's the one who finds this army's Achilles heel and destroys it.'

'Didn't you ever want his job? I thought kids wanted to follow in their father's footsteps.'

'I did, actually. My dad studied drama at college, but Mum said he quit when he found out she was pregnant with me. He wanted a real career, so he went to university to study microbiology. I sometimes wish he'd stayed with drama. I don't have much of an interest in microbiology, but I've picked a few things up because he talks about it a lot. Want me to prove it?'

'You love him, and that's important. But more so is that he loves you. He'd do anything for you. He was there from the day you were born, taking care of you. Making sure you were happy and safe. Kids need that. That's all you need to be the best dad in the world. Not everyone gets the best dad in the world, but you should feel lucky you did.'

Dressed, Julia grabbed the door to open it, but Katie's hand held it tight. She realised it was to avoid displaying those burns. 'Katie, I know why you have tingling hands.'

'It's just underuse, stiffness. Can you pass my other clothing out? It's on the floor.'

'You don't have to get dressed in the hallway.'

But Katie insisted. Julia fed the clothing through the gap.

'No, it's not underuse, that tingling. You're a strict vegetarian. Strict vegetarians miss out on certain foods like liver and eggs, which contain the vitamin B12. If you don't get enough, you get over-big red blood cells, and they can't carry enough oxygen around the body. There are a lot of symptoms of B12 deficiency.'

'Sounds fascinating.'

'I know that's sarcasm. But one of the B12 problems is par-aesthesia. I think you've got chronic paraesthesia. Long-term pins and needles.'

'You're smart. I'm jealous. I never had the opportunity to fill my brain like you have.'

Katie lobbed her nightclub outfit over Julia's head, into the wash basket, a perfect shot.

But Julia retrieved it. 'No, no, I have to hang this stuff back up, or Mum will know it's been worn. Besides, the washer's broken.'

Katie apologised and tried to step past Julia. Their shoulders touched. Julia raised an arm to block Katie, who turned her face. Inches apart, Julia couldn't stop herself. She leaned in to kiss Katie's mouth, but instead her lips touched the scar as Katie turned her head.

Julia backed off with her hands up. 'I'm sorry for that. Oh, God, I'm sorry.'

'I get pain in my back and neck, too,' Katie said. 'I get pain everywhere. I'm falling apart, even though I'm young.'

Julia thought Katie was rapidly trying to change the subject, and condemning that stupid kiss attempt to history was something she also craved. 'Paraesthesia is—'

'It's not that. It's nothing you could imagine, or ever guess. I could tell you what it is, if you want. And it's nothing to do with vitamins or food. I know my own body. You'll be shocked. You might think me weird suddenly. You might not want to be near me ever again. Sure you're ready to hear this?' Katie leaned against the doorframe, a grin on her face like a tease, or a taunt.

'We all like you, Katie, me especially. But not in that way, honest! You're like me in many ways, and like my big little sister.

So I don't even know what came over me. So hit me with what you've got, because I doubt you'll shock me.'

She was wrong.


'Eager for something?' Rose said as Chris hit the accelerator. He shook his head, but she grinned at him as if doubtful. She patted his leg. 'I need a shower. And I might need help.'

He said nothing. After half a mile in silence, she said, 'I have an idea. I think Katie has got no confidence about her achievements, about what she's made of her life, but she's proud of that go-karting trophy. It's a bit old and battered and the winner's plaque is missing. We could replace it. There's nothing to say who presented it to her, the go-kart place, but it was manufactured by a company called Cooper & Sons. I thought we could email them and see if they could make another one, with an engraving. A nice present for Katie.'

'By we, you mean me.'

'I mean you. It's old if she was under seven, but they might still have the mould or whatever they use, if they make a lot of similar trophies. Or if not, we could just get a new plaque. We can't really ask Katie where she got it because then she'd know what we were planning.'

He didn't really care at the minute, but he nodded. 'I'll do it.'

A few moments later, she asked him a strange question. 'When you took the socks up to Katie in the bathroom, was she dressed?'

'She was still in that smoke-smelling T-shirt. Why?'

'So not naked? She wasn't standing there naked?'

'No, why?'

'No reason.'

A lie. Carol's words still haunted her.

When they got home, Rose kissed her husband's cheek and said, 'I need that shower. And probably help with it,' and got out.

He followed her up the path. She threw a cheeky glance back as she unlocked the door.

It was half past midnight, but Katie and Julia were still up, watching TV. Rose dumped her bag.

'Good night? Did the women win again?' Julia said.

Rose ignored the question. She stared at Katie. 'You're in make-up. You're so pretty, did you know? Of course you know, sorry.' She slapped her own head, like a dumb cartoon character. 'We won, yes, of course, always.'

Chris sat on the sofa, next to Julia. He wondered if it might look like favouritism, but he could hardly sit next to Katie, could he? He saw Rose looking at him with wide eyes and figured she'd had the same thought. But no.

'You sit the same,' she said.

Chris realised he was cross-legged, and so was Katie. That propelled him to his feet before Julia could question Rose's comment.

He was about to leave, but Rose called Julia out into the hallway. Out there, he heard his wife apologise to his daughter. He watched the door as if it allowed better hearing.

'I'm sorry for trying to make you miss your gig, just to wait in for a package. It's just that it was important. It's for my pain and my circulation. But that's no excuse for selfishness. I'll make it up to you.'

'Mum, it's fine. There will be more gigs, and you needed that machine you bought.'

'No, it was bad of me, Julia. I could have collected the package tomorrow. Your gig was important. And I made you miss it. I want to make it up to you.'

Julia gave a laugh. 'Mum, really, it's fine. Just forget it. I'm glad you got your machine.'

'And it was wrong of me to think Katie couldn't wait for the package. It was only a signature. But I'm going to make it up to you for missing your gig.'

'Katie didn't take offence, if that's your worry. And I don't want anything. Just forget it. It's fine.'

'So I'll pay you. I'll give you two hundred pounds for lost money on the gig.'

'Okay. But it was two-fifty I lost,' Julia said without missing a beat.

Chris bit back a laugh.

As they returned to the room, Chris glanced at Katie, who'd remained silent. She was staring at him. She only smiled when caught looking.

He got up. 'I'm going to bed. You ladies have fun.'

He left the room, and Rose followed. He stopped in the hallway between the front door and the foot of the stairs. She appeared beside him and leaned close.

'Did you see that make-up? Why was she wearing make-up?'

He shrugged. 'Teenagers.'

She glanced at the living room door to make sure they weren't overheard. 'Maybe. But when I cleaned her smoke-stained jeans, I found a folded-up condom packet in the pocket. It was empty. Julia told me Katie said she has no interest in sex. She must have lied.'

Tomorrow he might give a hoot, but not right now. 'So?'

Not the answer she expected. 'Oh, I don't know. What a thing to say. But if she is sleeping with boys, then I don't think I want any of them coming round here. Can you have a word?'

He said sure, okay, and she went past with a pat of his bum. Halfway up the stairs, she stopped.

'What's wrong? Are you not coming up?'

He was still by the front door. He grabbed his keys off the rack. 'I need to go run an errand.'

She checked her watch.

He said, 'I want to go talk to Alan at home about something.'

Katie appeared in the living room doorway just as Chris said this. Sensing a private moment, she backed off.

'You mean go to his house? It's the dead of night. Won't I do instead?'

'If you can clear up a big problem at work.' She looked hurt by that, or just having her sexual offer declined. 'I need to clear up a problem and apologise to him. I need to do it tonight. I forgot earlier.'

She waved him off, annoyed, and clumped up the stairs.

Chris decided not to inform the others that he was going out. He got the satnav from Rose's car, because she had borrowed it, and climbed into his own vehicle. But then he thought of something. It sent him back into the house, to the cupboard under the stairs, for his toolbox.

Things might not go as easy as he hoped, so he took an item he thought might help. He hid it in his coat and then oozed out the door like a burglar.

# FRIDAY

# CHAPTER TWENTY-FIVE

He was home ninety minutes later. All the lights were off, which was good because he didn't want to meet anyone. He crept in. Rose was dead to the world and didn't stir when he turned the en suite shower on, although he washed in darkness in case the light stirred her. He dressed in an old T-shirt and jogging bottoms and took his dumped clothing downstairs. He stuffed it all into the washer, then remembered the damn machine was broken.

When he turned around to head back upstairs, he saw a faint glow from the living room. The door was ajar. He pushed it a little wider and saw Katie on the sofa, in the sleeping bag, with her face lit by the glow from her phone. Had the noise of water thumping the shower floor woken her? The kitchen light was off and the light from the phone would probably make it impossible for her to see Chris, so he hoped to get away unnoticed.

Didn't happen.

Katie looked up from the screen, then turned her phone to light him up.

'Hey. You're back. Pop the light on. Where have you been?'

Chris flicked on the living room light and leaned against the doorframe, hoping that this wouldn't take long. Being alone with Katie still seemed awkward, especially at night, and even after alcohol. She sat up. She was still wearing Rose's old long-sleeved top and jeans.

'Where have you been?' she asked again.

'Just an errand. Had to see my boss. Look, I'm tired, so can we chat tomorrow?'

She didn't respond, so he decided that was authorisation to leave. He turned to go.

'You can't change me,' Katie blurted out.

Sighing, he faced her again.

She continued. 'Babies are born blank canvases, and parents paint that canvas as they raise the child. But I'm already a painted canvas.'

It sounded like she'd been drinking too.

'We don't even look similar. That will always prevent a special bond between us. But I understand it. I'll accept it. I don't even have to call you Dad.'

He couldn't work out a response.

'The future isn't set until we get the results,' he finally said.

Katie nodded. 'I know you said you didn't want more children. Certainly not like this. And, like I said before, I don't even have to be in your life. I just want you to know that.'

'Rose couldn't have more children.'

Katie blinked at him, slow and steady.

'That's why we don't have a spare room. We wanted a second child. In fact, we wanted three. But after Julia… she lost the ability. Much later, when her arthritis got bad, she tried to pretend it was for the best. That she wouldn't have been a good mother being so immobile at times. But that spare room was like a… its emptiness was like a missing baby. It was always there, that empty space, a constant reminder that we were… incomplete.'

'Fateful,' she said. 'Thank you.'

What? What did that mean?

She said, 'Julia doesn't know this, and I won't tell her. And thank you.'

Thank you? For what?

She settled back and raised her phone to her face. Chris took it as permission finally to leave. He was eager to get this bizarre day shut away in history, but first he had something else to say, and after tonight he was worked up enough to not find an excuse to put it off.

'Katie. I saw your Facebook page. That line you put about being conceived during the Formula 1 World Championship. I think it's a little crude. Can you delete it?'

Katie said she would. No problem.

'Right now,' he snapped. Then he shut the light off and left.

\*

At not much past two in the morning, Chris woke with a bursting bladder which he blamed on Rose's healthy diet. In the bathroom, he was startled by a noise downstairs, which was a burglar with a knife until his dozy brain remembered that Katie was sleeping in the living room.

And then, a bizarre moment when he worried that it was a burglar after all and that Katie was in danger. Christ, he remembered being like that with Julia when she was a toddler. His worst fear had been waking to find that someone had slit Rose's and Julia's throats in the night, not a clue left. In one nightmare, the cops, sans clues, arrested him for their murders. He'd slept with a realistic-looking fake gun under the bed for about a month after that, until Rose found it.

He put on old tracksuit bottoms and T-shirt. He flushed the toilet, partly to let burglars know that other people were in the house. Then he went to the top of the stairs and cocked an ear.

Silence. He went down. The living room light was still off, no one in there or the dining room or the kitchen. Katie's sleeping bag was on the sofa, empty. Now he was awake enough to know he hadn't dreamed up a long-lost daughter, so he went to the window. He didn't see her motorbike. It could have been in the section of driveway running alongside the house, of course, so he turned on the light and looked atop the fireplace where Katie always put her keys. The trophy was there, the keys weren't. Katie had definitely gone out. But, this late, where?

He was about to leave the room when he spotted Katie's notebook on the sofa.

It was in his hands before he could stop himself, but restraint kicked in right there. He shouldn't look through this. Not because it was someone else's private property, but because he had no idea what he might read. What if there was something bad inside? About him or Rose? What if Katie didn't like them, didn't want to be Chris's daughter?

That disc was there, too. The one labelled 'MUM'. And something new: a folded sheet of paper. That he couldn't resist. It was a printout in PDF format titled, Overview of 'The Rise and Fall of Humour', from *Social Psychological and Personality Science*.

On a dentist's waiting room table, it would be something to be completely ignored. Here, now, he devoured it.

It talked about something called BVT: Benign Violation Theory. Apparently, humans found something humorous if it violated their view of the world, of cultural or social norms, but in a benign way. Too intricate? Laymen got a cartoon example: a monkey riding a motorbike. Now he thought he understood.

There was a theory that people could eventually see the funny side of tragedy. Deep and convoluted stuff about when a person's emotional response to a tragedy, or something dangerous, was diluted enough to make it 'benign' but still raw enough to create a 'violation', thus allowing humour. Too complex? Laymen got another cartoon: a bomb exploding with glitter. He thought he got that one, too.

Then the paper got a little far-fetched. It claimed to have pinpointed the exact time period it took for a person to overcome tragedy and look upon it with humour. Thirty-six days. What? Apparently, thirty-six days after someone got their leg cut off in a freak industrial accident, it was okay to take the piss about it. No cartoon illustrated this point.

Why did Katie have this? Had she been researching when and if she would ever get over the death of her mother?

As he was replacing the sheet, the disc slipped out. And of course, he found it hard to put back. With the book on his lap, and the disc atop it, he sat in debate and the clock counted twenty minutes. An internal battle which caution won. He put the disc in the book and the book on the sofa. He switched off the light and went upstairs.

Before getting into bed, he stopped and stood in the dark, and the debate raged again. He even headed back to the stairs, but thankfully Julia's door opened at that point. She staggered out like a zombie and said she needed the toilet; he said he'd just been and scuttled back into his bedroom.

He turned Rose onto her other side and got into bed. The book was trying to pull him, like moon and ocean, but he tucked the covers in around his body and closed his eyes. He hoped he wouldn't see the notebook again, because he knew his will would falter next time. Better not to know what was on that disc, or in that book. Better to keep his head buried in the sand.

But sleep would not come, and he got up and he slid his laptop out from under the bed. He was thinking about something Katie had said. About her mother wanting to film the suicide.

*

Eve Levine's arm went back and forth between her lap and her mouth, fingers clutching a pill on the way up but empty on the return journey. The room was dim, curtains drawn against sunlight, perhaps because a bright day would kill the black mood needed for the act of ending your own life. Dozens of dolls were scattered around the bedroom, and scattered was an appropriate word because they weren't sitting or leaning or propped, as ornaments should be. They were jammed in corners and draped across books and littering the floor, as if tossed like confetti, or a major earthquake had struck. And there wasn't a whole one he could see, either. They were in various stages of construction or deconstruction, or *dismemberment* – that was a better word. Legs here, arms there, heads all over the place. No earthquake had painted this scene.

The woman was in a nightgown, sitting up with her back against a wad of pillows, with pale and emaciated legs poking out. Dead centre of the bed, because the man who'd shared that bed had stopped doing so. Chris didn't recognise her against the memories in his head. She didn't even resemble the shambolic woman pictured at a charity fun day.

Her only movement was that arm. Up and down, robotically, like a captivated cinemagoer automatically crunching popcorn. It was like watching a looping piece of short film, except for one minor change: the pile of pills next to a bottle on her lap slowly shrank, one at a time. Her eyes were looking beyond him, so maybe, instead of lost in a trance, she was transfixed by something he couldn't see, something beyond the camera.

Twelve pills in, something changed. A glitch in the looped film reel. Her piston-like arm popped a pill and then those gnarly fingers spread over her face. She lowered her head as she rubbed her nose and eyes. Then she raised her head, seemed to yawn and laughed at something. And that was it. The loop resumed.

The loop glitched again at nineteen pills, and twenty-one, and twenty-four, and for a final time at thirty pills. Two pills later, the pile was gone, and the empty bottle was slapped off the bed, as if she blamed it for her lethal act. She shuffled forward, a supreme effort that made her grimace, then toppled backwards onto the pillows. Bony arms dragged the thick quilt up to her neck, which was also a great effort, and then she relaxed. He saw the quilt deflate as she released a heavy sigh from the exertion of moving. Or maybe it had been a breath of relief, of happiness, because the only task she had left in life was to greet the darkness.

# CHAPTER TWENTY-SIX

In the Manor, he didn't even sit before his first drink. He upended the whiskey bottle and took a giant swig. Throwing his head back cracked it on a wooden rafter, but it didn't interrupt his guzzling. He stopped for a breath only when the fire in his throat became too much. Then he sat, hard enough to hear a crack from the plastic chair.

He wasn't drinking to blot the shock but simply to sleep. And it worked because one second he was swallowing whiskey, and the next he was groggy and hearing what he thought was sniffling. He realised he'd fallen asleep.

He went to the trapdoor. Now the sniffling was definitely that. Rose, he knew. Upset. He slapped his pocket, realised he'd left his phone in the bedroom and got hit by a wave of dread. Now he understood.

Sure enough, he entered the dark bedroom to find Rose sitting up, crying softly, and with his phone in her hands. Its bright light displayed her grim expression. He had left the phone unlocked, screen lit up, and it must not have gone to sleep. She must have woken to see it alive and bright and displaying what he saw now.

The media player on his device showed a symbol of a square inside a circle, backdropped by the final frame of the suicide video. Eve lying, unmoving, with a big STOP symbol planted across her. He wished he'd deleted it.

She sensed him at the doorway and turned her head, which cast half of her face in shadow. 'Where did you get this?'

Even now he was unsure why he had set his phone to record the video as it played on the laptop. 'Katie had it on a disc.'

She didn't ask why. Only one person could answer that question. She wiped her eyes one at a time with the same palm. The other still held the phone before her face.

He got into bed and lay back, stared at the darkness above, and willed himself to talk in order to ease his wife. But she got there first.

'She was with Eve, wasn't she? At the end.'

He remembered what Katie had said about that night: how she'd pottered about, doing housework, *and while I did this my mother was killing herself ten feet above me…*

But when he started to relay this story, she stopped him.

'No, Chris. I mean she was *with* Eve. She was in the room. Eve is talking to someone.'

He sat up. She moved closer to him, arm touching his, and restarted the video. He couldn't not watch as Eve returned to life for yet another go at death.

The first time she spoke was when nineteen pills were gone. The second of what he'd called *glitches in the loop*.

Nineteen pills.

Eve flicks a glance to her left, beyond the camera, something there having caught her attention. A pause. Something happening behind that camera. A pause, and then Eve's mouth moves.

'She said *no*,' Rose said. He agreed. Eve had said *no* to someone. To Katie?

Twenty-one pills.

Eve puts her face in her hands, and he can see her jaw moving. More words spoken into her palms. Not a yawn, as he first suspected. Words, the last of which is uttered as she lifts her face to the camera.

'*Ron*,' Rose said. 'She's saying "Ron".'

He agreed.

Twenty-four pills.

'It looks like "And his whole family",' Rose interpreted.

And that final utterance, at thirty pills, while staring past the camera.

'"Let's hope you find your real father, then",' according to Rose.

He could hardly believe it, but there it was: undeniable proof that Katie hadn't been in another room, dismayed but accepting of her mother's suicide. She'd been right there with her. Had helped her commit suicide.

As if reading his thoughts, Rose said, 'There's no indication that she helped. She might have felt forced.'

He didn't know enough to have an opinion on that.

'She stayed out of range of the camera,' Rose said. 'I think someone edited the video to remove the audio.'

'Remove the audio? But why?'

'I think Eve probably didn't want to be alone at the end. If she was in pain, suffering, nothing to look forward to, and Katie agreed it was for the best, maybe she felt compelled to be there for the final moments. But there's laws against assisting suicide, and it probably counts as assisting if you intentionally don't stop someone. I think that's why Katie took out the audio. So no one would know Eve wasn't alone when she died.'

He couldn't get his head around any of this. Too many questions circled his brain.

'But why film it at all?'

Sitting up to look downwards at the video had hurt Rose's neck, so she rubbed it. Two hands. The phone got placed face down on the bed. They were in utter darkness.

'Maybe for proof that Eve chose to take her own life.'

Katie was worried the police might suspect foul play? 'But nobody has seen this video, Rose. The police don't have it. They'd question the lack of audio. They'd see what you saw – that someone was there. It would look bad.'

'Then I don't know,' she said. 'Maybe, right at the end of her life, when it was about to happen, Katie realised she didn't have any videos of her mother. Maybe Katie insisted on filming… something. Having *something* to keep.'

'But, like you said, this must be illegal.'

She put a hand on his shoulder. In the dark, blind, she caught his ear first. 'Is this your worry? That Katie will be revealed to be your daughter and then she'll go to prison?'

He shrugged and sighed, because he just didn't know. He told her he was trying to avoid thinking that far ahead. That he didn't like anything he was feeling right now.

'How do you feel about the euthanasia? It means "good death" in Greek.'

'And how on earth do you know that?'

'I don't know.'

He grabbed the hand on his shoulder and began massaging her misshapen knuckles. 'Anyway, it wasn't euthanasia. Assisted suicide, if anything,'

'Does the law see a difference, though?' she said. 'It's not the same as killing a sick pet at the vet's. It'll be a blow if you get a new daughter and you have to visit her in prison. That video goes against her. She's obviously there. The police—'

He dropped her hand. 'Look, we don't know what happened in that bedroom, okay? Maybe Katie stood by helplessly, forced to watch. Maybe Eve needed her to control the camera. Maybe Katie agreed suicide was for the best, or maybe she tried to talk her mother out of it. I don't know and neither do you. I don't want to talk about this anymore, okay?'

'I'm sorry.'

She turned away. He did the same, so they were back-to-back but two feet apart. He doubted either of them would sleep.

*

'Bloody hell!'

'What's up?' Rose said.

She sat up sharply as he rolled over in bed, clutching at his leg. His muscle was cramping which often happened if he stretched his legs after sleep. He beat at his calf with karate chops. Rose quickly realised what was happening and rolled her eyes at him. She took his calf and massaged it in both hands, which probably hurt her.

'Damn stupid dream about dolls,' he said once the spasm had subsided and he could think about something other than pain. 'They rained out of the sky and filled the streets.'

Rose grabbed her e-cigarette. 'Not sure that caused the cramp. But I had a funny one about buying a car with Boris Karloff. Anyway, we should get ready.' She patted his bad leg and got up and slipped into the en suite. He watched her naked figure walk away until it was gone.

In the night, he had felt Rose's touch, and her lips. And responded. Afterwards, without a word said, both had quickly found sleep. The sex must have had a medicinal quality, or it was the new, bright day, because he felt little of the dark disposition of last night. Clearly, Rose felt the same. It was as if the whole shebang with the suicide video had been a shared dream quickly written off. It wasn't, of course, so he'd have to see how his emotions held up when he encountered Katie, and as the day progressed.

'Do you think she's pretty?' Rose called out above the noise of the shower. 'Katie. She's not your daughter yet. Or if she wasn't. Do you think she looks pretty?'

He got up and walked to the window. 'No. I don't think anything like that about her. Why?'

No answer to that. A few seconds passed and then she said, 'Talking of dreams. You dream, like, based on things that happened a day or two before. I watched that Boris Karloff film a couple back, didn't I? Freud called it day residue.'

Of the two horror films she'd recently watched, a Boris Karloff movie had stuck? Then again, he'd dreamed about a downpour of plastic dolls smashing cars and holing roofs and crushing skulls. He looked out at his car, at the street. No dolls, of course. Day residue. Because of the doll he'd seen above the door of The Blue Swan, probably.

'Don't wear that River Island shirt because it's missing a button, okay?' Rose called out.

Realisation hit him like a slap. Eve Levine's funeral! This morning. He'd forgotten all about it, somehow.

'Christ.'

Rose poked her head out the doorway, hair soaked. 'You forgot, didn't you?'

He ignored the question. 'I don't want to go.'

She shook her head and vanished back into the bathroom. 'You're a little wimp at times.'

'And I don't want to write a speech.'

She was still naked, and wet and glistening when she came out the bathroom. 'I'll help you with it. Wimp.' She donned her dressing gown and opened the wardrobe. He was glad she seemed buoyant and the arthritis didn't seem to have a chokehold this morning.

'It's today, Rose, and we haven't got the paternity results. What am I supposed to say? Katie might not be my kid.'

'It's not about her, it's about Eve. And Eve you were definitely connected to, shared daughter or not. Talk about her. Here, think it's okay to wear this one?' She held up a red and black dress that he didn't ever recall her wearing or even buying.

'Ladies and gentlemen, Eve was a woman I knew briefly. She was sweet and lovely and a moment of passion has eternally bound us.'

'I dare you.' She shook the dress at him with a frown.

'Yeah, yeah, that dress is fine. Look, help me out here. I don't know what to say. I barely knew her and it was years ago.'

She hung the dress off the door. 'Lord. I'll write it. Tell me some of the things you found captivating about her. I don't want you embarrassing yourself in front of Katie.'

'Too late.'

# CHAPTER TWENTY-SEVEN

*To Whom It May Concern,*

*I am hoping to get a replacement trophy. You made one for an Under-7s go-karting establishment. It was Rider of the Year for someone called Katie Levine. This would have been in about 2007 or slightly before. Can you help?*

*Thanking you in advance,*

*Christopher Redfern*


Email sent to Cooper & Sons Ltd, Chris headed downstairs. The rolled-up sleeping bag on the sofa told him that Katie was out. The notebook was gone. In the kitchen, he found Rose at the table with a big smile on her face and pointing at the fridge door. Years ago, they'd bought Julia a bag of magnetic letters and he'd thought them long gone. But no. Except all the Os, it seemed.

*Gine fetch car fixed washer surry late nite uwt mther huse cllect stuff! Fixed washer t wash em*

That explained why Katie had gone out in the dead hours. Had she gone to The Blue Swan to collect her belongings?

'That's cool, right?'

She meant the fridge message.

'Easier to use the whiteboard,' he said, which he knew was a bit childish.

Now she pointed at the washing machine. Fixed indeed, because it was on a cycle.

'Isn't she just brilliant?' Rose said.

'She didn't put the whiteboard up, though, did she?'

The sarcasm was misplaced because it was a good thing that Rose had taken to Katie; all sorts of tension could exist if she hated her. But for some reason her morning glee grated on him. Maybe it was because he'd been promising to get the washer fixed for two weeks now and someone else had beaten him there. A man-pride thing. Whatever. He was annoyed.

'And she did the tree root. Maybe she can get a new ladder installed for the attic.'

Never. 'It's a shame she's not a bloke, because otherwise you two could have had a glorious white bloody wedding.'

One second she was virtually dancing on air, and the next she gave him a clock-stopping look and stormed out of the room. A wrecking ball of guilt instantly demolished his anger. He found her at the bedroom wall mirror, plucking her eyebrows, which was something she did when angry. He'd often referred to it as self-harm for the vain.

'I'm sorry about that.'

'You should be sorry,' she said. 'That could be your daughter and you're acting like she's in the way.'

He apologised again, and she tossed down the tweezers. She'd only plucked one eyebrow, so either she'd cooled or her fingers were hurting. He kissed her cheek and turned to go.

'You need to mention that video to her. The police will need to see it. She needs to show the police. It could hurt her if they find out another way.'

He nodded. He knew she was right.

'Today, Chris. Has to be today. Perhaps when you go to the pub tonight?'

He nodded again.

'Let's not mention it until then, and let's try to be normal around her until then. Maybe there was no way she could have stopped her mother taking those tablets. It might have been a long decision, carefully thought out, and we don't know what kind of pain Eve was in.'

A final nod.

Rose ran a finger down her nose. Like Julia's, it was slightly hooked. 'Think I should do some plastic surgery? I could have a nose like Katie's. It's so petite. Was Eve's the same? Was it what drew you to her?'

Before he could utter the sheer bewilderment he felt at this strange utterance, Rose turned from the mirror and waved a hand. 'Ignore me, I'm being silly. Come on, let's go.'

Downstairs, they got breakfast and awaited Julia. Chris had finished his cereal before she arrived, locked up with her phone. He was about to complain about her rudeness when his own phone beeped.

'Katie's got a car for the funeral. She'll be back in half an hour.'

'Why does she want a car?' Julia said. 'Does she not want to travel with us?'

'I don't know. Thinking time, maybe.'

'No problem,' Rose said. 'Half an hour, so let's hurry and eat and get ready, boys and girls.'

They were chowing down only for seconds when Julia, through a mouthful, noticed the washer on a cycle. 'Hey, you fixed the "useless bastard", Dad. About time.'

Rose almost spat her breakfast across the table. 'Language, miss. Katie fixed the washer, not your father.'

'How come she's staying with us, anyway? I mean, I like it. She's nice and she's not at my college, so we've got more than just studies to chat about, but I'm curious.'

'It's just for a short time,' Rose said. 'Katie is waiting for a letter that she's got coming here.'

She gave him a solicitous look. *Is that okay?* A pretty inert statement, he felt.

'How?' Julia said. 'Who would think she lives here?'

Maybe not. Chris gave Rose a glance. That one said: *Be careful, don't give away too much.*

'She had to give an address to someone she spoke to last night about the fire and gave ours.'

That seemed to do it. End of interrogation. Julia finished her food and announced she was going to get changed. Rose got up, too, but Chris was in no hurry.

With Julia gone, he said, 'Eulogy.'

Rose just nodded and took her bowl to the sink. He waited for a response, didn't get one.

'Eulogy?'

She finished washing her bowl, gave him another nod, and left the room. In the bedroom, she was standing by the mirror, still in her dressing gown and struggling to put on earrings. When she failed and shook her painful fingers, he stepped in to help.

'Stop messing about, Rose? Where's the speech? I need to practise it.'

'In my handbag, where it will stay until it's your turn to step up.'

'What? Why? I can't just read it fresh and—'

'Oh, but you can. It's better if it doesn't look rehearsed because you need emotion. If it's new to you, you'll pause and stumble and it'll look like you're suffering under emotion.'

A horrific idea. 'No way. Don't mess about. Where is it?'

'You need to look like you give a shit,' she said, then pulled away from him to get her dress.

Chris didn't argue, figuring there would be time at the church to talk her round, or snatch her handbag. He shifted to the mirror to fix his hair. Lord, he'd tried to mope about a bit but he was no actor. Twenty years ago, a woman he'd known for a day, most of it drunk.

Nobody could really expect him to vent tears.

# CHAPTER TWENTY-EIGHT

It happened on Herries Road South, the slash through the woods where, four days before, men with baseball bats had tried to rob them. Like before, Chris was driving and Julia was alone in the back.

'Gosh, she even drives like you, Chris,' Rose said as they turned onto that road. 'Something built into DNA that means you both can't use indicators. Wait, what's she doing?'

Katie's hire car was ahead, leading them. But it had started to slow and veer, and the outside wheels rumbled off the side of the road into the stones along the verge, and Chris realised something was wrong and it wasn't with the vehicle.

Chris slowed, too.

'Is she okay?' Rose said.

Katie's car stopped, like something dumped. The moment Chris's was at a standstill, Rose jumped out and rushed to the vehicle.

'What's Katie doing?' Julia said, finally noticing.

Rose didn't speak to Katie. She took one look through the driver's window and turned to Chris. Nothing said, no change of expression, but he got her message.

He told Julia to stay put and walked to the passenger side of Katie's hire car. She was slumped in her seat, hands in the lap of her black trouser suit, head down, as if asleep. She was chewing on her ponytail. Chris looked at Rose over the roof of the car.

'It's probably just hitting her properly,' she said. 'Perhaps we shouldn't have left her alone to drive.'

'She said she wanted time to think.'

Rose said nothing further, just walked away. He knew she wanted him to talk to Katie. He got in the hire car. Katie didn't look at him.

Chris was wondering how to start this conversation when she spat out her hair and said, 'I know I'm meant to be there. Everyone's waiting. It's been days in preparation. Everyone's expecting me.'

Chris waited. Something heavy in his gut lightened a little. The funeral no longer loomed ahead like a mammoth and bright tower – unavoidable.

'I can't go,' Katie said.

Chris knew that he could say nothing, do nothing, and he'd be released from today's horrible commitment. No awkward speech, no meeting a horde of distressed strangers.

But he said, 'It's to give you, give everyone, a chance to say some final words to your mother.'

'Do I need to adhere to some kind of social traditions to do that?'

'It's considered an acknowledgement to the deceased. That's why people go. But not everyone. It's not a law. Just a respect thing.'

'Do I need to attend this single event, and see my mother in a box, and witness everyone crying, to show respect? It's about honouring Eve, but can I not show honour in other ways? I went to Ron's and almost wish I hadn't. I hated it.'

'It's your choice, Katie.'

'I don't want to tarnish my image of her as vibrant in her living days. The final time I see her shouldn't be in a box. If I go, it would be for the other relatives, because they expect it, but why should I do this for them? They should respect rather than judge me. I have to do what feels right for myself. If somehow my mum's soul continues to watch this planet and the people who loved her, then her final moments with us should already have passed. They should be moments of laughter. Her final image of her loved ones shouldn't be one of people sad and mourning, but happy.'

'I understand,' Chris said. He couldn't say he disagreed.

'I would have liked to hear your speech, though.'

In that moment Chris almost wished his wife a bloody death. The damn speech was still in her bag.

'I didn't want to write one down,' he said, mind spinning. 'I thought it might be best to deliver it…'

Katie provided the words Chris couldn't think of. 'From the heart. Can I hear it?'

His prayer to God went unanswered. No sinkhole took the car into the depths. Chris reminded himself that a performance in front of Katie beat one in the presence of dozens of strangers. So he agreed.

'I want to record it, if you don't mind.' She had her phone already in hand. She aimed it at him. Watching, waiting.

Chris took a breath. One more time he reminded himself. It was just the two of them, in a box.

'Eve is a rare person, sincere, utterly—'

'No. Please. Use past tense. She's gone.'

'Eve was a rare person, quite sincere, and utterly genuine, able to communicate with anyone about any subject. One of those very rare people that was able to talk intelligently and confidently to any person on any subject. She was articulate, caring, funny and a fantastic friend to all who knew her, and wholly reliable and full of integrity, with strong principles. A woman whose essence imbibed those who came into her circle. A woman who was content with her life and didn't rue what she didn't have, or think herself unlucky for the terrible illness that consumed her. Strong even towards the end, she didn't let her illness get her down. She never complained, never wanted to burden others with her illness. She always put others first.'

Here he paused, hoping that was enough, but Katie said, 'Good. Now you. Now about what she meant to you.'

Nothing, she was nothing to him. But he didn't say that.

'I met Eve only briefly, a long time ago, but even then, even in that short space of time, I gathered all these things about her. I knew her friends loved her. I knew, if things had continued between us, that I would love her. And I know she loved her family. Her daughter, Katie, is her living testament, her legacy, and proof of her integrity and her love and her sincerity. As will all of you, I, even though I knew her so long ago, will miss her. But I know I am a better person, and this world a better place, for having been touched by her.'

Katie's head had slowly dipped, eyes now in her lap. 'That was lovely.'

Chris didn't feel the same. Eve's face was hazy, his memories of her diluted by time. He felt like a liar. Those exquisite words felt so wrong, and they cast some of their fakery into his fingers so that his touch upon Katie's shoulder seemed like an act, too. He felt like a man trying to make a home out of a hotel room. It all gave him a fresh reminder that Katie might be no one to him. Just someone passing through his life. But at the same time, he couldn't forget Rose's claims that he liked to bury his head in the sand.

'Is it okay if I can have some time alone?' Katie said.

'I'll wait in our car.' Chris got out, expecting to sit in his own vehicle for a few minutes before they turned around for home. But the moment he shut the door, Katie started the engine and peeled away. Rose poked her head out her window.

'What's she doing? Going ahead?'

Chris shook his head, watching Katie's car shrink. 'I gave her the speech. I think she just wants time alone.'

She got out, puzzled. 'I've got the speech. Did you do your own for her? There in the car?'

He nodded. They stood together in the dirt verge and she told him it was a sweet gesture. 'But we don't know where the funeral is.'

'She's not going to the funeral. Too much for her, I think. I don't know where she's going. So what do we do now?'

She didn't seem that astounded. 'Maybe it's the right thing for her. Maybe she'll regret it every day starting tomorrow. But it's her choice.'

He watched Katie's car approach the corner. The same corner she'd used to enter their lives. Maybe it now signalled an exit, for ever.

'I guess we should just head back,' Rose said. 'You're due into work and that will take your mind off it.'

The hire vehicle flicked around the corner, dangerously fast, and then it was behind trees. A wild image popped into his head: himself standing by a graveside, speech in one hand with Eve's name crossed out and Katie's replacing it – and a positive paternity result letter in the other.

'Yes, I can send other people for funerals.' He smiled to show he was joking.

'Give her time. I'll call you when she comes back.'

When they climbed into the car, Rose explained things to Julia.

'But we got all dressed up. I wanted to try my first funeral. We could find another one,' she joked.

But nobody in the car laughed.

# CHAPTER TWENTY-NINE

Louise was off. No call in sick. No answer on her phone. Chris was glad. He could have a rare peaceful day. Hopefully, she was feeling guilty after trying to shift fault into his corner about Raymond Monroe's death.

Not long after Chris arrived at midday, and the rest of the lab grabbed their jackets to head to lunch, Alan said that he was going to Louise's house to see if she was okay after yesterday. He announced it to all, but cast his gaze at Chris during the final part – *after yesterday*. Then he got his coat and went for the door.

Chris headed him off.

'Do you blame me for this?'

Alan looked puzzled.

'I mean Louise. You looked at me when you said you were going to see if she was okay.'

Alan understood now. His eyes met Chris's. 'See anyone else feeling guilty, Shakespeare? Are they all crowding me at the door?'

'So you do blame me? You think I caused this problem? And by the bloody way, it's my wife who's writing a book, not me, so stop calling me that.'

'Touchy. And it depends which problem, doesn't it? I don't think you're at fault for Louise missing the 0157 yesterday, if that's your worry. But she did ask you to order the kits, didn't she? Even though she really shouldn't have. But if *that* is *your* worry, then *you* worry *me*.'

'That makes no sense.'

Alan said, 'I'm worried about her state of mind. I'm worried that she's feeling like she killed a patient. All you're worried about is whether or not you could be blamed. Are you not concerned about your colleague's health?'

'I'll admit that I'm still pissed off that she tried to blame me. And you just basically admitted you do, too.'

'Maybe, Redfern, you have a cold soul. Is that why you've never phoned in sick after doing something that's affected a patient?'

Chris wanted to smack him. Instead, he said, 'Sickness due to guilt means an empty bench and many more poor souls who won't get necessary help.'

'And what kind of...' Alan started. And then stopped. And then turned his head to stare above his office door, at the plaque he'd nailed to the wall: *Sickness due to guilt means...*

'Smart-arse, eh? What if I come back and tell you that Louise is hanging from a noose in her house, Redfern?'

'Well, I'm sure you'll blame me for that, too.'

*

Because the boss was away, his staff got the big foam dice out and rolled to see who would go down to Specimens for the microbiology box. Knowing his staff sometimes detoured for a sandwich or cigarette, Alan had timed the journey between the two departments and berated anyone who took longer; but he was out chasing Louise, so today nobody was on the clock. The winner was back forty minutes later with a dot of mustard on his 'grill', as someone termed it.

'Grill?' someone else said.

'Yeah. Teeth. Slang. Like gnashers.'

'Or chiclets,' Chris said, his mind suddenly turning back time.

The team crowded round the treasure chest, even though it was nothing more than a big box of more work. Except Chris, who visited a computer and loaded Medway, the national medical database. He put the cursor in the 'PATIENT NAME' box.

'Chiclets'. The radiographer he'd overheard in the Pitstop had mentioned the term – as used by someone the radiographer had X-rayed. Katie had mentioned the term 'chiclets' to Julia. Chris had seen Katie checking her teeth in a mirror.

He typed 'KATIE LEVINE' and held his breath as the results loaded.

Katie Levines unfolded down the screen, and Chris quickly scanned, discarding those of the wrong age or wrong hospital. There were Katie Levines across the country with a welter of problems, but he found none who'd recently got an X-ray at Sheffield Royal Infirmary. Chris sat back with a sigh. The radiographer had said that chiclet woman was a freak, had something wrong with her mind. But that freak, thankfully, wasn't Katie.

That freak was someone else's daughter.

\*

'Aliens get a bad press, but I think…'

Chris's phone cut into a fascinating conversation between a Generation X grunger and his Gen Y goth girlfriend at the next table. He shifted to a desolate corner of the Pitstop to chat to his wife.

'Chris, you saw Katie's burns, didn't you?'

He knew this had been a looming conversation. 'Yeah. Did it as a kid farting around, playing dangerous games with fire. You only just seen them? I didn't think it was my place to talk about it. I was waiting for her to tell you.'

'Yes, well, she did tell me. And I felt the same way. That's why I didn't mention it to you. But here's the thing. Playing about with fire as a kid? That's not the story she told me. And I thought it was just her ankles. She told me her bike caught on fire while she was riding it.'

Katie had lied? 'When was this? Today?'

'Tuesday when she dropped off our stuff. I saw her ankles. But here's the thing. Julia just told me that she saw Katie's burns, too. She swore her to keep quiet.'

'As you would. It's embarrassing. And girls gossip.'

'But she didn't see her legs, Chris. She said Katie's T-shirt rode up and the burns she saw were on the lower back and belly. It's more than just her legs, Chris. It might be a big portion of her torso, too. Katie told her she fell in a bonfire. Why do you think she lied?'

Chris remembered that Katie had been careful to hide her torso the other night, after the flat fire. Because she was female, he'd figured. To hide the scars, he now knew. She must have left her legs exposed to him because Rose already knew about the damage to them, and would have informed Chris. But when Katie realised Chris didn't know, she must have felt compelled to explain. But why with a different story?

'Chris? You there?'

'Yeah, I'm here. She probably lied about the extent of the burns because she's ashamed, don't you think? The more someone is burned, the worse they probably feel about their appearance. I guess if I had my whole leg burned but someone saw only a burned foot, that's all I'd be happy showing them. And maybe I'd invent a story about how I burned just my foot. So each of us got to see only what we'd already seen. Maybe she told you about a bike fire because that could explain just her ankles. And then a different story for Julia. To explain just her torso, because Julia hadn't seen the leg burns.'

'Do you remember how scared she looked when those envelopes caught fire in our kitchen drawer?' Rose continued. 'She had something horrible happen to her as a child, and it's mentally scarred her. Made her terrified of fire. We should cancel the barbecue part of our anniversary party on Saturday.'

'That's a bit extreme. Everyone will ask why. We'd sound a bit silly saying it's because this girl here nobody knows is scared of flames. And we can't tell them who she is, can we?'

'Maybe we could by then. If the paternity results are in. But, Chris, those burns? How? She told three different stories to three different people.'

Chris thought he already knew the answer. 'I think it's only two lies, Rose. With you and Julia, she was put on the spot, so you got a tale about a silly accident. But to me she admitted it was a foolish error, her own fault. She believes I'm her dad and I don't think she'd lie to me. Is this a worry for you? The lies? I understand why she did it, but will this cause some kind of problem between you and her?'

'It's not a problem, Chris, of course not. That's silly. I just don't want her to have to hide anything. Especially if the paternity result comes back positive. She shouldn't have to hide things or lie. Not to any of us. Do you think we should talk to her?'

'Leave it for her to decide what to do.'

'Good. My thoughts exactly. I just didn't feel it was my place to keep this from you. We'll wait for her to tell us all the truth.' She bid him bye and hung up.

Chris put his phone down, looked at the next table, and saw the grunger and the goth turn away quickly. But he didn't care that his conversation had been overheard. He was thinking about truth.

There was a lot of that still to learn. He wasn't sure he was ready for it yet.

# CHAPTER THIRTY

*Dear Mr Redfern,*

*Thanks for your query about a replacement trophy. Unfortunately, it is not possible for us to trace the exact models given from the go-karting establishment to the race winners. I would suggest you contact the venue to see if they have any spares. On this, I'm happy to say I recall only one go-karting firm we designed for in that time period: Go-Racers. Sorry to disappoint.*

*Kind regards,*

*Dora Darlington – General Manager*

Alan was back with news – that he had no news. He announced to the whole lab that he'd got no answer at Louise's door, and now her mobile phone was off. As he walked to his office, he jerked his head at Chris, who followed.

'I apologise,' Alan said as Chris entered the office. 'Bad morning for me, even without the Louise thing. I didn't mean to say the things I said. My son got his leave cancelled.'

Chris relaxed a little. 'But he's in Cyprus, Alan. He'll be on the beach in his shorts, not in a jungle taking cover.'

Alan's son was part of No. 84 Squadron, Search and Rescue, based at Royal Air Force Akrotiri. Alan had often commented that his boy didn't face combat and likened the base to a holiday camp. But that didn't mean he didn't miss the kid and look forward to seeing him on leave.

The irony struck him. Alan's son had been in his life a long time, then he'd gone away; Katie had been away a long time and had now come back. Alan yearned for his son to give up the army life and return to the fold – but would Chris want Katie in the flock even if Redfern blood filled her veins?

'Chris?' Chris snapped back to now and apologised.

Alan said, 'So can you do it?'

'Do what? Sorry, I was daydreaming.'

Alan wanted something Chris could refuse, so Chris got only a grin for his ignorance.

'Louise's Saturday. Tomorrow. I'm taking her off because we can't guarantee she'll be back and I can't risk just waiting and seeing. Do her Saturday and I'll get you a day off next week. I'll get someone else for Sunday.'

The weekend. Of course. Louise had tried to get him to cover it. He didn't want Alan to go knocking on her door again.

'Yes. But you'll have to get someone else to do the on-call because it's my wedding anniversary.' Which he wasn't looking forward to.

'Done. Good man. Thank you. Now get lost while I call my boy. Don't forget it's a silver hollowware gift for sixteen years' servitude.'

Feeling much better, Chris returned to his bench and the business of saving souls.

*

Half an hour after the lab had cleared, his phone and the intercom buzzed at the same time.

Julia, miles away, said, 'Dad? Can I miss the party on Saturday? My friend, Donna, wants to meet and go over some coursework.' And a guy twenty feet away said, 'Delivery.'

He didn't know this Donna, but then he didn't know half her friends. At least it wasn't a boy. He wanted the whole family present for the anniversary party, but he also didn't want to upset Julia. So he put it on Rose.

'We'd feel better having you there. But ask your mother.'

Chris opened the lab door to see a guy with a transplant box. He put it on the floor and tried to hand Chris a slip of paper to sign.

'It's just a party. Mum said no.'

'What's this?' Chris said to the courier. And then, into the phone, 'Don't play us off against each other, Julia. If she said no, it's no.'

'Eyeballs,' the guy said, deadpan. Not a joke. 'A bagful. Just sign this for me.'

'I'm an adult, you know? I shouldn't need to ask permission,' Julia said.

'That's not for here,' Chris said, refusing to take the pen, even against the hypnotism the guy seemed to be attempting by waggling the item in front of his face. 'This is microbiology. You want the theatre department, don't you? They hand the eyeballs out.' Then, to Julia, 'We'll talk about this later.'

The courier looked disheartened, like someone whose last hope had evaporated. 'Theatre's shut. They're all shut except you lot. Everything shuts after five. Sodding cop shop near me shuts at five. No one gets ill or stabbed at night, obviously.'

To Julia, 'Sorry, what?'

'I said this is important. You can't control my life.'

And to the courier, 'Surgery as a walk-in centre? I'll mention your idea to the big cheeses. By the way, my daughter used to eat hair bobbles when she was a toddler.'

'Who are you telling that to, Dad? Stop playing around, this is important to me.'

'Won't help me now, will it?' the courier said. 'Sodding traffic, and now what do I do? Someone's gotta take this. I've been traipsing around with it. Can't take it back. Guy over there at haematology said no.'

'No to a bag of eyeballs? Is he mad?'

'Theatre's shut. Where am I supposed to put this, in the mailbox?'

'Dad, are you listening? It's rude to talk to someone while you're on the phone. I'm an adult and I want to see my friend on Saturday, not do some silly party.'

The courier was awaiting an answer. 'Find someone. Phone the theatre people or go to reception or something. I'm not taking that.'

Courier and daughter started moaning. 'The answer's no,' he told both. And he killed the call and shut the door at the same time.

Just before leaving for home, Chris googled 'Go-Racers'. Beneath the website name and URL was a description of 'The leading Go-Karting experience with twenty-two super fun and family friendly venues across England and Wales'.

He clicked onto the website and immediately knew he had the right place. The logo depicted a cartoon go-kart with wings, exactly the same as on Katie's trophy. It was a corporate chain, so he needed to find the Bradford site. The title banner had a 'SELECT A VENUE' drop-down list, but he didn't get that far. Because of three letters and four numbers located beside the GO-RACERS LOGO – 'EST 2015'.

*

At home, Rose was in the kitchen alone, massaging her own neck. Julia was upstairs, on her phone, and Katie, she said, had just run out to the shop. He took over the massage duties and told her that he'd been on the Go-Racers website. But, no, he hadn't contacted the Bradford branch.

'Est 2015,' Chris said, using his thumbs to gently unknot the muscles in his wife's shoulders.

'Est? Established? In 2015. You mean the company was formed in 2015?'

'Yep. Four years ago. Katie didn't go there and win a trophy, not as an under-7.'

'So you think she might have lied?'

'She *did* lie. Est 2015. The winged go-kart logo is trademarked. So it's not some other company.'

She put her head back as he kneaded her flesh. Eyes closed, a smile of content. She didn't see this thing as quite the problem he did, as proven by her next words.

'So she found it. It looked old and battered. The nameplate was missing because her name's not Donald Smith or whatever. No big deal. Drive me to the party, won't you? I want wine.'

'She lied to us, Rose. And what party?'

'Someone once told me he was captain of the college rugby team. He wasn't.'

'I thought they were on the verge of picking me. That's different. I was trying to impress a girl. Men do that.'

She used her hand to move his to a different part of her neck. 'And Katie is trying to impress the man who might be her father. Kids do that. Rub this left side harder.'

He rubbed harder, silent as he considered this. Was she right? Katie didn't run a company, hadn't starred in films or written books or climbed Mount Everest. Embarrassed, or thinking Chris might be embarrassed for her, had she sought some way of proving she'd achieved something memorable, something to be proud of? And lied because there was nothing?

'The party, Chris. Carol's party. It's tonight. You said it was okay. You're going out with Katie, aren't you? So film night is off anyway. And stop worrying about Katie and some silly trophy. It was just something to impress Daddy Dearest.'

He wanted to continue the discussion, but the front door opened and Katie called out that she was back. They met her in the living room, where she pulled a box of tealights from a bag. As Rose explained that Chris was driving her to a party before the pair hit the pub, Katie arranged the tealights long the windowsill. Scented candles, she announced. For promoting a happy mood.

Spiced apple, for relieving stress. Peppermint pumped through vents into the Tokyo Stock Exchange to perk up traders. And pumpkin, shown to enhance the libido.

That one made Rose blush.

# CHAPTER THIRTY-ONE

Carol's ex was standing outside the front door with a male friend, both holding bottles of alcohol.

'How come John's here?' Chris was surprised. 'I thought he was moving to Scotland. Are they back together?'

Now Rose was surprised. 'No. It's his party as well. It's a divorce party, isn't it?'

'A what? They're celebrating getting divorced? Both of them. Christ, look.'

Carol appeared at the door and handed her ex, John, a cracker loaded with cheese.

'Well, they have on-and-off days. Today they're fine. Have you never heard of a divorce party?'

'And all their friends are here? To have a good time?'

'Divorce parties are all the rage now, apparently.'

'Oh, well let's have one, then.'

Rose punched his arm on her way out of the car. 'Right, see you later.'

But Chris got out, too. 'I want to come in for a look. I just need a little more proof that this is the most bizarre thing I've ever heard of.'

Both waved at the people by the front door. When they turned back to the car, Katie was out.

'Can I come in, too? Sounds intriguing.'

Rose gave a nod. Chris gave her a fearful look. He'd met Carol and her cronies numerous times, mainly because of bowling, and he knew someone would ask who Katie was. She got this, but didn't share his concern.

'Katie,' she said. 'I hate to do this. But these are our good friends, and it's too early to tell…'

'I understand. I'm a family friend tonight, that's all.'

'Then let's go.'

At the door, Chris shook Carol's ex-husband's hand. He'd met John a couple of times over the years, but not enough to be called friends. It made it easier to ask the question.

'So. John. A divorce party?'

'Fresh start, my friend.'

John didn't ask who Katie was, but his hungry eyes scanned her up and down twice, slowly, like a roving CCTV camera.

They moved inside. It was thriving. Friends, even family. There was a 'JUST DIVORCED' banner across one wall. Once over his shock, Chris did a lot of handshaking. Heads turned to watch as Katie followed them around the room silently, but nobody asked any questions. Like a kid, Chris pointed, jaw dropped, at a wedding photo on the wall. Blown up onto A1 paper, cut down the middle and the two halves tilted to create a bride and groom leaning away from each other. Rose slapped his hand down.

'What, I'm not allowed to find it surprising?'

'You're not supposed to giggle like a kid in front of everyone.'

Carol's mother and father were there and so was Rose's mother, because the parents were friends. Rose and Carol hugged and shrieked. Chris slinked away and left the women to chat.

Carol said to Rose, 'I told John about your Chris and that girl in America—'

'What?'

'Don't worry, I didn't mention a baby. I just said a fling when he was young. I told the story of the car racing championship, and you know the only thing he said? The championship wasn't decided at that race. Talk about nit-pickingly obsessive!'

'Carol, don't ever tell him the truth. Ever. Jeez.'

'I won't, I won't. Jeez.'

Chris had sauntered over to a small cake and stared aghast at the two wedding rings inside mini coffins on top. Rose wasn't there to prevent his childish giggle this time.

He looked around, but didn't spot Katie. She wasn't by Rose's side. But he did see John walk past Carol and pinch her bum slyly, fielding a sultry wink from his ex. He almost barged people aside in his haste to get to Rose and tell her.

She didn't share his giddiness. 'Yes, they still have sex. They've got a hotel room tonight because Carol's mum is watching their daughter after the party.'

'I'm sorry, I thought you said a divorce party.'

'Oh, Chris, get with the twenty-first century.'

'So I can still be your sex toy after you dump me?'

'If you're lucky,' she replied with a wink.

It all got weirder for him when Carol called for quiet and, by John's side like newlyweds, made an announcement by the—

'Cake! They've got a proper cake!' Chris pushed past a couple of people for a closer look. White and fluffy, three tiers atop pillars, just like something from a wedding. These bride and groom figurines were facing away from each other, posed in mid-run, and each wore a manacle with broken chain.

'Is the father of the bride going to take her back?'

She blew on his nose and told him to behave.

'To new-found singledom,' John said. There was a round of applause.

'We hope to stitch up the gashes amongst our family and friends,' Carol added, to the same adoration.

'Your support would be great,' John continued. 'Remember that this is just like a business deal. It's been a great run, but now the future is open to both of us.'

'Divorcees are not lepers to be pitied,' Carol said. 'We are happy. Thank you. A toast to new beginnings.'

The applause again, wild and with cheering, as if war's end had been broadcast. Rose grabbed Chris's hands and clapped them together. He started laughing.

'You've got a child!' someone yelled. Heads turned. The clapping faltered. 'A poor child who's going to lose her father!'

The applause ceased. Everyone was focussed on the person who'd interrupted.

'Shit,' Rose murmured.

Katie.

Near the back of the room, she was holding up a framed headshot of John and Carol's five-year-old son, Carter. Rose started to move towards her. Chris tried to evaporate.

'Is this what we're celebrating?' Katie yelled across many heads, at a dumbstruck John and Carol. 'We're celebrating that this little girl's becoming part of a broken family?'

'Who the hell are you?' John yelled right back. A similar chorus filtered through the throng, while a woman by Katie's side snatched the photo from her.

'Two parents, a child needs two parents,' Katie said, quieter now that the noise had died down. 'You people are a joke. This party is a joke.'

Rose grabbed Katie's arm and led her quickly towards the door. The whole room was silent until they were gone, then myriad voices started making cutting comments. Chris didn't know where to look. Rose's mother grabbed his arm.

'You shouldn't have brought that obnoxious woman here. Who is she?'

Wilting under vile glares today, and seeing terrible tension in the future, Chris fled.

Rose was standing by the car, angry. Beyond her, Katie sat in the back seat with her head down, chomping her ponytail.

'I get it,' Rose said as Chris ran to her. 'I get her anger. Tell her everything is okay, and we understand. But get her away from here. I'll go in and make up some excuse.'

Chris got in the car and started the engine. Behind him, Katie stared at the floor and said nothing. Chris told her exactly what Rose had outlined, but it got little more than a soft nod. Chris left it at that for now. As he got the hell away at speed, he pictured all those people back there, their friends, family, talking about that hateful, strange girl. What a bitch! But at least she's gone, never to come back. Right?

# CHAPTER THIRTY-TWO

'Can I ask why you didn't stay with my mother?'

A question he'd been awaiting with all the joyful prospect of root surgery. Even the thought of the question, asked in the confines of his own head where the answer could be edited and moulded, had been too scary to complete. So he hadn't tried. But now he was on the spot and wished he'd prepared an answer. The hustle and bustle of the pub lounge helped.

'I didn't know about you, Katie. It was a holiday romance. I liked your mother, believe me, but we spent a day together and that was all. It was, I assumed, what we both wanted.'

'Tell me. I don't know how you met.'

He wasn't surprised by this. A deathbed admission probably didn't go into detail. So he recounted the tale of fake tickets bought from a tout outside a tourist spot, and a steward at the race track gates who refused him entry; of meeting Eve outside with the same tale of woe and no plans for the rest of the day. A walk through White River State Park. He left out the hotel romp, of course, although it was obvious that his term 'holiday romance' implied a sexual pairing. There was also the concrete evidence of Katie herself which satisfied a slant on Descartes's philosophical argument: I think, therefore they did it.

'And she didn't try to contact you when she was pregnant?'

They stared at each other across a pair of pints – water for Katie. 'Of course not, Katie. I didn't know there was a pregnancy. If I had, I would have contacted you.'

Jake Cross

'You never met her again after that? Didn't see her in the street or anything? In all those years?'

She was giving him a hard stare, as if doubtful of his version of history.

'Katie, I swear that I never heard from your mother again.'

'Makes sense.' Katie paused to take a slow pull on her water. 'I mean, seeing as you gave her a fake name.'

He couldn't work out if that statement had contained anger. They sat in silence for a few moments. For something to say, he brought up her drink. 'I saw you put salt in your water. And you did it back at our house. Why's that?'

'I get a metallic taste in my mouth, like I'm chewing foil. Salt water helps. And it's quite tasty.'

He saw a tenuous link into what he'd been building the courage to ask her. The past. 'Right. Katie, while we're on the past… your burns.'

Just for a moment, Katie looked shocked. But it became embarrassment. 'I knew this moment would come. Of course it would. Families talk. I was silly to think otherwise.'

'You told my wife, and Julia, and me all about those burn scars. But you gave three different stories. Are any true?'

'I didn't want to lie about my burns. But I was put on the spot… and yeah, sorry, I just made something up.'

'I understand if it's something you don't want to talk about. But that's what you should have said, Katie: "I don't want to tell you." Not a lie. Not three different lies. And it is three, isn't it? You lied to me, as well.'

'Yes. Do you want me to tell you the truth, is that it?'

'If you have to tell me something, it should be the truth, yes, of course. But I'm not saying you should tell me anything you don't want to.'

'I will. Soon. But not tonight. I don't want tonight to be ruined. Let's just move on. I'll get you another drink.'

The difficult conversation, then, was over. But as Katie stood up, Chris's hand snaked out, almost of its own accord, and snatched Katie's.

'I'm enjoying this, Katie. Whatever the result of the test, this is a good night. We're bonding. That means the questions you've asked are all important. It will mean a lot if the result is back positive. You agree?'

He released Katie's hand and sat back, thoroughly surprised by his sharp fork off-script. Katie looked equally surprised.

'We don't know each other and that should change. It's changing right now.'

'Exactly, Katie. I said your questions are important and they are. Sharing information is. So when you're ready to, tell me everything about you.'

'I will. But I can't promise you'll like it all.'

\*

Chris returned from the toilets, but the table was empty. Figuring Katie must have gone to the toilet, too, he sat to wait. But a minute later, he grew concerned. He figured she would have waited to tell him where she was going. What if she'd left because he'd given her a fatherly telling-off? He walked over to a window and stuck his face to the glass to block the room light. It was a long shot, but there she was in the car park.

With a man.

They stood near a car, backlit by a lamppost so that they were little more than silhouettes. He couldn't make out the male's features. He watched her step up and kiss the man's cheek. A boyfriend? Perhaps the man had been nearby, and they'd met so one could hand something over. Possibly Katie didn't want Chris to know about boyfriends yet.

Without warning, Katie started to jog Chris's way, back to the pub. Chris ducked out of sight and quickly threaded his way to his table. He got his ass on a chair just as Katie re-entered the room. A guy Chris had noticed appraising her all evening stepped in front of her to chat, but she blanked him and slid by.

'Cheers,' Katie said as she took her seat and raised her pint of water.

'Where did you go?'

She sipped slowly and watched Chris over the top of her glass. As if trying to read his mind. She burned more time by ripping open a sachet of salt lying idle on the table and tipping a little more into her water. 'I thought I saw a friend outside. It wasn't her.'

Her. He nodded and sipped his drink, unable to look at her. Why would she lie? She set her pint down with the solid thump of a woman who'd finally come to a difficult decision.

'It's time for honesty, Chris. So let me tell you a little truth about me that you don't know.' She leaned over the table. 'I lied to you and the family, and I'm sorry about that. My burns. I want to tell you about my burns right now.'

He didn't forget what he'd seen out in the dark, but curiosity, like a sea tide, dragged it a little further back. For the moment.

'I hope you understand why I didn't want to say this to the family. And I hope we won't talk about it again, not for a while. Not until I'm ready. I am internally damaged, like most people. But I deal with it by smoothing my dark past. I hope you understand that. So I will tell you this once, and then we'll move on from it.'

He waited.

'Before Ron came on the scene, my mother had other boy-friends. Until I was about four years old. One man was a monster. I hope I don't need to say more.'

She didn't. His stomach tightened, and the noise of the pub seemed to vanish. Did this horrible truth explain, condone, even force Katie to pitch lies about her disfigurement? Absolutely. Did he understand and accept this? Of course. Did he feel like a complete bastard for forcing Katie to re-open a slowly healing wound? With half his 100 billion neurons.

The remainder were still in the car park, watching Katie talk with the strange man.

'But don't feel sorry for me,' she said. 'I am a rock, tough and strong. I know you sometimes think I'm placid, or too stony, that I seem emotionless, that I never smile or laugh. How could I, after the life I've had?'

The tide once more drew the car park event towards deeper water. 'I don't think that, Katie. I...'

'Don't pity me. Anyone who endured the things I did as a child couldn't ever sink so low again. So don't pity me.'

This bizarre announcement caused a rip current that carried away all thoughts but one. It was devout regret that he'd come here tonight, and it might soon become a path into wishing he'd never met Eve Levine.

\*

For the taxi ride home, Chris wanted the front seat but Katie insisted they take the back together. She sat very close, leg touching his, and for the first time he was able to determine a smell about her. Something natural, not a perfume. Possibly a cream for her burns.

They were on the road just minutes, both sitting in comfortable silence, when Katie said, 'I told you a lie. About what the police said to me when I spoke to them. About Dominic Everton.'

Chris felt a spike of fear. 'What lie?'

'I told them that I knew him. I admitted everything, I honestly did. But I lied when I told you they claimed he was meeting lowlifes on the estate next to yours for a drug deal.'

'So he wasn't? He might have been on my street because of you after all? Which puts my family right back in danger.'

'I can see you're angry. I understand. I would be the same. First, he went after Ron, and now it's me. I wish I knew why, but I don't. Maybe he thinks I did something. Maybe Ron, in his final moments, gave him some line that tied into me. Maybe he thinks I know where treasure is buried. I don't know. But the police did say he'll be long gone and unlikely to return to the area.'

Chris said nothing. There was too much darkness in the back of the car to allow him to see Katie's expression. He couldn't get to grips with this. The alcohol was clouding his brain and he didn't know the correct response. Maybe all responses were correct.

Katie said, 'So I hired a bodyguard. He was watching us in the pub. I went out to thank him while you were in the toilet. He's been watching over us. He's been watching the family, all of us. No one is going to hurt us.'

Chris felt something tightly wound slacken inside him, like an anchor in his gut suddenly cut loose. A bodyguard? He was supposed to feel grateful, or at least without worry. But he didn't. He felt tricked, betrayed.

'You should have told me. But now we have to go to the police about Everton. He might be back. We're going to need a long talk about this, Katie. In front of the family.'

'I understand. We will have that talk. But, Chris, I promise no one is going to hurt you or your family. Ever.'

'You've already hurt the family,' he said, before he could stop himself.

# CHAPTER THIRTY-THREE

Katie told the taxi driver to pull into a bus stop on a bridge over the River Don. She got out and stepped to the rail, her back to the car, eyes out across the land. He knew she wanted him to join her, so he did. Fifty feet below, the river oozed under the bridge with a lullaby whisper. Over to the left, four youths were knocking a ball about in a school tennis court, with string between two traffic cones as a net and their phone torches for illumination. Behind, the taxi driver played on his phone, patient and content because he was earning for nothing.

'Why have we stopped?' Chris didn't like being out here, but the view of Sheffield and beyond had a calming quality. Seeing the lights of houses and the hills and white and red light trails on roads always made him think of the lives going on out there. Parties, sex, work, illness, laughter, sleep. It reminded him that he was a drop in the ocean, just a simple cog, and that his life wasn't the hell it sometimes seemed to be in certain fleeting moments. For every hundred people out there doing better than him, another hundred would swap their lives for his in a heartbeat.

But he was still curious as to why Katie had stopped the taxi. His question was soon answered.

'I want to show you something,' she announced. 'It's a video. A video of my mother.'

Katie was gazing out at the world, so Chris didn't need to feign surprise. He knew which video Katie referred to, of course, because he'd already seen it in secret. But he played naïve. 'What's on it?'

He took his hand out of his pocket, ready to plant it on Katie's shoulder in a reassuring, caring way. Because that would be the thing to do when Katie admitted it was a video of her mother killing herself.

But Katie said nothing. She pulled out her phone, tapped at the screen, and leaned the device against a rivet atop the thick handrail so they could watch. It showed a black screen with a PLAY icon.

'This might upset you,' Katie said. 'But I want you to see it. So you know what I know. Turn away at any time you like and I'll stop the video.'

He wouldn't turn away, though. He hadn't before, and he wouldn't now. The woman he was about to watch kill herself for the tenth time was a hazy memory, no more real than a remembered movie scene. He would have to feign shock for Katie.

But he didn't do that. They watched in silence, as Eve Levine swallowed pill after pill. Soundlessly. Chris counted them, but in reverse, because when nineteen became zero that video was going to hit its first glitch. That moment when, Rose had pointed out, Eve speaks to someone. To Katie.

Would she admit she was there? Was a confession the reason Katie was showing him this video?

Nineteen pills.

Eve flicks a glance to her left, beyond the camera, something there having caught her attention.

'I came into her room,' Katie said. She had her eyes closed, which spared Chris the act of surprise. It seemed less like an explanation than remembering out loud. Words not for Chris, but for Katie herself. Her timing was perfect, as if she was reliving the scene, faultless real time, behind her eyelids. 'At this point I was prepared. I was ready. I had had time to think, away in another room. There was a strange calm in the house, if you can believe that. I wanted to see if she was all right, which I know sounds silly…'

A pause. Something happening behind that camera. A pause, and then Eve's mouth moves.

'… This is where I asked her if there was anything I could do for her…'

Eve had said *No*, according to Rose. It fit with Katie's version.

'… Again, that seems preposterous, asking if she's okay, if she needs anything, because it's not like she's in bed with a stomach bug. She's killing herself. But I wanted her to be comfortable. And she was. She'd planned this for a while, and she was calm. She was going to end the pain. Going to go out on her terms. She knew what to do, and I knew what was coming. It was just a matter of taking the tablets and waiting. But I think I also came in just in case she might have something final to say to me. I mean, we'd spoken, we'd said our goodbyes, but…'

Katie's eyes were tightly scrunched shut, as her mind went spinning back. Chris's heart went out to her. He imagined those goodbyes Katie had mentioned. He remembered when his sister, Lindsay, had moved out of his mother's house as a teenager: the hugs, the goodwill wishes. Similar, except here there would be no promises to keep in touch, no hopes for a reunion. An eternal goodbye.

'… But I guess there could always be something forgotten in the heat of the moment. Or something new. Or maybe I wanted a fresher memory. I don't know…'

Twenty-one pills.

Eve puts her face in her hands, and he can see her jaw moving. More words spoken into her palms. Not a yawn, as he first suspected. Words, the last of which is uttered as she lifts her face to the camera.

'… And then she shouted at me and made me promise. Will I promise she'll be in Heaven with Ron…'

Eve had said *Ron*, according to Rose. The only word captured because Eve's hands had smothered the rest. Again, it fit with what Katie had said.

'… I'd already been told about you. She wanted me to find you, so you could know the truth, but I was worried…'

At twenty-four pills, Eve's mouth moved again.

'… And I promised I would find you. I said I hope he accepts me…'

In that moment, way back, Katie had been hoping Chris wouldn't cast her aside; Eve's response, according to Rose, was again a perfect fit: *And his whole family.*

'…The last thing I ever said to her was… not what I should have said. I should have said I would miss her, my mother. See, something forgotten after all. But what I said was that I already missed having a father.'

And, thirty pills down, that final utterance of Eve's, her last in this life. As she looked past the camera, right at Katie. If Rose's translation was correct, it was another perfect fit with Katie's words, to complete the jigsaw, and a flawless answer from a mother thinking of her baby's future once hers no longer existed.

*Let's hope you find your real father, then.*

Katie opened her eyes as Eve cast aside the pill bottle and lay back, the deed done. There was nothing further to remember. Or *worth* remembering, because her mother had said and done no more.

# SATURDAY

# CHAPTER THIRTY-FOUR

'Katie told me about her burns.'

Rose had been in bed, asleep, when he rolled home with Katie. Rather than wake her, he'd decided to wait until morning. But, with a mind filled with Katie, he'd forgotten to turn her and she'd stirred in pain after sleeping on one shoulder too long. She grumbled, not yet alert.

'I know why she lied. Before Eve met Ron Hugill, she had other boyfriends. I know how she got the scars.'

She gave rapid blinks and checked the time on her phone: 1.32 a.m. 'Video,' she croaked. 'Did you mention it? Police.'

'One of her mother's old boyfriends abused her.'

She sat up, eyes now attentive, police forgotten. 'Burned her? On purpose? You mean tortured her?'

'It explains the lies. She's a grown adult now. I reckon I'd be the same. Maybe I'd lie because I was embarrassed. I totally understand now.'

'Did he abuse her sexually?'

'She didn't say. I think she would have. So I'm guessing no.'

'It must be so painful to talk about.' She rubbed her aching shoulder. 'It must bring back horrible memories. The poor girl tried to avoid talking about it and we forced her to. We forced her by bringing it up. By noticing. It must have been hard for her to think about whether to tell us or not. She just wanted to keep it covered up, but we were bound to notice those burn scars at some point. So hard for her. Chris, we don't mention it again, not until she does. Not until she's ready.'

He nodded and they lay in silence for a short while. Since he'd retired to bed, he'd been surfing the Internet. When Rose had stirred, he'd brought forward a different Google tab. Now, her breathing got heavy and the eyes closed again, so he returned to his original Internet page. A website called *The Court Book*, where he'd been delving into the sentence archives of Bradford Crown Court.

A few minutes in: 'What are you doing?'

Awake again, this time staring right at his phone. A part of him deep inside had wanted to be caught. Needed to be so he could share this. And now he could.

It came easily. 'The old boyfriend of Eve's who did that to Katie. Maybe the guy had a history of it. Maybe he's done prison time for similar attacks on children.'

She sat up, pain forgotten. 'Why are you looking into that? To find him, is that it? Are you going to contact all these prisoners to find out which one is him?'

'I don't know.'

'If you find him, what then? You want to visit him in prison?'

'I don't know,' he said, a little sterner.

'Chris, my god. You're serious. And if he's walking around free now, then what? Pay a little visit and have it out with him?'

'Yes,' he snapped. 'If Katie is my daughter, then hell yes. You saw her burns. Who does that to a kid?'

She gave him a pitying look. 'Put that away, you idiot. That would be a police matter, wouldn't it?'

'Imagine if it was Julia.'

'Good Lord, Chris. I like that you're protective of her, because it shows you're getting used to the idea of Katie in your life, that you're no longer burying your head in the sand. I'm trying to do the same. But what good could this foolishness do? You want to bring more danger Katie's way? Even Katie isn't that stupid. Ever thought that Katie might have wanted to forget this animal, and now you're planning to bring him right back into her life?'

'Imagine if it was Julia who got—'

'Piss off. It's not Julia. She's been with…'

She tapered off, obviously realising she was about to say the wrong thing. Too late, though.

'I know, I know. If Katie is my daughter, it means I wasn't there to prevent this. I wasn't around to stop her getting abused. I ran away, and a sick bastard got hold of him. Trust me, I feel like a shit because of that.'

'That's not what I meant,' she said, but her tone said she was unconvinced by her own claim.

He threw his phone down. 'If Katie is my daughter, I'm not going to let this lie. No way.'

'I'm sorry. It's just… finding this man… that's no answer. It's in history. Leave it there. Katie has moved on.'

He turned off his bedside lamp, turned away from her.

But a few seconds later, she said, 'I need to tell you something about Katie. Something Julia said Katie told her. I don't know how you will feel about this. I didn't really want to bring it up. But I think she might need help. Mentally.'

He didn't turn towards her, but after a few seconds he said, 'Tell me.'

'It's about why Katie thinks her hands and feet tingle.'

'Paraesthesia,' he said. 'Julia already told me she told Katie that. B-12 deficiency. I saw Katie drink salt water to get rid of a metallic taste in her mouth, which can happen with low B-12.'

'No, it's not that, Chris.'

'You got a metallic taste a couple of days after getting pregnant with Julia, remember, and you had salt water to—'

'No,' she snapped. 'Face me, Chris.'

And he did. But when she started to explain, she found she couldn't meet his eyes. When Katie was a young girl, she smashed a vase with a small bouncy ball. She was forced to eat that rubber ball. It went into her body. It never came back out. Instead, it lived inside her, still bouncing, still causing damage. Across days and weeks and months, it flattened veins, it broke tendons and it smashed bones. Over the years, bits of flesh and bone and coagulated blood pummelled loose by the rubber ball floated about inside her, and gravity took them into her extremities. Her fingers and toes. Her hands and feet tingled because they were clogged up.

When it was told, Chris said nothing, and he remained turned away. But his chest rose and fell faster with quickened breathing.

Rose put her hand on his shoulder. 'We can get her help for that, if she's your daughter.'

'And sod her if she's not, you mean?'

'No, I didn't mean that, Chris. That's not fair.'

He didn't respond and heard her turn away from him, and felt her tug the covers to get comfortable. He shuffled so their warm backs were touching. His way of apologising. She pressed back. Her way of accepting it.

Sleep didn't come easily that night. Chris had worried about many things concerning Katie, but not this. Apart from one moment when he wondered if Katie had been that radiographer's Chiclet patient, *this* had never occurred to him. That he might inherit a daughter with serious mental illness. What if he couldn't handle the emotional baggage?

Chris buried his head under the pillow. There was no sand.

*

Eventually, Chris did manage sleep, but only briefly. He awoke and immediately wondered why. He didn't need the toilet, Rose wasn't snoring, and he wondered if an unknown noise had kicked him out. Possibly just Katie moving about downstairs, if so. But he had to know. He shuffled to the door and poked his head out. Immediately he noticed the attic trapdoor hanging down. And then he heard a voice from above.

'… Stepped into the light washing the steps, crouching to be seen…'

It was Katie, of course, not a burglar. He wanted to call out, but something told him to listen some more. So he stepped out, avoiding the part of the floor that creaked. He stood below the trap, looking up, seeing the light. The voice said something else, but he only caught a part of it:

'… Always dark because there was no sun…'

Chris quickly opened Julia's door and grabbed her wash basket, a sturdy plastic thing. Back under the trap, he placed it upside down.

'… I had patience though, because I had spent hours and hours here, over days and days…'

What? Katie had been in the Manor many times? Chris got on the basket. As he struggled to be quiet, to balance, he missed most of Katie's whispering. But as he squatted on the wash basket, and finally took a slow breath so needed by his thumping chest, he heard more.

'… I know you're down there…'

At first, he thought he'd been rumbled and considered fleeing back to his bedroom. But this was his house. So he stood up, head above the trap, and prepared to say *What the hell are you doing?* But what he witnessed locked up his throat.

The chair was for relaxing, but Katie was a world away from such a thing. Feet up on the seat, head between her knees. One arm was hooked under a knee. Her blonde hair was loose, wild, and her fingers were fisted in it pulling, forcing her head down, as if she was trying to fold herself into a ball. He knew he hadn't been heard. She was still talking in that loud mumble.

'… The monster stepped into the light—'

Mid-sentence, she stopped. Her feet hit the floor with a thump. Thinking she'd sensed his presence, Chris ducked. He clambered off the wash basket as he heard the creak of footsteps above.

He scuttled quickly into his room and closed the door, quietly. He was in bed seconds later, and debating whether or not to wake Rose to explain what he'd just experienced. But he left her to sleep.

What had he just observed? A symptom of mental illness? Self-harm? He was no expert on either. For all he knew, it had been an ancient and exotic exercise routine. Despite the strange things she'd said, maybe there was a logical and rational explanation, so he knew his best response was to wait and see. The daylight hours might deliver answers. The pair of them might be laughing about this come breakfast time.

Still, he balanced Rose's phone on the door handle, so it would fall and make a noise if someone tried to enter.

# CHAPTER THIRTY-FIVE

When Chris woke, his first thought was if the strange behaviour he'd witnessed last night had been a dream, or he'd misread it with a sleepy brain. Rose was still out like a light. His phone said it was 6.32. It was still dark out in the second-to-last month of the year. He decided that he would wake Katie and have a chat, because a little bit of normalcy would help him to forget the scene in the Manor last night.

Unable to remember if he turned Rose in the night, he did it now and then headed out. He nearly walked into Julia's wash basket. Shit, it was still upended under the trap, which was now shut. Katie couldn't have missed it when she climbed down. She would know why it was there. Chris had been rumbled after all. Now that chat was inevitable.

Katie was already up, eating cereal at the kitchen table. Her hair was again in a bun at the back of her head and she wore a tracksuit. Not one of Chris's or Rose's. He strolled in nice and relaxed and patted Katie on the shoulder as he went for a glass of water, and he asked about her clothes. All to show he wasn't unnerved by last night's event.

'An old one of mine from Mum's house,' Katie said. 'I went there Thursday night, grabbed a few things. I've just been for a jog.'

'How was it, going back there?'

She shrugged. 'It was home for a long time. It was okay. I'm getting through it. Listen, I hope you don't think I was intruding, but I went into your attic last night.'

That wash basket would be the reason Katie was admitting this. And the reason Chris couldn't lie.

'I know. I heard the ceiling creaking in the bedroom. I put a makeshift step out for you, because it makes a racket dropping down.'

'I was looking to see if I could sleep up there. You know, to get out of everyone's way because I'm taking up the living room. And I got relaxed. When I'm relaxed, I like to quote from an old storybook my mum used to read to me as a kid.'

'I didn't hear any of that, so you didn't wake anyone. I was awake anyway.'

They dropped into silence. Katie chewed, Chris drank and considered small talk subjects. Further awkwardness was interrupted by movement and voices upstairs as Rose and Julia met the new day. Chris grabbed a frying pan to make eggs as they filed into the kitchen with sleepy voices and wild hair. They danced around him to get their own breakfasts as he cracked eggs, and nobody gave him strife for having a greasy meal.

The first egg exploded against the side of the pan and he swore, which raised laughter and applause. Chris took the pan to the bin, but Rose yelled at him.

'What are you doing? That's a waste.'

'It cracked. The yolk'll go hard.'

'It's still an egg. All the yolk is still there.'

Through a mouthful of cheese spread scooped straight from the carton by a finger, Julia said, 'That's sixty boxes of eggs a year wasted if you toss one egg a day.' She waved her phone to show she'd accessed the calculator in the blink of an eye.

That started something. Rose put her hand on Julia's shoulder, forming a tag-team. 'Just think of the farmer who picked it, and the people who packaged it, and the driver who delivered it, and the Tesco staff who put it on the shelf. All that hard work wasted.'

'And we haven't even got round to Third World starvation yet.'

'Get lost,' Chris said. He was still standing over the bin, frying pan in hand. He motioned to tip the dead egg out, but it got a chorus of moans.

Rose said, 'Remember those alternate universe branches. If you cook another egg, you'll be a minute behind for the rest of the day. If you're driving to work and you see a crash behind you, just think about how you would have been back there and caught up in it. And then we'd all be sad.'

'So an egg is somehow going to save this family sorrow and heartache?'

Julia furrowed her brow at this. Rose laughed. Katie just watched. Chris relented and put the pan back on the hob. A minute later, he was at the table with everybody else, and eggs had been replaced as a subject of conversation. But he bristled and couldn't help himself.

'It's not a waste of their hard work, by the way. Their work was rewarded when we bought the box. They don't get paid when I eat.'

All three rolled their eyes. Katie had been watching the show with intrigue and now offered her first remark on the subject. 'True, Chris, true, nobody loses out if you don't eat the egg you bought. Except the chicken. Not her ideal dream for her little boy to be eaten. But at least he's serving a purpose now. Little Sammy thanks you for not binning him because he wasn't what you wanted.'

Rose and Julia nodded like her damn backing singers.

Chris said, 'It's not little Sammy. It's just a bloody egg.'

Julia said, 'How about human eggs, Dad? Sometimes they don't cook right, so are you saying the government should get rid of disabled? It's not 1940s Germany.'

The humorous atmosphere stammered as everyone failed to work out whether Julia was trying to be funny. Annoyed, Chris got up with the last of his toast smeared in crappy solid egg yolk and stomped out of the room. He knew it was childish, but he didn't care.

*

The timing of his puerile exit was perfect, though, because he was two seconds into the living room when he got a Messenger call from Lionel Parrott.

'Cops found Louise,' he said. 'Beaten within an inch of her life.'

Chris's mouth moved only to chew crap egg. He let Lionel ramble. Lionel was happy to do so, because he'd been calling everyone from work about this story.

An online newspaper in Louise's area had run the story on their website, which Lionel subscribed to. A reporter for that publication had been headed to his other place of work and had spotted the cop cars and crime scene vans on the street. The whole scene was packaged up like a Christmas present. But the cops were saying nothing, so the guy loaded up his laptop and wrote a story with the blanks filled neatly in. In that version, unknown intruders, perhaps as many as five, broke in and raped and killed the Bible-worshipping family inside. The reporter was boastful about using this trick to scare a young and naïve cop guarding the gate into giving up the truth: lone young female occupant, beaten badly in her kitchen. Comatose, no obvious sexual assault, no stolen items. Boyfriend claimed he found her when he popped by. Maybe he did, but he was down the station giving up his skin cells because there was no forced entry and that suggested she knew her attacker. She'd opened the door to him. The police were lurking around Doncaster Royal Infirmary in the hope that she'd emerge from that coma and provide a description. Or a name.

Chris said, 'So they think he did it?'

'We all thought she'd been off because of that patient who died,' Lionel said. 'I guess you can stop worrying about that. She was probably off work because of this boyfriend. Some long-term argument that came to a head. So that Enterics kit mess-up had nothing to do with this. Everyone's gone on to her Facebook to leave messages. You going to?'

'Maybe.'

'You okay, man? I know this is a shock.'

'Yeah.'

'Okay. I'll chat later, okay? I've got to call some others about this.'

'So the cops definitely think it's the boyfriend? They're not looking for anyone else?'

'Looks that way, I'm afraid. But, hey, that's not why I called. Can you bring some milk for the fridge? Later, dude.'

Chris put down his phone and crunched more toast. He put Louise out of his mind when he heard the mail thump through the letterbox. He didn't dare move. He heard someone scrape the letters off the hallway tiles, and then Rose appeared in the doorway.

She held a letter up.

'Results.'

# CHAPTER THIRTY-SIX

Not an ideal place, but they needed to be away from Julia. In the bathroom, Rose looked from Katie to Chris, knowing each wanted to see the reaction of the other before showing their feelings to what she'd just read out. Nobody moved.

'It's that bum chin you both have. Now hug, silly people.' She pushed them both together.

Official, then. Father and daughter.

She knew the hug might be an uncomfortable affair, but she'd thrown them at one another so she could slip out of the bathroom unnoticed. They needed time alone, but to be honest, she needed the same in order to let her own emotions adjust. That letter, that result, had officially announced that Katie Levine was going to be a big part of her life now, for a long, long time. She'd spent days picturing this moment, analysing it, breathing and believing it, and had concluded that she was prepared for the scales to tip either way. But now it was here, real, in her face, and she didn't know how to feel. Although she felt regret that she'd told Chris she hoped Katie wasn't his because she wasn't hers. Hopefully he wouldn't remember.

She sat in the living room and stared at the letter, and at Katie's stern face on the driving licence attached to it. A 99.998 per cent probability that Chris was the biological father. Undeniable, but that made acceptance no easier to swallow. She knew time would help. Or hoped so.

She dropped the letter and went back upstairs, but not to see Katie and Chris. She wanted to be alone. She stopped halfway up the stairs, in a dead zone where she couldn't hear Julia below or Chris and Katie above. There, she sat and stared at a family picture on the wall. A photo from three years ago, taken at their garden table. Three of them in a circle, fixated on the camera, drinks before them, green grass below, blue sky and hot sun way above. The memory of that day stirred a warmth in her belly – did that mean something?

It was a four-seater table.

It had meant nothing at the time, of course – it was simply a spare chair that Chris had assembled in case another broke, and nobody made three-seater tables. Now, though, that empty chair looked like a void, as if someone had been airbrushed into nothingness. Or, conversely, like a hint, as if something heavenly had sent her a forecast. She imagined Katie in that empty seat to see how it affected the picture. It didn't look right, and it didn't look wrong. She was still undecided.

She wiped away a tear as Julia appeared at the bottom of the stairs.

In her hands was the letter.

*

Chris and Katie came out of the bathroom, laughing about something, but they stopped when they saw Rose on the bed, with Julia lying with her head in her mother's lap. Rose made a motion that meant *close the door*. Katie looked puzzled, but Chris, in tune, granted her wish. Rose heard her husband tell Katie they should go downstairs and wait. She could hear a deadness in his voice, as if he'd been concussed. Well, he had, hadn't he?

'When I said all those years ago that I wished I had company in the house, I meant a dog,' Julia said, giggling. Rose stroked her daughter's brow.

Julia wiped her eyes with the back of her hand. A few seconds later, she spoke again.

'If there's something in your will about a bonus for the eldest child, that's got to change.' Another joke, a typical Redfern reaction to shock. Rose remained silent, still willing to wait.

Another half minute passed in silence, then Julia said, 'She's not taking the top if we have to get bunk beds in my bedroom.' Another laugh.

Again, Rose silently waited for her daughter's emotions to acclimatise to the new atmosphere. Julia got up and walked to the window. 'They're in the garden. My dad and my sister, who I barely know but is taller, and older than me by a few weeks.' She paused. 'Since it's a day for big news, I have some. Think you're ready?'

'Is this about how you like girls?'

Julia's jaw dropped.

'I've suspected for a while, Julia. Mums can sense things. Now you can relax and stop hiding it.'

'Does Dad know?'

'It took him a week to notice the big birthmark on your back, Julia. He has no clue. But you can tell him. Perhaps not right now. Let's wait for the Katie news to settle. But don't worry about his reaction, okay? You're our daughter and whatever you want, we want for you. I'm guessing it's this Donna friend you mentioned, right? She's your girlfriend? You wanted to miss the anniversary party and see her, right?'

'Yes. At first. But when you guys said no, I rearranged. I'm seeing her later this morning.'

'I'll drive you. Your father always said he'd vet any boys you brought home. But since it's now girls, I'll be taking the reins on that one.'

'You want to vet her?' Julia was surprised, but a little happy.

'It's what parents do. But try this idea. Tonight, why don't you bring her to the party? If this lady is going to be in your life for a little while, everyone needs to meet her. Oh, don't look so nervous.

You stand in front of dozens of drunken men in nightclubs and tell dirty jokes, you'll be fine.'

It was a few seconds before Julia found her voice. 'You knew about that, too?'

'That one we'll keep from your dad for a little longer. I don't want him to bust a blood vessel with so much shock in one day. Now, come, how about we go interrupt what's probably awkward silence between father and daughter.'

'I suppose I should go hug my big sister for the first ever time.'

*

Chris led Katie into the back garden. Out there, he peered across the high fences to make sure no neighbours were in their gardens.

All clear given Katie said, 'She knows, doesn't she? Julia knows already. The way she was crying on the bed. Rose told her.'

'Seems that way.'

'Do I still call her Rose? Or…'

'Let's just stick with Rose for now.'

'How do you think she's taking it? Julia. She didn't look happy to me.'

'She just looked dumbstruck,' Chris said as he sat at the garden table. Katie sat opposite. 'Just as I'd expect.'

'Do you plan to tell other family members about me? And friends.'

Chris quickly outlined the situation with his sister – errant and unreliable – and his grandparents – ancient and remote. 'But we can tell our friends. Rose wants to do it at the anniversary party tonight. Her mother will be there, but that's all the family Rose has. How does that sound?'

This made Katie smile. 'You could wrap me up. Look, a special birthday present for you all.' She lost the smile. Somewhat nervously, she dug a perfect fingernail into the wood of the table. 'But are you sure you want me at the party?'

'Why wouldn't we?' Chris noticed that Katie's finger was tracing over Rose's name. All their names were by his hand, carved there the day they bought the table. Rose, Chris, Julia. The whole family. Back then.

'I just thought… I thought the invite was thanks. You know, for finding your wallet. You being nice, but deep down hoping… Maybe you didn't want me to be your daughter. I thought you might just want me to go away now you know… now you got the wrong answer.'

All along her seeming ease amongst the family had been bravado, he realised. A bottling-up of nerves. Katie's shows of vulnerability often boosted Chris's resilience, and right now was no different.

'If that was the case, Katie, I would never have allowed you in the door. I would have waited for the result. But I did that because I wanted to get a head start on getting to know you, just in case.'

'But was it what you wanted? If you had the choice, what result would you have picked?'

'Wait here a second.' He got up and walked quickly into the house. He was back in his chair half a minute later. With a sharp knife. Katie eyed it with a frown.

'What would I have picked? It wasn't my choice, Katie, was it? It wasn't anyone's choice. It was as it was. You were my daughter or you were not. I wasn't picking a daughter, or buying a daughter, or doing anything else that could cause regret. I was waiting to find out if I had one. I have one. Now things change according to that.'

'What's going to change?' Katie traced her fingernail across Julia's name.

'On the day I met Rose, we didn't know each other. There were nerves, and doubt. Now she's my soul mate and all the awkwardness of years ago is like a half-remembered dream. In fact, it's hard to imagine I existed on this planet for nineteen years without her.'

'I think I understand. You're saying that we've got a lot of catching up to do.'

'I know I wasn't there when you were young, but think about Julia. All my memories of Julia when she was young, they're just feelings and pictures in my head. If some scientist scanned my brain and told me most of it was dreamed, how could I know the difference? That make sense?'

Katie nodded and dragged her finger around Julia's J. 'I think so. In the future, it won't matter that you missed me as a young girl. By then you'll know everything, and that information will be in your head. Like real memories.'

Chris nodded. 'I'll think of them and it'll be like remembering the good times.'

'And the bad,' Katie said, sitting up straight.

'We're going to get past that.'

'That's why I'm bringing it up. I'm already over it. I was reading online about something Julia mentioned. Benign Violation Theory. Have you heard of it?'

Chris nodded. He remembered the printout he'd seen in Katie's diary, but he wasn't about to admit that. So he said he recalled something from some Open University programme on TV.

'It's fascinating,' Katie said, almost gleeful. 'Part of what those researchers were saying was that, over time, humans come to accept and are able to laugh about tragedy. It's been years since that abuse, and I'm no longer bothered by it. Now that we know I'm your daughter, I don't want you to dwell on that. I want you to think of that abuse as a remembered nightmare, that's all. Like your saying, "white noise." Just background chatter, or something I dreamed. It's nothing, so we'll treat it as such. Those researchers said that it takes thirty-six days to get over tragedy and be able to joke about it. Starting now, try to put it out of your mind. To accept it. Thirty-six days from now it won't bother you, same as it doesn't bother me.'

Chris doubted it was all so cut and dried, but he agreed, just to get Katie off the subject. Then he put the knife on the table. Katie looked at it, then at the names scraped into the wood. Then at Chris, who gave another nod.

Katie picked up the penknife and jabbed the blade into a spot below the bottom name, Julia's. She started to cut a straight line. The letter 'K'. There was a smile on her face.

# CHAPTER THIRTY-SEVEN

Katie was deepening the 'T' in her name when she caught a stiffening from Chris and looked round. Julia and Rose came into the garden, holding hands. In Rose's other hand was the letter. Katie stood up. 'Julia, I'm sorry for all the secrecy, but I—'

There she stopped as Julia reached out to grab her in a giant hug, tearful. 'Sister,' she said. 'God, that sounds so weird to say. I lied, by the way. I don't think having a sister would be a living hell.'

'I lied, too. I wasn't at your college to find a computer course. I went there to see what my possible sister looked like.'

They broke the hug and Rose went next, clutching Katie tightly to her. Into her ear, she whispered a warm welcome to the family. The four of them sat at the table. Rose put the letter down and tapped it. 'We're going to reimburse you for that, Katie. It's a lot of money.'

Katie shook her head. 'The best money I ever spent.'

The wind tried to take the letter, but the driving licence weighed it down. Noticing, Julia pulled the plastic card away and held it up. 'It says here Katherine Jane Hugill. Is your name not Levine?'

Katie took the licence from her and looked at each of them in turn. 'My mother changed my surname to Hugill when she realised she would be spending the rest of her life with Ron. But they never did marry, so strangely, she always remained Levine. Far as I remember, I always was Hugill. I was too young to remember anything else. But since I found out Ron wasn't my dad, I started using Levine again. Not officially, but it's the name I used. It didn't feel right to stay as a Hugill, so I never told you it was my actual name. Not until today. I'll have to officially change it back soon, I guess.'

Julia pulled her mobile. 'Maybe you could go for Redfern.'

Rose said, 'From a very young age? Didn't you say that your mother had other boyfriends?'

Katie glanced at Chris, for unloading information told in confidence. He couldn't think of an excuse.

'My mother and Ron split for a while when I was older. She had other boyfriends. But I don't want to talk about that.'

'Of course, of course,' Rose seemed embarrassed by her error. 'Look, we'll leave you two alone to chat. Julia, come on inside and help me with the washing now that Katie has magically fixed the washer.'

Rose stood, but alone. Julia was playing on her phone.

'Julia, come on.'

Julia looked up now, grinning. The child in her was back. 'I know how you got your scar, Katie.'

'Not now,' Rose warned her.

'Trying to rescue people from a burning building.'

'Julia, ceasefire,' Chris said.

'You cut your face escaping from a burning building! The story is on the Internet.'

Katie took a long swallow of water. 'I was going to tell you all. You deserve to know everything about me.'

'No, Katie,' Rose said, stern. 'You don't have to respond to Julia's rude outburst. This is a story you can tell us when you're ready. And when we're ready to hear it. Which isn't today.'

'It was a Saturday night, years ago.' Her eyes were on the table. 'A building on an industrial estate was on fire. I saw it while walking past a parallel street, and I rushed over there. By this time the fire brigade was already there, and a mass of onlookers. The flames were high, loud, vicious. All any of us could do was watch the professionals trying to extinguish the inferno. But then we all heard what was unmistakably a scream from inside.'

Rose leaped into Katie's pause. 'You really don't have to tell us this. Not right now.'

'Loads of us rushed forward, wanting to help, but at that point a large window on the first floor seemed to explode due to thermal mismatch of materials. The frame basically warped and broke the window. A number of people, myself included, were in the cascade zone. And when we heard the sound, I couldn't help but instinctively look up.' She touched her scar. 'I didn't rescue anyone, but the reporters who turned up realised a number of us had been about to enter, in response to the scream, and they painted us as heroes. Maybe the others were. I wasn't. I failed to rescue her.'

'Katie, you can stop right there.'

'No,' Julia barked. 'Who? Who did you fail to rescue?'

'Julia!'

'Everybody got out except one,' Katie said, fingering her own carved name in the wood. 'A woman in the bathroom. Too scared to exit. Until the room literally heated up so much she had to try to flee. That was the diagnosis, after the investigation. By the time she got over her fear and knew she had to run, the doorframe had warped. The door wouldn't open. Not until the fire brigade had broken it down long after the fire was out.'

Silence. Katie broke it when she saw long faces. 'Hey, it was a long time ago. I'm over it.'

A few moments later, a new conversation had started, and smiles had returned. Chris didn't miss the fact that Katie had witnessed a family argument, but nobody had felt embarrassment about it. Was that because they all felt Katie was no longer a guest? That she now lived here, belonged here as much as any other member of the family?

He was surprised to find he didn't mind that idea.

*

Before Rose and Julia left for Julia's meeting with a 'friend' they both hugged Katie again. Julia handed Chris the letter. Alone with Katie, Chris found the nerves creeping back. He was relieved when his phone beeped with a text message.

'Just a second, got to answer this,' he said. He got up and walked a few feet, his back to Katie, then read the message. It was an update from Lionel Parrott.

Now the cops were saying that Louise hadn't been attacked the previous evening. It had happened the night before, on Thursday. Because of the reporter's story, which named Louise, the police had been forced to divulge information a little quicker than they would have liked. They'd released Louise's boyfriend: no charge, cast-iron alibi for the attack period. In proud capital letters, Lionel reckoned there could be two serial killers out there.

*'SO COOL. Oh, and don't forget the milk.'*

'Louise,' Katie said.

Chris jumped and the letter slipped from his grasp. The wind took it into foliage at the back of the garden.

Katie was right behind him, staring over his shoulder. 'Was that who you went to see? Late on Thursday night?'

Chris put his phone away and took a step away from her. He gave a long pause before he answered. 'Yes. She must have been attacked later that night.'

Katie glanced back, as if to make sure they were alone. 'The day of that argument. When she threatened you.'

'I didn't speak to her. I didn't even go to her house. I just sat outside in the car. What are you trying to say, Katie?'

'I'm your daughter. Dad. I can help you.'

Now Chris glanced around to make sure nobody could over-hear. 'Help with what?'

'This must be a scary time for you.'

'Scary? Why? I'm not sure I like your tone, Katie. What can you think I need help with? What are you trying to say?'

She put a hand on his shoulder. 'I understand your worry. You can't shake the horrible thought that you might have sat outside her house, while inside dangerous men hurt her. Is that it?'

Chris said nothing.

'You didn't know,' Katie said. 'Cancel the guilt. There was nothing you could have done. And even if you had gone inside, it's not as if you could definitely have saved her. You'd probably be in the news, too. And maybe never able to read about it. This is a tragedy, and we need to get you through it. Perhaps you could read up on Benign Violation Theory?'

'I don't need help, Katie. But I need to get to work. Louise isn't part of our lives. We should concentrate on our family.'

Katie nodded. But her eyes were unable to meet her father's.

# CHAPTER THIRTY-EIGHT

The police wanted people seen around the area of Louise's home two nights ago to come forward with information. A process of elimination, they called it. Get rid of all the innocent ones until the guilty sod remained. Dog-walkers would give their tales, and taxi drivers would submit to DNA tests, and pedestrians would volunteer that they'd walked down the shops, and they'd be eliminated one by one. But not everyone would come forward. Burglars weren't likely to admit they were out and about casing targets, for instance. Some people would need finding, including the owner of a brown Ford Mondeo seen parked on Louise's street right around the sweet time.

A horn snapped him out of his reverie. He was surprised to find himself parked in a bus lay-by, and a bus was waiting to pull in and pick up people who had worries no bigger than avoiding shop queues today, or to drop off people who had no police interrogations planned for the near future. He cleared the space and drove on.

The satnav. There would be a record of all his journeys. He snatched the device out of its cradle, ready to start deleting entries, and then he tossed it onto the floor as if it was burning hot.

'You can't take two spaces.'

He was standing by his car in the hospital car park, and a woman in a Mini was motioning at him out her window. She repeated her moan: *can't take two spaces*. He realised he'd parked across a dividing line. But she drove on and he left the car where it was.

What the hell was he doing? If he deleted information from the satnav and the police got it anyway, from a server perhaps, then they'd see his actions as suspicious, as evidence of something.

'Chris?'

'Sorry. What?'

'I said how's the kid?'

He seemed to have time-jumped again. Now, he was in the microbiology lab's doorway with his coat half off, and Lionel Parrot, the MLA he would be alone with today, was staring at him.

'You mean Julia or my new daughter?'

'New daughter? What?'

'Nothing.'

'Whatever. There's an urgent joint fluid for you. Hey, did you get milk?'

'I'll get on that joint fluid. And there's some milk jiggers in Alan's bottom drawer that he nicked from the canteen. Alan's already said I'm gone at five, okay? You'll have to stay if we get anything urgent and last minute. Five, I'm gone from here. Understand?'

Lionel nodded. He didn't press on the new-daughter news. Chris had considered trying his big secret out on a colleague, but as a lab rat this lab guy was all wrong. He'd either not care or paste it across social media. Chris sat at his bench and tried to get his mind off dark things.

The wanted man was trailing another vehicle towards the train station and Sheffield Hallam University. He'd been following the car from the house. At first, he'd kept far back to avoid being spotted, but in the city centre he knew red lights and side street injections of traffic into the main veins could thwart him in seconds, so he hugged the target car's ass and hoped the two women inside were only paranoid about the dangers lurking ahead.

The target car pulled into a bus lay-by between the Wagon Bistro and the Coachlight Bar, and the target got out of the passenger side. Dark hair, tall. And matching the picture he'd seen on her Facebook profile. Julia Redfern. The train station was a hundred metres away, but there was nowhere legal to park down there. He pulled in in front of Julia's car, which was a bad idea because she would have to walk past his vehicle and might see him. Bad if this all went wrong and she was alive to identify him.

Julia bid goodbye to her mother and the car left. Julia started typing on her phone and walked away. Towards the rendezvous. Towards his car.

The phone had her attention, so all he had to do was sit still and she'd pass him by, danger over. But, Lord knew why, he didn't just *not* sit still – he got out. And she didn't just see him, but had to jump aside when he climbed into the passenger seat and swung the door wide in order to exit.

They stood face-to-face for a moment, and he smiled at her. She tutted and moved on, eyes back on her phone. He crossed the pavement and went into the bistro, where he shouted across the whole shop for a fried egg sandwich and waited by the window, watching the girl saunter away. Nice ass. Shame she pitched for the other team.

When he left two minutes later, he couldn't see her amongst the students, commuters and shoppers on the pavement ahead, but it didn't matter. He knew where she was going. Towards the spot where she would die before his fried egg sandwich was gone.

'It's all over Facebook,' Lionel Parrott said, waving his phone. He was talking about Louise, of course. Now Chris remembered something from his fugue state as he walked through the hospital. His inquisitive ears had latched onto snippets of conversations – nurses he passed in the corridors, porters pushing beds into lifts, doctors lurking in alcoves – all of them had been talking about the same subject. The buzz of the story of Louise's beating permeated the entire building.

On Facebook, some of the hospital staff had mentioned their own theories, and the fact that the police had already contacted them for information. Authorities were rightly looking into her social circles for enemies, for people with motive and opportunity.

'They'll come chat to us two, I bet,' Parrott continued, eyes glinting. 'They'll probably come here to the lab. You'll be intriguing, what with that fight you had with her.'

Chris wanted to slap him, but he had a point. The cops would doubtless find out that he and Louise had quarrelled. Then they'd have their story, so clear-cut. A car spotted outside her house on the night of the attack belonged to a guy she'd had a brouhaha with. A guy with a record they'd already known about.

'He let her live,' Parrot said, 'but she was lucky. They start like this. A warm-up. He's a monster in training. And now we've got two with the same MO. Louise and Meadow Moll.'

*Why were you there?* they'd ask. They'd know he and Louise had never hung out socially, so they'd want to know what he'd been doing outside her house so late. They'd never buy his apology story: *But she didn't accept your attempts to say sorry, did she? And that got you angry, did it not? It sparked a brouhaha, am I right? You wanted her to shut her mouth, isn't that correct? Well, you shut her mouth for her, good and proper, didn't you?*

'The Bedroom Beast, that's what he'll be known as. The next one will die. Louise and Moll got lucky because he's honing his art. They won't catch this guy for years and he'll be the next big British serial killer. You just watch. It's about time. Oh, shit, wait – unless it's two guys working together? You think having two serial killers is better than—'

'Shut your bloody mouth,' Chris barked at him.

*

The wanted man pulled into the traffic, into the left lane, alongside a BMW X6, a big vehicle that would suit his purpose well. Ahead, opposite the train station, there was a bench by a fence advertising The Outdoor City. The bench was wooden, perhaps in testament to the Steel City's attempts to rebrand itself as a prime spot for tourism and the outdoor way of life. It was just a couple of feet from the road, sitting there like a boil on the pavement because there was no bus stop or anything else to sit and wait for. Maybe it was there to commemorate the site of someone's death, like in a cemetery, which would be ironic. Or for those who liked to watch traffic.

Julia Redfern, just as he'd been informed, reached the bench and dumped her sweet ass. The next second, she was lost from sight as he bore down on a beer delivery truck parked on the pavement a hundred metres away. Ten seconds until he reached her, and then there would be no more Julia left, unless they built a bench from her bones.

The X6 driver, a glossy woman in a suit, gave him a look like she'd found him on the bottom of her shoe, and he made a big show of taking a giant chomp into his overcooked fried egg cob. He made damn sure she saw the whole mushy mess all over his teeth and tongue as he chewed like a cow. It was his way of avoiding screaming at her that she was about to have a bad day, which could have been dangerous for him in the long run.

At the right time, he'd swerve too close, clip the X6, pretend to overcompensate, or bounce off, then precisely mount the kerb and splat Miss Bone Bench dead. A hit-and-run, a crime for sure, but no one would suspect the killing was intentional, and certainly not pre-planned. X6 lady would spend a couple of hours talking to the cops, and many more thinking she was partly to blame, even though the other guy involved in the car crash had scarpered. If they ever got him, he'd simply say he had lost control after being struck by the lunatic in the big German car and hadn't thought to stop at the scene because of numbing terror. Maybe back that last bit up with a story about bedwetting and nightmares after being run down by a BMW as a kid.

Or maybe he'd just admit it, because then he'd be a double-killer and that would get him a bit more respect in the slammer.

X6 lady was still glaring at him, so he bit into his breakfast again and wrenched his head away from the food like a coyote tugging at flesh. The overcooked egg came free in one piece and dropped into his lap. He swore and his foot came off the accelerator, and the X6 pulled a couple of a lengths ahead.

As it passed the truck, a delivery guy trying to get a barrel off the tailgate misjudged his strength or the weight or got ballsy in front of female students, and sixty litres of Dutch Courage hit the kerb with a gong-like clang. It immediately ricocheted into the road. Into his path.

He stamped the brake, but he was too close, too fast, too hung-over to react quickly enough, if there had ever been chance of that. The barrel clanged again as it was sent bouncing down the road by his bumper, then again as an oncoming vehicle struck it.

His car had stalled. The X6 was past the beer truck and safe, heading onwards as planned. The delivery guy was chasing his spinning barrel.

Fifty metres ahead, Julia Redfern got off the bench to move away from the noisy traffic, to make a phone call. Against the shops, out of range, pedestrians between her and the road.

He put his window down and angrily skimmed the egg away like a frisbee. Nobody was building a bone bench today.

# CHAPTER THIRTY-NINE

Like a reminder, the scratch on his neck started to itch. The one Louise had put there. As she fought for her life in her blood-soaked bedroom – how could the police see it any other way? Right now, skin from his neck would be in a lab similar to this one, transferred there from under her fingernails, and soon the results of DNA testing would light up a computer screen. He could almost see the bright flashing red word MATCH and his own ugly mug pictured above it. A klaxon would send armed cops sliding down a chute and into a vehicle with his address already in the satnav. The evidence against him was mounting up. The handcuffs were coming.

For the next two hours, until lunch, Chris could barely concentrate and got no work done. It didn't help that he was in a damn hospital and periodically heard the approach of screaming ambulance sirens, easily mistaken for police cars.

Just before lunch, Rose called. 'I just got back from dropping Julia off in town and Katie isn't here.'

'So what? She took that hire car back. It was due today.'

'I know, but she's been back since. Her bike is gone. Has she not been in contact? She seemed a bit off today. Do you think she regrets missing her mother's funeral?'

'I don't know.' What he meant was, he didn't care. Bigger worries. 'Give her time to have a ride around to clear her head. We had some big news today.'

'Okay. You sound funny, too. Are you okay? Any worries now you have a new daughter?'

'No. I'm fine.'

Rose paused. He could hear heavy breathing, a sure sign that she was preparing to broach a tricky subject. 'Chris, remember how I got that metallic taste in my mouth with Julia?'

Of course he did. Only a couple of days after they'd first had sex, she had informed him she might be pregnant. Not because of anything so scientific as a missed period or morning sickness, or even a strange food craving. No, it had been a constant metallic taste, which she'd described as feeling 'like I've got a penny stuck in my cheek.'

'Sure. But what's your point?'

'What if Katie's metal taste isn't this *parenthia* thing you mentioned? Remember that empty condom packet I found in her trousers?'

He felt a lurch in his stomach. At first words wouldn't come, and what he eventually managed was a little razor-studded. 'It's pronounced paraesthesia. It's my job to know these things, and that's what she's got. She's not pregnant. She's probably had that funny taste for a long time. And I'm a little busy here, Rose.'

'Oh, well, pardon me. Anyway, I also phoned because I was just going to do that DIY thing you get so protective over and hang the whiteboard. The hammer is gone. It's not in your toolbox. Have you moved it? Have you hidden it so I can't do your precious DIY?'

Tense, Chris said he hadn't touched the hammer and hung up.

*

'Afterwards, I think of ways I could have avoided getting attacked…'

Chris felt trapped, as if the young woman and her mother at the Pitstop table next to his held him in some kind of traction beam. His eyes stared ahead as he sipped his coffee, but they saw nothing. Everything was internal and it was as if his brain had shut down his eyes in order to soak up the information coming into both ears. The young woman's words reminded him of his own to Rose: alternate universes and big what-ifs.

'What if I hadn't been one of the last off the train? If I hadn't paused to fix my shoe? Had got a later train? If I had made just one change to that day's events, I could have delayed or brought forward my appearance in that dark park at that exact time, and the rest of my life would have mapped out differently. Five minutes earlier and I would have been on my way before he arrived. Sixty seconds later and he would have been past, beyond, gone about his way. But I arrived there at that exact time because of choices I made, so my collision with the man who attacked me was my fault.'

The young woman was in a nightgown, barefoot and tapping a nervous beat on the floor with all toes. Her face was mostly shielded by a ball cap pulled low and thick sunglasses. But what skin he could see on her cheeks was bruised. She looked like a withered shell, as if every day alive had been a struggle.

'An absurd viewpoint, of course, but in the moments right after the attack, my brain isn't spinning how it should. As I slip in and out of consciousness and crawl to a bush, meaning to hide, to stay safe, I feel the calm coming over me. Strangely, I am alone in the dark in the middle of nowhere, but I feel safe. Attacks like this make the newspapers because they are rare, and much rarer still is the tale of twin attacks by different perpetrators upon the same woman in the same night. That is why I am calm. I have had my attack, and it cannot happen again. I am calm because I am probably the safest woman in the world right now.'

He glanced across as the young woman finished her story. Simone Baker. Julia's friend. Meadow Moll. Up and about now that the boys in white had taken their samples and the boys in blue had asked their questions. Telling the story of her attack to her mother. Maybe she was doing it right here in the Pitstop as a method of ingratiating herself back into the company of strangers, or as a form of catharsis.

Something was wrong with her brain still because she'd seen him as she entered the café, but without recognition. Maybe she had put his shocked expression down to the state of her face. He hadn't dared introduce himself to her, or even look her way, in case old emotions about him, about their argument, caused a… brouhaha.

Simone and her mother spoke quietly, unable to be heard by anyone else. Only Chris. And maybe their openness suggested he shouldn't have been able to overhear, as if his ears had developed a superhuman sense purely for this practised routine of his.

Two men in hi-vis jackets entered the building, loud, and Simone Baker's head jerked their way in terror so quickly it almost broke her neck. Chris could see her try to shrink into something smaller as the guys approached. They passed her table, passed behind her, and she leaned forward as if fearful of a blow. One guy did raise his hand, but not to strike a stranger. He called out to someone at another table, who waved back.

Chris scraped his chair back and got out of there so fast he caught the table and knocked over the remainder of his coffee. The sound made Simone jump again.

*

Soon afterwards, Ricardo, a man born in France and given a Brazilian name by his *Afrodeutsche* father, entered the lab, and behind him were two uniformed police officers, one male, one female.

'Oh, man, this is about Louise,' Lionel whispered to Chris, with sheer glee in his voice. Now he could boast at parties about helping the police to capture the Bedroom Beast. 'Let's try to get some information out of them.'

Chris stiffened. From their bland expressions, this was just more legwork for the two officers, more of the monotonous and the mundane, and they weren't expecting bombshells. They'd siphon information out of Lionel, and then thank him for his time, which would kill him, and then they'd turn to Chris, still in the routine. They would not be expecting to crack this case in the next few seconds.

He had his lie ready. He had been at home that night, all night, and he watched *Top Gun* on Netflix, because it was a film he knew well. Just in case they tested him by asking about the plot.

'Chris,' Ricardo said, and all three aimed straight at him. Chris went from petrified tree to wobbly jelly in half a second. They weren't here for information from Louise's colleagues. They were here for Chris.

'Police from Bradford,' Ricardo said as they closed the gap. 'They want to ask you some questions.' The consultant looked puzzled and angry and scared all at once. It was clear he didn't know what was going on, but was pissed off at Chris for this interruption to a working day, and worried about a black mark against his lab's great reputation for not having criminals as staff.

The officers stopped six feet away, but Ricardo moved closer to Chris because he hadn't been trained to stay out of knife range. The officers said nothing at first, clearly waiting for Ricardo to get lost. He clearly didn't want to. He didn't leave when he was thanked for his time by the male cop, either. It took an order from the female for him to wait outside. Not something that pleased him, but he didn't look half as dejected as Lionel when he was ordered out too. Chris managed to get his ass above his chair just as his legs gave way.

The woman was quite young and quite pretty. Maybe she'd been sent to butter him up so he'd come quietly. If the butter didn't take, the guy with her was big enough that they'd get their man down the station regardless. Chris rubbed his hands together to hide their shaking.

They waited until the lab door shut behind Lionel, then the female officer opened her mouth to speak. Chris got there first.

'I was driving to work…' he blurted, the beginning of an explanation. But the puzzled faces stopped him. Right then he knew this wasn't about Louise – West Yorkshire Police, not South – and they weren't here to arrest him. 'What's this about?'

'Do you know a woman called Katie Hugill?'

There was a strange seismic shift in his gut as two emotions competed. Relief, because he wasn't about to go into handcuffs, and trepidation. Because Katie might be hurt. Or might have done something.

'She my… yes, I know her. What's happened?'

'How do you know her?'

Despite the bubbling anxiety, his mind was on point enough to develop a careful answer. 'I knew her mother from way back. Katie found me through her and she's been staying at my house for a few days. With my wife and daughter. Look, what's happened?'

He ground his teeth as the female officer explained. A motorbike registered to Katie Hugill had been found in Neepsend, just a few miles away. On a quiet street, partway up an embankment opposite the river, as if the driver had lost control. There was no damage to the bike, but it lay on its side. Could have happened when the rider hit a dead stop and pitched forward… but maybe not. Ms Hugill was missing, but her mobile phone had been found in the bike's top box. There were only two numbers stored in the device: CHRIS MOB and CHRIS WORK. The work number had led police here. Did you see her this morning? Did she say where she was going or who she was meeting?

Chris's mind was way behind. 'Did you say her phone only had my numbers in it?'

His question was ignored. The male officer said, 'Staff at Baldwin House say she left without warning and they haven't heard from her in eight days, but that she seemed quite anxious on the day she left. Did you notice anything like that? Did she meet anyone you didn't know recently? Did she have any enemies? Do you know of any threats against her recently or strange phone calls?'

Enemies. He stiffened at the thought that Katie might have been attacked. That it had occurred because Chris had refused to talk to the police about the dangerous foe she'd dragged right along with her into the Redfern world. He jumped to his feet, about to unload all he knew about the fugitive killer Dominic Everton, but his slow mind was playing catch-up and it now latched onto something the officer had said earlier.

'Baldwin House? Wait a minute. What's that?'

What they told him sank in like ice water. Baldwin House was a homeless shelter in Sheffield. Katie had self-referred a month ago and been offered a room two weeks ago. She'd been there just a few days, until last Sunday, when she packed her belongings without a word and vanished.

'I thought she had a flat,' Chris croaked.

The officers said no home was registered to Ms Hugill, but of course it could be privately rented, maybe cash-in-hand, and they asked for an address that Chris couldn't provide. He didn't mention the fire that was supposed to have burned her flat. Because that, it seemed, was a lie. Never happened. There was no flat. Instead, he gave them The Blue Swan.

'She used to live there, but moved out a couple of years ago. I saw it the other day. It's closed up and for sale, but I thought I saw movement inside. I thought it was a squatter, but…'

But could that have been Katie? Had Katie been living in the pub since her mother's death, just like a squatter?

The police asserted that they'd look into the pub, then immediately returned to the subject of Katie's enemies. Chris shook his head. No enemies. No strange phone calls. *Can't help you.* Soon they decided they had all they were going to get. They told him not to worry, that residents of homeless shelters sometimes went missing without warning, but they also gave him a direct police station number and a call-us-if-you-learn-anything request. Then they left.

Parrot came back in, firing questions, but at least Ricardo had gone. Chris ignored the asshole's questions because he was asking himself a whole bunch of his own. But not about whether Katie was hurt, or if she'd abandoned her bike after being chased by Dominic Everton. Everton, despite his danger, didn't even figure.

But the fire did. Why had Katie lied about a flat fire when there was no flat, even going so far as to smoke-damage her own clothing? He had a theory. Maybe Katie had felt an aura of rejection pulsing off Chris and had created a fiction in order to get into the house, get closer to the family. To sort of force them to accept her. If so, he could understand that, which helped to take the shady edge off what was otherwise a very big, very scary lie. Only the edge, though.

Not the case with Katie's phone, though, because he had no clue how to explain it. Why Chris's numbers were the only ones stored in the phonebook was cause for a lot more worry.

# CHAPTER FORTY

'KATIE HUGILL'

The results unfurled down the screen. A lot of Katie Hugills on Medway, with a lot of ailments. In the 'location' pull-down box, he selected Sheffield Royal Infirmary and got what he expected.

*Wednesday, Katie Hugill, X-ray department.*

In the notes for the appointment, the referring GP, visiting the homeless shelter called Baldwin House, had backed up the story that Katie had complained of a set of teeth growing beneath her external ones. A symptom of internal damage following a fall as a child. The doctor, it seemed, hadn't been given the same story Katie had told Julia, of a rubber bouncy ball ricocheting about, wreaking havoc inside her. Based on the bizarre teeth claim, the doctor had recommended a visit to Handleway Home – which Google said was a psychiatric hospital – but Katie had refused. The doctor might not have known about the rubber ball, but he had information about various other claimed symptoms of this 'fall' and it was a shivering read. Chris was surprised the doctor hadn't insisted on a little time in a special ward.

Her eyes turned upside down when she closed them.

Her stomach couldn't digest meat, and there was twenty-year-old rotten flesh in there still.

She sometimes saw the future in her dreams, in which she was an old woman, just a head attached to a life-support machine.

Sometimes people's speech echoed in her head for hours afterwards.

Chris seemed to die inside as memories of Katie alone in the Manor that night bubbled up. His girl. His blood. He had inherited a daughter. A daughter who needed more help than he knew how to give.

*

Lionel wouldn't let up, so to save the guy from a broken nose, Chris went down to Specimens to get some breathing space. He decided he shouldn't worry about Katie being missing just yet, until he knew more, but that became impossible when something popped into his head. He hauled his mobile as he walked.

Sixty seconds later, his fear was staring him right in the face. A Google map showed him that Neepsend, where Katie's Suzuki had been found, was neighbour to Netherthorpe.

Where Dominic Everton had tried to chop up police officers with a machete.

*Everton might be after me*, Katie had said. Everton had killed Ron Hugill, the man Katie called Dad for her whole life – had he also now got to Katie?

Using the stairs while carrying the pathology box was a big no-no because some idiot miles away and years ago probably fell and broke samples, but Chris rushed into the stairwell to make a phone call. Despite his earlier reservations, and his promise to Katie not to mention her childhood connection to Everton, he was planning to tell the police everything. He regretted not doing so earlier. But before he could dial the first of three nines, Rose called him.

'I'm sorry for snapping at you earlier,' he blurted before she could say a word. He expected mirrored regret, but Rose's tone was as sharp as the one he'd apologised for.

'The police have just been to the house,' she spat.

He forgot about their argument. 'Don't worry about Katie until we have more news. I'm going to call them in a minute and explain about—'

'They wanted to talk to you about that girl you work with, Louise. Why, Chris? Why do they want to talk to you? Because of your argument? Tell me you don't know anything about this horrible attack.'

So, she didn't yet know about the police finding Katie's bike. Or she did, and that problem wasn't as urgent as this one.

'Are you there, Chris? Did you hear me?'

'I don't know anything,' he said, with a monumental effort at implanting calm in his voice. 'They want to talk to everyone she knew, that's all.'

'No, Chris, that's not it. Not now, anyway. They mentioned your car. They're tracing Ford Mondeos because one was seen in the area and their eyes lit up when I told them you had one. Now they're very interested that a Ford Mondeo belongs to someone Louise worked with. Someone she argued with.'

His throat was desert-dry. 'What did you tell them?'

She started to cry. 'They wanted to know where you were on Thursday night into Friday morning. Chris, I had to tell them that you went to see Alan. That's what you told me.'

He said nothing.

'But they've already talked to Alan. He's already said he was in bed all night. You didn't go to Alan's, did you? Chris, please, did you go to Louise's on Thursday night?'

'Rose, I didn't go to Louise's house. Why would I? I just went for a drive to think about Katie, about all of this, which is messing up my head. That's all. You don't think I did this, do you? That I attacked Louise? You can't think that, surely?'

'The police just left and they're coming to the hospital to talk to you.'

'Rose, you didn't answer my question. I didn't do this. Jesus, you really don't believe that, do you?'

A pause, which was bad, but when she came back, her tense tone had loosened up. 'Chris, just talk to them and get it over with. Tell them the truth. They came to the house and I don't like the neighbours seeing that.'

She hung up. No goodbye, no see you later. He almost dropped the pathology box. His own wife was suspicious of him, which didn't bode well.

As he pushed open the pathology door, he froze and his heart jumped like a scratched record. Ahead, Ricardo, leading two men in what Chris could only call serious casual. He knew instantly that they were detectives. All three turned to stare at him. The scratch on his neck suddenly burned like a fresh brand.

The Louise police, finally.

Game over.

*

Chris and the two detectives waited outside the microbiology door until Ricardo had gone, and then ID got pulled and mouths opened, but he started talking before they could say a word.

'Listen, I know you already know about my record, but it was bullshit. I was driving to work, and I see this pair of teenaged girls, mean-looking ones, hassling another girl, a small-looking one, and then she tries to get away from them and runs right in front of my car, so I stop and get out, and the girl jumps into my car and shuts the door, and then the two bullies start yelling for her to get out, and one of them actually opens the door to get her out, and they're both dragging her from the car, so I tore their hands away, and then the bigger one, about eighteen, she pulls out a knife, right, a knife, right at me, and she looks like the sort who might use it, and so I punched her in the head, and they ran off, but they got my registration and then the police came and arrested me for assault, but the charges got dropped and so I have a caution on my record, that's all, a caution for an assault that wasn't a bloody assault at all, so I do not hurt people and I liked Louise and I had nothing to do with her attack, okay?'

While Chris took a breath before he fainted from lack of air, one of the detectives made a quick call to base. The other guy said, 'I'm sure the officers on that investigation will contact you in due course. But we're not here about that. We're Bradford CID and we're here about a man we think you might know. He's been in the news, as I'm sure you've seen. Dominic Everton. We'd like to know if and how you know him.'

Dominic Everton? The police thought Chris knew him?

'What's going on?' he said, suddenly a lot more nervous than if this pair had been here to question him about his movements on the night Louise was attacked.

# CHAPTER FORTY-ONE

The police had been gone barely two minutes when the wall phone rang. It was Ricardo, the consultant. Enraged with news that another pair of detectives was here to see Chris. First Bradford bobbies, followed by Bradford CID, and now a couple of detectives from Doncaster. Doncaster: the Louise ones for sure this time.

'I'm bringing them up. This is starting to officially piss me off. What the hell have you been up to, Mr Redfern?'

'Nothing,' Chris said. 'It's research for my wife's book. Don't be nosy. Bring them up.'

When he hung up, he pulled his mobile away from his chest, where he'd planted it so that Rose didn't hear the conversation with Ricardo. Now, he continued a conversation he'd started as soon as the Bradford detectives had left.

'I'm back,' he said.

'Okay. Look, what do you mean, meet?' she said.

He'd called her to say that he'd spoken to the police, and they had evidence that supported his claim that he'd never been inside Louise's house. She had calmed after that little lie, until he asked her to meet him and failed to hide concern in his tone.

'Is Julia back from the town centre?' he asked.

'Yes. Her friend, Donna, who me and you need a little chat about, texted her to say she couldn't make it, so Julia got the bus home. She's here now.'

'Good. Get Julia and meet me.' He gave her a location near their home.

'Chris, what's going on? What did the police actually say? Is this to do with that? Are you in some kind of other trouble?'

'Think I'd be talking to you on my mobile if I was in trouble with the police? It's fine. I'll explain when we meet. Just come.' An idea jumped into his head. 'I've got a surprise. A celebration of the fact that I'm a new dad, kind of, at thirty-eight.'

She took a little more convincing, given his secrecy and the urgent tone he couldn't hide. But she agreed, and he hung up pleased with the way the last couple of minutes had turned out.

Lionel, sent out, came back into the lab now that the police had gone. Obviously, he was desperate to know what had been said. Chris said nothing.

Before he left the hospital, he had one thing to check on the Internet.

*

In a tense escape from the hospital to avoid the policemen who wanted to talk to him about Louise, Chris found humour in the fact that a squad car was parked next to his. He didn't laugh when his car failed to start, but soon he was on his way to meet Rose and Julia.

Half a mile away from their house, outside a salad place called Tossed, which would have better suited a massage parlour, Chris pulled up behind Rose's car and got out. He found Rose and Julia in the store.

'So what's this about?' Rose asked.

'Remember Wooderland? We got a free weekend there. I just got the email. I told Katie to meet us there tonight. So we can do our anniversary party out in the woods.'

Julia didn't share his glee. 'But you paid for the function room. The landlord won't refund that. My friend Alex was going to have her eighteenth—'

Rose had something else on her mind. She cut in. 'Katie's okay? But where is she? I tried her mobile and it was dead.'

'She got a new mobile and called me.'

She furrowed her brow, uncertain about this. 'A new mobile? And she said she's okay?'

Scorn was evident in her tone, but he pretended not to register it. 'Yes, she's fine. Missing the funeral upset her, though, just like you said. She wishes she'd gone now. So she's having an afternoon of catching up with the family and explaining. She doesn't want any interruptions, so she told me nobody's to phone her until she phones us first. That's what she wants. She withheld her new number. But she thinks the idea of a weekend away is good. A change of surroundings for a few days. She'll meet us down there.'

'But we can't just abandon the party,' Julia said. 'You've planned it for months.'

Rose gave him a long stare that was half puzzled and half suspicious. He'd never claimed to be a good actor.

'All very impromptu,' she said, loaded with scorn. 'After we booked the room at the pub, too. And a DJ.'

'I couldn't pass it up. Mr Jernigan said we could have Wooderland until Monday morning if we agreed to drum up interest by posting what a great time we have on social media. So who's up for it?'

'But you've got all your friends coming to the party,' Julia said. Clearly, she didn't want to go. He was surprised by his daughter's reluctance to have a weekend away. She'd even asked him if she could miss the party.

'How about we text everyone and say they can come down?' Chris said. 'They can't stay, though, so it's come and go. How's that? It's a free weekend, Rose. That place costs four hundred normally.'

'That's less than you paid for the wasted party,' Julia moaned. 'And you can't expect your friends to do all that travelling.'

Rose looked between them both, carefully. He awaited more questions, but she said, 'Well, we'd have to go home and pack.'

So he showed her the boot, which was loaded with bags of clothing. For all of them. It boosted the suspicious expression on her face, but she didn't object or question him further. She ordered Julia into the car and within thirty seconds they were driving.

But her frequent sideways glances at him confirmed she was highly doubtful of everything that had exited his mouth in the last few minutes. Maybe even the whole day. He kept his eyes glued to the road and tried to look happy.

# CHAPTER FORTY-TWO

On the A61, heading south towards Derbyshire, Rose kept looking into the back seat, where Julia was playing on her phone. Chris had a funny feeling he knew what his wife was looking for.

And sure enough, just a few miles later, she gave another look back and then turned the radio up a little. A quick glance in the rear-view mirror showed him that Julia had her eyes down on her phone but now wore headphones. He could hear the tinny thump of music from them.

'Just like that. A nice holiday?'

So here it was, the moment Rose had been waiting for. He tried to gulp but his throat was too dry.

'I didn't think we could pass it up. It will be nice for us all have some space to—'

'Bullshit.'

He nearly jerked the Mondeo into a caravan in the next lane. 'What's wrong?'

She was burning a hole in his cheek with those eyes. He could almost feel the anger pulsing off her. But she kept her voice calm because of their daughter. 'I don't yet know what's wrong, and that's why I'm keeping my cool. Because you haven't told me. Something *is* wrong, though. I know you better than you do, Chris. Ever since this morning, you've been cold and robotic, and in a rush, but since we got in this car, you've relaxed a bit. So, tell me, or we turn around at the next chance. We're not holidaying, I know that much. Is this about that criminal, Everton? Have we been threatened?'

*

In Birchover it was an eastern run through fields, out of this small pocket of civilisation and onto Lees Road and into an empty pocket in an old pair of trousers lost in a loft for decades. The final part of the journey was a northwards burrow through thick woodland, possibly to give virgin visitors the impression that they were getting deeper and inextricably lost before a cut east delivered them into Stanton Lees. Perhaps by design the meek would be so thankful to God that their first man-made sight apart from the road, the Chapel on the Hill ('A small church with a big message'), would impel them inside. But the Redferns had never got that far on their first trip out here, and again didn't make it. Where the woodland section of road flicked east, there was a padlocked farm gate barring a track jutting away northwest into dead country. This was their route.

Two years ago, the old gate had been padlocked to a heavy wooden post on one side and that old chain with a spattering of green paint was still there. On the opposite side was a new post and fresh hinges which gave the impression that someone had bust that side to gain illegal entry. Mr Jernigan had had a problem with thieves for years.

The code was the same, so in they went without trouble. The going was bumpy because tyre tracks made in rain-softened mud had frozen hard over the last few days. Two years ago, the route had been lit with patterned tinplate lanterns hanging in the trees, but today those were gone, and cat's eyes ran down the centre of the track. It was like following a trail of stars in space. They wound to the right, then straight, then left, ever downward. Three hundred metres in, the track widened into a clearing. On the left was a wooden house, with a wooden sign calling it ECLIPSE and an ornate streetlamp by each front corner. Very quaint, and a little spooky at night, like something that might be on a Christmas card if there was snow. The track continued ahead, beyond a sign with an arrow and two names: SAVANNAH and WOODERLAND. Chris remembered that the original sign had listed four cottages. Another change was a large boulder blocking progress.

'What's this?' Rose said. 'Is the cottage out of bounds?'

'Maybe he moves it when people come. It'll be fine.'

'I don't see a bulldozer.'

An old man came out of the house, already shaking his head. Chris got out to talk to him. A minute later he was back. 'Place is rented from Tuesday, so we can have it until early that morning,' he said. 'Big Ray died.'

'Who's Big Ray?' Julia asked.

Rose answered. 'Big Ray is Mr Jernigan's boyfriend. Was. That's a shame.'

'What's he doing?' Julia pointed.

Mr Jernigan squatted beside the boulder and dug his fingers under one end. It was twice his size.

'He's had spinach today,' Chris said.

Amazingly, the old guy stood up and one end of the boulder rose with him. A hundred times his weight, but he flipped it over and it rolled into the undergrowth. Rose and Julia started howling with humorous disbelief, of the sort you might do if you saw a monkey riding a bike. It was obvious from the way it didn't crush plants that the boulder was a foam prop. Obvious to everyone, surely.

'I want spinach, Mum,' Julia said.

Wooderland was so-called because it was in the woodland and was a wonderland retreat, according to its entry in *Treat Retreats* magazine. It was a two-storey wooden cottage hugged by tall trees about a hundred metres down a track jutting off the main route, a mile from Mr Jernigan's house and half a mile past Savannah. The two names missing from the sign, Moonlight and Ocean, belonged to houses now gone. Both on the left side of the main track, their dead pathways were blocked by corrugated iron fences. Chris had read online that Mr Jernigan had sold two of his properties to an amusement park that was planning to build rides nearby.

A few hundred metres in, they passed Moonlight on the left, whose track was barred in preparation for demolition of the cottage. They drove on into the black void. The next offshoot track came on the right: SAVANNAH. Unbarred, and tonight home to a family of eight called the Sandersons, according to Mr Jernigan.

Deep in the trees they caught the flicker of light from the cottage.

Half a minute later, Ocean's no-go track slipped by on the left. For a short period after that the trees on the left thinned and allowed glimpses of a high wooden fence deep inside. Next up, on the right, the sign for WOODERLAND.

Mr Jernigan seemed to have misjudged how much land to clear for Wooderland because the trees were so close their branches touched the walls and roof. Or maybe nature had clawed some space back. Or maybe the builders had simply dropped the building into the woods using a crane.

They parked and Chris got their bags. Julia still looked glum. Just inside the front door, above a mirror, was a key rack and an old laminated A4 sheet with the house's address and 'House Rules'. Number one: 'All damages must be paid for.' Chris tried to hang the keys on one of the hooks and the whole rack came right off the wall, nails with it. Everything clattered to the floor.

'No wonder he put that rule first,' Julia said.

Chris picked up the keys and the rack. 'Like playing Buckaroo,' he said as he slammed the rack's nails back into their holes in the wall and then carefully hung the keys.

'You two, living room now, please,' Rose said.

It was time, he knew.

Time for questions to be answered.

# CHAPTER FORTY-THREE

They sat Julia down on the dusty sofa. Chris stood facing her. Having already got the story in the car, Rose stepped back. The floor was all his. He didn't want time to think, to back out, so launched straight into it. Julia listened with growing horror as he told of a man called Dominic Everton, a lowlife scumbag who was on the run for a gruesome murder. His victim had died. And his victim was Katie's dad, her first one. And the cops had found Katie's abandoned bike and suspected foul play.

Rose, unimpressed with Chris's jerky telling, knelt before her only daughter and grabbed her hands. 'The police came to see your father about this. They have evidence – and your father says they wouldn't tell him what – that this man, this Dominic Everton, might be after us. After your father. The police don't know where he is, but they have proof that he knows where we live and might do something. So we've had to sort of go on the run, too.' She flicked a glance round at Chris as she added, 'Also like criminals.'

'Wait a minute.' Julia was shaking her head. 'You said Katie was planning to meet us here. You said you talked on the phone. Was that a lie? Is Katie in some kind of danger from this man?'

Rose stepped forward. 'We don't know where Katie is,' she said, careful not to use the word *missing*. 'Yes, the police are considering that Katie might be in danger. There's a chance he could have hurt her. So we came here because your father didn't want to take the risk with us. But we might be overreacting. Katie did say she had errands today and maybe she crashed her bike and couldn't ride it.

It's a little strange that she'd leave her mobile behind, but that's not proof she's hurt. She might be fine. The police have no evidence she's been hurt. And this man, this Everton, he can't stay on the run for ever. Everyone knows his face. He'll be captured soon. Meanwhile, we just wait here and see if Katie calls us.'

'But how did Everton find out about you and Katie, Dad? We only found out the truth today.'

Rose said, 'Eve, her mother, has known a long time. Everton is from the same city, so it's possible that he heard a rumour somehow.'

Julia said, 'Does Katie owe this man money or something? Did she do something to him? Why does he want to hurt her? And us, just to get Katie?'

'The police didn't say,' Rose answered. 'According to your father.'

Julia got up and went to the window, to stare out at the darkness. But the room light showed her only her own reflection. 'Wow. I remember the story you told me about when you two met, Mum. How my granddad interrogated Dad and phoned the police to find out about him. See if he had a criminal record, or any other scorpions in the closet. And Dad, you told me about how you worried that Mum's ex-boyfriend might be a wild man and still have a thing for her. Baggage, that's what people call it. Well, Katie, she's certainly come into this family with some baggage. A weirdo out to hurt her. That's the baggage she brought when she moved into our lives.'

'Julia, I'm so sorry about this, truly. But it's important we try not to think about this right now. We do the best we can to try to pretend this is actually a holiday. It won't be easy. Can you do that, Julia? Until the winds change.'

Julia nodded. The glass reflected the face of a girl twisted by tension and she yanked the curtains to shut her away. 'Are the police protecting us? Why aren't they here?'

Rose stepped up and put her hands on Julia's shoulders from behind. 'You father had the bright idea of not telling the police we were run—'

'I said I was going to call them tonight,' Chris cut in.

'Be quiet, Chris. Julia, they know all about Everton and his plans, and they're going to watch the house in case he shows up there. All will be fine. And Katie, I'm sure she'll be fine when she calls us. It's just awkward we can't call her. But there's one more thing. Chris?'

She'd told him he had to do this part. Take Julia's phone and block all incoming calls from any numbers not listed in their contacts, just for tonight. Chris and Rose had already amended their mobiles. As expected, Julia clearly didn't like the idea. 'It probably won't happen, but it's just in case this Everton criminal gets our numbers. We don't want him calling us. If he got our numbers somehow.'

'You mean off Katie. If he hurt Katie and got our phone numbers.'

'That hasn't happened,' Chris said. 'I'm sorry I lied about Katie having a new mobile, about saying I talked to her. But when she does get hold of a new one, she'll call us—'

'How will she call us if unrecognised numbers are blocked?'

Both women turned to look at him. His mind raced. 'Facebook. When she can't call us, she'll contact us through social media, and then we can bring her here. We just need patience for that. And for a few days until Everton is captured. I'll be telling the police everything I know when I call them later.'

Julia shrugged her mother's hands away and pulled out her phone. 'Fine, I'll do it. I'll block calls. Whatever. But what are you leaving out? There's something. You haven't told me everything.'

'That's everything your father told me,' Rose said, her piercing stare locked on Chris. A careful line that said the unsaid.

*

The vibe soon mellowed. After all, they were safe here in this woodland retreat, by definition a place designed to excise worry. Julia got help in that department from Simone, who texted to say she was to be freed from the hospital tomorrow; she would stay with her parents in Sheffield for the next week and hoped Julia could drop by for a chat.

They unpacked and then tried to settle into their stopgap home. But Julia was restless because her father had neglected to pack any of her underwear or toiletries, and her complaints were quickly followed by Rose's discovery that the cupboards were empty of food. A shopping trip meant leaving the house, going out of the light and into those dark woods. But they quickly got over this irrational fear. If the man called Everton hadn't attacked their home yet, he was unlikely to have tracked them here. And if he had, he wouldn't just lurk behind a tree and wait for someone to step out. Besides, Julia *needed* some new personal items.

Rose remembered a small supermarket they'd passed a mile away and they hopped into the car. Irrational fear, yes, but still they watched the woods carefully and ran between the house and the car. Mr Jernigan was on the porch of Eclipse when they arrived at the foam boulder, back in place to deter the unwanted. As Chris was sliding it aside, Rose wound down her window and asked the old chap what time the supermarket shut.

'Food yer after? Surprised ye didn't bring any. It's only a mile and a bit, but you can raid the guest house if ya like.'

'He won't have what I need,' Julia moaned.

'I'll share,' her mother replied. She called to Mr Jernigan. 'That would be so kind of you. Where's the guesthouse?'

He led them down a pitted concrete path between a chain-link fence and the side of his house. His backyard was a long oval cut into the trees. The chain-link fence ran off in a jerky line deep into the woods, but he'd erected a small one along the treeline. The uneven, grassy ground rippled like a green sea. The only real garden feature was a rockery. On one side was a kids' playground, the equipment in good nick but clearly made of old materials.

Twenty years ago, when they bought the land, Mr Jernigan and Big Ray had wanted to adopt a son. The playground had been part of their sales pitch for why this pair of middle-aged men would make good parents. Never happened. Two years ago, when the Redfern family was here last, Mr Jernigan and Big Ray still held the dream, and they'd kept that playground equipment painted and oiled and wiped just in case. Earlier, Mr Jernigan had told Chris that bowel 'hammer-on' cancer had taken Big Ray away, but a fear of upsetting Mr Jernigan had prevented him from asking how the old chap was faring alone. Now, he saw another chance to inspire answers without appearing insincere.

'You've kept the playground.'

'Just in case I get guests wi' kids,' was the reply. Somewhat sharp. But not biting. More like a practised answer. But of the invented sort. Chris suspected that the playground was a reminder of Big Ray, since they'd built it together. Maybe that explained the upkeep: letting it slide would be akin to losing a grip on his dead lover, of letting pieces of his memory of the man peel away as paintwork peeled away.

'There's the guesthouse, as you can see.'

It was nestled in the corner of the oval. A two-storey wooden erection with a sloping roof. He led the way. 'Looks good from 'ere, eh? Like Big Ray.'

Inside, the guesthouse was bare walls, no carpets, all wood that was beginning to warp. Wall cupboards had no doors, nor the doorframes. No plug sockets, no skirting boards. An incomplete shell left to rot. The living room had a hole in the wall for a missing fireplace, and an actual fire sometime in the past had painted a big black spot in a corner of the dining room. It struck Chris as the perfect setting for a haunted house movie, highlighted by the fact that in each room was hung one of the old tinplate lanterns that had once lit the road into the property. Mr Jernigan ignited them with a kitchen gas lighter, after filling each from a bottle of Bartoline lamp oil as they moved through the old wreck.

'Inside, though, a diff story, eh?' Mr Jernigan said. 'Like Big Ray.'

It wasn't all rotten. The broken kitchen had a row of three modern freezers plugged into a generator. And there was one piece of carpeting here, which was a blue rug. The Artexed ceiling was cracked and bulged downwards as if under a great weight of water.

'Big Ray reckoned the guy who built this place hid an antique eighteenth-century sword under one of the floors. Well, it wasn't antique back then.' Mr Jernigan raised one end of the blue rug. It didn't curve or bend, but lifted like a door. Solid. 'Wooden inserts. Got matching rugs in all three houses. Ray's idea. They hide the cellar doors and they're sturdy. Ray was so big he worried he'd crash right on through if he stepped on the cellar door in the night. You need to wash your rug, take the inserts out first, eh? Look in the freezers, then, and take what you want.'

They loaded the car and thanked the old guy, but he insisted on showing them the top floor of the guesthouse before they left. No one doubted he missed company. Upstairs, a bathroom and two bedrooms. The main bedroom had a metal baby's crib built right into the wall and the back bedroom, above the kitchen, had a mammoth pull-down wall bed. Contrary to the kitchen ceiling, the floor was flat, but it was missing floorboards and those that remained were badly warped and broken, and in a neat, foot-long line, eight feet from the raised wall bed, some were snapped and blistered. The ceiling was covered in damp. Here, though, was the only window frame that actually had a window with glass, not a sheet of opaque Perspex jammed into the hole. The last room to see, so Mr Jernigan lit the lantern and put the oil bottle and lighter on the windowsill.

They went to the window, stepping carefully, every footstep seeming to sink a shrieking floorboard two inches. Mr Jernigan proudly pointed out Big Ray's old house, way across the fields and woods where there was a scattering of building shapes and pinprick lights. There was no way to determine which building he was pointing at, but Chris and Rose both nodded.

'How does this open?' Julia said from behind.

They turned. 'Don't touch that!' Mr Jernigan suddenly yelled. She had her hands on the king-size wall bed, running them about, looking for a way to open it. She started to step back and he grabbed her to yank her out of range.

'No dampers, an' an iron frame. Heavy as heck, girl. Push-latch, but it's flimsy. Walk into this hard enough and it'll free fall and crush ya like something out of an ol' silent comedy fillum. Big Ray used to use it for weight training. He dropped it once from about waist-high, and look where it smashed the floorboards.'

That explained the line of damage: right where the bed's legs would have repeatedly hammered the wood as Big Ray exercised. Mr Jernigan walked carefully but fast across the smashed wood and put a hand on the bed. He ushered Julia away and shook the frame to make sure the bed was locked in place.

'Has it got a mattress?' she asked.

'It has, yay, but we keep away from this. Big Ray needed my help to slot it back usually. Now let me show you something.'

Back at the window, Mr Jernigan pointed into the backyard, at a barbecue pit. 'Having a dear acquaintance over tonight with her grandkids. Sausages an' stuff. Ya welcome to join us. About seven? Gives ya an hour to get the grub into ya freezer and get changed. If you want, that is.'

He looked like he'd tried hard not to beg – besides, they had nothing planned. After a nod from Chris, Rose said they'd be happy to attend.

Julia barely heard. She was still looking at the wall bed.

*

Rose and Julia got a chance to dress up, but Chris wore a tracksuit because Mr Jernigan wanted him to chop wood for the barbecue. Except the old guy's dear acquaintance brought kindling, so there he was looking like a car thief who'd crashed a grand ball. Even Mr Jernigan had put on a suit in order to impress.

His new lover, Sally, was a woman in her fifties with a lithe body from years of running, and her grandkids had inherited her action gene. Julia got run ragged playing tag with the small dynamos. Rose and Sally drank wine and chatted about the art of writing, because Sally had self-published two detective fiction e-books on Amazon. Chris and Mr Jernigan supped his sugar-loaded homebrew and discussed the benefits of country living. Chris totally agreed that the peace and quiet out here outweighed any single yield from urban existence, but tonight the solitude only reminded him how far they were from help… if someone got hurt.

Rose approached Chris with a glass of whiskey. 'It's not the same brand you have in your attic Ivory Tower, but maybe this will chill you out just the same.'

He grinned at her and took a mighty swig. Rose glanced around to make sure nobody was within earshot. 'I was thinking, perhaps we should call the police for an update on what they know? About Katie. They might know where she is.'

'A waste of time, I think. The police said people can sometimes vanish for a while without telling people. I don't think they're out searching for her yet. There was no evidence of foul play. She's an adult. Remember your "missing white woman syndrome" thing. She fits the criteria for a massive search if the police really thought there was danger.' Yeah, homelessness and mental instability aside.

She took a little more convincing to agree to wait for news, but he got her back into the party spirit. Around nine, the four-year-old whirlwinds had to be returned to their parents. Minus Sally, Mr Jernigan's smile turned upside down and he decided to call it a night. The peaceful countryside was a double-edged sword, it seemed. The Redferns returned to their cabin, and Rose prepared cake and candles, but it was all a far cry from the function they'd passed up in order to come here. They ate and smiled and tried to pretend they were having a grand old time, as you might if not stalked by a lunatic.

Afterwards, Rose decided to take a bath. It was while searching Chris's car for her earphones, because she couldn't bathe without an audiobook, that she found damning evidence that would ruin the homely atmosphere.

# CHAPTER FORTY-FOUR

When he walked upstairs, she was sitting fully dressed on the side of a full bath, looking grim.

'What's wrong, Rose?'

'Thursday. Your errand. Where did you go, again?' She had her phone in her hand, and shook it, like a sign. Like a message. He felt a lead weight settle in his stomach at the knowledge that this conversation was coming back upon Louise.

'Where do you think I went?' He was careful not to outright lie, because he didn't know what she knew.

What she knew was a lot.

'I checked your satnav for Thursday night. I don't even know why, but I did. I googled the address and found a news story about Louise. It's Louise's address, isn't it? You went to Louise's house on Thursday night.'

A band seemed to tighten around his throat, making words hard. 'What are you saying? That I'm having an affair with Louise?'

He knew she didn't think that, but he wanted her deflected. Or, at least, he didn't want to give her a suspicion she might not already have.

She already had it. 'She was attacked that night, Chris. The night you claimed you were going to your boss's house, but instead went to hers. The night someone saw your car in her area.'

He looked at the floor. 'I shouldn't have to explain anything, should I? I'm your husband. You already know the truth, or you don't. Tell me right now if you think I half-killed Louise. A woman ten inches shorter than me.'

'Where's the hammer from the toolbox, Chris?'

He was angry. 'So you've made up your mind. I'll be around when you decide you've made a big mistake and are willing to apologise.'

She got off the bath and approached. For a second, he thought she was going to grab him, bury her face in his chest and spout apologies through tears. One second only, though, because that was all it took for her to cross the bathroom and slam the door in his face.

*

Like a form of 'hammer-on' cancer, the darkness started in nooks and crannies beneath trees, and welled up in corners of the rooms and beneath chairs, and stained the sky in blooming shapes and then settled in Chris's gut. By the time the visible universe was black, Chris was in a mild panic. It got worse when his phone vibrated. He hadn't set his to block.

He ignored the call, made sure Julia wasn't likely to remove herself from in front of the TV, and then slipped out the back of the house and stopped on the garden path.

His shadow was on the ground in a square of light. He looked up and around. The bathroom light, where Rose was locked all alone and wondering if her husband was a would-be killer. Rose. He would have to talk to her soon. And tell the whole, sorry truth.

The call was from a Sheffield number he didn't know. He returned it.

'South Yorkshire Police,' a voice answered.

Police? His heart thumped. 'My name is Chris Redfern. You just called me. What's happened?'

'Hold a moment, Mr Redfern,' the operator said.

'No, I want—'

But the beeps of hold took over. It was a long moment. Then a voice was back, but not hers. Not even female. And not a lowly constable.

'Mr Redfern, this is Superintendent Butlin. You're not at home, right? Where are you?'

A superintendent. Top guy in a division. Chris felt his heart jump because right then he knew something was badly wrong. He knew this wasn't about Louise.

'What's happened?' he said.

'Your house caught fire a little while ago, Mr Redfern. Are you telling me you didn't know this?'

Now his legs felt weak and he had to sit on the cold garden path. He could see his shadow shaking. 'What do you mean? How?'

'Where are you, Mr Redfern? Where are your wife and daughter?'

Obvious concern in the man's question. He was worried about Chris's family. Worried that Chris had hurt them?

'I didn't burn my own house,' he barked, losing his nerves, the fear making him impatient and angry instead. 'My family is fine. Listen. I was waiting until I got my family safe before I called you. I was planning to call. I'm in trouble. There's someone after me. I'm with my family far from home to keep them safe. If you say my house burned down, then I know who did it. That means you need to take me seriously and listen to what I have to say.'

'I do, Mr Redfern. Very much so. But I need to know your wife and daughter are safe.'

'What do you mean, safe? Do you think – right!'

Fired-up, Chris ran to the living room, where Julia was attempting to get a fire going in the grate. With a forced smile, he told her to shout what she thought of the cabin.

'Spooky.'

'What about your wife?'

*She's busy* wouldn't have gone down well, so he told the Super to wait a minute and made a nervous trek up the stairs to knock on the locked bathroom door.

No answer.

'Mr Redfern, what's going on? Where is your wife? I need you to put her on the phone.'

Feeling silly, he said, 'Rose. I need you to say aloud what you think of the cabin.'

No answer. But it beat some outburst about Louise – imagine if she'd asked him again if he'd attacked her?

'Rose, can you just confirm aloud for the police that you're not dead and buried in the garden?'

The lock clicked and the door opened. Rose was wrapped in a towel, wet, still angry and numb. She pushed past him, but thankfully, she also told him to get out of her way. Nice and loud. She slammed the bedroom door behind her, and Chris rushed into Julia's room.

When there were two shut doors between him and another's ears, he said: 'There. My family is fine. I haven't hurt them, they're not kidnapped, and I didn't run off after burning my house down. I ran with my family because there's a nutter out there who wants to hurt me. Understand? Now you need to listen to me because I have quite a shocking story.'

The Super said, 'I understand. But if you feel you're in danger, Mr Redfern, then you need to come in. There are questions to answer, and there will be no safer place than in a police station. It doesn't help you to be off hiding somewhere if there's someone who means you harm. Do *you* understand?'

'Yes, but—'

'And I want you to let me speak to your wife.'

'No, not yet. You don't understand. They're calm and settled. I'm not dragging them back there, not tonight. We'll do this tomorrow. But you haven't even asked me who's after me. This nasty mess involves Dominic Everton, that fugitive everyone is after. There, now you've got a chance to stop being hounded by the public. So will you listen to me?'

'Mr Redfern, you need to come in. Listen to *me* carefully. There was a body found in your house. Do you understand what I just said?'

Suddenly, Chris couldn't feel the phone jammed hard against his ear, or in his tight fist. Everything went numb. 'Dead body?' he wheezed.

'Mr Redfern, you need to return to Sheffield this instant. Tell me where you are and I'll arrange for officers to be with your family while you and I speak about this. Where are you?'

He blurted: 'Have you IDed the body? Who is it?'

'I was hoping you could answer that. Who burned the house, Mr Redfern? Do you know who's lying burned to a crisp in your home?'

Now he felt dizzy. 'Katherine Hugill. My daughter.'

# SUNDAY

# CHAPTER FORTY-FIVE

Three times over the years had Julia known her mother to do the bedroom thing, where she locked herself away after a raging fallout with Dad. She knew Mum wouldn't come back downstairs this night, and her father was in an armchair, trance-like and stiff, like a criminal in an electric chair. With her parents engaged, Julia finally succumbed to the urge that had been eating her for the last hour.

Donna had messaged through the dating app earlier, wanting to meet. Julia sent a reply.

*'I'm miles from u babe and deep in the woods sorry.'*

A message from Donna flashed up almost instantly.

*'Never done it under the night sky.'*

Julia smiled. The clock on the wall rode past midnight, into a new day, and she decided it was time. She got up and went into the hallway, sending her girlfriend another message.

*'No need for us to b cold I know a place.'*

At the front door, she lifted the keys from the hook to expose the House Rules sheet.

*'Sounds good will bring wine where are you?'*

Julia took a photo of the House Rules – or at least the important portion at the bottom, with the postcode. She sent the photo
along with a specific location in the woods.

*'Cant wait babe.'*

As she tried to hang the keys, the rack fell away, just like before,
and clattered to the wooden floor. She heard her father grunt, and
the creak of the chair as he jumped up. A moment later he was in
the doorway, staring at her.

'What's going on? You can't go out this late.'

She gave him a look like he was being an imbecile. 'I know,
Dad. Why would I be going out in the woods this late anyway?
I was taking a photo of the House Rules for a joke I'm sending
someone. Calm down. How come Mum isn't downstairs?'

She knew that question would get rid of him. He mumbled
something she didn't catch and went back into the living room.

*'Ill be there see you soon wrap up n keep that body warm 4 me.'*

It had started to rain outside. But that text from Donna made
her smile. She went back into the living room to try to kill time:
113 minutes until the 2 a.m. rendezvous. Dad was still giving
that thousand-yard-stare, but he didn't look sleepy yet. He was
probably thinking about the argument with Mum and worried
about this Dominic Everton guy.

'I'm going to bed,' she said. 'It'll be worse if you stay down here
and Mum wakes in the night alone. In this place.'

She went to her room, closed the door and put her ear to it.
Beautifully, her warning had worked and she heard him head up
the stairs. Then enter the main bedroom. Then shut the door.

Then nothing, except the rain battering the house.

Julia quietly got dressed and sat on her bed to count the minutes down.

*

Rose's phone was on the pillow, trailing earphones to her head. He could hear the tinny rasp of her audiobook. The light illuminated her face, making her look beautiful as well as ravaged by anxiety. He hated himself for what she had been through. Was still going through.

He slipped into the bed, naked, and close to her. She was turned away, wearing pyjama bottoms but no top. Warm. As he snuggled up, slowly, carefully, she grunted. He put a hand on her hip.

'There's something I can't get out of my mind about Eve,' Rose said softly.

Chris slid a few inches away from her, worried.

'In America. September 24th, 2000. Your holiday, when you met her. You said, being with her, you didn't mind missing Michael Schumacher win the World Championship. But he didn't win it in America. He won it in the next race, in Japan, with one race to go. Carol's husband said that. I looked. He's right. Japan is eight hours ahead of us, so an early afternoon there would be the middle of the night here. You got your races mixed up. What was in the envelope, Chris?'

'What's wrong, Rose?' But he had a feeling he knew exactly what was wrong.

'The eighth of October 2000. That was the date of the Japanese Grand Prix. That was two weeks after your America holiday. A week after we conceived Julia. The same day I told you I suspected I was pregnant. What was in the envelope, Chris?'

'A chain,' he said, sitting up. 'Just a necklace chain. You saw it. I don't understand what you're saying, Rose.'

She remained turned away. 'You were with Eve when Michael Schumacher won the World Championship. Katie's Facebook even confirmed it: the eighth of October. The second time, when you gave her a false name again. After me. *After* Julia. You were there. With her. This was in the envelope.'

Her right hand, buried beneath her right flank, came up and deposited something on her left shoulder. In the light from the phone, he saw it was a tiny silver book, an inch high, with hinges and letters in bas relief saying 'OLIVER TWIST'. It was open and he could see a little tuft of white. The corner of the slip of paper bearing a phone number, torn away when he pulled it free.

'It's tacky silver junk. It could have been your anniversary gift to me.' That line was dripping with sarcasm.

'Rose, listen—'

'I remember that locket on a necklace you had when I met you. Found it, you said. Gave it to a friend, you said, when it was gone. But it was gone because you gave it to Eve Levine while you fucked her as men raced around a racetrack. While I sat waiting for you with Julia in my belly.'

# CHAPTER FORTY-SIX

'We used protection in America. Eve left her necklace behind by accident. The hotel we booked for the afternoon returned it to my hotel later that night, after I'd said goodbye to Eve. Neither of us knew where the other was staying, so I kept it. I started wearing it. Yes, a week later, when I met you, I told you I'd found it in America.

'Then a week after that, I bumped into Eve in Sheffield. A bar was staying open late to show the Japanese Grand Prix, and we were both fans, and she was there. We drank all night because the TV was showing scenes from before the race, like the warm-ups. It was five or six on the Sunday morning in Britain before the race, but long before then we were very drunk, too drunk to stay up. So we went to a hotel.

'She saw the necklace and I said I'd been holding it for her. She liked that. She thought I'd come to the bar just to find her, that I'd been hoping to find her and return the necklace ever since America. One thing led to another. This time we were very drunk. It was one time.

'Afterwards, we argued because I told her it was a mistake, that I was with you. And I abandoned her. Again.'

She didn't speak.

He continued, 'I'd suspected after looking online at the name of her pub, but when I saw that necklace in the envelope, I knew for certain who Eve was and that the woman who gave it to me was her daughter. And that she must be contacting me because she thought I was the father. I suspected Eve had probably made a deathbed confession. When you asked what had been in the envelope, I had to give you something, but I knew you'd recognise the locket. So when I put my hand in the door pocket for it, I ripped off the locket and showed you only the chain. I'm sorry.'

He waited for her to get out of bed, take the car, leave with Julia, abandon him here. But she didn't.

He said, 'Julia should have been born first. But she was nine days late, and Katie must have been premature by a few weeks. But I wish it had been Julia, because then you would have known the truth straight away. I wouldn't have had a chance to get caught up in this awful lie, which I'm so, so sorry about.'

Again, he waited for her to climb out of bed and begin the process that would see him abandoned here, homeless, wifeless on his anniversary, hated by his entire family.

Instead, Rose said, 'And those were the only two times you ever met her?'

'Yes,' he said, and he was glad of the darkness and that she was facing away. He didn't trust the look in his own eyes.

'In the morning you tell me everything.'

It puzzled him. 'What do you mean?'

'I found that locket in your car at the same time that I discovered your satnav, that you'd been to Louise's house. Two lies. One of those we can maybe get past. I don't know about the other. So you will tell me everything. But in the morning.'

He understood. Next to her suspicions that he had attacked someone, an ancient affair paled. 'I will. I know you were suspicious of how quiet I've been. It's just because with Katie in our lives…'

'A ripple in your neat, ordered life. I know. It's hard for you. It's hard for us all.'

'Yes. That's all it was, though. But about Louise… I—'

'Stop,' she cut in. 'I need sleep. I don't want to worry this late. Don't tell me another word.'

'I will. I'll tell you everything.' He pressed his hand harder onto her skin, just in case she couldn't feel it, and awaited a reaction. 'Are we okay? Until then? I can sleep downstairs if you want.'

Her hand lay on top of his. He waited for her to lift his, but she didn't. She left it right there on her flesh. And hers atop it. He didn't realise how tense he was until he relaxed and his head sank two inches deeper into the pillow.

In the morning. Then he would tell her the entire truth, and together they would deal with a transformed and painful future.


At ten to midnight, Julia made her exit. She chose the back door, because the key for that was left in the lock. She left the door unlocked, figuring that burglars wouldn't be skulking in the back of beyond. It was a ten-minute walk to Mr Jernigan's house, so she took the old bike in the back garden. It creaked, so she carried it to the main track before climbing on.

The going was rough because of stones and gouges from car tyres, and the rain was softening the miniature hills and valleys into muddy plains, but her adrenaline was flowing and the sweat on her skin felt good, and the rain kept her from overheating. It was a tough, long ride. She hoped Donna didn't mind a little female stink.

Mr Jernigan's house had a light on in the living room, so she decided to forego her promise to wait at the foam boulder. Instead, she continued up the track fifty metres, where she found a tree stump that made a nice seat. She laid the bike in the undergrowth and sat, holding her warm phone between both hands.

No message yet from Donna. But if she was driving, then—

A noise in the woods, behind her. The crack of still-dry wood snapping, so familiar from a thousand horror films. Someone stepping on a fallen twig. She stood and turned, and stared. The light from her phone had killed her night vision, so it took a few seconds for her eyes to make out a squat black shape against the tall, thin trees. Someone there, twenty metres away. Rain was bouncing off its shoulders.

It raised a hand, and waved. She waved back.

'Donna? Where's your car?'

Donna tripped and fell forward. Stifling a laugh, Julia moved into the woods. She had to sidestep around a tree because of a tangled foliage patch ahead, and in the instant her vision was blocked by thick black wood, Donna had got to her feet. On the ground one moment, upright the next, like a pair of images in a flick book.

'Are you okay?' Julia said, and turned her phone to illuminate her friend.

And then she tripped. She landed hard, but on twigs and sodden leaves, and it didn't hurt at all. In fact, she laughed, even though her phone skipped out of her hands.

Donna stepped closer as Julia got to her knees and reached for her bright phone.

'Well, it's not happening under the starlight,' Julia said. And she held out her hand to meet the two reaching for her.

But they didn't take her hand.

They slipped past, and grabbed her head.

'You came here for a party, little bitch-ass. So let's have one.'

The horror pulsed like something electric, something painful. Not Donna at all – that powerful grip, that rugged voice: a man.

She tried to get to her feet, and that happened easily because the figure yanked her up, but she also tried to turn and run, and that didn't work because it still had hold of her head in both hands.

One hand let go, and then she did turn, because the figure spun her. She tried to move forward, towards the track, towards freedom, but was jerked backwards instead, and then a hand clamped over her mouth.

# CHAPTER FORTY-SEVEN

One thing nobody out in the boondocks wants is a late-night noise in the house. Chris jerked into a sitting position to find Rose already awake and staring at him.

'What was that?'

'Julia,' he said aloud. He dearly hoped he was right. She'd been the only one awake when he went to bed. The good news was that he stuck his head out and saw her bedroom door wide open. The bad news was that—

'Her phone's going straight to voicemail!' He turned to see Rose with her phone at her illuminated ear.

'Maybe it's out of charge,' he said, but he knew, absolutely knew he was wrong. Rose's look said the same. Julia never put her mobile out of reach. To do so, she had once said, was like disconnecting yourself from the world. The phone hung in her pocket in the shops, lay on her pillow at night, and sat on the side of the bath while she soaked. She even had a portable charger in case it got low on juice. He had never known her to let her phone go flat. Ever. There was more chance of getting no answer from the emergency services than from Julia.

'Maybe you accidentally blocked all numbers on her phone,' Rose whispered. That calmed him a little, despite Rose's accusing tone. 'Check downstairs.'

He dressed while she slipped into a bathrobe, and they both went to the top of the stairs, in the dark. Light would have helped, but it would expose that people were awake if a stranger was in the house. Instead, he padded quietly but quickly down the stairs. Rose was right behind him.

A small window in the front door splashed a ray of moonlight onto the bottom of the stairs, and he quickly rushed through the beam as if it were burning hot. Rose, again, was right on his backside.

Down the short hall, but slower this time, dead quiet, listening for more sounds. Somehow, it was worse that there was nothing to hear. No TV, no voice, no noise of something cooking. He knew, dead centre of his thudding heart, that Julia wasn't in the house.

But someone was.

He pushed open the door to the living room and slapped the light switch, all in one movement, no pause, still moving forward.

But then he froze.

Rose crashed into him.

There was someone in black clothing sitting on the sofa, facing them, and aiming a gun.


'In the stolen car, abandoned when a fugitive attacked police with a machete on Wednesday night, there was a £20 note with a bloody fingerprint,' Chris said. 'The police traced it because it might belong to another victim. And got a match. To me. They came to see me at the hospital. But the bloody print wasn't blood. It was a dye called neutral red which is used for staining samples in the microbiology lab. On Monday I was using that dye and it put my thumbprint on that £20 note. The same note that was in my wallet when it was stolen on a dark road on Monday night. By Dominic Everton.'

The figure behind the gun said nothing. Rose, shaking her head, muttered, 'I don't understand, Chris. Please, what's going on? Where's Julia?'

'Katie's bogus father's killer, her real father, and Katie herself, by sheer coincidence all together on that sliver of the planet at that exact moment? She set it all up, Rose.'

Still Katie said nothing.

Rose looked between her and Chris, numbed by shock, by an inability to digest what she was hearing. She dropped to her knees on the wooden floor, still staring at that gun in Katie's hand. It was the detail that twisted everything into an incomprehensible mess.

'What's he saying, Katie? Is it true? Where's my Julia?'

But Katie continued her silence. She just watched, intrigued.

'Rose, all along she's been in league with the two men who killed Ron Hugill. She had Ron killed. She set up that robbery so she could play hero and get into our lives. And she sent Everton to our house tonight. We were supposed to think Everton had hurt her and that he'd come for us. But I suspect she would have arrived in the nick of time yet again. She would save us from a murderous fugitive and we'd all be together for ever, and in awe of the magnificent Katie.'

Still there was no emotion from Katie. Rose had to plant a hand on the floor to avoid crashing down dead-weight. Chris stepped forward to aid her, but in the next moment she leaped to her feet, pain ignored, and launched herself towards Katie, planning Lord knew what. In the nick of time he grabbed a trailing arm and enveloped her, holding her tightly as she struggled to be free.

'Police found our house burned down, Rose, and a body insi—'

With a wail, she went limp in his arms, instant shutdown, like a computer crashing because of overload. His mind darted back to his conversation with the police superintendent...

*I was hoping you could answer that. Who burned the house, Mr Redfern? Do you know who's lying burned to a crisp in your home?*

*Katherine Hugill. My daughter.*

Scrambled, he had been answering the superintendent's first question, not the second. Now realising he was creating the same shudder in Rose that the superintendent had felt before Chris had explained, he turned her face to his.

'It's okay, it's not family, it's Dominic Everton. When Katie found us gone, she got Everton to burn our house down. He died inside. And then she came here to hurt us. I don't know how she found us, but she did, and she's taken Julia. I'm so sorry, Rose. I brought a monster into our home, Rose. I'm sorry.'

'It's too late for apologies—' Katie started.

'Shut your mouth,' he roared over Rose's head. Putting this woman into his heart had been a sluggish affair, like wading through quicksand, but ejecting her from it took an atomic second. 'The police know everything, Katie. You're being hunted. Thin blood binds us, Katie. You are not my daughter.'

'Your own sister, you bitch,' Rose screamed at her. 'What have you done to her?'

Katie stood.

Chris stepped in front of Rose, partly to shield her, and partly in case she tried something stupid again.

'Julia went to meet a girlfriend,' Katie said. She arched her spine, as if sitting had hurt. 'A lady called Donna. Donna doesn't exist, though. A fake profile. I'm Donna. You didn't know Julia was a lesbian, did you?'

He didn't care about that. But he thought back to when Julia had knocked the key rack off the hook in the hallway. He'd seen her looking at the House Rules poster on the wall. But not actually the rules. The address and postcode for the house. To give to this Donna, so they could arrange a secret woodland meet late at night. He tried not to imagine Julia's terror when, out of the eerie blackness, Katie had appeared instead of the girl she was meeting. Her own sister, who had then attacked her and done… God knew what.

'If she's hurt, I'll kill you,' Chris said. Quietly.

'She's not hurt, but that changes if anyone tries anything. Lift the blue rug.'

The blue rug. Katie knew where the cellar was. He realised she was planning to put Rose down there. But not him. She would have something different planned for him. So he went to the rug and yanked it aside, almost eagerly. It would be dark and cold down there, but his wife would be beyond the reach of that gun.

'Open it,' Katie said. 'And help your wife down there. Don't try anything wacky.'

Rose shook her head. 'No, what's she going to do to you, Chris? No, I'm not going in there. I want Julia.'

But he threw open the trapdoor then grabbed her under the arms, hauling her to her feet. She kicked liked an abductee, but he was far too strong.

Katie seemed fascinated by the show.

'No, Chris, no, please, I can't, she'll kill you.'

'No, I'll get Julia back. She's going to take me to her.'

She still struggled, but he lifted her right off the floor and carried her. Her thrashing head caught his lip and he felt blood run over his chin. But he didn't pause. Across the room. Down the cellar stairs. Into a black hole as cold as deep space. All the while, he whispered into her ear promises of a reunited family, oh so soon.

Rose's nails raked his back and shoulders as he tore free of her grip. He felt like a monster as he grabbed her painful wrists and forced them towards the pitted concrete floor, which made her fall to her knees.

'Rose, we have to. Please trust me.'

The fight in her evaporated. She collapsed onto her side, sobbing. The chilly cavern suddenly felt like her grave, as if he was entombing his wife.

But he had to.

What little light seeped in from above was blocked as Katie appeared at the top of the stairs, just a silhouette aiming a gun.

'Get out of there, and lock the trapdoor.'

He kissed the side of Rose's head, swept her hair off her face and pulled her dressing gown tight around her for warmth. She continued to sob, staring dead ahead, at nothing.

'Everything will be okay, I promise. The next time that trapdoor opens, you're going to see Julia standing there. Both of us. I swear.'

Now she looked at him. He wasn't confident of his promise, but his resolve took a boost by the belief in her wet eyes.

'I love you with everything I have,' he told her.

And then he buried her alive.

# CHAPTER FORTY-EIGHT

The cellar… something about the cellar… but he couldn't place it.

He knelt on the trapdoor, creating an additional barrier between Katie and Rose. But Katie ordered him into the kitchen. And he went. The further he was from Rose, the less chance she would hear the gunshot that killed him.

She followed him into the dark and flicked on the light.

'If you won't tell me where Julia is, please tell me if she's hurt?'

'Sit at the far end of the table.'

Chris took the seat she indicated. Katie took the chair opposite. As she sat, she blocked his view of the cellar trapdoor in the living room. He could finally focus on the woman. She looked pasty, and tired. The eyes were blank. No, cold. On TV, *cold* was a popular description of the eyes of psychopaths by their victims.

She laid the gun down on the oak, but kept her finger on the trigger. The barrel pointed across eight feet, right at Chris's gut. She ordered him to put his hands on the table. Something wildly optimistic inside him clenched them into touching fists, creating a barrier across the bullet's path.

'Is my Julia hurt?'

'She's not dead, if that's what you mean. I told you that.'

'I should believe a single word that comes out of your face, that's what you think?'

'Antagonising someone with a gun is good, that's what you think?'

'I think you're dead inside. I think you have a plan and it doesn't matter what names I call you.'

She gave him a thumbs up. 'There's a chance you could do something heroic and save Rose, because she's right here. Just over there, well within reach. But not Julia. You don't know where she is and it's going to stay that way until I've shown you what I want you to see.'

Unable to rend flesh from bones, Chris wanted to spit and curse, but he knew that would only waste time. 'What do you want to show me?'

'It's not here. We need a short journey. But once you've seen, I'll let you all go. Go free. Just like that. How's that sound?'

'Is this about Ron Hugill? He was the man who abused you, wasn't he? You slipped up when you said the abuse happened after Ron got with your mother, and you had to give that lie about her having other boyfriends. Ron abused you, and when you found out he wasn't your father, you decided it would be fine to kill him in revenge. Using Everton.'

Katie took time over her answer. 'The storm in here,' she tapped her head, 'is there to stay. I didn't have a home. I wasn't a daughter. It was a prison. I was a prisoner.'

'I can't imagine how you must have suffered.'

'Obviously, with your perfect family. But it wasn't physical abuse. Mental abuse leaves eternal scars.'

The act of sympathy became ever-harder as Chris said, 'I know. Katie, you need help for—'

'One time, though, when I was eleven, I did get hurt, and I was glad. Finally, it was out of my hands. Teachers would see bruises. I was ready to tell everything. I told the story over and over in my head, and I practised it in the mirror. It became like a scene from a novel. I rewrote it and rewrote it, for maximum tension, for intrigue, all those things writers do when they tell a scene. I was eager to tell the story. I couldn't wait. It would be the end of all my problems.'

Katie closed her eyes. Chris had to placate a sudden urge to pounce across the table, to snatch that gun. If he failed...

'I moved four feet through the black, knowing where to step to avoid pits in the brick floor. I felt out for a switch and flicked it. Nothing happened. The cellar light had blown. From high above, muted by brick, came that voice again. "I know you're down there! I heard you down there!"

'A sick feeling in my stomach at that voice again. My hand slipped off the wall into a hole that sucked me in. For all my memories of this dark place, I forgot the corner where I'd played so many times. Minus toys, I had had to improvise. The cellar was my alien world, always dark because there was no sun, the corner my spaceship. As I fell, my head hit the old fireplace and I dropped to my knees onto the broken pieces of an old radio.

'My head swam for a moment. Black dots darker than the cellar exploded in my vision like bloated raindrops striking a window. Then another shout from an alien monster cut through the gloom, through the endless ticking of expanding and contracting pipes, which was a symphony I came to love, even need.

'Before, I had twisted and linked the wires of that radio in an attempt to repower the engine of my spacecraft and blast off from this cold, dark, desolate planet; now, I huddled and hoped the beast in the atmosphere above didn't find me. I grabbed the wires, hoping to restart the engine and fire off from this world, and to burn up the beast in my fiery jets. I had patience, though, because I had spent hours and hours here, over days and days, cramped, aching, pain everywhere, but never giving up, never condemning myself to a life alone, lost, abandoned here on this planet.

'Then the throbbing in my injured head faded, to be replaced by growing fear. The spaceship dissolved, too, and I was back in the cellar, in a recess that had once been home for a fireplace. The dream had been replaced by a living nightmare.

'"I know you're down there!" came the voice again, slurred by alcohol. Light flooded my dark world as the cellar door was yanked open. The monster stepped into the light washing the steps, crouching to be seen…'

Chris remembered when Katie was in the Manor, his attic hideaway, and telling this same story to herself. But not practising it. Reliving. Maybe punishing herself given the way she had tried to painfully fold herself up in the chair. Like a form of exorcism. Chris had ignored this very succinct warning sign. Until it was far too late.

Katie's eyes flicked open and blinked rapidly, like those of someone jerked from sleep. There was more to the story, but she looked at him a little fearful, as if worried because she'd momentarily forgotten that she had a real enemy before her. He saw her relaxed fingers tighten again on the gun.

'Of course, I was kept off school, kept locked away. Until the bruises faded and no one would believe my story.'

'And your mother never knew? Is that why you had Ron killed? Once you knew he wasn't your father, that bond was gone? There was nothing to stop you, no reason not to. I can understand that. You couldn't forgive. But fathers can forgive their children a lot. Maybe we can get over this, Katie.'

Katie took out her phone, pressed a couple of buttons and slid the device across the table.

It smacked his knuckles and sat there. He didn't want to touch it.

But touch it he did. It was part of her plan, and antagonism was wasted time.

She watched him carefully, clearly eager to see his reaction to what was on the phone.

It was a video. As he pressed the play button, he thought about Katie's cellar story. And the cellar entombing his wife.

The video was of Eve Levine, to camera, just her. Still ragged, clearly ill, but more kosher than in the suicide video. And dressed as if for a day outdoors. An earlier moment. She was in the bed surrounded by dolls again, but this time they were whole, unbroken, sweet. No one had yet taken offence.

The video started. Eve was pointing something at the camera. She squinted at the lens, nodded and put aside the thing in her hand. Small, black. A remote for the camera. She was aware that the machine had started filming. She spoke directly to it. She took a doll from the bed and cradled it in her hands.

'I'll come right out with it. Ron's not your dad. He knows he's not. We met when you were about one. He helped to take some of the load. Lord, I always said you were a handful, but before he came around it was so much worse. I didn't tell him about you at first, when we met, but in the end I had to. He seemed fine with it. He came into the house and he accepted you. Not love, of course. Nobody's ever loved you, have they? A freak like you, how could they? Not even a sweet man like Ron could really love you, and so what does that say about you? Pathetic, and horrible. A waste of space. A lunatic. What does it say about me that I could give birth to such an animal? Donkey killer!'

At the end, she became so animated, so angry, that spit dribbled down her lips. Or maybe it was because of the cancer storm raging beneath her skin. She wiped her lips, composed herself, and continued.

'Here is the evidence of your real father,' she patted a scrapbook by her side. 'He's a man with insight, that one. Maybe he knew what kind of freak his daughter would be. He did what I wish I'd done years ago and abandoned you. He wanted nothing to do with you. Maybe there was something rotten inside him and he knew it would be in his daughter, too. Anyway, here's the evidence. I'll be gone by the time you get this video. I don't want my final days to be ones with you around. If you want someone to lash out at, lash out at your real father. He provided the seed of your warped mind. Maybe he's a raving weirdo like you and you can live in the loony bin together. He made me this way, by the way. He did it by leaving me alone with you. I hate you because you're his. Goodbye, donkey killer.'

Offscreen, a noise. A door burst open. Katie's voice.

'I heard it all. You think I didn't suspect something as soon as you asked where the video camera was? So you want to leave? You want to be free?'

Katie stepped in front of the camera, blocking most of its view. Only her back and upper legs showed. She snatched the doll from Eve's hands and tore the head off in one quick motion. Then she turned to the camera, giving a brief look at her face, which was a bizarrely calm blue sky despite the black storm of her words. There was a crashing sound, and the picture flipped and went off.

Chris's senses reeled from this hammer blow. He willed himself to disbelieve it, but it was impossible.

'It wasn't Ron at all. Ron didn't abuse you. It was your mother. But you blamed him. Was this because your mother was dying? You couldn't bring yourself to blame her but you had to lash out at someone. Was that the real reason you had Ron murdered?'

'Keep watching,' was Katie's reply.

Within seconds another video was playing. This one he'd seen before. Chris found himself again watching Eve Levine's suicide. Surrounded by broken dolls, all Katie's work, he now knew. But this time something was different.

This time there was audio.

# CHAPTER FORTY-NINE

Nineteen pills.

Eve flicks a glance to her left, beyond the camera, something there having caught her attention. A pause. Something happening behind that camera. A noise. Loud. A door crashing open, maybe under a foot. Katie coming into the room, but not into shot. A grunt of annoyance clearly picked up by the camera.

Last night, on the bridge, Katie had said: 'This is where I asked her if there was anything I could do for her.'

But what she actually said on camera was: 'Do you need me to ram those pills down your throat with a knife?'

A pause, and then Eve's mouth moves. 'No.'

Twenty-one pills.

Eve puts her face in her hands, and he can see her jaw moving. More words, spoken into her palms. Not a yawn, as he first suspected. Words, the last of which is uttered as she lifts her face to the camera.

According to Katie: 'She shouted at me and made me promise: will I promise she'll be in Heaven with Ron?'

But what Eve shouts on camera is: 'Why did you have to kill Ron?'

'Because I'm the monster you created, remember?' Katie responds. 'A beast from your belly. Now eat those pills.'

And a mere few seconds after that, when twenty-four pills are gone, she appears to speak again.

According to Katie: 'I hope he accepts me.'

But on the video, Katie says: 'Hurry up and die. And don't you worry, Ron won't be rotting alone. The other will pay for what he did. But for me, not for you. He'll pay for me.'

Eve's response is: 'And his whole family.'

And then, at thirty pills, again just a few seconds later, she jerks her eyes to a point past the camera, to Katie.

According to Katie: 'I told her I already missed having a father.'

But the camera tells a different story: 'Nearly there. Nearly time for you to leave. And look at me, look at me! Like that, yes. So look at your legacy. I am a beast from your belly. Alone, I survive and thrive, and I am unstoppable. I am a tornado of destruction that you unleashed, and I will destroy anything that hurts me or ever tried to in this life or a thousand before it.'

And Eve's response, her final captured utterance in this life: 'Let's hope you find your real father then.'

When the video ended, Chris needed a second to recalibrate, to remember where he was. The overwhelming danger came back hard, like a meteor strike in his core. It created an instant hot flush. And a sense of disbelief.

'You forced your mother to kill herself. Because she abused you.'

'For as long as I can remember, the only thing I wanted was to watch her die. I wanted to be there. I needed that. I was a small, weak child but it didn't stay that way, did it? I got bigger and stronger. She got older and weaker. I could have killed her. I could have crushed her skull probably. But I didn't want that. I wanted to see the woman turn old and weak and fade, while I got big and strong and watched.'

'I understand your resentment, but my family—'

'Donkey killer, that was what she called me. Not Katie. Oh, she could have been something, Eve. She could have been in those African countries, working in animal sanctuaries, preventing donkeys from being worked to death, but instead I was born. She could have saved those poor animals from having their skins turned into medicine for the rich Chinese middle classes, but I came along. She could have put a stop to donkey torment for fun in America. But I had the breath of life, selfish old me. So thousands of donkeys were tortured or worked to death, and it was all my fault. I killed them all. She even wanted to flee to the donkey sanctuary in Devon, to offer help in her final days, but I stopped that, too. Although that one was my choice, and something I never regretted. Not once.'

'Katie, please, listen to—'

'You know who's getting the money from the sale of the Blue Swan? The donkeys. That's who she left it to. That's what she told me after Ron was gone. That place should have been mine. Didn't know that, did you?'

'I know you've been living there since your mother died. After you fled from Baldwin House, the homeless shelter. Not at some phantom flat. I saw you inside.'

He expected surprise at what he knew, but she responded without missing a beat. 'I have been living there, you're right. Once I hit adulthood at sixteen, Eve threw me out. I claimed I had a flat, but it was a lie. I continued to visit Ron at the pub, always when it was busy so I didn't have to endure the presence of her near me, but when I left to go home, I simply sneaked back inside after closing time and slept in the cellar. I did that for a long time. Even after Eve got ill and they stopped trading as a pub, I sneaked inside every night to sleep. But Ron started to spend time late at night clearing out furniture from the bar in preparation for selling the place, and he nearly caught me. After that, yes, I did settle into a homeless shelter.'

'I feel for you, Katie, I really do, but—'

'But after Ron got killed, I left Baldwin House and once again started sleeping at the Swan,' Katie continued, as if she hadn't heard him. 'Eve was alone and too ill to come down to investigate noises. So I wasn't there alone. It wasn't me you saw through the window. It was Everton. That's where he's been holed up. He had to hide when you appeared. He told me it took great willpower not to kill you right there.'

Chris's throat closed up at the thought that he'd been standing just metres from Everton, a man who had planned his murder. And the thought of Eve sleeping in the room above the man who'd killed her lover. In Katie's eyes was clear enjoyment at the shock she'd injected into his blood. 'Katie, please, Julia is—'

'You made me diverge,' she cut in with a tut. 'She worked out how much money she'd spent on me. Nappies, food, medicines, clothing. Over the years. All worked out, like some audit. Written down, added up. Thousands of pounds. I owed it all back. And I paid her. I paid her whatever I had. I worked the bar as a young teenager, and I worked a building site once I'd left school, and I fixed computers. And I paid her back. She wanted it all. I owed her money for nappies. You believe that?'

'I do, Katie. Hell on earth. But Julia—'

'But then she tried to run. Run and die in some silly donkey sanctuary. Die in comfort, where *she* wanted, and deny me the one thing *I* always wanted. No. It was going to be my way. Well, I got right on it after that. Don't you understand that?'

He did, but he didn't care. Yet he knew he stood a better chance of getting to Julia, and freeing Rose, if he pushed Katie to the end of this purging.

'So you murdered her. But Ron did nothing to you, yet you had him killed, too. Why?'

Katie was on a track she wouldn't be deflected from. 'I did consider going to the funeral. I know they preserve the bodies, but there would have been some sort of decay, surely. That would have been nice to see. Real, physical fading away. But I couldn't go. I couldn't have her black soul thinking I cared. All that crap I spurted in the car on the way to the funeral, I felt none of that. I don't want you thinking I cared, either. That was just a bunch of lines and quotes from soulful idiots that I found on the Internet. That funeral trip was an act, just like when I went to Ron's funeral. Different reasons, though. I went to Ron's funeral to pretend I cared. But Friday's sham was just to get your speech. I wanted to hear what you thought about her. To see if you mentioned me. That, I did care about.'

'You murdered Ron, Katie, and now you want to kill me and my family. To pay for what I did. But what did I do? What did Ron do?'

Katie's eyes had been hazy, ethereal as she flicked back time, but they quickly refocussed. 'Nothing. Ron did nothing. Literally. He allowed that evil bitch's lie to perpetuate. Pretending to be my father when he wasn't, he perpetuated the stinking life I had. If I'd known about you, I could have come to you as a child. Instead I was sentenced to a hell existence with that bitch. Because of him. And because of you.'

'You blame me because I didn't stay with your mother? You think I somehow condemned you to a horrible life. That I made you end up feeling so alone?'

'No. Very much no. Alone, I survive and thrive.'

'Then what? You wormed your way into my house to get close enough to kill me, you sick bastard. Was that your plan?'

'No, you should have died the same night as Ron.'

That threw him.

Katie stroked her chin, as if calculating how much to reveal. 'The same night they killed Ron, Dominic Everton and his friend drove to your house. Dominic was still lusting after blood. He was still lusting after me. Funny what a guy will do for a pretty face. I sought out a wild animal to do my bidding, and he was tamed in no time. They were coming to kill you…'

Chris could almost see the processes occurring in Katie's rotting brain. She had killed Ron, for the lie, and she had forced her mother into suicide, for the abuse. Two parts of the triangle down. The final piece: Chris Redfern, the father who'd abandoned her, who'd caused it all by condemning Katie to a life of abuse, to a rotting mind, to pulverised dreams.

Except…

'But they messed it up. There you were, slippers and coffee, enjoying your comfortable sofa, sixty seconds from a grisly end… and they crashed the car into a fence just down the street. They had to abort. You don't know how close you came.'

The Swifts' fence busted by a stolen car late at night. The same night that Ron Hugill had died. Killers with Chris's blood in mind, but a freak accident had saved his life. But they could have tried again, and again, and again, the next night, or the next.

Except…

'Even as they were coming for you, I wondered if I had rushed into this. So that failure, it made me think. I didn't know you, so maybe I was being rash. I even wondered if maybe, possibly, we could have a life together after all. As a family. So I decided to give you a chance. I spared you. I spared your family. I gave you a chance to prove that I might mean something to you.'

'And you do. You do, but Julia—'

'No, I didn't, Chris. I didn't mean anything to you at all. Did you really think I posted that note through your door as part of some silly idea to give you big news piecemeal? No, no, no. That was a test. If Eve had meant anything to you, you would have considered that daughter of hers, conceived right around the time you were together with her. And you would have searched for her. You would have found her on Facebook. I created a profile the very day I spared your life. I mentioned exactly where and when I was conceived. If I had mattered to you, you would have made the connection from the note and would have sent a message immediately. But you didn't. Because I didn't matter…'

His voice started to fade as Chris retreated inside himself. But not for security, not like Simone Baker withdrawing behind the walls of a protective cocoon. Instead, he locked himself away like an artist who needed solitude to create, to think…

'But even then, I gave you another chance. Maybe you hadn't read the article correctly. Maybe your Facebook account was down. So, after I'd got the sham of Ron's funeral out of the way, I decided to introduce myself to you. I still held the idea that… maybe we could even become a family after all, a new family after all this time.'

'And we still can.' He leaned forward, staring at the lunatic across the oak table. 'We can get over this. I know you're just angry, not thinking straight. There's a chance for us, because you are my daughter and blood is thicker than water. But Julia is your sister, Katie. Part of the family. Why would you want a family without her? Please tell me where she is.'

The words almost burned on his tongue. The whole thing was like vomiting broken glass.

Katie said, 'Julia is too like me. Adult, same height, same knowledge of the adult world. She even likes bikes. She would be like another me. Two of us. Split affection. She's a challenge, being another adult child. I can't have that. No, no.'

'Katie, fathers can forgive children almost anything. But not for Julia. Not if you hurt Julia. Do you understand? Where is she? She has to come back if you want to become part of this family. And be loved.'

He felt he'd overdone it with the last line, but Katie sat back in contemplation. Or suspicion. 'I planned to let Julia live a while, you know. Then she would have an accident. Maybe a year in or so. But then Julia told me about Benign Violation Theory.'

Where was this going? 'Katie, please, where is she? Let me take Rose out of the cellar and—'

'Thirty-six days, those researchers said. For someone to overcome tragedy. To see the funny side of that tragedy. I thought the death of Julia might have a lasting effect, until I looked into that BVT a little more. Thirty-six days. Well, I got right on it after that. Little more than a month, and we could be a normal family with Julia gone. That can still happen. Can you suffer for thirty-six days?'

Now he knew where this was going and it chilled him. But he remained outwardly calm. 'You're talking about a car crash or a house that falls down, Katie. Not murder. Not my daughter. I can't forget that. Can't forgive it. That wound can't heal. If you want me to accept you, you can't kill my daughter. You can't hurt any of us. Do you understand? If you want me to accept you, I can. I will. But only if my family is released, unhurt. All of them. Your stepmother and your sister. Please understand that that's the only way. Where's Julia?'

'We'll double it and add a few days. Call it three months. Three months, Chris, and you'll be over her. Those scientists know what they're talking about. I bet after three months we could even joke about it. How does that sound?'

'I would never get over it, Katie. Where is she? Think about this, please. Don't hurt…'

Something Katie had said ignited in his brain. An admission of planning to murder her mother: *Well, I got right on it after that.* But she'd used the same line shortly afterwards. About Julia.

Praying he was wrong, Chris asked her, 'Did you try to kill Julia? Before today?'

'Of course,' Katie said, looking at Chris as if he was being dumb. 'Yesterday morning, Everton was five seconds from crushing Julia to death with his car, but fate intervened there, too. The BVT process should have already started. But your recovery is going to be delayed by half a day.'

He tried to remain calm – outwardly. 'Where is my daughter, Katie?'

'Mind you, it's lucky for all that you ran today. The plan sounded so good. This evening, Everton was supposed to storm your wedding anniversary in the pub and kill her. I couldn't be there for that, because Everton might have given the game away by how he acted around me. And I didn't trust myself to give a good performance of shock and terror. So I dumped my bike and pretended Everton had got to me. I would be found the next morning, unhurt. While you grieved for Julia on day one of thirty-six, you'd also care for me, your hurt and terrified new daughter. It seemed like a good plan, but I wasn't thinking straight. Seeing your Julia *slaughtered* in front of you? Christ, that could take *six months* to get over. Half a day extra I can manage, but not an extra three months.'

Chris closed his eyes. It made it easier to deal with the clearly psychopathic animal facing him. 'But she's alive, Katie. That's all that matters. We can be a family again, all of us. You can experience real love, which you never have. It's the best feeling in the world, Katie. Having someone to care about, and knowing others care about you, is something special. I pity those who don't have love in their lives. You will come to love Julia like a sister. I say again: fathers can forgive their children almost anything. It's not too late. But only if Julia is released unharmed.'

'Fathers forgive their children, you say?'

'Of course. Wholeheartedly yes. And we can help you, Katie. I know what you told Julia. About all those things you think you have wrong with your body. And we can get you help for that.'

'Fathers trust kids, believe their word, even if evidence points the other way?'

'Katie, listen to me. You need help, and as a family we can get it for you. The pain in your neck and back, the tingling in your hands and feet, and that metallic taste in your mouth. It's not circulation, you're right, and, it isn't about a lack of vitamins. But you were wrong, too. It isn't bits of your body falling into your hands and feet from some bouncy ball you swallowed. You spent hours cramped in that cellar, in pain. Chronic pins and needles, Katie, from day after day of bending your neck and spine too much. Chronic neuron and nerve damage, that's all it is. We can help you treat that. We can treat you for everything that's wrong. Including in your mind. The things you told Julia, they're symptoms of mental illness, Katie. Your mind needs help as well as your body. We can fix it all.'

Again, Katie ignored what was being laid on the table. 'Do fathers also give kids the benefit of the doubt?'

'Yes, Katie. I promise. We can be that family you always craved. We can get you help, to make you better, comfortable. Help with your mind, and your body. An end to the pain. But Julia's pain has to end, too. You have to tell me where—'

Katie slammed the table with her hand. It was the first piece of real emotion he'd ever seen in the girl, and it was neon bright, as if a long build-up had burst a dam.

'*How stupid do you think I am?*' she screamed. 'After Julia, after I admit about Ron and Eve, you still try that bullshit? But you're missing one vital point, Chris. You've already showed your hand. You ran from me. Again. You could have had doubts about that stupid £20 note thing. You could have sought my version of the story. Benefit of the doubt? Remember how I gave you the benefit of the doubt when all the evidence pointed to you as the man who attacked that woman you work with, Louise? You didn't give me the benefit of the doubt, or forgiveness, Chris. Instead, you did what you did the first time, all those years ago. You ran. We should have been having family bonding time right now, but you dumped me. I even killed Everton to make you think he'd perished by accident when he burned your home. Still you didn't try to reach out to me. With Everton gone, you were supposed to think the threat was over and come home, to try to find your missing brand-new daughter. But you continued to hide. You didn't give me the benefit of the doubt. You've proved you don't want me, and it angers me that you're trying this trick now, playing on my emotions. On my desires. It's too late. By eighteen years it's too fucking late.'

The rage on Katie's face hit Chris like frigid water, and he was more fearful than ever for Julia, for Rose, for himself.

'Do you know what I did for you, Daddy? I found that old army buddy friend of your father's. I gave him a letter that I wrote for you, to give to your father. Because I wanted you to bond with him again. But look how you repay me.'

Katie gave him a smile. Big, and wide, and obviously fake, like every single other he'd ever seen split her face. 'Don't be so shocked by my act. I, this empty shell you created, can pretend when I need to. It would seem I inherited acting abilities from you, too, given the bogus emotion you showed when eulogising my bitch mother. The Internet, as you well know, is beautiful for researching cliched endearing terms and when to use them.'

His shock had been at her admission of trying to help him reconnect with his father, not the flash change in her temperament. But he would never admit that. 'You're no empty shell, Katie. You're packed with corruption, stripped of everything humanly good. I tried to reason with you, but I might as well tell a lion not to kill. So what happens now? You kill us all right here?'

'Maybe I should. I'm sure you'd kill me if you had the gun.'

Chris shook his head. 'No. You're my daughter, monster or not. I don't want to see your name on a headstone. But you should be locked up for the rest of your life. You're a danger to the world.'

From her reaction, Chris could see that Katie didn't know how to react to this news, that he retained a level of care for his daughter still, despite what had happened between them. Then she shook it off, like casting away a daydream.

'You would be dead already if I wanted it. Nobody will die if you do what I say. I just want to show you something. Something that will prove to you that I was right to kill Eve. You might even wish you'd done it yourself. There's something nobody bar me in the whole world knows about that woman. We're going to the old guesthouse down the road. And then I will set you all free. No more darkness.'

Darkness. He thought of the cellar again. And this time something finally clicked into place.

'Okay,' Chris said.

# CHAPTER FIFTY

'You agreed so easily, Daddy. A trick planned, perhaps?' Katie said, watching him carefully across the table.

The denial was right at the edge of his lips, ready to plummet out, but he stopped himself. There was no guarantee that Katie's cesspool brain was up for rational thinking. She could kill him in one second and regret it the next. So when the gun was lifted and aimed at his skull, he made a strange decision.

'Maybe. Perhaps there's a weapon in the guesthouse.'

Katie thought long and hard. Chris waited for the irrational bullet. But Katie lay the gun down again. Flat on the table, not aimed anywhere lethal, but her hand remained on it. On that trigger. Bad news was still only one second away.

'And when you've shown me this thing, what then?'

'You'll never see me again. I'll be out of here. Unfortunately, you won't get your wish to see me behind bars.'

Chris doubted that very much – the first part of Katie's claim – but he nodded.

Again, Katie thought for a long time. Maybe she was visualising her plan, playing it out dream-like in her head, seeking holes and fragile sections and testing responses to whatever tricks Chris might have in store. Or maybe she was simply battling against the black neurons in her brain that preferred the fire and brimstone scenario of killing everyone. Chris could only wait. It seemed like an eternity.

There was a scary moment when Katie swapped the gun into her other hand, because he got the wild idea that she was removing the weapon from a limb she didn't trust, couldn't control.

But then she stood and said, 'Any wacky trickery at all, I kill your wife and Julia. Let's go.'

*

They exited Wooderland, out of the warmth and into the chilly rain. She'd walked out behind him, but now moved past and got in the back of the Mondeo, leaving him standing there, as if unconcerned that he might run. Maybe she just hated rain.

With Rose imprisoned and Julia's location in Katie's head alone, running was no option. So Chris got behind the wheel. Katie shifted into the middle of the rear seat and told him to turn the interior light on and twist the rear-view mirror so that they could see each other. In that moment, Chris heard once more the ticking of Katie's clock, which stayed with her always. That rhythmic pulse, echoing the noise of old water pipes back in that cellar long ago. Maybe, like her old story relived in the Manor, the clock kept the memories constant, thus becoming another form of self-punishment. Or it was a sort of lullaby, to tranquilise vibrating nerves. But it was the last thing that mattered right now.

The moment Chris started the engine, the satnav kicked into life and displayed his recent journey history. In a flick of the eyes, like Rose hours earlier, he noted the entry for Louise's house. It had the number two next to it. Twice the satnav had been ordered to go there.

'And don't even consider the old crashed-car-sudden-stop-trick, Chris. If we survive, I'll come right back here and make Rose suffer in a way that will make hardened detectives puke.'

The satnav had made two journeys to Louise's house. The first had been during his failed trip to bury the hatchet, because he'd had to input the postcode. The second? That was now terrifyingly obvious.

Later that night, when Katie had left the house on her bike.

'You attacked Louise,' Chris rasped. He knew now why Katie had fixed the washing machine that same night. It was to wash her bloody clothing. And he remembered the toolbox item that Rose had discovered missing. 'With my hammer.'

She didn't even consider denial. 'The police were right. She did open the back door for me. No threat, another woman. I apologised for you, by the way. I told her you felt bad. But the silly bitch-ass was mean to my dad, wasn't she? What kind of daughter would stand for that?'

Chris could hardly believe his ears. A woman who had wanted him dead had then been prepared to kill to protect him. And now the circle had closed. 'Yet here we are,' he said.

'You're all mine, aren't you? What business does anyone else have to hurt you? Besides, that was when I thought there was a chance for us. Before you abandoned me. Again.'

Chris shut down, reminding himself, once again, that this human-shaped animal's mind was rotten.

He felt in the driver's door pocket for the voice recorder. He'd taken it from his toolbox the other night in order to record his conversation with Louise, just in case she tried to lie later about what he'd said. He'd chickened out of knocking her door, so hadn't needed it. But now he flicked it on, wanting a record of what Katie said.

Partly in case he needed proof for the police.

Partly so the police had evidence if Chris and his family suddenly vanished off the earth.

He set it to record and tossed it under the seat. Then he put his eyes on the road. And drove into the unknown.

# CHAPTER FIFTY-ONE

The car slowly rolled past Ocean.

'You feel sorry for Eve? You think I'm a monster?' Katie asked, glaring. 'You don't know the suffering I went through. My burns? They were down to her. Yes, I developed a habit of setting fire to things, but how do you think Eve dealt with that? Professional help? She locked me in the bathroom, which was all tiles, no paper, no towels, every time I got the urges. She said if I wanted to burn things, then I should burn myself.

'And I did. I couldn't help it. She made sure I burned only where my T-shirts and trousers would cover it. She marked me. Marked the lines where T-shirts and shorts would sit. Anything outside the pen lines, anything that people on the street, or at school, could see, there was hell to pay. Maybe you think she tried to burn it out of me, like that old trick of forcing a kid caught smoking to smoke until she's sick? No. She liked it. But you won't ever believe that, because you see only a sexy young woman on holiday, before the madness took her.'

Chris said nothing. He concentrated on driving. Coming here earlier, the car had bucked and jerked on solid ground. Now the land was wet and soft and the vehicle glided like a boat on water, with just as little control.

'What makes you think you can trick me, Chris? I know you plan to.'

Louise was still in his mind, and he was making room amongst the terror for anger. The correct response would be denial, but he said, 'Throw a drowning guy a straw, see what happens.'

Katie considered this veiled threat. 'Surely even a drowning man knows a measly little straw won't help?'

'I got you away from my wife, didn't I?'

Katie nodded, admitting Chris's neat little point.

But then she said, 'Guy still drowns.'

Captive and captor drove past Savannah.

'This guy might have five kids,' Katie said. 'Quintuplets all in wheelchairs, and all waiting for Daddy to get home with birthday presents and pain medication.'

A black shape had stepped out of the woods and right into their path, forcing Chris to hit the brakes. A shaggy-haired guy in ripped denim and carrying a rucksack, with a dog that squatted to do its business right in the headlights. The guy raised a hand, as if to say *Wait a minute*, as if he was walking the queen's dog on Her Majesty's land and nothing else was as important. One of the Sanderson clan, from Savannah.

Katie's message was clear. Chris could have called out for help, two on one, or three if the dog had a killer sense of loyalty towards its master. But Katie had that gun. So Chris only raised a hand in return.

The dog finished watering the ground, then dragged its owner towards the trees on the other side, and both vanished from the world and their lives.

Chris drove on.

As the Mondeo slid past Moonlight, the rain let up.

'Christmas, every year. No presents,' Katie said. 'But I got no abuse. She would leave me alone. That was my present each year. Getting left alone. In my room, just me. One day. She had to bite her tongue. Literally. There was a backlog for the next day, though. If presents or money came from relatives who never visited, then Eve got rid of them, or spent it. The only presents I got for my birthday were bags of sweets from school. One time, when I turned seven, she forgot about it and told me three days later. I had no clue. Three days! "By the way, you little shit, you were seven three days ago."'

As the car pulled up alongside Eclipse, Katie sat bolt upright.

'Stop right here. And stop looking at that guy's house in hope. He's old and was no match for me.'

In other words, don't call to him for help. Then Chris realised that Katie had used the past tense: *was*. Not an assumption, then. Katie had already learned that Mr Jernigan was no match.

'Did you kill him?'

She exited and opened the driver's door for Chris. There was no answer to the question. But she had her back to the house and didn't seem at all worried by standing in the glare of the ornate streetlamps.

Answer enough.

They trekked towards the house Chris first, Katie behind, gun between. Then alongside, down the path, into the gloom.

'Was it worth it, Daddy Dearest? You gave me up, chose this life instead. But this life, look at it now. You thought you'd be happy without me. You could have lived to a hundred, but now there's a real chance that you'll die before you reach half of that. Think about the fear Rose and Julia are experiencing. Was it worth it? You cut me out of your life and ruined mine. You expected a long life, but you cut me out and now look! Are you happy now without me?'

A memory fired a dreadful realisation that almost buckled Chris's knees. Still walking, still looking ahead, still praying that an opportunity to strike back would materialise, he found his voice. Barely.

'You tried to kill Simone Baker. It was you all along. Why?'

Again, no lie was entertained. 'You chose her over me. You were going to give her a room, and give me, your flesh and blood, nothing. That's what I was to you: nothing. You wished then, and you wish now, that you could have erased me. Turned me into, as you say, white noise, at the press of a button. Into nothing. And I didn't try to kill her, by the way. I covered the pipe in foam, just in case I lost myself.'

'You lost yourself years ago.'

Such a line could have made Katie lose herself, but by now he was well aware that her unbalanced mind was resistant to insult.

'I did envision killing *you* with each strike, though. It was a kind of release, although I'm not sure why because by then I believed I could win you over. I heard her statement about what I'd said during the attack. My words were directed at you, but she tied them into a boyfriend that she recently dumped. I wanted her to blame a man, and of course she would, but it fit so sweetly, and her ex-boyfriend was arrested. I never did want Julia to be upset by that, though. But if not for her sorrow, we would never have discovered BVT.'

Chris said nothing further. He walked on.

Katie behind.

Gun between.

# CHAPTER FIFTY-TWO

Mr Jernigan's backyard was moonlit, which didn't help. He wanted darkness because it amplified his chances of a counter attack. But Katie was too far back, able to see everything, and he knew he had to wait. But he couldn't wait long. There was something wrong, but he couldn't figure out what. He stopped and turned.

Katie stopped, too. Eight feet between them.

'You have some great trick planned to hurt me and save your family. You have the car keys. You can strike me down and get back to Rose and call the police. But what about Julia? She could be anywhere. She could be in a hole in the woods, buried alive with just a straw poking out so she can get air. Hard to see a freshly dug grave in the dark. Maybe she's whistling through the straw poking out of the ground and you could hear her that way. If you get within ten yards, that is. Could take you all night to run around these woods. Better hurry up and do your trick.'

Chris turned to face the guesthouse again, which rose before them like a giant clock ticking down. He approached the door. It was already open. Ten feet out, he recognised a familiar smell, thick, encompassing. From the walls inside, from the floor, from everywhere. He stopped again.

As did Katie. 'And here we are. Time for your trick. Better hurry in case Julia's out there somewhere, dying.'

Chris stepped into the doorway and immediately saw two petrol cans in the gloomy hallway. Now there could be no denying he'd been tricked.

Katie hadn't come here to show him something.

This was where the lunatic wanted to burn him up.

Katie ordered him up the stairs.

Chris didn't even pause.

'So willingly. You still rely on your plan, don't you? I can't wait to see it. Go in the main bedroom.'

It was to the right, but at the top of the stairs, Chris darted left. It didn't panic her, because there was no shout or thump of running feet – where could he run? She took the last few stairs casually, although she was careful to enter the smaller bedroom with an arm raised in case of a surprise blow.

No blow, but she got a surprise.

Chris was in the centre of the room, holding the bottle of lamp oil that Mr Jernigan had left on the windowsill. He flicked it, sending blue-dyed fluid towards Katie, who instinctively put up a hand and took a splash there.

Chris lifted the lighter and flicked it on.

'Now we'll go get my Julia. Turn around. Any wacky trickery, I'll put you in a living nightmare.'

She sniffed her wet hand. 'This is it? This was your great trick? To threaten me with fire?'

'Let's go, now.'

'This is the problem with the modern world, Chris.'

'Shut up and turn around.' Chris moved the lighter a little closer. But Katie didn't flinch.

'Our ability to create heat and fire-making tools, that's our problem. In parts of the world where they don't have that technology, where they have to rely on an actual flame, they've learned to accept fire. They master it at a young age, so it holds no allure or intrigue; they don't treat it like a dangerous animal, or a lethal weapon, and that means they don't fear it like we do.'

'Stop talking and take me to my damn daughter. Last chance. I swear I'll burn you up.'

At first it appeared she was slotting the gun into a pocket. But then she pulled out a lighter of her own, a cheap disposable thing. Still aiming the gun with that same hand, she touched the flame to her soaked palm, instantly setting it alight. Orange light danced in her captivated eyes.

'Fire is new life, like a newborn baby, and I adore it. The most powerful form on this planet, because there is no barrier to what it will destroy, and it never stops devouring. It is my only friend, and I do not fear it. I master it. But not you. You're in over your head. Go ahead, create that new life. We'll both be devoured. One of us will scream, and the other will laugh.'

Despite her claims, the pain soon became too much and she clapped her hand against her chest to kill the flame.

Chris took a step backwards. Katie closed the same distance.

'I know you don't fear fire, Katie. Because of this.'

Chris touched his face, drew a line. Puzzled, Katie drew the same line, but along the ragged scar on her cheek.

'Because of my heroism in a burning building?'

'I did what Julia did and searched online for the name Katie Hugill. I saw that article about the fire. Three people, cut by glass and willing to tell an on-scene reporter about their heroic attempt to get inside a building burning because of a fire that started in a storeroom.'

Katie gave a long stare, analysing. She took another step forward to match Chris's backwards one.

'That building was the Bradford branch of a go-karting club called Go-Racers, three years ago. Someone broke in on the night of that fire and took a memento, a trophy, to relive their actions long after the event. Literally: a trophy. The cause of that fire was loose nine-volt batteries and paperclips.'

For the third time, Katie chose the truth. 'It wasn't the only one. Four burned dead, and never been caught. For your home, by the way, I used the old-fashioned tealight candles left next to a curtain. A classic. And yes, I bought them for that reason. Just in case.'

Chris already knew Katie had set that fire, but it was still a thump to the chest to learn the method. To know that she had planned it for days. He took another step back, towards the wall holding the big bed. A small section of floorboard creaked under his foot.

But this time Katie didn't match it. She looked around the room. 'You know I don't fear fire, but you rushed up here for this little threat. Which means you didn't come here for a bottle of lighter fluid.'

Chris quickly bent down to remove the broken floorboard he'd stepped on. Seeing this, Katie stepped forward and aimed a kick, which missed as Chris fell back and rolled into the wall bed. He scrambled, and got to his feet out of her reach.

'I knew you'd try something else. Stand right there.' Aiming the gun, Katie knelt and yanked up the floorboard piece. She fed her hand into the hole, eyes and gun on Chris.

Seven feet away, Chris pressed himself up against the wall bed.

Katie's hand found nothing, so reluctantly, she let her eyes have a try.

The moment she looked down at the hole in the floor, Chris took a step forward then launched himself backwards, hard into the wall bed. Over the thud of his flesh hitting the solid iron base, there was a click. A lock disengaging. He jumped aside as the great slab groaned and started to topple.

But it moved only an inch, maybe two, and one corner stopped dead, still engaged by a catch. The other shivered as free as a bird. In the next second, something snapped with a pinging sound. And gravity got its moment to create, as Mr Jernigan had said, a scene from an *ol' silent comedy fillum*.

But that one-second delay had given Katie all the time she needed to fathom the danger and dart aside. Fast as a kicked cat, she rolled out of the bed's shadow, beyond its crush zone.

The giant bed thundered down, slicing between them, and slammed into the floor with a thunderclap. The legs knifed through ruined floorboards like blades into butter, and the base connected hard enough to create a wide laceration in the floor. The whole world seemed to shudder. Then there was silence. They faced each other across the bed. The rolling motion had snapped the elastic band holding her hair in a bun and blonde waves lay across her face and shoulders.

Piercing eyes spiked him through the curtain.

'You'd do this to your Julia and Rose? Just as I always knew. You're no father.'

She raised the gun.

# CHAPTER FIFTY-THREE

What happened next was quick, like a tumbling house of cards.

It started with mighty snapping sounds beneath Chris's feet, too thick and meaty to be simple floorboards breaking. Immediately the laceration under the footboard expanded. The floor instantly fell away from the break point, like water down a plughole, spreading outwards as giant cracks became fissures. Like breaking ice. Broken floorboards vanished out of sight, and whole floorboards tipped away. A giant opening, like a sinkhole, exposed the kitchen below. The floor seemed to melt away right under Katie's feet and she was sucked down with a scream, disappearing between snapped joists.

As the world fell away beneath Chris, he grabbed the footboard, digging his nails in. The bed continued past ninety degrees, past 9 o'clock, forcing stubborn floorboards to bend or snap free. It jerked to a stop at 8 o'clock and a mechanism connecting it to the wall gave a loud shriek, but held.

Chris slipped into the void and felt his arms almost wrenched from their sockets as he kept a lock on the footboard. But they held, too.

Below, Katie was swamped in a lake of wood and plaster, just her right arm and head visible. Like an animal, she screamed and started to pull herself free. Chris's feet dangled just a few feet above the littered floor, and he knew Katie could reach him. With extreme effort, he hoisted himself up, over the footboard, and lay in the 'V' it created with the mouldy mattress.

But her thick hair was caught in a number of places, anchoring her. She twisted, placed her arms somewhere solid, and heaved, like doing a press-up. The effort raised her back, but bent her snared head forward. With a yell, not of pain but frustration, she got her knees under her and gave a final push, and was free.

Chris heard the sound of her hair tearing away, but not in clumps. All of it. It came away whole and he realised it was a wig, tightly glued in place. There were thick, misshapen patches of dried glue all over her bald head. She turned to him and started to get to her feet.

But her jacket was also snagged by sharp wood. She unzipped and shrugged it off and tossed it aside, with only a vest beneath it. Now, he saw the torso burns Julia had described to Rose, but so much more. The scars extended partway down her arms and stopped in a neat line around her mid-biceps. A similar neat line cut a curve of ruined flesh at the base of her throat. The giant wound resembled a T-shirt.

The burn boundaries Eve Levine had marked on her daughter so many years ago.

But Katie had found another part of her body to ravage. The patchwork of discoloured lakes and rivers across her scalp wasn't glue residue but more burn scars, with short tufts of blonde hair in the landmasses between.

In thirty seconds, she had turned from pretty girl into disfigured beast.

Katie started to kick at wood, searching, and he realised she wanted the gun. It must have slipped through a gap, under a floorboard or chunk of plaster.

She stared up at him, all rage. So she did have that emotion in her after all. But amid it she managed a frustrated laugh.

'That definitely counts as wacky trickery.'

She turned and stomped across the wood carpet, the going tough, like through deep snow. Chris looked at the bedroom doorway. The chasm between the bed and the doorway was vast, no way across the ragged, gaping hole unless Katie attempted a great leap. But Katie wasn't going for the hallway stairs, he realised. Nor was she going to attempt to haul herself up using snapped joists pointing down like gnarled old fingers. And she wasn't going for a weapon.

She was going for the back door.

Back to the cottage, for Rose. As promised. To make her suffer. To make murder detectives puke.

And Chris would never catch her in time.

Katie had to scoop aside wood to clear the back door, but she stopped and turned when Chris shouted.

'You know, I did meet you once as a baby. Your mother found me, came right into my college and confronted me. You were with her, in a pram. I wanted you. I was ready for a family. I even held you in my arms. She never told you that, did she?'

Chris saw Katie's eyes narrow as she tried to figure out if he was telling the truth. Still, she gave no reaction that she believed it; she kicked aside the last of the wood, and the door was clear.

Leaning over the footboard, Chris shouted at Katie's ravaged back, 'But I took one look into those little blue eyes of yours, and I knew.'

Deafened by her focus, Katie yanked the door open, exposing the black night beyond…

'I knew there was something out of whack in that brain, even as a one-year-old. I saw it in your eyes. I knew you were an egg that didn't cook right, Katie. So what did I do?'

She stopped, her back still to Chris. And didn't move. Torn between two decisions, with one hand still on the door and one on the frame.

'I chose to bin Sammy and try again, didn't I?'

Katie jerked backwards and slammed the door in one fluid motion.

And then she turned to face her father.

# CHAPTER FIFTY-FOUR

Katie stomped across the debris and leaped for the bed. Caught the dangling footboard, and started to pull herself up. The bed sagged, the angle widening, and Chris felt himself about to tumble off. The mechanism holding it all together shrieked again.

Lightning fast, and with shocking strength, the sinewy, light young woman hoisted her body up so that her chin raised above the footboard, even before Chris could attempt to scramble up the mattress, his plan to get high enough to be able to reach what remained of the upper floor. In the next second, Katie let go with one hand and grabbed Chris's hair. Tight, hard. The bed rocked.

She threw up her other hand. It locked around the back of Chris's neck. With no anchor on the bed, Katie fell, but her weight dragged Chris forward. His throat was forced into the top of the footboard, hard, and he felt his air immediately shut off.

And then he heard his own neck snap.

No, something behind him, higher. Another snapping sound, even above Katie's abusive yelling. The bed sagged lower. Then a final shrieking, grinding snap.

Like a clock hand, the bed cut fast downwards, eight to six, free end thudding hard into the sea of busted wood. The jolt bounced Chris off the mattress and he hit wooden water hard enough to lose the deep breath he sucked in when the pressure was removed from his throat. Ignoring the pain, he rolled and got to his knees, and he saw the bed sticking up out of the wooden sea, connected still to the frame on the upper floor by twisted tentacles of metal.

And he saw Katie trapped beneath the bed, her legs lost behind it.

She was screaming in pain, breathing rapidly, hands trying to shift the mammoth weight. Her coarse bald head was tilted back, pushed down into the busted wood so that she could watch Chris.

Chris stepped across sharp, jagged wood. Standing over Katie, he saw that the bed had crushed his daughter's hips into the floor. Staring up, shock numbing the pain, she tried to speak. It took two attempts to audibly beg for help. She didn't want to die, please, father.

'It's just your legs,' Chris said. 'Not your belly. Breathing isn't constricted. Just broken hips. You'll live.' He turned and moved away.

He grabbed Katie's jacket and fumbled out the phone. He hit 999.

'But Julia won't,' Katie croaked, her voice a little stronger now. 'You did me, and you can drive to Rose and you can hug her while the police put me in chains, and I can't stop that. But there's nothing you can do to help Julia. Unless you burn me.'

Chris stared at her.

'She might be taking her last breath now, a mile from here, buried in soil, trying to scream for her daddy.' She made a scream of her own as she tried to move and something badly damaged didn't like it. 'Burn me. End it. Let me go my way.'

Chris moved again. He started kicking and scooping floor-boards and plaster aside.

An operator answered the phone. Chris gave the address and said, 'There's been a murder. It's my daughter. Get here quick.' He listened, then said, 'No, the killer. The killer is my daughter.'

He hung up and continued to scoop wood and plaster aside, until he exposed what he was looking for. The reason he had tricked Katie into bringing him here.

A blue rug.

He yanked it partly aside to expose the trapdoor beneath, flicked the bolt and hoisted the door open against the weight of wood.

Jake Cross

'Julia will die, Daddy. Burn me up. Give me this one thing, the only thing you've ever given me. Show you care. Please.'

Blue rugs, one for each cellar in each house. Exactly how Katie had known where the cellar was in Wooderland: because she'd seen this one, here in Eclipse's half-built, empty guesthouse, perfect for a night-time rendezvous, whose postcode was listed on House Rules.

'Burn me!' Katie yelled.

Chris ignored her and aimed the phone's flashlight downwards.

There. At the bottom of coarse wooden steps, lying curled at their feet, dazed and bleeding from her face, and lit up, and alive and staring up with a face creased in fear that what she was seeing wasn't real.

Julia.

ONE WEEK LATER

# CHAPTER FIFTY-FIVE

When Katie appeared, Chris noted that she had another wig, this one brown, functionally short. It reminded him of Eve, as pictured during a fun day photo shoot for a newspaper. A cut designed only for comfort, screaming that there was no one in her life to impress. Katie's new wig wasn't this time a disguise, just something to allay attention. She sat awkwardly in the chair, probably because of a freshly fixed broken hip.

'This is the last time we ever see each other. And I didn't set this meeting up as some kind of goodbye. I came to make sure you understand that you're nothing to me.'

He had considered imparting his information by post. But he needed to know he'd done this without restriction, to face and overcome his nerves. Even if the sight of him put a smile on Katie's face.

And there it was, thin, almost invisible, but a smile, nonetheless. But it was yet another piece of fakery, because the eyes were out of her control and they told the truth. They displayed anger.

She was a hundred miles away, in a soundproofed prison suite, but those cold eyes, as glassy as the laptop screen she stared out from, made him shiver. He had to steady a shaking hand in order to pull a folded sheet of paper from a pocket.

'This is going nationwide tomorrow. The police are going to announce it. There are still people who blame me, blame my family, for what you did. Hopefully, this final thing will end the persecution of my family by people who associate your evil blood with me. But I wanted to show you first.'

Just then, someone knocked on the door. Chris crossed the storeroom and slipped out, careful not to let anyone see what he was doing.

It was Lindsay. 'Big bro, your boss is so drunk he's asleep. I said I'd take him home, since I'm the only one sober.'

True to her word, she hadn't touched any of the alcohol scattered around. For the two days since she'd arrived on his doorstep, she hadn't touched a drop, or asked for money, and the eyes had the clarity of the drug-free. Chris was sober, too. He'd been pretending to drink vodka, but it was water, to keep a clear head for his chat with Katie.

'Thanks. Take him, please.'

At the back of the crowded function room Alan was slumped over a table and being ignored by four of Chris's other work colleagues. Simone Baker was in the process of tying one of the helium-filled '16TH ANNIVERSARY' balloons to his ear and being watched with intrigue by Carol and John.

When Lindsay left, he checked his watch. It was nearly time for Julia's stand-up routine, which she'd promised to tone down for the few teenaged sons and daughters present. He'd also promised to watch, since it was her first performance in front of her parents. So he had to get this thing done.

Back in the storeroom, he took his seat once more. Katie had waited patiently. But of course. There was only a lonely cell to return to. He gave a little smile at the person sitting in front of him and behind the laptop, silent, just listening. Rose had refused to see or be seen by Katie, even by video. But she had wanted to watch her husband do this.

He picked up the sheet of paper again, so Katie could see it. She gave it only a flick of a glance, but the eyes showed no confusion. They knew what it was.

'This survived the fire. It was in the garden. The police wanted an explanation. I gave it. They were quite shocked. So they contacted Gene Genie, the testing lab. They wondered if you'd performed other paternity tests, in case there was another dead non-father out there.'

Katie said nothing. Behind her, Rose watched the lid of the laptop, as if she could see the back of Katie's head. She remained silent, unwilling to let Katie know she was there, but determined to watch this happen.

'The lab didn't have a paternity test with my name on it, Katie. We both signed that application form, but you didn't send it off. This result sheet here is a fake, a copy, cleverly made by someone with a computer. You made it look very official, with the cheque and the licence included, and you posted it to my house. You didn't need to do that test, did you? Because you already knew the truth. Because the lab *did* have a test for Katie Hugill. But not a paternity test.'

Katie said nothing.

'Why were you at Julia's college a couple of weeks ago, that day she saw you? Not to find a computer course. And not to get a first look at a woman who might be your brand-new sister. Could it be you were waiting for her to shed a hair, or break a fingernail, or toss a tissue in a bin?'

Katie didn't react. Chris took another sheet of paper from his pocket. Another DNA test. Katie didn't look at this one. Three columns, one for a gobbledegook of numbers and letters, one for a CLIENT/SIBLING named Katie Hugill and one for an ALLEGED SIBLING called Julia Redfern.

'You performed a half-sibling DNA test on Julia, without her consent. Once you had an answer, you introduced yourself to my family with that bogus robbery and your ceremonial paternity test. But something was puzzling.'

Now Katie looked bored. She even yawned.

'So many times I stopped you talking about this subject until we knew the truth. I was a little cold with you. I shut you out, so you had to beat a young woman half to death, and lie about a fire and pretend to be homeless, just to get into my house. Why, when you could have presented the test results on Julia and made one instant happy family? Just add water.'

Again, Katie said nothing, but her eyes strayed slightly. It might have been a trick of the camera, but it appeared she was looking somewhere narrowly past Chris's ear.

He pointed at the only fragment of the letter that mattered. Not the disclaimer that the names couldn't be verified because they were supplied by the client, or the warning that samples collected without a legal chain of custody couldn't be defended in a court of law. And not the technical four-sentence result at the bottom, either.

Just one word of it. And one number.

PROBABILITY 0%.

Katie looked. She looked for a long time, as if trying to work out a way around this new problem. The she stood. She smoothed her clothing.

'Why, Katie, if I wasn't your father? Still you came to me, but why? Because you rested your hopes on me but Julia's negative test result burned all that, like everything else in your life? Because you had nowhere and no one to turn to? Did you decide I would do anyway because otherwise you had nothing?'

Katie leaned forward and grabbed her laptop. Her room shook. Her face filled the screen. It was one of disappointment. 'I must have a problem with my DNA. Something that happened inside me. It ruined me. It made the test fail. Or it was him, Everton. Everton did this to me. His vile seed. I'm pregnant with his demon.'

Chris felt a shiver as he realised Katie did not accept the truth. This knowledge suffocated her shocking news. Beyond the room, he heard the whine of microphone feedback. Julia was preparing for her routine. He put a hand atop the laptop, ready to slam it shut, and end this. He had chosen to do this here, now, during his belated wedding anniversary party, because immediately afterwards he wanted to drown himself in people he cared for, who cared right back. But he had one more thing to say first.

'I hope the pregnancy makes you happy, Katie. But now I need to tell you something. My story about meeting your mother when you were just a couple of months old. That was true.'

He glanced over the laptop, at Rose. If she had heard Katie's claim to be pregnant, then she didn't show it. Katie was nothing to her. Instead, she nodded at him to continue his story. The day after the terrible events of the previous Saturday, he had admitted this final piece of the tale to his wife. She had taken it well, although there was residual tension between them, but he hadn't felt clean. He'd known then that to cleanse himself fully, he needed to confess to one other.

'But I lied to you about how it happened. Your mother did indeed find me at my college. She told me I had a little girl. She wanted us to have a life together. A family. But I already had a new family. I had Rose and a new baby. I didn't want to lose them. So I abandoned you. I was a coward, and I ran from my responsibility. Literally, I ran. I ran out of college that day, and I never went back. Just in case she found me again. It was utter weakness on my part, and even though I know now I may not be your father, for that I am sorry.'

Trance-like Katie didn't respond. The glassy eyes seemed to hold no emotion.

'Will you be okay, Katie?'

She said nothing. If not for the slight rise and fall of her chest, he might have assumed the video feed had frozen.

'Dad!' Julia called out. 'Come on, you're going to miss my show.'

Behind Katie, Rose stood.

He leaned closer to the laptop.

'Katie, I really am sorry. I mean it when I say, I hope things work out well for you. Especially with the baby. I hope you're both healthy. But I have to go now.'

Again no response. He wasn't even sure she had heard. Maybe, like him, she was thinking about the life in her belly, about the terrible hand she had dealt it before it had drawn a first breath. A killer for a father, himself murdered by the mother. And then there was Eve... It was almost too much to comprehend.

He put his hand on the laptop, but couldn't find the will to shut it. A desire to say something positive suddenly forced him to impart a piece of information he'd had no intention of telling her. 'I got a letter from my father. He plans to phone me soon. I have you to thank for that.'

Those dead eyes seemed to show a flicker of something, just for a moment, but he was unable to decode it. It could have been gratification, but it might have been envy, or disappointment. Her enduring silence conceded nothing.

Then Rose placed her hand on his, and pushed the lid down, and Katie became white noise.

# A LETTER FROM JAKE

Hi All,

Nothing I've ever written went through as many changes as this book, and I barely recognise it as the novel I started two years ago. I reshaped plots, added and replaced scenes, and erased characters off the face of the earth. But finally, I got this thing into the shape it is, and I hope you like it.

If so, please leave a review on Amazon/Kobo/Goodreads/Facebook/Twitter, or your blog or website. They all mean a lot.

If you'd like to keep up to date on other great titles like mine when they're on special offer, then sign up to Bookouture Deals here:

www.bookouture.com/bookouture-deals

Jake.

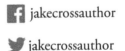 jakecrossauthor

jakecrossauthor

# ACKNOWLEDGEMENTS

Thanks to everyone at Bookouture for yet more sheer brilliance. Noelle and Kim gave great advice and this author's had back-slaps and reality checks at all the right times. Despite having done this writing lark for a while, I still made the mistake of thinking my first draft of this novel was good to go. So the biggest thanks go to my editor, Leodora, who sat me down and said, 'Not so fast.'

And thanks to my partner, Jen, who was my source of research into all the medical details.

25/6/19

Lightning Source UK Ltd.
Milton Keynes UK
UKHW040620091019
351290UK00001B/85/P

9 781786 814432